STARS
of
CHAOS
SHA PO LANG

STARS of CHAOS
SHA PO LANG

WRITTEN BY

priest

ILLUSTRATED BY

罐一一

TRANSLATED BY

Lily & Louise

Seven Seas Entertainment

STARS OF CHAOS:
SHA PO LANG VOL. 2

Published originally under the title of 《杀破狼》 (Sha Po Lang)
Author © priest
English edition rights under license granted by 北京晋江原创网络科技有限公司
(Beijing Jinjiang Original Network Technology Co., Ltd.)
English edition copyright © 2024 Seven Seas Entertainment, Inc.
Arranged through JS Agency Co., Ltd
All rights reserved

Cover and Interior Illustrations by 罐 一 一 (eleven small jars)

Seven Seas press and purchase enquiries can be sent to press@gomanga.com.
Information regarding the distribution and purchase of digital editions
is available from Digital Manager CK Russell at digital@gomanga.com.

Follow Seven Seas Entertainment online at
sevenseasentertainment.com.

TRANSLATION: Lily, Louise
COVER DESIGN: M. A. Lewife
INTERIOR DESIGN & LAYOUT: Clay Gardner
PROOFREADER: Stephanie Cohen, Hnä
COPY EDITOR: Jehanne Bell
EDITOR: Kelly Quinn Chiu
PREPRESS TECHNICIAN: Melanie Ujimori, Jules Valera
MANAGING EDITOR: Alyssa Scavetta
EDITOR-IN-CHIEF: Julie Davis
PUBLISHER: Lianne Sentar
VICE PRESIDENT: Adam Arnold
PRESIDENT: Jason DeAngelis

ISBN: 978-1-63858-935-8
Printed in Canada
First Printing: January 2024
10 9 8 7 6 5 4 3 2 1

TABLE OF CONTENTS

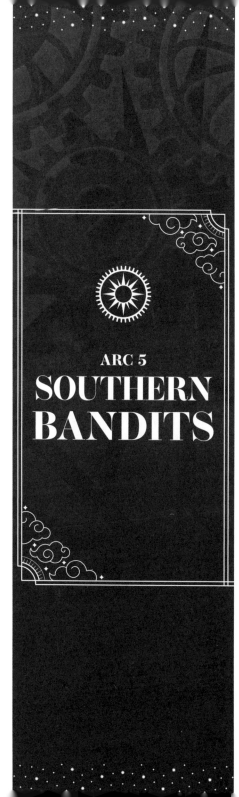

ARC 5

SOUTHERN BANDITS

MARCHING ORDERS

HOWEVER GREAT the sum of a ruler's achievements, the life of an emperor leaves behind no more than a page in the annals of history.

Since brush was first put to paper, no two emperors have been the same. Some governed the nation and brought stability to the land, while others brought calamity upon the country and people. Some washed their hands of mundane affairs and retreated from governance to seek immortality, while others stepped up to the throne to make waves.

The late Yuanhe Emperor was undoubtedly a seeker of immortality. He was magnanimous and kind, but muddle-headed and incapable. Yet his son, who held political opinions much like his own, was undoubtedly a maker of waves.

The Longan Emperor Li Feng rejected that Daoist saying, "Ruling a large nation is like cooking a small fish": interfere too much in the process and one spoils the whole project. He was diligent in administration and firm in character. The day he ascended the throne, he turned the tide on the late emperor's soft habits of neglecting government affairs and kicked off his tempestuous political career with a fiery vigor.

In the first year of the Longan era, the emperor ordered the Marquis of Anding, Gu Yun, to escort Tianlang Crown Prince

Jialai Yinghuo back to the northern border. At the same time, he established new branches of the Silk Road connecting multiple small nations in the Western Regions and opened a corridor of trade with the area, leaving the Marquis of Anding to supervise all necessary arrangements. Whether it was compelling the marquis to treat with the northern barbarians or dumping him in the arid Western Regions, the emperor's resentment for the nation's empty coffers was abundantly clear. He may as well have said, *Gu Yun, earn that money back or sell yourself to make up the difference.*

In the second year of Longan, Prince Wei colluded with Dongying nationals in an ill-fated plot to strike the capital from the sea, and threatened the empire with a fleet of dragon warships. His plot was exposed halfway through, and the Jiangnan Navy launched a blitz attack to capture the rebel leader under Prince Wei's employ aboard his vessel. Prince Wei was imprisoned and later "committed suicide" by drinking poison.

In the aftermath, the Longan Emperor purged the leadership of Jiangnan with extreme prejudice. Eighty-six major and minor officials were implicated in the incident, and over forty of them lost their heads. When the season of the harvest ended and the season for beheadings arrived,[1] there were too many to execute at once: three rounds of executions were scheduled. The remaining prisoners were sentenced to castration and penal exile, banned from working as government officials in perpetuity.

That same year, a comprehensive implementation of new laws began in Jiangnan, which cracked down on the illegal occupation of lands by local gentry and landlords. These seized lands were not

---

1   Traditionally, spring and summer were the seasons to give rewards, and fall and winter were the seasons to serve punishments. 秋后问斩, "to be executed after the autumn harvest," was one way death sentences were served.

redistributed to the commoners and the tenants but returned to the possession of the imperial court, while the rights to their usage were returned to central authorities in the capital. By the third year of Longan, determining what to plant or build on any given patch of earth required endless layers of approvals. Power was centralized to a degree even Emperor Wu had not achieved, and restrictions on violet gold usage tightened to a stranglehold.

No one dared object—those who did were treated as members of Prince Wei's party, and were fated for either a cut above the shoulders or a cut below the belt.

In the fourth year of Longan, Li Feng implemented the Token of Mastery Law. This edict required all civilian artificers to register themselves with their local government and receive a "token of mastery," which would authorize them to work. Each token had a seal carved at the bottom with an identification number, and the holder of the token was to use it to mark any object they repaired or created. The court created five ranks for artificers based on experience and skill. Strict rules governed the work an artificer of each ranking could do, and unregistered artificers were prohibited from practicing their trade. Non-military artificers were forbidden from working on armor or engines for military use. Any who violated this law would have their fingers cut off and be sent into exile.

The pronouncement of this law touched off a storm of debate within the court. But no matter what reasoned arguments officials brought to bear, the emperor and the cabinet—the members of which, after yet another purge, were to a one in the emperor's palm—sang the same refrain: If tight control wasn't maintained over the artificers, how could the government staunch the outward flow of violet gold?

Before the debate over the Token of Mastery Law had reached a conclusion, Li Feng tossed down another thunderbolt—the Marching Orders Decree. This law targeted the army.

Great Liang's military forces were originally organized into eight military branches, each with a different specialty. These divisions were split between the five regions of Jiangnan, the Central Plains, the frontier north of the Great Wall, the Western Regions, and the southern border, and each region was presided over by a commander in chief. The appointment and dismissal of military officers, as well as the allocation of salaries, provisions, armor, and engines, was managed by the Ministry of War, while all else fell under the purview of the commanding general of the military region. Furthermore, the Marquis of Anding held a Black Iron Tiger Tally invested with the authority to command all military forces in the nation in the event of an emergency.

Li Feng did not alter the composition of the five military regions, nor did he recall the Tiger Tally held by the Marquis of Anding. He merely created roles for a handful of military inspectors to aid the commanding general of each region. These military inspectors served three-year terms and reported directly to the Ministry of War. They had but one duty: to request marching orders decrees from the Ministry of War. If the commanding general ordered his troops to move so much as a single step without a marching orders decree in hand, it would be considered an act of treason.

All regional garrisons had to abide by this law—with the exception of the Black Iron Battalion.

The moment the Marching Orders Decree was announced, the nation exploded with debate. Everyone soon lost interest in the trivial matter of civilian artificers.

The emperor and his civil and military officials argued straight through the New Year, squawking at each other like chickens and ducks. The day it was announced, three of the five regional commanders declared they were retiring due to old age, and the clamor was such that it reached even the ears of the Marquis of Anding far away in the northwest. Before the marquis could express his own concerns about the emperor's new decree, he found himself forced to reassure the soldiery of each region. It took all his patience to listen to the old generals sit clutching their hearts and wailing mournfully as Gu Yun himself ran around putting out fires all over the place.

On the night of the Lantern Festival,[2] Gu Yun returned to the capital to report on his duties. The girls and young ladies crowding the streets buried him in more than fifty tossed handkerchiefs, but he had no time to be smug about it—within the span of a few days, he'd handed every last one of them out to wipe others' tears. These perfumed tokens turned out to be more economical than the coarsest diaper cloth.

Even the civilian world got in on the ruckus. Scholars in academies throughout the land talked of little else; they dragged this and that decree out to argue and retread the same ground in endless circuits. The imperial court, which had been so stagnant for the entirety of the Yuanhe era, finally provided the literati some material to quarrel over.

The chaos persisted until the sixth year of Longan. No conclusion had been reached on the Marching Orders Decree. The emperor refused to repeal the law, but he had yet to appoint any military inspectors. The law hung suspended in midair, a threat without action, like a dangling sword ready to leave one side battered and bloody at any time.

---

2   A festival held on the fifteenth of the first lunar month, the first full moon of the year. It marks the coming of spring and is the last day of the extended New Year's celebrations.

Autumn chill rolled across the land once again. It had been four years since the dragon threat in Jiangnan. Prince Wei's corpse had cooled in its grave, and the incident he provoked had expired as a topic of conversation. No one brought the matter up anymore.

Beside the official road through Central Shu, there stood a small tavern called Apricot Blossom Village.[3] It was no more than a shack erected to sell wine. Wherever one found such humble establishments, eight out of ten were guaranteed to be called something like "Apricot Blossom Village."

A young man gently lifted the curtain hanging above the doorway and stepped inside. He was no more than nineteen or twenty, on the cusp of adulthood, and was dressed in long, tattered robes like a poor scholar. His face was incredibly handsome, almost violently so—he had a high nose, a hairline so neat it might have been carved by a knife, and deep-set eyes that glimmered like cold stars. On anyone else these features might have seemed aggressive, yet this young man had an aura as warm and gentle as jade. One glance at him and a person's eyes would light up in pleasure; nor would those who looked longer tire of his appearance, but would, upon closer inspection, find a certain remote tranquility in his countenance.

The tavern was so small even a large dog would have to bend down to enter. There were only two tables inside, and the seats at them had already been taken. The proprietor, who also worked as the waiter and bookkeeper of the establishment, was lazily flicking the beads of his abacus back and forth when his gaze was drawn to this young man. After internally exclaiming at how handsome he was, the proprietor stepped forward and greeted him with cupped hands.

3　This common name for taverns is a reference to the poem 清明, "Tomb Sweeping Day," by Tang dynasty poet Du Mu.

"Honored guest, my apologies. You've come at a bad time; there's nowhere to sit. There's another place to rest about two and a half kilometers down the road. Perhaps you might take a look there?"

"I was just feeling parched when I came across this establishment," the scholar said, good-natured. "Could I trouble you to fill my jar with fine wine? I don't need a seat."

The proprietor reached for his wine jar. When he opened the lid, the scent of the dregs of wine inside poured out. "Bamboo leaf liquor, got it."

A customer at one of the tables waved the scholar over. "Young master, come rest your feet here, I'll make room for you."

The scholar accepted this offer and cupped his hands in thanks.

Yet before he could take a seat, he heard a voice from the second table. "What's your problem? I think our current emperor is great. He's the emperor; isn't it right for him to keep power in his hands? With all due respect, can you really say the one who never managed a single thing, and spent all his time practicing Buddhism and fooling around with the palace maids and concubines, was a good emperor?"

The scholar didn't expect to find someone making grand observations about the world here in this modest tavern. He looked up and found an older fellow with brawny arms, pants legs rolled up, and engine oil smeared between his fingers. He appeared to be a low-ranked artificer.

The old farmer next to him was quick to agree. "Exactly! Just look at the cost of rice these days. Has anyone seen such low prices since the founding of our dynasty?"

Seeing he had support, the artificer grew still more pleased with his own opinions and prattled on self-importantly: "I went into the city the day before yesterday and heard a bunch of scholars from the academy discussing current affairs. When they came to the Marching Orders Decree, some young lad without fuzz on his upper lip said His Majesty was weakening Great Liang's border defenses. Ridiculous; what sort of armchair strategist does he think he is? Didn't he see what happened when Prince Wei tried to revolt? These generals' posts are in remote lands where the emperor is far and central control is weak. If any one of them felt the urge to rebel, never mind the stability of His Majesty's nation, wouldn't it be us commoners who suffer the consequences? I heard people say that, with the Ministry of War keeping a tight leash on the generals, military expenses will plummet, and we civilians won't have to shoulder the burden of all those taxes. Isn't this a good thing?"

At this point, everyone in the tavern nodded. The older man who had invited the scholar over also spoke up. "The Marquis of Anding hasn't even come forward to oppose it, yet everyone else is already flying off the handle in his stead."

The scholar, who hadn't been following the conversation closely, instinctively looked up at the mention of this individual. "What does this matter have to do with the Marquis of Anding?"

"Young master," the older man said with a laugh, "let me explain. On the surface, it looks like His Majesty hasn't touched the Black Iron Battalion with this decree. But in truth, he has divided the military power available to the Marquis of Anding. Think about it: If from now on, the soldiers of the nation can only be mobilized with a marching orders decree, what of the Black Iron Tiger Tally held by the marquis? If mobilizing soldiers without a marching orders decree is treason, and the Ministry of War refuses to issue one, who should the five regional commanders listen to—the Ministry of War or the Marquis of Anding?"

The scholar smiled. "So that's how it is. I have been enlightened."

Seeing that the proprietor had finished fetching his wine, the young man turned away from these country bumpkins' nonsensical conversation, politely thanked the older man who had allowed him to sit, and made his exit, leaving his payment behind.

As he stepped out of the tavern, he saw that a man had appeared on the previously deserted road. The newcomer said nothing, but seemed rather embarrassed to have been caught by this poor scholar. He bowed neatly in greeting, then moved off to the side of the tavern where he proceeded to do a convincing impression of a mural.

The scholar pressed a hand to his forehead in mild exasperation. *They're catching up faster and faster.*

This "scholar" was none other than Chang Geng. After his row with Gu Yun four years ago, he had been escorted back to the capital by a Black Hawk. After refusing every one of the emperor's awards and commendations, he proceeded to spend half a year clashing daily with the Marquis Estate's guards before successfully making his escape.

Gu Yun had sent people after him more than once. But after engaging in a painful stalemate for over a year, the marquis had finally realized that this child truly was like a hawk chick that could not be caged or tamed by force. He had no choice but to compromise and let the boy do as he pleased. Still, wherever Chang Geng went, he would encounter a few soldiers from the Black Iron Battalion in plain clothes, coming and going like ghosts.

Later, with a recommendation from Liao Ran in hand, Chang Geng took an obscure civilian martial expert as his master. He joined his shifu in his elusive ways, traveling throughout the land and visiting all sorts of uninhabited places—and, in doing so, lost the Black Iron Battalion completely. But every time he appeared near a relay station, his tail would appear again...and just as expected, the instant he set foot in Central Shu, he found this young soldier waiting for him.

The Chang Geng of today was no longer that mulishly stubborn youth who housed a heart piled with uncertainties. He led his horse up to the soldier, a genial expression on his face. "You've been working hard, brother. How is my yifu doing?"

The soldier was a man of few words, and never expected Chang Geng to strike up a conversation with him. Fumbling, he stammered, "Your High...Young Master, the master is doing well. He says if everything is peaceful on the border at the end of the year, he will come celebrate the New Year at home."

Chang Geng nodded. "All right, then I will depart for the capital in a few days." Whether his face held any joy or reluctance was difficult to discern. As he spoke, he handed the full jar of wine to the young soldier. "You've had a difficult journey, coming all this way. Please warm yourself with a sip of wine."

No matter how oblivious the young soldier might be, it was plain that he was a thorn in Chang Geng's side. He was surprised. Not only did Chang Geng speak kindly to him, he even graciously offered him a drink. The young soldier was rather stunned by this favorable treatment. He didn't dare touch his lips to the jar and nervously poured a mouthful of wine from midair, careful not to spill a drop. He politely returned the jar with both hands and picked up the reins of Chang Geng's horse.

"Last spring," said Chang Geng, "I actually paid a visit to the northwest, but Yifu was busy with military affairs, so I didn't bother him. The Silk Road really is flourishing. To think that endless sea of sand could become a place so bustling people must walk shoulder to shoulder—I've seen few places more prosperous in all Great Liang."

After peering around to ensure they were alone, the young soldier said quietly, "With the marshal at the helm these past few years, the desert raiders have gradually disappeared. Many people have settled down at the entrance to the Silk Road to do business, and you can find little trinkets from all over. The marshal said if there's something you're interested in, he'll bring it back for you the next time he returns to the capital."

Chang Geng paused, then said, "So long as he comes back."

The young soldier didn't catch the deeper meaning within his words and thought he was only being polite. He had spent many years in the military and had no knack for flattering others in conversation, so he fell silent instead.

Chang Geng walked down the official road through Central Shu. Though his face was impassive, his chest was beginning to feel a bit hot. He had once thought that separation was like water, and with a splash of it, affections sketched in shades of cinnabar, saffron, viridian, or ochre could all be washed clean. But now he found that his feelings for Gu Yun weren't painted but carved; after all his washing, he had only etched these traces deeper.

Although it was only the beginning of autumn, when Chang Geng heard Gu Yun might return to the capital at year's end, he discovered to his surprise that he already felt anxious about this reunion. He had blurted out that he would "depart for the capital" like someone in a hurry to return. Now he regretted it to no end, and wished to go back on his word and flee to the ends of the earth.

As he was caught up in these flustered thoughts, he spotted a frail matron trudging toward them down the road with someone on her back. The woman struggled to walk, stopping every few steps and panting like an ox. As Chang Geng watched, she tripped over a stone lying on the road and tumbled to the ground with a cry.

Chang Geng came to his senses at once and rushed to help the fallen pair up. "Auntie, are you all right?"

The woman was too tired to speak—who knew how far she had walked? Before she could utter a word, tears began to roll down her cheeks.

Chang Geng started in surprise but didn't press her for answers. He lifted the unconscious old man she had been carrying off the ground and felt for his pulse. After a moment, he said kindly, "This elderly gentleman is only suffering an excess of internal heat[4] from spending too long immobilized. A simple round of acupuncture should solve the problem; it's nothing fatal. If you are willing to trust me, please come along."

The young soldier from the Black Iron Battalion hadn't expected this prince to be proficient in medicine. He hurried forward to hoist the sickly old man onto his own back. Chang Geng set the woman atop his horse and took the lead with the reins in hand.

Before long, they arrived at a village. Near the entrance stood a house of elegant construction with a strip of cured meat hanging from the doorway to dry in the sun.

Chang Geng tied up his horse with the ease of familiarity and walked straight in. He carried his patient to the inner chambers and laid him on a small couch, then retrieved a case of silver needles from beneath the couch's pillow. Without further ado, he rolled up his sleeves and began to personally administer the treatment.

"Are...these your lodgings?" the young soldier asked cautiously.

Chang Geng looked up and flashed a quick smile. "No, this is just the house of a friend..."

---

4 In traditional Chinese medicine, an excess of internal heat, which can be caused by uncontrolled emotions, hot temperatures, heating ingredients in food, or other factors, can give rise to symptoms such as fever, thirst, insomnia, and redness of the face.

Before he finished speaking, a new voice called from outside the room, "I see you've invited yourself in again."

A tall and slender woman in white lifted the door curtain and stepped inside. The young soldier flinched, and his body tensed unconsciously—she had gotten all the way to the door without him sensing a thing. Her martial abilities were undoubtedly superior to his.

Chang Geng didn't pause in his work, nor did he look at all abashed to have let himself in. "Miss Chen, I thought you weren't home."

This woman was, of course, Chen Qingxu, the Linyuan Pavilion member they had met on a rebel ship in the East Sea four years ago.

38

A CHANCE MEETING

OR ALL CHEN QINGXU COMPLAINED, she didn't look annoyed. Perhaps she was used to guests barging in uninvited. She set the medicinal herbs she was holding to the side and greeted Chang Geng's companions. "My surname is Chen. I am a physician of the jianghu."

This woman claimed to be a jianghu physician, but she moved with the composed grace of a well-bred lady. She also didn't smile, and her face was icy-cold. The older woman grew timid at the sight of her. She mumbled for a while yet failed to speak, and in the end only managed to curtsy again and again. Chen Qingxu glanced at Chang Geng, who was placing the acupuncture needles. "He's a half-disciple of mine, and although he can't snatch anyone from the jaws of death, he is competent enough to handle your common illnesses. Dajie,[5] this man is in good hands."

It was impossible to tell Chen Qingxu's age from her face, but she dressed, at least, like a young, unmarried woman. Standing off to the side, the young soldier felt his heart pound at the sight of her.

Their prince had just walked into the home of an unwed young woman without a word of greeting. Even if she was a doctor...

---

5   大姐, *dajie, is a word meaning "eldest sister." It can be used as a casual term of address for an older female.*

was that *proper*? And he was clearly familiar with the place—who knew how many times he had been here?

Back in the capital, families that were strict about etiquette required notice be sent through servants before even a married couple could call upon one another. Granted, people did say the sons and daughters of the jianghu cared not for these trivialities...

This was the young soldier's first time tailing Chang Geng on his own, and he was soon entirely absorbed in trying to deduce this mysterious woman's relationship with the fourth prince. How angry would Gu Yun be if he found out about this? The young man was so distressed, it was as if a pot of water were boiling in his chest. He was practically on the verge of tears wondering how he would report this to the marshal.

While they were talking, the old man on the couch groaned and coughed heavily a few times before slowly opening his eyes. Heedless of the filth, Chang Geng retrieved a nearby spittoon and helped the man hack up a mouthful of thick phlegm. The matron with him was overjoyed and poured out a stream of thanks. Chen Qingxu handed Chang Geng a handkerchief. "Go write a prescription," she instructed. "I'll review your work."

Her tone was light, but the words were quite obviously a command. Chang Geng took out paper and brush without a word of protest and, after a moment of thought, began to transcribe a prescription. The young soldier's eyes nearly bugged out of his head. When this soldier had served at Gu Yun's side, he had heard Marshal Gu lament more than once that the fourth prince had grown up and refused to listen to him anymore. Yet he clearly followed this woman's orders to the letter, more obedient than the young students at the academy—where was that untamed spirit who had dared to defy the Marquis of Anding as a youth?

While the young soldier stood frozen in confusion, Chen Qingxu had already struck up a conversation with the matron, who finally relaxed after seeing the improvement in her companion's condition. Gradually, the matron explained her situation: After the farming puppets had been widely deployed in this region, no one had land to farm anymore. The court had decreed that local gentry were not to mistreat their tenants, but as time went on, what landowner would be willing to support a bunch of free-loaders? Late and reduced payments became increasingly common, and later, those who were still forced to toil even with the puppets around began to find it unfair. In the end, the farmers formed one faction, the artificers another, and the businessmen who ran small shops joined with minor landlords to form a third. Everyone thought they were at the greatest disadvantage, and everyone was dissatisfied with the rest.

The woman's husband had no desire to sit around at home with nothing to do but attract others' ire, so he set out with some fellow villagers to look for work in the south. After he left, the woman's family lost all contact with him. Her elderly father-in-law was ill, her children were too young to help, and the barefoot doctor in their village had left long ago, bored for lack of patients. She had braced herself to carry her old father-in-law on her own back and set off on a long journey to seek treatment.

Chen Qingxu frowned when she heard the matron's tale. "The south? There was a great flood in the south this year. They haven't even gotten around to sending disaster relief; what work could there possibly be?"

The woman looked lost. She was a resident of a mountain village who plainly had no idea what lay beyond the few acres of land before her doorstep.

"Auntie," Chang Geng asked as he wrote the prescription, "have you received this year's grain rations?"

The woman gazed down at the sick old man on the bed and a look of distress came over her face. "To tell you the truth, we have not. I...I'm getting on in years. And I'm a woman. How could I cause a scene by showing up at the official's door to demand rations? At least grain prices have been low this year, and we still had some stores left at home, so we could purchase what we needed to get by."

No matter what the woman said, Chang Geng understood that these farming families were accustomed to a frugal lifestyle. They never dipped into their savings unless circumstances were dire, and each coin spent was like a knife to their hearts. Otherwise, why would she have walked all this way carrying her father-in-law on her back, step by step, rather than hire a carriage?

"Are there no public fields?" asked Chen Qingxu. "The harvest from public fields is turned over to the national treasury for distribution to government officials, but I've heard surplus can be claimed by local residents."

The woman laughed bitterly. "Our public fields aren't planted. They've been left fallow the last two years."

Chang Geng started. "Why? Is the land barren?"

"They say it's because the fields were close to some official's ancestral home," the matron explained, "and the county magistrate wanted to build an ancestral temple on that plot. For some reason, the higher-ups didn't agree, so it ended up going back and forth, and in the end no one can say what the land is supposed to be used for. Now it's simply been abandoned."

At that, all three people listening to her story fell silent.

"In an area cut through by mountains and rivers, there's so little arable land, and now these fields have been left fallow." Chen Qingxu sighed. "Honestly, these people..."

Whatever Chang Geng was thinking, he kept his thoughts to himself. He briskly finished writing the prescription and handed it to Chen Qingxu for her inspection.

"Mm, this will do—Dajie, please come with me. I keep some common medicinal ingredients here; you won't need to buy them yourself."

She led the woman, who was still thanking her effusively, to the rear courtyard to fetch the medicine.

The moment she left, the young Black Iron Battalion soldier sighed in relief and sidled up to Chang Geng. He followed the prince around without saying a word, rolling up his sleeves to preemptively perform every task he saw Chang Geng about to do. In short order, the soldier had washed the spittoon and tidied up the paper and brush on the table. Only then did he manage to squeeze out a few words. "Young Master...you're quite familiar with this place," he stuttered.

Chang Geng hummed in assent. "I often stay here when I'm in Central Shu."

What?! An unmarried man and a single woman staying in the same house? The young soldier's face turned red from the effort of choking down his words. Now he fully realized the gravity of his mission. If he didn't get to the bottom of this, the marquis might carve *him* into a spittoon when he returned with his report.

Only when Chang Geng saw the young soldier looking like he'd been struck by lightning did he realize what the poor man was thinking. He said with a smile, "Don't get the wrong idea. This may be Miss Chen's house, but she usually isn't here, and the house is often empty. It's common for her jianghu friends to stay a few days when they're in the area. If she happens to be in, the women stay with her, and the men lodge elsewhere. I was going to bring you to stay here for a few days, but since the owner is home, we'll go find an inn."

The young soldier relaxed slightly. *Oh, so that's how it is.*

But before he could relax completely, his worries were rekindled once more. The young soldier thought to himself with a hint of woe, *So even someone as highborn as the fourth prince must avoid staying in inns to save money.*

Glancing at Chang Geng's ratty clothes, the young soldier blurted, "If the mar...if the *master* knew you were living like this out here, he'd be worried sick."

This young soldier had a sharp mind and was swift to action, but was hesitant and sparing with his words. Whenever he managed to break his usual silence to say something like this, he sounded incredibly sincere. Chang Geng's heart skipped a beat, and he couldn't think of how to respond.

Just then, Chen Qingxu and the older woman returned from making up the prescription. The physician glanced at Chang Geng's face and frowned. "Compose yourself. What have I told you?"

Chang Geng came back to his senses and bent his mouth into a smile.

It was true that Chen Qingxu half counted as his teacher.

Two years ago, Chang Geng's shifu had walked in on him during one of his wu'ergu attacks. The heavy secret previously known to none but the heavens, the earth, and Chang Geng himself finally had another witness. His shifu had no knowledge of medicine, so he dragged Chang Geng on a long journey through multiple destinations before finding Chen Qingxu in the old eastern capital. Unfortunately, the wu'ergu was a closely kept secret of the barbarian shamaness, and even someone as widely read as Miracle Doctor Chen couldn't make any immediate headway. All she could do was prescribe him some calming medicine while she continued her slow investigation.

While she was treating him, Chang Geng had inquired about Gu Yun's condition in a roundabout way.

"Miss Chen," he had asked, "do you know of any patients whose sight and hearing come and go?"

Chen Qingxu naturally grasped the meaning behind his question, but it wasn't her place to say too much. She gave only a cursory response. "I do."

"Then, can deafness and blindness be alleviated with medicine?"

"If the disability is congenital, they cannot be. If it is a condition acquired later due to injury, it depends on the cause...if the cause is poison, it may be possible to mitigate its effects."

She had thought that, after circling the topic so many times, Chang Geng would eventually ask about Gu Yun outright. But in the end, he never did. Chen Qingxu realized then that she had perhaps underestimated this young man's intelligence and insight.

Chang Geng asked not a single question further. Instead, he earnestly begged her to accept him as a disciple.

The Chen family had produced miracle doctors for generations. In some ways, the traditions of this clan were very particular, yet in other ways, they were not. They had only one family precept: "Dedicate your life to relieve the suffering of humanity." Any member who tried to imitate the eccentric so-called "miracle doctors" in storybooks and take only the most rare and difficult cases, or who discriminated based on a patient's identity, would be driven out of the clan without exception. Chen Qingxu treated grave injuries and illnesses, but would just as readily attend to a child's common cold or a woman's difficult labor. Nor would she hold her lifetime's learnings close to her chest—the family had no rules prohibiting their knowledge from being divulged to outsiders. If someone sought her tutelage, she would teach. Since Miss Chen hadn't finished her own apprenticeship yet, she claimed she couldn't take official disciples. Thus, she could only half-count as his shifu.

The Chen family resided in Taiyuan Prefecture farther north. Chen Qingxu usually didn't linger here in the south through fall and winter, so Chang Geng surmised that she must have some business that kept her in Central Shu this late in the year.

He produced a money pouch from his lapels and handed it to the young Black Iron Battalion soldier with instructions to hire a carriage to convey the old man and his daughter-in-law back home. The young soldier didn't dare take a single coin from this poverty-stricken prince, and hastily refused the proffered pouch before running off to carry out his orders.

Once all the outsiders had left, Chen Qingxu pulled out a small cloth sack and handed it to Chang Geng. "It's a good thing I ran into you. This is my newest formulation of pacifying fragrance. Take it with you and give it a try."

Chang Geng accepted it with a word of thanks and, after transferring a portion of the medicinal powder to his own sachet, put the rest away. Chen Qingxu's eyes lit as they landed on that sachet. It wasn't embroidered with dizzying designs like mandarin ducks playing in water or butterflies flying in pairs. Rather, it had a lining of clean silk and an exterior constructed of a thin piece of soft leather tooled with filigree patterns. The design appeared to depict an iron wrist cuff with interlocking gears, with a blade peeking out from its edge as if perched to take flight. The entire piece was exquisite.

"Where did you get this sachet?" Chen Qingxu found herself asking, "It's quite unique."

"I made it myself. Would you like one?"

Miracle Doctor Chen, whose composure was unshakable even in the thick of battle, revealed a slight hint of shock.

"It's quite sturdy." Chang Geng continued to recommend his work. "That's right, I meant to ask—mid-autumn has already passed, so what are you still doing in Central Shu?"

"The Marquis of Anding plans to pass through Central Shu on his way south; he asked to meet me here. What, you didn't know?"

Now the shoe was on the other foot, and it was Chang Geng's turn to be shocked.

It was a long interval before Chang Geng managed to find his voice again, aided by the lingering scent of pacifying fragrance. "I—I didn't know. My yifu...why is he heading south?"

Chen Qingxu was mystified. "If the Marquis of Anding is leaving the northwest, he must have military affairs to attend to. I only got the chance to exchange a few words with him because of his connections with my elders. There's no reason for him to give me his itinerary."

"But that young man from the Black Iron Battalion just told me he would return to the capital for the New Year..." Chang Geng said, a bit lost.

Chen Qingxu was still more mystified. "The Double Ninth Festival[6] hasn't even arrived; what do his plans now have to do with whether he'll return to the capital for the New Year?"

Chang Geng didn't know what to say. He fell silent for a spell, then couldn't help but laugh. Only someone waiting in such great

---

6   重阳, Chongyang, a festival held on the ninth day of the ninth month in the lunar calendar. Nine is a yang number, so the Double Ninth may be a very auspicious date.

expectation and fear would utterly disregard three, nearly four, months' time.

"I thought that was why you were here, but it turns out it was just a coincidence," said Chen Qingxu. "In his letter, he said he would arrive within the next few days. If you're not in a rush to be on your way, you may as well stay and wait."

Chang Geng hummed distractedly in response, his mind already a thousand kilometers away.

"Chang Geng, Chang Geng!" When he finally came back to his senses, Chen Qingxu was calling sternly into his ear.

"I've told you," Chen Qingxu said with a grim expression, "pacifying prescriptions are *not* a cure. They can only assist you in your fight. When it comes to dealing with wu'ergu, the worst thing you can do is lose your peace of mind. Every stray thought is fertilizer for that poisonous sprout. Your thoughts have wandered twice in such a short time today. What is going on?"

Chang Geng begged her pardon and lowered his eyes, face inscrutable. He didn't wish to discuss this topic any further, so he casually changed the subject to the prescription he'd just written for the old man. Chen Qingxu traveled the world practicing medicine. She had healed countless wounds left by knives and swords, and alleviated the suffering of lingering chronic illnesses. But did she know how to mend a person's heart?

After sending the old man and matron on their way, the young soldier returned in haste. When he saw Chang Geng hadn't abandoned him and disappeared again, he sighed with relief. Chang Geng borrowed a few volumes of the *Classic of Medicine* from the house, then said his goodbyes to Chen Qingxu and took the young soldier to book a room at the inn in a town nearby.

The autumn insects were especially pervasive in Central Shu, and they were even noisier in the dead of night than during the day. Chang Geng placed his sachet with the new pacifying fragrance beside his pillow, but he soon found himself disappointed by Miss Chen's new formulation. Not only did it fail to calm his spirit, the overpowering scent of it kept him awake half the night before he finally climbed out of bed to spend the lingering hours before sunrise reading by lamplight. He depleted a full bowl of lamp oil and managed to memorize two and a half of the three volumes of the *Classic of Medicine* before day finally broke, yet felt not the slightest hint of fatigue.

It was as if a gold tank had appeared in Chang Geng's chest, puffing out steam as it burned through a bottomless supply of violet gold. No matter if he recited *compose yourself* in his head tens of thousands of times, tried to convince himself to view Gu Yun's imminent arrival as an ordinary occurrence, or indeed, tried not to think about it at all, eagerness and anxiety intertwined and wound themselves tightly around his bones. Their thorny vines lashed at his heart throughout the night, eliciting pain and numbness in turns. There was no use lying to himself.

The next morning, Chang Geng called the young soldier over. "Little brother, when you're traveling south through Central Shu on your way to the southern border, which roads do you usually take?"

"If it's for official business, of course we take the official roads. As for everything else, it depends on the circumstances, so it's hard to say. If necessary, we might even crawl in through some mountain ravine."

Chang Geng nodded in silence.

A short while later, the young soldier was stunned to discover that Chang Geng had changed out of the tattered robes he wore while traveling the jianghu and into a new set of attire. Though his new clothes weren't ostentatious, they were of a very fine make—one could tell at a glance that their wearer must be either wealthy or of noble descent. In the blink of an eye, Chang Geng had metamorphosed from a destitute scholar into an out-and-out noble young master. Even the innkeeper unconsciously spoke to him in a more respectful tone.

Dressed in this young master getup, he went out to walk his horse on the official road every day—it was hard to tell if he was waiting for someone or just showing himself off. His fine clothes were easily dirtied, so after pacing around in the dust all day, he'd arrive home in the evening covered in a layer of grime. Chang Geng didn't want to trouble others with his laundry, so he washed the clothes himself—he had to, because he only had two sets of this "young master" attire, and if he wasn't diligent with the washing, he would soon have no clothes to wear.

Every day when Chang Geng mounted his horse, he would think to himself, *Maybe I should just leave.*

But he hadn't seen Gu Yun in more than four years. Day after day, his longing had piled up into a mountain, and now he worried the entire thing would collapse at the slightest breeze.

Chang Geng wanted to run, but he couldn't bear to do it. He spent every minute of the ride out from the inn fighting with himself in his head, and would arrive each day at the official road before the battle had come to a conclusion. Then, since he had already come, he could only linger in the area getting whipped by the wind and tasting sand, failing to encounter even a single rabbit for all his waiting.[7] When he returned to the inn in the evening, he would think to himself, *Tomorrow, I'll settle my bill and leave.*

---

7   A play on the idiom 守株待兔, "waiting for a rabbit beside a tree stump," which refers to waiting foolishly for an unlikely coincidence. The idiom draws from a fable in which a farmer sees a rabbit collide with a tree stump and die, then hopes he will get lucky enough for it to happen a second time.

But the next morning, he would eat his words and head to the official road once again, fighting with himself the whole way.

He spent several days in this state of temporary madness. One evening, four or five days into the whole affair, Chang Geng turned his horse back toward the inn and gazed upon the bloody glow of the setting sun in the west. It was a beautiful scene, and he found himself slowing his pace to let his horse stroll and graze along the way. Thinking back on all he had done these past few days, Chang Geng didn't know whether to laugh or cry. *If Liao Ran knew, he'd probably laugh until his teeth fell out.*

Suddenly Chang Geng heard the thunder of hoofbeats approaching from behind. He turned his horse to make space to pass and looked back to see several large and handsome horses fly past, pulling a carriage behind them.

At a distance, he could only see that the riders were all in the everyday clothing of commoners, no different from any other travelers who hurried along the road. Yet for some reason, Chang Geng's heart began to race.

39

BANDIT SCOURGE

EVEN WITH FIERCE WINDS whipping past his ears and the horses' hooves thudding across the ground, Shen Yi's keen senses picked up the abnormal sounds inside the carriage. He spurred his horse to overtake Gu Yun, then placed one hand over his chest and mimed a retching motion, asking Gu Yun with his eyes—*What do we do if that guy pukes?*

A faint smirk crept across Gu Yun's face, clearly expressing his stance. *Serves him right, and he can clean it up himself.*

Gu Yun was heading south because Fu Zhicheng, the commander in chief of the Southern Border Army, was in mourning. General Fu's elderly mother had recently passed, so he had submitted a memorial to the court claiming that he would hand over his seal of command and return home to observe the mourning period. Being in mourning was an innocuous excuse—someone in mourning could take leave or not, and there were adequate explanations for their decision either way. Historically, however, regional commanders did not make such requests.

If a commanding general went home for several years, who would lead the troops if war broke out?

Furthermore, the entirety of Great Liang knew that General Fu had gotten his start as a bandit chief. The old Marquis Gu had beaten him into submission, and he was offered amnesty in exchange for service. Even today, the old general sometimes forgot himself and let a few cusses slip in front of the emperor. He wasn't overly concerned about propriety. This so-called mourning was clearly an expression of General Fu's dissatisfaction with the Marching Orders Decree. What's more, there had also been flooding in the south this year, and the southern border was a mess. The general had chosen this timing to quit in an attempt to compel the court to back down.

Within the carriage was Sun Jiao, the Assistant Minister of the Ministry of War and a staunch supporter of the Marching Orders Decree. The emperor had intended to send him as an imperial envoy to the southern border to "offer condolences" to the bereaved, meritorious General Fu, only for the minister's balls to shrink up into his body at the prospect. Tears streaming down his face, Sun Jiao submitted a memorial to the emperor stating that he was prepared for this to be his final voyage, and that he was ready to lay down his life for the nation. The emperor, helpless, had no choice but to send a messenger with a golden arrow token of command all the way to the northwest, and toss both the useless sniveling minister and the mess on the southern border at Gu Yun's feet.

Gu Yun had spent the better part of the year on the run, toiling away to wipe the emperor's ass. By now he was roiling with anger. He could not defy the emperor, so he instead went to every effort to torment the shameless Assistant Minister Sun.

As they drove the horses onward, Gu Yun caught sight of a young master walking his horse at the side of the road. He paid no attention at first, and only when he was riding past did he happen to glance at him. Their eyes met. It was a brief glance, like the flash of wings when a bird takes flight, and in an instant, Gu Yun's swift horse was already some dozen meters down the road. Before he realized it, his hands had already yanked hard on the reins.

The horse whinnied, and its front hooves reared high in the air before landing back on the ground, having turned a quick semicircle on the spot. Gu Yun stopped and stared at that young master—he looked somewhat familiar, yet Gu Yun was hesitant to call out his name.

Surely this is too much of a coincidence. Gu Yun thought, still uncertain. *Am I overthinking? Do I have the wrong person?*

While Gu Yun was wavering, Shen Yi had galloped up behind him. "What...aiyah!"

The young soldier accompanying Chang Geng finally reacted and dismounted from his horse. "Sir!" he called out in excitement.

Startled, Gu Yun's horse lifted its front hooves and snorted, pawing at the ground.

In that moment, even if Chang Geng were to be tossed into a pile of pacifying fragrance, his heart would've still beat hard enough to rattle his chest. He sat numb atop his horse, his mind a blank white, as if his silver tongue had melted into a pool of liquid metal and sealed every skillful word inside his mouth. Out of pure instinct, a stiff smile appeared on his face.

"Chang Geng?" Gu Yun called out hesitantly.

These two syllables hit Chang Geng's eardrums with a peal like the tolling of a great bell. Despite making every effort to remain composed, he ended up awkwardly rubbing his nose. "I happened to be passing through Central Shu when I heard from Miss Chen that Yifu would arrive in the next few days, so I decided to stay a while. I never expected I would run into you while I was just out walking my horse."

The young soldier's chin was about to drop onto his toes. *You have to bathe and change your clothes every day and show up at this exact time and place just to walk your horse?*

He looked at Chang Geng's unremarkable mixed-breed horse with new awe, suspecting that there was some godly steed hidden beneath its mottled coat.

Just then, a figure tumbled out of the nearby carriage. Heedless of this moving reunion between father and son, he stumbled to the side of the road and puked.

The interruption finally gave Chang Geng a chance to catch his breath and temporarily return it to his chest. He turned to glance at the Assistant Minister of War, who was trembling like a baby chick, and affected a look of gentle and refined surprise. "Have I said something nauseating?"

Gu Yun began to laugh. Although he had been vaguely aware of Chang Geng's activities over the years, he had never expected Chang Geng would grow into someone like this. It was like the youth he knew had become a whole new person. For a moment, Gu Yun forgot their unhappy parting, forgot their long standoff, their cold war, his distasteful actions in sending people to tail Chang Geng through all his travels, his refusal to let go. He was surprised that he managed to recognize Chang Geng at all. This child really had changed too much—the character of his every action, his every expression, had all changed.

Gu Yun quickly counted back. *That's right. It's been over four years, hasn't it?*

Shen Yi led his horse up to them with a smile. "My heavens, the little prince has really grown up in the blink of an eye... Do you still remember me?"

"Hello, General Shen." Chang Geng said with a smile.

Shen Yi sighed. "If it were me, I wouldn't have recognized you there. It's all because your yifu has been thinking about you every day. At this point it's turning into a complex; he can't stop himself from taking a second glance whenever he sees someone who looks like you..."

Gu Yun interrupted, unable to stand it any longer. "What nonsense are you making up now?"

Shen Yi looked at one, then the other, and finally spurred his horse past them with a chuckle to help pull Assistant Minister Sun back into the carriage. He waved a hand in front of the man's face. "Assistant Minister Sun, are you all right? Hang in there a little longer, we're almost at the inn."

Sun Jiao leaned against the side of the carriage, panting like a dying man, and almost kicked the bucket right there in the middle of the road. Yet the minister soon discovered that Chang Geng was his lucky star. After encountering Chang Geng on their way, those Black Iron beasts slowed from a wild gallop to a steady walk, as leisurely as an after-dinner stroll. Even the clangorous sound of their hoofbeats softened. Following Chang Geng's lead, the party soon arrived at the small town's inn. But the humble inn only had so many rooms; even if they booked the entire establishment, everyone would have to double up.

Gu Yun left them at the entrance. "I'll stay with my son," he said airily, "we can leave a single room for Assistant Minister Sun."

Sun Jiao courteously refused on instinct. "No, no; how could I impose on the marshal..."

Shen Yi reached from behind to pat Sun Jiao's shoulder, then lowered his voice and said, "Minister, accept the gesture. The marshal has run into the fourth prince and is in a great mood— or would you rather watch him think up ways to murder you all night?"

The sweat on Chang Geng's palms never dried, and his reins had nearly slipped from his hands several times. It was almost like he

BANDIT SCOURGE ☼ 45

was drunk—he knew he should stay alert yet couldn't help but sink deeper into his intoxicated state. Before laying eyes on Gu Yun, he was still wavering between *stay* and *run*, but the instant he saw him, every single thought flew from his head.

At this point, Gu Yun finally remembered to settle the score with Chang Geng for his misbehavior. As they entered the room, he closed the door behind him, his face dark. "You're really getting more and more out of line. The old housekeeper said you haven't returned to the Marquis Estate once these past four years. Last time I entered the palace to report on my duties, even the emperor asked after you. What was I supposed to tell him?"

In the past, any shift in Gu Yun's expression had made Chang Geng anxious—anxious to admit his faults, or anxious to stubbornly retort. But after so many years of separation, he found that all the caution and panic in his heart had disappeared. Now, he wanted to carve every one of Gu Yun's expressions into his heart—smiles or anger, he wanted the complete set.

Four years ago, he had swallowed down his misery and affected a calm façade as he declared, "The Marquis Estate can't detain me forever."

Today, he looked at Gu Yun and carefully revealed just the right amount of emotion. "If Yifu isn't there, what reason is there for me to go back?"

What could Gu Yun say? He never could manage to stay angry for more than three sentences, and hearing this, he couldn't even maintain the cold look on his face. His iron heart softened into a wad of cotton. Gu Yun looked around the small room, and, seeing a few medical texts tossed on the table, grabbed one at random and riffled through the pages. "What are you reading these for?"

"I've been learning some medicine from Miss Chen. I had hoped to become skilled so I could care for Yifu in the future. My talents are limited, unfortunately; I only know some basic techniques."

Gu Yun was speechless. *When did this kid become such a sweet talker?* he thought, helpless. *How lethal.*

After years spent guarding the Silk Road, Gu Yun's keen aura had gradually faded, like a legendary blade stored in its sheath. It seemed that his temperament was steadier as well. Calling an unspoken truce, neither mentioned their unhappy parting, but conversed good-naturedly about all they had seen the past few years.

Chang Geng talked and talked, until he realized the sounds from beside him had faded away. Gathering up his courage, he turned and looked—the beds in this inn were too narrow, and nearly half of Gu Yun's body was hanging off the mattress. He had carelessly pulled a bare corner of the blanket over himself, and his feet were crowded at the foot of the bed, while his head was pillowed on one hand. The exhausted marquis had actually fallen asleep in this position as he rested his eyes.

Chang Geng's mouth snapped shut. In the dark, he stared at Gu Yun's side profile for a while. He raised his hand, then lowered it again, several times, up and down, his fingers hovering hesitantly in the air for who knows how long. Finally, he held his quivering breath and laid his hand against Gu Yun's waist, patting the man's side as lightly as if he were brushing away dust.

"Yifu, scoot in a bit. You're going to fall," he said quietly.

Gu Yun started awake, but was quick to recall his whereabouts. With a hum of acknowledgment, he turned in the direction Chang Geng had nudged him and mumbled without opening his eyes, "I drifted off while we were talking; I must be getting old before my time."

Chang Geng pulled the blanket more firmly over him and reached over to remove his hair crown. "It's because I put pacifying fragrance beside the pillow. You must be tired from such a swift journey; get some rest."

This time Gu Yun said nothing because he had truly fallen asleep. There was very little space on the bed, and when two people lying on it spoke in low voices, it was like lovers whispering in each other's ears. Chang Geng nearly dipped down to kiss Gu Yun's temple—as if it were the most natural thing in the world—then flinched back as he realized the disgraceful direction of his instincts. He hastily shifted over to lie squarely on his own side of the bed.

The pacifying fragrance seemed to be a success: Gu Yun had fallen into a deep sleep the minute he relaxed. But its potency must have been selective because it had no effect whatsoever on Chang Geng. With Gu Yun lying beside him, every time he closed his eyes, he felt like he was dreaming, and couldn't help but open them again to make sure this dream was real. After a few rounds of this, every trace of fatigue evaporated. In the end, Chang Geng gave up on sleep and stared quietly at Gu Yun instead.

He stared the whole night through.

Chen Qingxu arrived at the inn the next morning. First, she grabbed the still desperately ailing Assistant Minister Sun as a case study and tossed him to Chang Geng to play with—that is, care for—before going up to see Gu Yun. Chang Geng glanced at her retreating back as she ascended the stairs, but showed not the faintest hint of curiosity, as if he had no interest in her patient at all.

Gu Yun had been on his way south for official business when he heard Chen Qingxu was in Central Shu, so he had sent someone with a letter asking her to come examine his eyes. Chen Qingxu didn't pause to ask about his symptoms but began her own examination directly. After a moment, she asked, "My lord, is your vision already weakening?"

"I would have usually taken my medicine last night, but I put it off so Miss Chen could examine me."

Chen Qingxu hesitated before speaking. "My lord, when my grandfather gave you this prescription, he must have told you that this medicine is not a cure, and likely wouldn't be a permanent solution."

Gu Yun showed no sign of surprise. "How long do I have left?"

Chen Qingxu's expression was grave. "If you use it sparingly from now on, you might be able to stretch it a few more years."

"Using it sparingly may be impossible," Gu Yun shook his head. "What do you think of increasing the dosage or switching to a new prescription?"

Before Chen Qingxu could reply, Shen Yi, who had been sitting nearby, spoke up in a low voice. "Every medicine is part toxin, and you take it constantly. Even if you change prescriptions, your only option is a more aggressive one. At that point, wouldn't you just be quenching your momentary thirst with slow-acting poison?"

"He's right," said Chen Qingxu. "I am ashamed to say that although our family has touted ourselves as a clan of miracle doctors, we've been unable to cure your eyes and ears all these years."

Gu Yun smiled. "What are you saying, Miss Chen? It is I who have made you all go to so much trouble."

Chen Qingxu shook her head. "For too long we have looked down on the foreign tribes around us as ignorant and uncivilized, restricting ourselves to the Central Plains. My lord, give me a few years. Very soon, I plan to set out on a journey beyond our borders. Perhaps I will stumble upon some solution."

Gu Yun was taken aback by her words. Aside from having a member of the Chen family check his condition, the main reason he had asked Chen Qingxu to meet him in Central Shu was as a plausible excuse to delay for a few days—he wanted to ensure a certain someone knew he was in the vicinity. He wasn't counting on a young lady like Chen Qingxu to resolve a condition that had stumped even her grandfather. "Miss Chen," he hurried to say, "you mustn't. It doesn't matter whether I can hear or not; the northern barbarians have been our enemies for generations. How could I possibly face the Chen family if you take such a risk for this trifling matter of mine?"

Chen Qingxu was quiet for a beat. She brought over her small satchel and took out a handwritten booklet. "This is an acupuncture treatment I devised. It's nothing miraculous, but it may alleviate the headache caused by your medicine. His Highness has studied acupuncture with me for some time; he will understand."

Seeing Gu Yun's frown, Chen Qingxu added, "I didn't tell him, he guessed on his own."

Several expressions flitted across Gu Yun's face, but in the end, he sighed. He felt like his head was beginning to hurt already.

After a few more words of instruction, Chen Qingxu retrieved paper and a brush and wrote a handful of nourishing prescriptions. "These are better than nothing. If that's all, I'll be taking my leave. Take care, my lord."

"Wait," Gu Yun called after her. "Miss Chen, please think carefully before you decide to cross the border."

Chen Qingxu turned to look at him, and a faint smile appeared on her ice-cold face, like blossoms on an iron tree.

"It's not only for your condition—some things simply must be done. If I may speak boldly: although my position is low and my power is weak, my aspirations are as lofty as yours. I was born into the Chen clan and chose the way of Linyuan. How could I spend my life in the shelter of my ancestors' accomplishments, seeking safety behind others' backs? My lord, may we meet again."

With that, she turned away and floated downstairs without giving Gu Yun another chance to call her back.

Chang Geng had become quite considerate after many years wandering the jianghu, and quickly stepped over to her. "Miss Chen, I'll see you out."

Chen Qingxu waved away his offer and looked searchingly into his eyes. He was young and strong; one sleepless night wouldn't do him much harm, but his face still showed signs of fatigue. Chen Qingxu asked in puzzlement, "Is there something wrong with the pacifying fragrance?"

"I'm afraid the problem is with me," Chang Geng said, smiling bitterly.

Chen Qingxu considered for a moment. "I always tell you to compose yourself, but in truth, I don't know the cause of the restlessness within you. Perhaps my solutions are impractical—a person can't really be without emotions and desires. If you truly can't restrain these restless feelings, perhaps you should let nature take its course."

Chang Geng flinched and unconsciously pursed his lips. *How exactly am I supposed to let nature take its course?*

Chen Qingxu took no responsibility for cleaning up after her kill. She departed right on the tail of that fatal blow, *let nature take its course*, and left Chang Geng wandering in a daze for the rest of the day.

Gu Yun remained in the small inn for two days and nights. Sun Jiao was eager to hurry on their way, but when he recalled the high-speed journey that nearly jostled his insides up and out of his throat, he was afraid to urge the others to leave. Yet when they finally did set out again, he found that Gu Yun no longer barreled along like he was rushing to be reborn. With the fourth prince stuck to his side every day, the pair strolled like holidaymakers out on a spring excursion. Sometimes their party even mixed with merchant caravans on their way back from trading in the north.

The people of the southern border were fierce, and bandits in the region ran amok. Minister Sun had ostensibly been sent to offer condolences to the regional commander, but that was merely a pretense. His true goal was to borrow the Marquis of Anding's might to uncover evidence that Fu Zhicheng, an appointed official of the court, was colluding with lawless bandits, and turn the Southern Border Army into a stepping stone for the advancement of the Marching Orders Decree. But as soon as Gu Yun entered Shu, their journey was delayed by one thing after another. Everything south of Central Shu was Fu Zhicheng's territory, and by now there had been plenty of time for the local tyrant to learn of their whereabouts. How were they to catch him off guard at this rate?

Once Minister Sun arrived at this question, he stopped puking, and instead acquired a bloody ring of blisters at the corner of his lips from anxiety.

"You can offend upstanding gentlemen, but you oughtn't offend petty people," Shen Yi whispered to Gu Yun. "Enough is enough. You'd better watch out if that bastard tries to get back at you when you return to the capital."

Gu Yun only smiled.

The sight of that careless grin made Shen Yi itch to concoct a long-winded speech. But Gu Yun replied, nearly inaudible, "Neither an upstanding gentleman nor a petty person will be a problem for me."

"It'll be a problem if you make a blunder," Shen Yi snapped back.

Gu Yun didn't stoop to Shen Yi's level but lowered his voice even further. "That guy is the real problem... Clashing with the Ministry of War like fire and water is the best way for me to be, don't you think?"

Shen Yi stared blankly for a long time, then sighed and spoke no further. Since when did Marshal Gu, who thought himself number one in the world, begin to spare attention for these kinds of under-handed maneuvers?

"I shan't be listening to an old maid like you ramble on any longer," Gu Yun said with a dramatic toss of his head. "I'm off to find my son."

He spurred his horse forward, ignoring whatever else Shen Yi had to say.

Shen Yi felt that those two were becoming far too nauseating.

In the south stood two verdant mountains, their lush slopes show-ing no sign of decline even as autumn turned to winter. A winding road, so long its end couldn't be seen, was pressed between them, circling its way up to the peak.

Horsewhip in hand, Gu Yun pointed out the scenery to Chang Geng as if he were discussing important matters of state. "Soldiers always get nervous when we see this sort of terrain. If an enemy set an ambush here, forging our way straight through is practically asking for a beating—even within Great Liang's borders, bandits will often come and declare themselves king in a place like this..."

Before the last words were out of his mouth, the shrill blare of a horn sounded from up in the mountains.

Shen Yi was on the verge of collapse. "Sir, are you a crow in human form?!"

40

HUNTING MONKEYS

P ON THE MOUNTAIN'S PEAK, a large flag was slowly hoisted into the air. At first glance, it appeared to be the banner for yet another "Apricot Blossom Village," but when the wind unfurled it fully, the words "Apricot Grove" became clear. The figures of numerous mountain bandits, large and small, showed themselves from their hidden places behind trees and foliage. All wore crude homemade armor and stood with arrows nocked and pointed at the group at the foot of the mountain.

Silver flashed on the slopes above. When Chang Geng squinted upward, he spied a suit of heavy armor, stolen from who knows where, standing at the mountain's peak. The face of the person in the armor was concealed beneath their visor, but they stood out in the open like a target waiting to be hit. Chang Geng almost wanted to laugh at this gang of highwaymen who had managed to set their sights on the Marquis of Order. But when he turned around, he found that Gu Yun wasn't smiling at all. Far from it—his expression was frighteningly dark as he squeezed one word from between his teeth: "Fools."

Chang Geng did a quick mental calculation, then lowered his voice. "So it's not just a rumor that the southern border officials are colluding with bandits? It's actually true?"

Gu Yun didn't speak, but his face grew still more grim.

For as long as there had been a Great Liang dynasty, the local specialty of the East Sea had been pearls, the local specialty of Loulan had been fine wine, and the local specialty of the southern border had been mountain bandits.

Due to the deployment of the farming puppets in recent years, farmers could no longer find work. Some joined the itinerant merchants and went north to make a living, while others decided for incomprehensible reasons to turn to crime and joined the mountain bandits in the south. Goods were becoming cheaper and cheaper, so silver seemed more and more valuable in comparison. Fewer people kept stores of goods and grain, and more began to keep stores of gold and silver instead. This, in turn, greatly increased the efficiency of the mountain bandits' robberies.

The culture of banditry flourished here, and the bandits' nests outnumbered even those of the wild hares. They were like prairie grass, ineradicable by wildfire and shooting up again with every spring breeze.[8] It didn't help that the Ministry of War treated the Southern Border Army like an unwanted stepchild. The army's funding was never enough, and they had no way to keep up with the bandits. Yet though the bandits had the advantage in numbers, their abilities in battle were limited. In the face of a proper army, their nests would fall one by one, so they were still wary of the local garrisons. Once a person came into money, they would naturally pursue peace and stability. No one wanted to spend their days getting chased around, constantly at risk of having their heads struck from their necks—and bandits were people too.

Thus, as time went on, the Southern Border Army and the local bandits developed a curious symbiosis.

---

8   A line from the poem 賦得古原草送別, "Ode to a Parting on the Ancient Prairies," by Bai Juyi, a Tang dynasty poet.

Fu Zhicheng, the commanding general of the Southern Border Army, had started out as a bandit in the first place. On the surface, he strived to keep the bandits in check and ensure they took only money and not lives—but what was this if not a method of shielding them? And with the Southern Border Army in dire financial straits year after year, tributes from the local bandits had played no small part in their ability to scrape by all this time.

Collusion between officials and bandits was nothing to be proud of, but Gu Yun understood the ins and outs of the situation. Over the past few years, the emperor had implemented farming puppets and thrown the gates open to new trade routes. Both were good policies that should have enriched the nation and strengthened its people—but for some reason, the national treasury didn't fill up. It emptied instead, and military funding was reduced once again. And now, the south had been struck by floods, and had yet to receive disaster relief. If fighting between the army and the bandits were to start on top of everything else, the common people's suffering would only intensify as bandits scuttled through every city and town. And even if the court wanted to appoint a new commander in chief to the Southern Border Army due to Fu Zhicheng's indiscretions, Gu Yun couldn't think of a single person other than General Fu who could keep the southern border under control.

Caught between two evils, Gu Yun chose the lesser of them. It was hardly a choice at all. He had to find a way to protect Fu Zhicheng for the time being.

In a few more years, when the construction of the Silk Road was complete and Great Liang's inland trade routes were fully opened, silver would flow in from overseas, and the nation could catch its breath. When that time came, not only would Gu Yun mobilize troops, he'd build a proper road from the Ba-Shu region to the southern border and strengthen government supervision over this faraway region where the emperor's control was weak. Only with this two-pronged approach could the bandit scourge be brought under control once and for all.

Unfortunately, none but he seemed to understand this situation, leaving Gu Yun to worry on his own. Or perhaps it wasn't that they didn't understand, but that to them, the Marching Orders Decree and future opportunities to kiss the emperor's ass for power and money were more important than the stability of the region.

Gu Yun had spent the entire way here pondering how to protect Fu Zhicheng. He had even sent him a secret missive, only for the general to pull this move on him before he'd even reached his destination. What gang of bandits emptied their whole lair for a highway robbery, and even showed up with flag flying and drums beating? They clearly knew who he was.

What difference was there between violently intercepting an imperial envoy of the court and outright insurrection?

Chang Geng had spent these years down among the people as he traveled the world. He had a good grasp of the current political climate as well as the everyday concerns of the populace. With some thought, the general outline of the situation became clear. He glanced at Gu Yun's face, then said under his breath, "Yifu, I think this may not necessarily be General Fu's intent."

"No kidding," Gu Yun said coldly. "Since when was Fu Zhicheng this stupid?"

These bandits who declared themselves king of the mountain likely recognized a handful of characters at most. If they wanted someone who could write and do sums, multiple peaks would have to share a single accountant. Perhaps these bandits had heard rumors leaked from somewhere or other and decided to act on their own.

They'd intercepted Gu Yun as both a test and a threat, so they could later go to Fu Zhicheng and brag about their accomplishments.

Unfortunately, they were idiots. And if their idiocy wasn't handled properly, responsibility for this incident was likely to fall directly on Fu Zhicheng's head.

High up on the mountain, a bandit raised a crude copper squall, bellowing at Gu Yun's party down below like he was singing lines in an opera. "Who goes there? Identify yourselves!"

Next to them, Shen Yi seemed torn between laughter and tears as he drew an arrow from his quiver. "Sir?"

"Shoot him down," Gu Yun ground out.

Shen Yi's arrow leapt from its string the instant Gu Yun's words left his mouth, piercing the bandit with the copper squall like a hot knife through lard. A startled bird squawked as it shot into the sky, its cry echoing through the mountain pass.

The valley exploded.

Minister Sun had no chance to rejoice that he'd grasped some leverage against Fu Zhicheng, as he was too busy being scared stiff. He tumbled from the carriage, babbling, "You mustn't, you mustn't! Marshal, you mustn't, there's at least a hundred bandits in these mountains. We only have a handful of people with us, and no one is wearing armor. We're practically defenseless! And the fourth prince, the fourth prince is of noble status, we can't let anything happen..."

Gu Yun didn't deign to look at the man as he waved Chang Geng over. "Your Highness, have you been keeping up with your training?"

Chang Geng said with a bow, "I should at least be qualified to serve as a modest cavalryman under the marshal's command."

"Come, I'll teach you how to hunt monkeys in the mountains." Gu Yun spurred his horse straight up the slope, and Chang Geng followed without hesitation. The seasoned Black Iron Battalion soldiers understood their commander's intent the instant Gu Yun moved and urged their horses to follow.

Minister Sun was left in their dust, his screams lingering in the air behind them. "Marshal, you mustn't—"

Someone snagged the back of his collar, lifting him bodily off the ground. Shen Yi hoisted the minister up with his sword hilt and tossed him onto the back of his own horse. Sun Jiao let out a squeak, and his eyes rolled back in his head at the impact.

"Minister Sun, stop yelling. This humble general will preserve your life; never fear," Shen Yi said in exasperation.

He glanced at Minister Sun, who had fainted dead away, whites of his eyes showing. *This is the first time I've seen an assistant minister who seems so much like a eunuch.*

On the mountain's peak, a young bandit turned to his chief. "Dage, I heard that eunuch yelling, 'Marshal.'"

Entombed inside the heavy armor, the bandit chief pushed the iron visor up and snapped, "No shit! If it wasn't a 'marshal' down there, I wouldn't be ordering an attack! Just shoot already! Surround them! Surround them!"

The call of a horn once again echoed through the valley, and the bandits surged forward in a wave, charging straight toward Gu Yun's meager forces.

Perhaps they'd attempted such a dramatic encirclement in an effort to bolster their courage. One side was already running down the mountain while the other was still banging pots and pans and yowling on their way over from the opposite peak, their headlong rush kicking clouds of dust up into the air. Unfortunately, most of their horses had been stolen from passing merchant caravans. How could they hope to keep up with the Black Iron Battalion's incomparable warhorses? The bandits were quickly left in the dust.

Gu Yun gave a hand signal, and the soldiers following him scattered in all directions. Now that the targets of the bandits' arrows had split, they rapidly lost any semblance of order.

Facing the throng of fierce bandits, Gu Yun dispassionately drew his sword, the blade flashing like snow. Without turning, he said to Chang Geng, "Remember this: on the battlefield, whoever clings to life is the first to die—"

Chang Geng was nearly blinded by that sword. Gu Yun's blade moved like a soaring dragon, drops of blood splattering in its wake. With a few strikes, the bodies of bandits and horses tumbled to the ground. He smoothly finished his sentence. "...Even if your enemies aren't worth a damn."

High on the peak, the bandit chief gazed down through a field scope. Seeing their plans had gone awry, he roared, "I told you to surround them! What's going on?!"

Distress was written across the face of the young bandit next to him. "Dage, I don't know!"

A deeply tanned bandit ran over to report. "Dage, it's not looking good!"

Seconds later, a light cavalryman charged through a gully. The bandit holding the horn didn't even have a chance to shrink his neck back before his head was parted from his body with the flash of a blade.

Gu Yun had outstanding riding skills and could gallop through mountainous terrain like he was riding over a flat plain. As he crossed a narrow mountain path, his sword whipped out in an arc. A blood-curdling scream sounded from behind a large boulder—someone had been hiding in ambush. Gu Yun flicked blood from his blade, using this action to give Chang Geng a chance to catch up. "There are plenty of obstacles in the mountains, and the local thugs often hide behind them. Even if your martial skills are good, you may not be able to avoid a trap."

Scanning the area, Chang Geng saw that a mechanical crossbow had been set up behind that rock, ready to shoot some unsuspecting passerby. His horse was no godlike battle steed, and he was having some trouble keeping up with Gu Yun. But he still felt every drop of blood in his body grow warm. "Yifu, how did you know?"

The corner of Gu Yun's lips curved up in a smile. "It's simply a matter of practice."

He had hardly finished speaking when a boulder suddenly came loose and rolled down the mountain toward them. Like there were eyes on the top of his head, Gu Yun dug his heels into his horse's flanks. The warhorse sprang forward as the falling stone practically brushed against its tail. At the same time, Gu Yun stood up in his saddle, grabbed a nearby vine, and swung through the air, flipping himself up into the canopy. Chang Geng heard a squelching sound and instinctively reared back, narrowly saving himself from getting a face full of blood courtesy of his savage godfather.

Gu Yun raised one eyebrow and smiled down at him from above. He whistled for his horse, and the well-trained animal trotted directly over to him. Chang Geng's heart pounded in his chest. That smile from Gu Yun had nearly sucked his soul from his body.

Gu Yun called down, "When hunting monkeys in the mountains, remember to first take the high ground—"

By now, the bandits' joke of an encirclement had already devolved into complete chaos. Gu Yun's men seized control of the mountain gullies at lightning speed, and the bandits transformed into a bunch of headless flies, which scattered in all directions as they were joyously slaughtered by the arrows raining down from above. By the time Chang Geng caught up, Gu Yun was once again mounting his horse, swiftly drawing a special arrow from his quiver as he did.

Both bow and arrow were thick and sturdy. The bow had to have weighed dozens of kilograms, and had a box the size of a thumb affixed to it. Chang Geng's eyelid jumped. *The bow has a gold tank?*

A moment later, a burst of white steam confirmed his guess. The shaft of Gu Yun's arrow seemed to be made of iron, and when it flew from the string, it let out a piercing shriek like twenty fireworks frantically racing toward the sky. As if shot from a miniature parhelion bow, the iron arrow sprang forth with enough force to pierce the sun and, with a clang of metal against stone that rippled throughout the entire valley, buried itself in a giant mountain boulder above that heavy armor.

There was an uproar like the galloping hooves of wild horses as the gargantuan rock quaked, then fell down the mountain's slope.

Troops of monkeys scattered, but the bandit chief was hindered by his heavy armor and looked up a second too late. Before he could see a thing, he and his armor were buried together.

"Yifu, I know this one." Chang Geng smiled. "Cut off the head, and the body will follow?"

Protected at Gu Yun's side, not a single hair on his head was out of place, even after swooping through hundreds of bandits. With his hems flying behind him, Chang Geng looked every inch the elegant young master.

Gu Yun clicked his tongue in dissatisfaction. *This is it for me. Next time I return to the capital, I'll be lucky if I have half as many young ladies throwing handkerchiefs.*

Just under an hour later, Gu Yun gathered up his "practically defenseless" Black Iron Battalion soldiers and strutted into the bandits' den.

Most of the bandits had scattered after the death of their shiny-armored leader. They were intimately familiar with the terrain and disappeared as soon as they melted into the mountain forests. Gu Yun had only a small force with him; it would be inconvenient to chase them one by one. He settled for capturing the few that hadn't run quick enough, stringing them together as they huddled like quail.

Gu Yun sat down in the bandit chief's tiger-pelt seat. Feeling that something was off, he stood back up and lifted the tiger pelt, then laughed. "This mountain king of yours has quite a unique throne." Beneath the magnificent tiger pelt draped over it, all four legs of the chair had been sawed off and replaced with a pile of gold bricks topped with a wooden board.

"If you sit on this thing, will you start laying golden eggs?" Gu Yun quipped.

Shen Yi coughed a few times, signaling to his marshal to please cut the crap.

By now, Minister Sun, who had been terrified into pissing himself, had finished changing his pants and returned looking prim and proper once again. He looked around and, realizing that this was his best opportunity, instantaneously transformed from the pathetic creature he had been when he was yelling "You mustn't!" without end into a stately minister of the capital. He stepped toward the prisoners and barked with righteous fury, "Who gave you the courage to intercept an envoy of the court? Who ordered you to do this?"

Chang Geng, who had been fiddling with Gu Yun's special bow, looked up at this and smiled. "Intercepting an imperial envoy is tantamount to treason. The chief's crimes speak for themselves, but ordinary bandits might get off with just banishment and penal service. Ones as heroic as all of you, though..."

Chang Geng trailed off with another meaningful smile. He didn't spare the trembling bandits a glance, as if this were just an offhand remark, and turned to direct his attention elsewhere. Grinning at Gu Yun, he asked, "Yifu, this is such a good bow. May I have it?"

Gu Yun waved an imperious hand. "Take it."

Sun Jiao paused. He had never met this fourth prince and was unsure what he intended. His first impression was of a man who didn't put on airs, who was gentle in temperament and skilled in conversation, yet wasn't especially shrewd. Now, he realized he may have been mistaken. The bandits weren't stupid; after hearing these words from Chang Geng, they at once began to beat their chests and wail.

"This lowly citizen didn't know the imperial envoy had arrived, please spare me!"

"It's not easy to fill our bellies on the road. In a remote place like this, we might not see a single traveler for half a month! How could we know we'd run into an imperial envoy as soon as we stepped out to work? I'm innocent... Actually, I'm not innocent at all—but I have old parents and young children; It's not like I have it easy!"

Sun Jiao was speechless.

Just then, a Black Iron Battalion soldier marched in on rapid steps and leaned over to whisper in Gu Yun's ear. "Sir, we've received a letter from Inspector General Kuai of Nanzhong. He heard you were harassed by bandits and has set out with two hundred men from his personal guard to assist you. They will arrive in short order."

Gu Yun looked up, expressionless, and happened to meet Sun Jiao's gaze. The blood on Marshal Gu's body had yet to dry, and the sight of him frightened that momentary smugness right off Sun Jiao's face. Kuai Lantu, the Inspector General of Nanzhong, had been put in place specifically to keep Fu Zhicheng in check. He commanded two hundred elite personal guards and could deploy them as needed in a crisis. In the event of a true insurgency, although two hundred personal guards alone couldn't hold off the Southern Border Army, individuals among them stood a chance of breaking through a siege to bring word of the attack.

Kuai Lantu and Fu Zhicheng were enemies forced to rub elbows on a narrow road, and both desired to force the other down a dead end. It was unlikely that this newcomer was arriving with any good intentions.

"Inspector General Kuai got word the very second I broke into the bandits' nest," Gu Yun said lightly. "He must get news even faster than the soil god of these mountains."

Sun Jiao knew Kuai Lantu had misjudged the timing and appeared too soon. He hurried to say, "Marshal, I must tell you the truth: ours should have been a secret journey, but we encountered the fourth prince on the way. How could I allow an imperial heir to expose himself to such peril? I took the liberty of notifying the Inspector General of Nanzhong and requesting assistance…"

"I see. Minister Sun has been very thoughtful," Chang Geng said with a smile. "But how did you know this journey would be so perilous?"

With reinforcements on the way, Sun Jiao's back grew straighter. He cupped his hands and said, "Your Highness, to be honest, before setting out on this consolatory mission, I had already heard that bandits were rampant along the southern border. To prepare for all contingencies, I requested a marching orders decree from His Majesty before my departure—only for the worst to actually come to pass! How fortunate we are that the marquis has fought countless battles and remains unflappable in the face of danger."

At these words of flattery, Gu Yun looked at him with a smile that didn't reach his eyes and said nothing.

Sun Jiao's voice took on a sanctimonious tone. "These bandits maraud unchecked. If they are so brazen as to intercept even appointed officials of the court, how must they treat the local commoners? If we don't eliminate this scourge, the southwest will know no peace. It seems I was right to make this request of the emperor. This is the first marching orders decree in the history of our Great Liang—and it seems the honor has fallen to General Fu."

41

OPENING MOVES

I N ADDITION TO HIS two hundred personal guards, Inspector General Kuai of Nanzhong had at his disposal ten suits of heavy armor and fifteen light pelts. If he added a giant kite, his forces would be no weaker in terms of armor and engines than the guard of Yanhui Town on the northern border. When he received Sun Jiao's letter, Kuai Lantu knew the day he'd waited for had finally arrived.

Fu Zhicheng was a rough and arrogant character who had gotten used to life as the local tyrant. He had refused to show Kuai Lantu respect in front of others multiple times, and a grudge had long been fermenting between them.

Now the emperor had his heart set on centralizing the nation's military power and enacting the Marching Orders Decree, and His Majesty would surely need a sacrifice to his cause. The northwest was Gu Yun's domain, so he couldn't touch it, at least for now. Jiangnan's primary military force was its navy, which undertook the important mission of supervising merchant ships traveling to and from the Far West. In addition, there were still wokou pirates stirring up trouble in the East Sea, so this area, too, was an inappropriate place to make sweeping changes. The Central Plains Army stabilized the nation from its center, so it would be the last piece to tackle, if at all. The backward hinterland of the southern border was the single remaining option for an opening move. If Fu Zhicheng were smart, he would hunker down on the southern border and pretend he didn't exist—but instead, he had sprung up to pressure the court under the pretense of mourning.

One of Kuai Lantu's personal guards approached and reported in a low voice, "Sir, the kerosene has been prepared."

Kuai Lantu accepted the field scope from the guard and surveyed the charming scene of verdant mountains laid out before him. The master of the mountain in the distance was a Daoist priest who went by the title Jing Xu. Most of the common people followed the lead of the emperor in his Buddhist faith, so not only had his Daoist temple struggled to stay open, the local ruffians had also seen him as an easy target and showed up time and again to rob him. In a fit of rage, Jing Xu had beaten one of these robbers to death, and with nowhere left to go, his only option had been to turn to banditry. As someone who was both literate and ruthless, he had made quite a splash, and later became the leader of all the bandits within a few hundred kilometers' worth of mountains along the southern border.

Kuai Lantu knew Jing Xu and Fu Zhicheng were birds of a feather. If he wanted to kill Fu Zhicheng, he would have to start with this Daoist priest. Kuai Lantu and Sun Jiao had formulated their plans long ago when the emperor first used a golden arrow token of command to summon Gu Yun to the south. They would make the first move and spread news that the court was sending an imperial envoy to investigate Fu Zhicheng's collusion with mountain bandits on the southern border. For his part, to make certain that no one attacked the imperial envoy, Fu Zhicheng was sure to warn all the great bandit chiefs about the incoming consolatory delegation and order them to keep a tight leash on their subordinates—Kuai Lantu and Sun Jiao were counting on this.

Now, should these bandits trust General Fu about the nature of this envoy? Or should they trust the rumors?

If these bandit chiefs harbored the tiniest mote of doubt, what would they think when Fu Zhicheng tried to pass off investigators sent by the imperial court as envoys of a "consolatory delegation"?

Just as the imperial envoy was about to cross into the southern border region, Kuai Lantu received Sun Jiao's letter warning of their approach. He sent a group of his men disguised as soldiers of the Southern Border Army to Jing Xu to tell him the entourage of the Marquis of Anding and the imperial envoy had been ambushed. Kuai Lantu's instructions were clear: they were to tell the bandit chief that, lest prying eyes spot the connections between General Fu and the bandits, the general could not personally intervene and therefore sought the Daoist priest's assistance. Jing Xu and Fu Zhicheng were friends of long standing, so whether he was suspicious or not, there was no question that he would cover for Fu Zhicheng at such a critical juncture. Placing brotherly loyalty above all, Jing Xu rushed over with his men the instant he heard the news.

The minute they left, Kuai Lantu and his lackeys emerged from the mountainside where they'd been lying in wait and blockaded every road out of the mountain with heavy armor infantry. Thousands of arrows dipped in kerosene were nocked onto bow strings, and Jing Xu's lair burned to the ground in a great blaze. At the same time, Kuai Lantu sent light pelt and heavy armor units to patrol the mountains and send any escapees to join their compatriots in the afterlife with a short cannon blast. Both the bandits who poured out to guard the mountain and the helpless elderly, women, and children who stayed within received the same treatment. None were spared save a few survivors intentionally left alive so they could bring Jing Xu the news.

Looking over at the distant mountain peak, which had now been reduced to a pile of rubble, Kuai Lantu stroked his whiskers and smiled in satisfaction.

"That's enough. Let's go; it's time to call on Marshal Gu." With a wave of his hand, heavy armor infantrymen, light pelt cavalrymen, and two hundred elite soldiers fell into formation with practiced ease and prepared to set out. Kuai Lantu mounted his horse and glanced back at the peak mangled by flames. "Fu Zhicheng always said the mountain bandits were wily; 'ineradicable by wildfire and shooting up again after every spring breeze,'" he observed absently. "Well, this humble official has set the wildfire, and we'll see if they shoot up again now." With that, he urged his horse on.

Now every bandit in the area would see that, to save himself from the imperial envoy's investigation, Fu Zhicheng had launched an attack on his former brothers as a stalling measure. Kuai Lantu was determined to have Fu Zhicheng and the mountain bandits at each other's throats—wasn't Fu Zhicheng the one who thought so highly of his own cunning, and was so sure no one could find anything to use against him?

Sun Jiao and Kuai Lantu had carefully plotted every detail of their plan. To guard against Fu Zhicheng doing something so desperate as actually rising in armed rebellion when backed into a corner, Sun Jiao invited the Marquis of Anding to personally oversee the consolatory mission. Gu Yun had yet to reach the age of thirty, and his abilities might not be sufficient to counter Fu Zhicheng, a regional commander who had battled his way through mountains of corpses. But whether they were or not mattered little—it just so happened that Fu Zhicheng owed a debt to the former Marquis of Anding for recognizing his talents and supporting his military career.

Kuai Lantu was certain that Fu Zhicheng wouldn't dare touch a hair on Gu Yun's head.

Although most of the former Marquis of Anding's men had retired from the military in their old age, the influence of that complex network of relations lingered. If Fu Zhicheng really were so ungrateful as to attack the old marquis's only son, the backlash from the Southern Border Army would be more than enough to teach him his lesson. Furthermore, no matter how reckless the man might be, even he wouldn't think his insignificant Southern Border Army had the ability to raise a rebellion and shake the foundations of Great Liang—right?

Minutes after Kuai Lantu left the mountainside, a palm-sized wooden bird arrived. It swiveled its eyes and flapped its wings, then took off once again amid the thick smoke and crimson splashes of blood, shrinking into a small black dot before disappearing entirely.

At the same time, inside the Southern Border Garrison, Fu Zhicheng had just received word that the Marquis of Anding's entourage had been ambushed. Thunderstruck, he leapt to his feet and grabbed the scout by his collar. "Where is the Marquis of Anding now?"

"The Marquis of Anding slaughtered his way through Apricot Grove," the scout said in a rush, "but for some reason, he remains in their lair and refuses to leave. He even swapped out their flag for the commander's banner of the Black Iron Battalion."

When Fu Zhicheng heard this, his face twitched, and he swept all the wine glasses and teacups on the table to the floor. He spat in fury, "Those whoresons haven't done a worthwhile thing in their lives; all they know how to make is trouble!"

The scout was afraid to even breathe too loud. He stepped to the side, knelt down on one knee, and watched as the commander in chief of the Southern Border Army paced back and forth across the room like a caged beast. Fu Zhicheng wasn't surprised that Gu Yun cut down the Apricot Grove bandits. It would be a far stranger tale if he were successfully ambushed. But that still left him with the question...what was the Marquis of Anding thinking?

Why did he stay at Apricot Grove, rather than hurry along on his journey? If he was staying only to interrogate the bandits, why swap out the flag? Was he waiting for someone? Was he waiting to *do* something? Not to mention...Gu Yun's official reason for coming south was to offer condolences to a general in mourning—so why had he brought the commander's banner of the Black Iron Battalion? If the commander's banner was here, was the Black Iron Tiger Tally here too? Did he really bring only a handful of guards and a useless assistant minister?

Some hundred kilometers from here, that Inspector General of Nanzhong had without a doubt prepared a full bucket of mud to smear on him. Had Gu Yun made contact with him ahead of time?

As it stood, Fu Zhicheng couldn't tell which side Gu Yun was on. His eyelid began to twitch. Although he had indeed served under the former Marquis of Anding, he hadn't interacted with Gu Yun much over the years. He knew well that Gu Yun disapproved of his involvement with the bandits. Fu Zhicheng couldn't begin to guess the true reason for Gu Yun's visit.

"Saddle the horses." Fu Zhicheng broke the silence. "The Mountain Tiger, White Wolf, and Spirit Fox Divisions come with me; we will go see the Marquis of Anding and the imperial envoy. The Forest Leopard will gear up and await orders. Watch for smoke—that will be your signal to move in. Be prepared to march at a moment's notice."

The scout stared at Fu Zhicheng in shock—with this, General Fu had mustered almost half the Southern Border Army. Were they planning to behold the Marquis of Anding or besiege him?

Pulling a long halberd off the wall in one smooth motion, Fu Zhicheng barked, "What are you waiting for?!"

Three quarters of an hour later, the Southern Border Army's forces set off for Apricot Grove. There was no going back now.

As night deepened over the official road through the southern border, merchant caravans that had missed the chance to stop at an inn set up temporary camps at the side of the road. These itinerant merchants traveled throughout the land and were used to roughing it in the wild. They left a single night guard with a burning torch to watch as the rest dropped off to sleep.

At the third night watch, the lilting call of a cuckoo sounded from inside the forest. The night guard and several "merchants," who had only been pretending to sleep, stood up one by one. They exchanged no words, but communicated with their eyes as they brushed past each other, then slunk behind the wagons without a sound.

These wagons had secret compartments built into them. After the men shoved aside the goods piled on top, they lifted a board to reveal the hidden cargo beneath: cold armor that reflected no glint of light. In small groups of three to five, these nocturnal travelers swiftly donned the steel armor. Among them were hawks, carapaces, and even some light pelt cavalrymen.

Then, they turned and disappeared into the night, dispersing in all directions. The rustling of the forest as they departed startled a few sleeping birds awake, but within minutes, all returned to stillness. Only the points of light from the merchant caravans' torches remained, scattering over the darkness like a handful of gold pieces strewn across the southern border's mountainous terrain.

Under the cover of night, multiple unseen forces, each with motives of their own, sped toward Apricot Grove. The Apricot Grove bandit chief, crushed beneath that giant boulder, had never in his wildest dreams imagined that his singular stupid decision would become the spark that lit the fuse on the southern border.

Inside the bandit lair within Apricot Grove, the bandits under Sun Jiao's interrogation doubled down on their story: they had no idea the imperial envoy was coming. The assistant minister spun his wheels for half a day with little to show for it. Defeated, he was left with nothing to do but sit, eyes drifting toward the door again and again.

Gu Yun took a few bites of food, then wiped his mouth and set down his chopsticks. Watching Sun Jiao, who looked so antsy he may as well have been sitting on a bed of nails, he laughed. "Assistant Minister Sun, you've looked at the door seven or eight times since we sat down to eat. Do you really miss Inspector General Kuai that much?"

Sun Jiao cycled through several expressions before molding his face into an ingratiating smile. "Marshal, don't be absurd—is the food not to your taste? Why don't you have some more?"

"I'll pass." Gu Yun shot him a pointed look. "Overeating slows one's movements; this is plenty. Oh right—Jiping, if you have nothing else to do, count up all the gold and silver in this bandit lair. If we're going to the trouble to rob bandits, we can't end up with nothing to show for it. Pack it up and take it with us."

Sun Jiao stared.

Gu Yun turned back to him with a smile. "Assistant Minister Sun, you won't impeach me when you get back, will you? Ay, to be honest with you, given how stingy the Ministry of War is these days, times have been tough for the Black Iron Battalion," he said with a sigh. The trussed-up bandits were quick on the uptake, and when they heard this, they hurried to speak. "We have account books! We do! They're...they're up there!"

Shen Yi turned to look where they pointed and found that this place even came with its own semi-secret hideaway. A tall ladder stood in the corner leading straight up to the ceiling, where a pile of hay concealed a small attic constructed on top of the rafters.

Great, Shen Yi thought. *I've once again become the accountant of a chicken coop.*

It was at that moment that Kuai Lantu arrived at Apricot Grove.

Kuai Lantu strutted in with his personal guards in tow. The scent of blood and fire on him had yet to disperse, shrouding him in a murderous aura. He stepped forward and announced in a booming voice, "This lower official Kuai Lantu, Inspector General of Nanzhong, greets the Marquis of Anding, Assistant Minister Sun, all the generals, and this..."

Chang Geng smiled at him. "Li Min."

Kuai Lantu trailed off.

Sun Jiao hurried to remind him in a low voice. "Show some respect, that's Prince Yanbei, His Highness the Fourth Prince!"

Kuai Lantu started in surprise—Li Min, the emperor's youngest brother, had never shown himself before the eyes of the world. Most people only knew that he had once been lost among the commoners. After he was found, he kept to himself deep within the Marquis of Anding's estate and rarely left. He was rather young, and had no achievements to speak of... What was Commandery Prince Yanbei doing *here*?

As if Prince Yanbei's sudden appearance was some ill portent, Kuai Lantu's eye twitched fiercely. But before he could respond, one of his personal guards hurried inside and whispered into his ear.

"Inspector General Kuai," said Gu Yun, "How precious the spittle of your subordinates must be. May we not even listen?"

Kuai Lantu kicked the personal guard away. "Insolent! To whisper in front of the marquis and His Highness; unthinkable!"

Even after suffering a solid kick, the guard's face showed no resentment. He dropped to one knee without hesitation and reported, "My lords, tens of thousands of soldiers are marching toward Apricot Grove. It appears to be the Southern Border Army!"

The words had barely left his mouth when an unfamiliar vanguard captain arrived on the slopes of the mountain. The inspector general's personal guards raised swords, spears, and halberds as if they were trying to light up the night with the cold gleam of their blades. The vanguard captain, however, showed no sign of fear. He called out, "Fu Zhicheng, Governor of the Southwest, leads his troops to welcome the marshal!"

Gu Yun's face was impassive as he thought to himself, *This Fu fellow really knows how to seek his own demise.*

Kuai Lantu sneaked another surreptitious look at Chang Geng. The fourth prince offered him a smile, then turned, unhurried, and ascended the ladder in the corner, disappearing up into the attic where the account books were stored.

Kuai Lantu saw his chance and stepped forward. "Marshal, this lower official has something to report!"

Gu Yun looked back up at him.

"As the defending general of this region, Fu Zhicheng has neglected his duties and colluded with local bandits. He treats the peasants like livestock and conspires with foreign nations to the south. His traitorous intentions are clear. Marshal, you must be prepared!"

"Oh? Is that so?" Gu Yun did not look at all surprised to hear such accusations. He spun his worn prayer beads around his fingertip a few times, as if lost in thought. After a beat, he said, "Well then, let's invite him up. I would like to see exactly how he plans to commit treason."

Kuai Lantu and Sun Jiao looked at each other, both suspecting their ears had malfunctioned.

Gu Yun repeated, "I said, let's invite General Fu up here. Do the two of you have some objection?"

Chang Geng had climbed into the attic and found that it was quite a change of scene from the dim lair down below. The small space had a window and even a skylight, through which he had an excellent view of the mountain below. The Apricot Grove bandits had previously raised their flag right above this skylight. Shen Yi had set up a tall torch off to the side, and Chang Geng found him burning some unknown substance that released a pillar of white smoke, which rose straight into the sky without being diffused by the wind.

Chang Geng smiled. "I thought General Shen was here to examine the accounts and came up to lend a hand. It turns out you came up here to light a smoke signal instead."

Shen Yi leapt down from the skylight. "Your Highness, you understand accounting too?" he asked with interest. "What have you been up to all these years?"

"Nothing much. I studied medicine with Miss Chen for a while, and sometimes ran some errands for my jianghu friends. I've also joined up with merchant caravans here and there. I've learned a bit of everything."

It was an obvious nonanswer, but Shen Yi tactfully asked no further. A person couldn't fake experience or knowledge. No matter how a green youth might work to put on an act of composure, those who were observant would see the cracks in their façade. Chang Geng's experiences traveling the jianghu could not have been so simple, or he never would have acquired such an enigmatic aura. As he was now, he was impossible to read.

Chang Geng pushed open the attic window and looked out. A grand procession of troops snaked their way up the mountain, their commander's banner whipping in the wind like a ship's sail. Their armor gleamed coldly under the glow of the torches, and a cloud of steam rose from their ranks and wound down the mountain for kilometers, like a living, breathing dragon. Fu Zhicheng had commanded the Southern Border Army for nearly ten years and was all but a local tyrant on the southern border. If he had brought a few hundred soldiers to slay bandits and welcome the imperial envoy today, he would have room to explain and maneuver. But the man had actually dragged half the Southern Border Army out for this errand.

Chang Geng watched the procession for a while, then sighed. "Yifu may have been inclined to protect General Fu at the start, but now it will be difficult do so."

"He has not only failed to appreciate the favor, it looks like he's coming here to throw down the gauntlet." Shen Yi gazed curiously at Chang Geng's serene profile. "Your Highness has the demeanor of a seasoned general, steady in the face of danger. And at such a young age—you are a rare talent indeed."

"It comes with experience," Chang Geng said evenly. "Back when I infiltrated the East Sea rebels' lair with Yifu, I truly had no confidence that we would make it through. That time, those of us at his side were more burden than help, and we had no idea when the navy would finally arrive—nor did we know if they would receive the letter we sent en route in the first place. Yet he still laughed with ease as he always does, and we made it out in one piece. I learned something back then."

"What?"

"There's no point in being afraid."

Shen Yi thought for a moment, then shook his head with a smile. "Well of course, everyone knows that there's no *point* in being afraid. But it's just like how everyone gets hungry at mealtimes and cold without clothes. It's a natural reaction of the body. How can someone suppress the reactions of their own body?"

A faint smile appeared on Chang Geng's face. "It's possible."

Shen Yi blinked in surprise. He suddenly had a vague feeling that quite a lot was hidden within Chang Geng's, *It's possible.*

"It is my belief that, as long as you are willing, there's nothing in this world that can defeat you—not even your own flesh and bones," Chang Geng said in a soft voice.

These words sounded ordinary, but Chang Geng's expression and tone as he said them were too resolute—so resolute that they were oddly bewitching, in a way that made others unconsciously believe them too.

"Your Highness, when you and the marshal were trapped in the East Sea, you still had some dozen experts from the Linyuan Pavilion at your side. It was a collaboration from within and without. But this time is different. We only have Assistant Minister Sun, who has his heart set on advancing the Marching Orders Decree, and Inspector General Kuai, who is harboring his own ulterior motives. Fu Zhicheng is about to fight his way up the mountain with the thousands of soldiers under his command. Isn't the situation even more desperate than last time? Your Highness, are you not worried?"

Chang Geng flashed him a self-possessed smile. "I'm not worried. Seeing the commander's banner of the Black Iron Battalion flying above this attic, I feel as if there are three thousand Black Iron divine cavalry hidden within these southwestern forests. I can't help but feel reassured."

Taken aback, Shen Yi laughed awkwardly and pressed his hand to his forehead. He broke out in a cold sweat on Gu Yun's behalf—their little highness certainly lived up to his bloodline as the descendant of imperial dragons. He was quite a handful.

"Besides," Chang Geng spoke up again. "General Shen knows too, right? That my yifu might not be dead set on saving Fu Zhicheng."

Shen Yi was speechless.

He actually didn't know that part!

42

ONSET OF CHAOS

KUAI LANTU'S PERSONAL GUARDS obeyed the order to make way for the Southern Border Army, but they did not sheathe their weapons. They left Fu Zhicheng a narrow, blade-studded path up the mountain. Bandit Fu also dropped all pretenses of subtlety. He brought more than a hundred of his elite soldiers with him, each and every one armed to the teeth. They marched in two long columns, baring their blades to ward off the personal guards flanking them.

Both sides clashed the whole way up, and Fu Zhicheng gritted his teeth and pushed his way through amid the clamor of metal on metal. He didn't look like he was coming to beg forgiveness, but rather like *he* intended to arrest and interrogate Gu Yun.

The remaining Southern Border Army soldiers surrounded Apricot Grove in a solid wall, glaring menacingly up toward the mountain's peak. Kuai Lantu clenched his jaw. He hadn't expected such audacity from Fu Zhicheng—this man didn't even perform the most basic niceties before charging straight in with weapons drawn, disregarding completely the presence of the Marquis of Order.

Fu Zhicheng charged up the mountain like a wild storm and appeared at the peak in a gust of thick bloodlust. Sun Jiao, acting as the guard dog, bore the brunt of his initial attack, and, in his hasty retreat, accidentally trod on one of the tied-up bandits lying on the ground. The bandit yelped, and the ferocity of this cry made the pair of chopsticks Assistant Minister Sun used for legs go weak with fear. Fu Zhicheng had yet to open his mouth, but the opposing side had already suffered one casualty.

Chang Geng looked down from the attic with clear interest. "I remember now," he said to the stupefied Shen Yi.

Shen Yi's ears perked up.

"Assistant Minister Sun's younger sister from his father's primary wife married Imperial Uncle Wang as his second wife after he became a widower...*tsk*, what is the emperor thinking, allowing his uncle's brother-in-law to enter the Ministry of War? Isn't it more punishment than reward to make the man deal with a bunch of dissatisfied generals all day?"

"Your Highness," Shen Yi asked carefully, "you said just now that the marshal might not be set on saving Fu Zhicheng. Could you please enlighten me?"

Chang Geng shot him a sidelong glance. "Why else would we remain in this bandit stronghold? If he had his heart set on protecting Fu Zhicheng, he would have already hastened to the Southern Border Camp to interrogate him."

Shen Yi was silent. In all honesty, he had wondered about Gu Yun's decision as well—but he had been accustomed to trusting Gu Yun unconditionally for many years. He'd thought Gu Yun still had another card up his sleeve.

"I'd guess that when Yifu saw these lawless bandits blocking our way, he was already beginning to weigh the pros and cons. If Fu Zhicheng had appeared in person to confess his crimes, Yifu may have considered letting him off out of respect for his years of labor and service, but now..." Chang Geng chuckled. "It isn't a crime to be greedy, cunning, or even foolish. But Fu Zhicheng should never have openly challenged the Black Iron Battalion."

The Black Iron Battalion was the product of three generations of painstaking effort. Regardless of whether the nation's true military power rested in the hands of the emperor or Gu Yun, every day the glory of the Black Iron Battalion persisted was another day Great Liang maintained at least a superficial degree of security. A public challenge to the Black Iron Battalion was an attempt to shake the foundations of the nation. This alone was intolerable to Gu Yun.

Below, Fu Zhicheng gazed at Gu Yun in silence. It seemed that he still retained some small measure of reason, for he returned his sword to its scabbard and dipped into a bow. "It has been many years since we last met. I'm glad to see Marshal Gu safe and sound after all this time."

Seeing Fu Zhicheng bow his head, his guards sheathed their own weapons and arrayed themselves behind him in a loyal wall of flesh. The tension in the room eased at once. Kuai Lantu and Sun Jiao both inwardly cheered—bringing Gu Yun here had been the correct move after all.

Yet after watching Gu Yun stare at Fu Zhicheng for a moment, they never expected his next words.

"I haven't been entirely safe. General Fu, Inspector General Kuai has just informed me that as the Governor of the Southwest, you have colluded with local bandits and conspired with foreign nations to the south, with clear intent to commit treason. What do you think of this?"

No one expected Gu Yun to be even blunter than Fu Zhicheng. With the Southern Border Army knocking at the mountain's door, he didn't mince words, and instead interrogated the man outright. The atmosphere thickened once again.

Up in the attic, however, Chang Geng was relaxed. He seemed quite fond of the bow Gu Yun had given him. It weighed several dozen kilograms, yet he hadn't put it down for a single second. He had strapped it to his back earlier, and now he unshouldered it and held it in his hands, carefully wiping it down with a handkerchief he had produced from who knows where.

Shen Yi thought for a second. "But if he intends to give up Fu Zhicheng, won't he have no choice but to watch as His Majesty pushes through the Marching Orders Decree?"

"General Shen," Chang Geng said placidly, "haven't you considered this before? Even rural farmers know that once the Marching Orders Decree goes into effect, it will divide the military power invested in Yifu's Black Iron Tiger Tally. All the regional commanders oppose it. So why won't he say a word against it?"

"Why?" Shen Yi found himself asking.

"Because he grew up with His Majesty, and he understands His Majesty's headstrong nature better than anyone. Every day the Marching Orders Decree is delayed is a day His Majesty is unable to personally control the nation's military power, a day he'll fail to eat and fail to sleep. Opposing it will merely intensify the conflict within the court, and the most Yifu will achieve will be to turn lord and subject against each other, leaving an opening for vile characters to gain his coveted position. He must make this compromise eventually; it's only a question of how..."

Chang Geng's last words were drowned out by a furious shout from below. Kuai Lantu had made his move right before Gu Yun's eyes!

Kuai Lantu wasn't as timid as Sun Jiao. The moment Gu Yun spoke, he knew this wasn't going to end well. Either he or Fu Zhicheng would die in Apricot Grove today. The Southern Border Army stood ready at the foot of the mountain, and the more words he wasted here, the faster his demise. He might as well capture this Fu bastard before he had a chance to act.

No matter how many Southern Border Army soldiers waited at the foot of the mountain, without their leader, wouldn't they be lambs to the slaughter? Kuai Lantu had made a snap decision to go over Gu Yun's head. He pointed at Fu Zhicheng and shouted, "Arrest this traitor!"

The inspector general's personal guards, who had been on a hair trigger since they entered the bandit's lair, surged forward at his command.

Chang Geng sneered. He took a heavy iron arrow from his quiver and slowly drew his bow from where he stood in the attic. A thin trail of white steam hissed from the bow tip and puffed against the side of his face. As the condensation beaded on his jade-like skin, he looked all the more handsome and gentle.

Shen Yi was privately shocked. This bow had been custom-made for Gu Yun, and even though it was equipped with a gold tank that allowed it to achieve the effect of a parhelion bow, it was still far too heavy for any normal person to draw. Chang Geng was no more than twenty, yet when he drew the bow and took aim, his arms were as steady as stone, without the slightest tremble. This young highness had been doing far more than "keeping up" with his martial training.

"Even if the marshal did intend to compromise," Shen Yi ventured, "who would be left to clean up the mess on the southern border in General Fu's place?"

"What do you mean?"

Shen Yi ran down the list of all the major and minor military generals in service. "The newly appointed Jiangnan Army and Navy Commander Zhao Youfang is relatively competent, but aside from him, the others aren't up to the task. We may not be short on fierce generals, but the position of commander in chief of an entire region requires more than just combat ability. Both experience and a record of service are a must, and they'll need to hold their own against both local powers and those useless idiots in the Ministry of War. His Majesty can't very well dump a naval commander into the southern border's mountain ranges, can he?"

Chang Geng laughed, but his gaze remained fixed on the scene unfolding below. Fu Zhicheng wasn't going to let himself be arrested without a fight, and the seasoned general of the southern border indeed lived up to his valiant reputation. With one sweep of his sword, he took off a man's head, then turned to face the charge of a guard in heavy armor head-on. He made no move to dodge, swinging his sword to meet the attack, then leapt up, landed with one foot on the heavy armor's shoulder, and flipped in midair. Three of his Southern Border Army soldiers charged after him, the heel ropes they carried snaking out like whips to ensnare the heavy armor between them.

Fu Zhicheng and the steel machinery let out twin roars. The general gripped his iron sword in both hands and slashed down, the blade finding with fatal precision the chink in the heavy armor's nape and severing the neck of the soldier inside. The heavy armor took one last stiff step and fell still.

Only then did blood start flowing from the armor in streams.

Fu Zhicheng sat atop the heavy armor's shoulders and wiped blood from his face, then turned his hawklike glare toward Kuai Lantu.

Kuai Lantu finally took an involuntary step back.

At that moment, an arrow streaked down from above with force enough to shoot down the sun, slicing through the air with a shriek that rang through the bandit lair.

Fu Zhicheng's pupils contracted, but it was too late. The arrow brushed the top of Kuai Lantu's black official's hat, bursting it into two halves with the force of its passage. Shaken from its bun, his hair spilled down like an unkempt ghost. The arrow had yet to reach the end of its flight—it punched straight through the chest of the heavy armor, pulverizing the sheet of iron on both sides, before nailing itself into the ground with no loss of momentum. Rocked by the force of the impact, Fu Zhicheng tumbled from his perch.

The ground around the arrow's landing site exploded, leaving only a pit behind. The three Southern Border Army soldiers simultaneously leapt back. The arrow had embedded itself perfectly at the intersection of their heel ropes.

The nock of the arrow was still trembling with the force of its impact, buzzing like a hornet's nest.

"How impertinent." Chang Geng muttered under his breath. Beneath the shocked gazes of everyone in the room, he drew a second iron arrow and nocked it to the string. At the same time, he quietly continued his conversation with Shen Yi. "General Shen, don't forget, there is still one more person."

Shen Yi was still deep in shock at his breathtaking shot. It took him several seconds to find his voice again. "...Forgive me, I am unable to recall anyone else."

"So close, yet so far."

"What?" Shen Yi blurted out in shock.

The corners of Chang Geng's eyes curved in a smile. "Yes, I mean you."

Down below, Gu Yun's face was devoid of his usual easy confidence. His taut features made him seem especially cold. "Kuai Lantu, I have been meaning to ask you a question. Where did you find the guts to keep so many private soldiers?"

Kuai Lantu's face was ashen as the buzz of that iron arrow echoed in his ear. Unsure whose side Gu Yun was on, he began to panic. "M-Marshal, there are some things you don't know. Because the Inspector General of Nanzhong works on the border, the court granted me special permission to maintain a guard to protect against mob uprisings…"

Gu Yun wouldn't be put off. "With the exception of His Majesty's Imperial Guard, no guard detail is permitted steam-powered armor with firepower greater than light pelt cavalry. Even the heavy armor used by the Imperial Guard is not allowed gold tanks over sixty centimeters in size. Kuai Lantu, whose memory is failing, yours or mine?"

Kuai Lantu sucked in a sharp breath.

Of course he knew he was breaking the rules, but while this infraction wasn't a minor one, neither was it especially major. Someone could make a fuss about it and write a nasty impeachment against him, but if he could take out Fu Zhicheng and make way for the Marching Orders Decree to be enacted, it would be but an unfortunate footnote to a great achievement, easily forgotten. Now that he had come this far, there was no going back. Kuai Lantu clenched his fist and returned fire with some insinuations of his own. "My lord, with a traitor to the nation before us, is it really the time to be quibbling over the specifications of my guard detail?"

A slight frown creased Gu Yun's brow, as if he were unused to arguing face-to-face.

Kuai Lantu didn't miss this fleeting change in his expression. Now that he had thrown caution to the wind, Inspector General Kuai found that the legendary Marquis of Anding wasn't so scary after all—he was merely a young man with high status. What was Gu Yun without the former marquis's people behind him?

On the other side, Fu Zhicheng roared with fury. "You bastard—who are you calling a traitor to the nation?!"

Kuai Lantu raised his voice. "Everyone, we have been surrounded by the rebel army. Our only option now is to capture their leader before they have time to react! My lords, I hope you will control your subordinates and show you will not tolerate treason!"

Fu Zhicheng was so angry he could only laugh. He had an ugly face, and his laughter made him look still more like a wicked devil. "Capture me? I'd like to see you try!"

Fu Zhicheng's personal guards moved first—they surged forward and charged into the main hall to bring a close-quarters fight to the Inspector General's guard. Apricot Grove's tiny bandit nest was shortly packed full of armor and weaponry.

Why was Gu Yun still feigning cowardice, merely watching the commotion? Shen Yi didn't understand. The earth-shattering din of battle cries spurred him to action, and he made to jump down from the attic. But as soon as he turned, he saw that young prince's unaffected expression. His arrow's aim never strayed from Gu Yun. If anyone should get too close, he would skewer them on the spot.

"General Shen, don't worry. I'm keeping an eye on things." Chang Geng's voice held a subtle yet unquestionable conviction.

A terrifying thought crossed Shen Yi's mind: was Gu Yun deliberately arousing the bad blood between Fu Zhicheng and Kuai Lantu to kill by the hand of another? And before Shen Yi had figured it out himself, the fourth prince had already seen through it?

"If Fu Zhicheng is captured today, the position of commander in chief of the southern border will be vacant," Chang Geng said calmly. "His Majesty may be stubborn, but he understands where his priorities lie. An important region like the border needs a senior officer to guard it, and across all the court, no one is more qualified than you, General Shen.

"His Majesty is only undermining my yifu's military power because his paranoia runs too deep. There is still affection between them from growing up together, and the security of Great Liang still rests on my yifu's shoulders. Once the Marching Orders Decree is enacted, the Black Iron Tiger Tally will be an empty symbol. No matter who becomes commander in chief on the southern border, they will have only administrative and not true military power. Yifu has already made his stance clear—isn't it only right for His Majesty to offer his marshal a sweet to soothe the pain of this beating?"

Chang Geng paused, then smiled. "General Shen, consider this: even though His Majesty has little fondness for me, his discount youngest brother, he won't reduce the yearly reward he grants me by a single coin. Altogether, it's even more than Yifu's annual salary."

Shen Yi set aside the complicated question of who, exactly, was the Marquis Estate's breadwinner for the time being, and looked at Chang Geng in shock. Several expressions flickered across his face. Finally, he sighed. "Your Highness, you truly have changed."

The teenager they had brought back from the small town of Yanhui was pure and stubborn, every emotion worn on his sleeve. Shen Yi had inwardly applauded his tenacity of spirit many times. Any normal child who transformed from a country bumpkin into a prince overnight would have long been spellbound by the splendor of the capital city.

But now, this young man—who spoke passionately to him about the direction of the nation in the middle of pitched battle—had shed all the tenderness of youth. The extent of his transformation was frightening.

Chang Geng didn't reply. For the last four years, he hadn't dared let up on training either his body or his mind for a single day. It wasn't because he wanted to accomplish great things. It was because he wanted to become strong as quickly as possible; strong enough, one day, to exchange witty repartee with the wu'ergu... Strong enough to protect a certain person.

"Our nation's greatest difficulty right now is a lack of money," Chang Geng said. "Although our ports are open, the Central Plains people rarely make sea voyages, and our coastal defense is lacking. We depend on the Westerners to travel back and forth and bring commerce to us. The Western merchants who make the trip reap the big profits, and the silver that trickles into our coffers isn't even enough for His Majesty to spend secretly buying the Westerners' violet gold."

"That's true," Shen Yi agreed. "But this is only a temporary situation. There are a number of ways to remedy it."

Chang Geng laughed. "That's right. This spring, I visited the Silk Road. The entrance of the Silk Road in Loulan is so prosperous it fills one with awe. And when I thought of how my yifu had fostered this growth with his own hands, I, too, was filled with pride. In another three years at most, the Silk Road will be fully connected and span the breadth of Great Liang. Once the common people profit from the trade it brings, gold and silver will flow into the national treasury. The Lingshu Institute won't have to fret over funding, there will be plenty of money for military salaries, and with a strong army, who would dare to invade? By then, it won't matter to my yifu who is in charge, himself or the Ministry of War."

Shen Yi fell silent. He didn't understand how after a four-year separation, Chang Geng understood Gu Yun better than before. Everything he said was true.

A few years ago, Gu Yun had oozed bloodlust, always privately muttering about how he'd beat up this or that person. Yet ever since he took charge of the Silk Road, he said these things less often. Part of it was that, as he grew older, he began to think more and lose his temper less...but another part was that Gu Yun had never wanted to cling to military power in the first place—what point was there in swaggering about like that?

The only thing he wanted in life was peace for his nation.

If this could be achieved in battle, he would don his armor. But if defense was all that was needed, he was also willing to be a poor and humble guard along the trade routes.

Watching Shen Yi lost in thought, Chang Geng recalled hearing someone say that no one could get between a general and his mechanic—such was the trust and understanding between them. A hint of sour envy creeped into his heart. But before he could finish brewing this vinegar,[9] there came a flutter of wings, and a bird landed on the windowsill. Chang Geng started, then put aside his bow and arrow. The bird obediently flew over and perched on his palm.

Upon closer inspection, it was fashioned of wood, though exquisitely lifelike in construction. The movements of its neck were cute and clever, not unlike a living creature.

Shen Yi was a former member of the Lingshu Institute, and the way his hands itched at the sight of machinery was a chronic condition. Upon seeing the bird, his eyes nearly popped out of his head. He all but fidgeted with greed, but had no good reason to ask Chang Geng for the little machine. Chang Geng lightly tapped a particular rhythm into the bird's stomach, and the panel sprang open to reveal a roll of paper inside.

---

9   *Drinking vinegar is used as slang for jealousy, usually in the context of romantic relationships.*

When Chang Geng read its contents, a shift came over the immovable calm of his face.

"What is it?"

Below, Gu Yun spotted a flash of light out of the corner of his eye. He raised his arm and placed his hand, slender and pretty as a noble son's, on the sword that hung at his waist.

A small southern border soldier had sprung up and charged at Kuai Lantu. Gu Yun's Black Iron guard rushed to his aid, but before Kuai Lantu could react, the soldier opened his mouth and spat something out. The Inspector General turned to dodge, instincts sounding the alarm—but it was too late. A blow dart the size of a finger buried itself in his neck. At the same time, the Black Iron guard's sword slashed down on the southern border soldier's head, as if the man hadn't seen the blow dart flying toward Inspector General Kuai at all.

Kuai Lantu's throat spasmed, and he raised his hands as if to grasp something—but within a split second, both assassin and mark had lost their lives.

Sun Jiao hadn't expected this mishap. He stepped back and crashed into the wall behind him with a clatter, petrified.

Then, with a shriek that pierced the skies, half of the high ceiling of the bandits' nest burst open. Countless Black Hawks swooped down onto the scene.

Kuai Lantu and Sun Jiao had plotted to use Gu Yun to force Fu Zhicheng into rebellion, but Gu Yun had refused to follow their plans. He had exacerbated the conflict before they could make their move, goaded Fu Zhicheng into killing Kuai Lantu, and produced the Black Iron Battalion—which had somehow infiltrated the southern border—to handle Fu Zhicheng. He had deployed troops with good reason and killed two birds with one stone...

But something was wrong!

Chang Geng dashed down from the attic. This wasn't over yet!

Now that he thought about it—the one who started all of this wasn't Kuai Lantu, the Ministry of War, Sun Jiao, or even Gu Yun...

43

THE SOUTH

THE BANDIT CHIEF Jing Xu had accompanied the message-bearing "Southern Border Army" soldier to assist Fu Zhicheng. But as they rushed toward their destination, the veteran bandit sensed something was wrong—the group's leader seemed to be taking them down a path where the bandits often sounded the bells.

There were many such places in the mountains of the southwest. The terrain was craggy, a natural maze, and any outsider who entered would soon find themselves hopelessly lost. A complicated series of tunnels spread in all directions below the earth, and once the locals went to ground, they could appear and disappear at will. The bandits often found ways to lure people into these twisted mountain passages, then hemmed them in and robbed them. A robbery in such a place was a guaranteed success, and this tactic was well-suited for countering certain famous armed escort forces and jianghu sects. In the bandits' slang, they called it "sounding the bells."

Jing Xu may have been in a hurry, but his mind was clear. As they approached the area, he realized that this was one such "bell jar." Cold sweat trickled down his back. He screeched to a halt and sent someone up to interrogate the soldier leading the way. It only took a short exchange to find that this so-called soldier's story was riddled with holes. Caught out, the soldier attempted to launch a surprise attack. The mountain bandits subdued him in a flurry of limbs, only for him to commit suicide by poison.

Startled and suspicious, Jing Xu ordered his subordinates to return the way they came. On the way back, they ran into one of their comrades from the stronghold they had just left, covered in blood. Only then did Jing Xu learn that their lair had been demolished. By the time they rushed back in a panic, all that remained were broken tiles and crumbled walls around a ground strewn with burnt corpses.

The work of ten years had turned to ash overnight.

"Dage!" A distraught bandit staggered over and clutched Jing Xu's arm. "The tunnels. Don't panic; we still have the secret tunnels!"

The southwest was mountainous, and the bandits were like wily hares with three exits to their burrows. Many of them had excavated secret tunnels deep inside the rocky peaks, where they could disappear into the earth. If enemies fought their way up the slopes, the locals could vanish into the mountain ranges after a feigned attempt at defense. Even Black Hawks in the sky couldn't snatch a gopher in its burrow. The other bandits' eyes lit up at this reminder.

Jing Xu swayed on his feet, face blank, without a single trace of joy. He watched his subordinates eagerly leave to search the tunnels, hoping for a lucky break—but he knew it was useless. If their assailants had only come to kill with swords and spears, the majority of the mountain's residents could have escaped through the tunnels, and the attack wouldn't have shaken the foundations of their stronghold. But they had burned the mountain down.

Even Kuai Lantu didn't know what he had sent up in this blaze.

Jing Xu stood frozen for a long time, until a shrill wail sounded from the direction of the tunnels. The people who had gone to search shouted in despair, "The tunnels have all collapsed!"

The great bandit chief closed his eyes. *Of course.*

Below this unremarkable mountain, hidden in the secret rooms, there was no gold or silver of the kind stored in Apricot Grove, but violet gold.

Never mind the Southern Border Army, even the Black Iron Battalion struggled to make ends meet with the scant amount of violet gold they were supplied by the court. Fu Zhicheng naturally had his own black-market suppliers. Kuai Lantu had been tipped off that Fu Zhicheng and the great bandit chief Jing Xu were close, but he didn't know that the Daoist priest Jing Xu was the "shopkeeper" from whom Fu Zhicheng purchased his black-market violet gold.

A bandit's business was robbery; he never missed an opportunity to skim off the top. Jing Xu was doing business with the black markets and smuggling violet gold for Fu Zhicheng—of course he was getting something out of it himself. Jing Xu didn't consider himself an avaricious man, so he kept only a tenth of the goods with each transaction. Fu Zhicheng was well aware and had tacitly permitted him to continue.

Shortly before this incident, Jing Xu had delivered the latest batch of violet gold to the Southern Border Army. The tenth he kept for himself was stored in his hidden chamber below the mountain. Now, ignited by the fires scorching across the mountain, it had become the fatal blow that detonated the tunnels and killed every last soul in the stronghold.

Was this a coincidence? How *could* it be a coincidence?

Jing Xu recalled something he'd heard long ago: "The gentleman is moved by justice; the miscreant is moved by profit.[10] Those who come together for the sake of profit will fall apart because of the same." He and Fu Zhicheng had come together for the sake of profit, and now that their unsavory business had come to light,

10   *A line from* The Analects of Confucius.

Fu Zhicheng would abandon him without a second thought. The mountains were lousy with bandits; even if he discarded Jing Xu, there were countless others he could patronize in his place.

"Dage," one of his subordinates sobbed. "Let's dig out the tunnels, maybe there're still some survivors."

Jing Xu stood, silent, and shook his head.

"Dage!"

Cries and wails rose from all around.

"That's enough!" Jing Xu roared. The survivors standing on the scorched earth stared at him. "Come with me." His eyes gradually reddened, like those of a ferocious beast about to sink its fangs into its unfortunate victim. He lowered his voice and said through gritted teeth, "If Fu Zhicheng shows us no humanity, he can't claim I'm acting without justice. After so many years, he really thinks I'm defenseless against him?"

Back in the bandit lair at Apricot Grove, Chang Geng was speaking:

"The southern border has numerous mountains and numerous strongholds within them. The bandits do not each govern themselves but follow an established hierarchy of authority. As far as we know, there are three great bandit chiefs." Chang Geng produced a ragged sheepskin map and pointed several features out to Gu Yun. It was densely covered in complex notation that indicated the terrain, climate, types of roads, what carriages could pass through each road, and all sorts of other information.

Gu Yun had seen this kind of map before in Jiangnan. There was no mistaking it—it was unquestionably the work of the Linyuan Pavilion. He considered Chang Geng with a pensive look beneath the lamplight but said nothing. He signaled for him to continue.

Gu Yun had planned for three thousand Black Iron Battalion soldiers to disguise themselves within the southbound merchant caravans traveling the mountain roads. With the smoke signal as their cue, they moved secretly under the cover of darkness and dropped from the sky once Kuai Lantu's guards had trapped Fu Zhicheng on Apricot Grove's peak. Over two dozen Black Hawks, aerial assassins, got the brawl on the summit under control while Black Carapaces and Black Steeds split into two and divided the forces of the Southern Border Army at the foot of the mountain. The Southern Border Army had the advantage in numbers, but with their commander captured and facing the Black Iron Battalion in the flesh, Gu Yun rounded them up as easily as a flock of defenseless sheep.

When a commander took a great army on the march not to slay his opponent, but to bolster his own courage, even if he brought an army of tigers and wolves, they would turn into nothing but a cartful of sheep in the end.

Yet before the chaotic battle at Apricot Grove could reach its conclusion, Chang Geng relayed another piece of news.

"Yifu, look: the factions of the three great bandit chiefs split the southern border into three. They usually coexist peacefully, each keeping the bandits within their own territories in check, and all three have some connection with the Southern Border Army. The most notable among them is the Daoist priest Jing Xu, whose territory is here, farthest to the north."

"Why is this person special—because he is the most powerful?" asked Shen Yi. "Or because he has the closest relationship with Fu Zhicheng?"

"Because he smuggles violet gold for Fu Zhicheng," Chang Geng said quietly.

Gu Yun's eyelid jumped, and his head shot up. "How do you know? Why *did* you come to the southwest?"

Four years ago, when the monk Liao Ran lured him to Jiangnan, Gu Yun had already begun to harbor suspicions. The Linyuan Pavilion was embedded deep within the jianghu and stood outside political affairs; it couldn't monitor every interaction between the highest officials of the court. They had likely discovered the dragon threat in the East Sea by tracing the civilian violet gold black market.

Chang Geng smiled but seemed unwilling to explain further. "The people of the jianghu have their ways. Yifu needn't worry…"

Gu Yun cut him off with a lift of his hand, face overcast. "You know what sort of a crime smuggling violet gold is under our laws. Getting caught means certain death. Everyone in the violet gold black market is one kind of desperado or another. Don't you know the saying, 'A gentleman does not stand beneath a crumbling wall'?"[11]

Listening from the side, Shen Yi wished he could blush on Marshal Gu's behalf. Look how righteous he sounded scolding others—as if he had nothing to do with smuggling violet gold himself!

Chang Geng didn't become upset or argue back. He merely looked at Gu Yun with the ghost of a smile, the words, *I know what you've been up to, but I won't expose you before an audience*, written plainly on his face.

Gu Yun flinched in surprise; he instantly caught the meaning of that look. *What, this little bastard is even investigating me now?*

Chang Geng pressed Gu Yun's hand back down. "Yifu, don't get angry yet. Let me finish."

When Chang Geng laid his well-formed hand over Gu Yun's own, his palm was warm and his touch gentle, as if he were holding a baby

---

11 A quote from the eponymous philosophical text Mencius meaning that wise people foresee and mitigate risks.

bird. He let go at once, but for some reason, the whole interaction felt strange. Gu Yun was suddenly a bit awkward. Between close friends and brothers, embraces, joining hands, horseplay—even a kiss or two was unremarkable. Military officers didn't care for meaningless etiquette, and the rank and file cared even less. But... this gesture was really too clingy. Gu Yun's fingers twitched, and he forgot what he was about to say.

Chang Geng, seemingly unaffected, continued. "Ge Chen sent me a message via wooden bird just now. Someone has burned down Jing Xu's mountain stronghold."

"...Ge Chen?"

"Ah, Ge Pangxiao."

Gu Yun shot a look at Sun Jiao. Since the moment of Kuai Lantu's death and Fu Zhicheng's capture, Assistant Minister Sun had turned into a pathetic little quail and forgotten how to do anything but tremble. Gu Yun had set someone to guard him.

The situation looked complicated at first glance, but with a few moments of thought, the whole unraveled. Fu Zhicheng was aware of Gu Yun's party's itinerary, so if he really wanted to clear himself of suspicion on the matter of colluding with bandits, there was no way he'd choose this time to act against Jing Xu. Doing so would be the same as a confession that he was silencing witnesses to cover his own tracks. This fact, along with Sun Jiao's foolish confidence in the plot he had hatched with Kuai Lantu, made the truth clear: The Ministry of War wanted to advance the Marching Orders Decree at all costs, and Kuai Lantu wanted to get rid of Fu Zhicheng. Thus, the two joined hands to exacerbate the conflict between Fu Zhicheng and the bandits and force the two parties into a cockfight right under the Marquis of Anding's nose. No matter how much Gu Yun might want to protect Fu Zhicheng personally, there was no way he could turn black into white when the truth was so stark before him.

The cruel bastard who had set fire to the mountain was most likely Kuai Lantu. But there was no way Kuai Lantu knew the true nature of Jing Xu and Fu Zhicheng's arrangement. If he had, he never would have chosen to burn the mountain. Even if Fu Zhicheng's collusion with bandits was made manifest, it might not be such a severe crime that the Governor of the Southwest and commander in chief of the Southern Border Army would be condemned to death. If Kuai Lantu knew Fu Zhicheng was using Jing Xu to smuggle violet gold, he wouldn't rashly lend him a hand in destroying the evidence. Smuggling violet gold was treason, enough to send ten Fu Zhichengs to their death.

"The violet gold black market has three major sources," Chang Geng began. "First, the official government stores. Even with the law as strict as it is, there are always profiteering rats willing to take the risk for personal gain. They steal from the official violet gold stores, then sell an adulterated product to civilians. The second are the 'black panners,' the suicidal prospectors who travel beyond our borders to hunt for violet gold mines and risk death to extract it. The third comes from overseas. We have been investigating the third trail because this particular batch of violet gold originates in the foreign nations to the south."

Gu Yun sat up straighter. "You're sure?"

Chang Geng nodded silently.

Shen Yi's expression also grew grave. Everyone knew that the nations to the south did not produce violet gold.

The foreign violet gold flowing into Great Liang's black markets came directly from Far Westerners, along set routes and through a set cadre of black-market traders. The suppliers wouldn't complicate things by opening a side branch of this operation and passing the contraband through new hands—it was too risky. If there really was some interest using the southern nations as a screen while manipulating the southwest's violet gold market from afar, those behind it almost certainly weren't taking such a great risk, nor concealing themselves so well, just to trade a few kilograms of illegal violet gold.

"Since the southern nations lie beyond our borders, our ability to intervene is limited," said Chang Geng. "We've sent people south to investigate several times, but all have returned empty-handed. And that Daoist priest Jing Xu, who has yet to show his face, is another wild card. Yifu, I doubt a vicious bandit who has gained access to violet gold is planning to cover the mountains with farming puppets and plow the wilderness into fertile fields."

Gu Yun pondered for a moment, then stood up and whistled. A Black Hawk circling overhead descended on silent wings and landed in front of Gu Yun. A frown furrowed Gu Yun's brow, and he issued three orders in quick succession.

"Take this map and dispatch two Black Hawk scout squadrons to locate the three great bandit chiefs of the southern border. We capture them first.

"Arrest the Inspector General of Nanzhong's guards and find out which lawless thug gave Kuai Lantu the brilliant idea to instigate conflict between Fu Zhicheng and the bandits this way.

"Interrogate Fu Zhicheng. Jiping, you take this one."

After giving everyone their orders, Gu Yun inadvertently squinted his eyes. Before even Shen Yi could notice anything amiss, Chang Geng had already caught his arm. "Yifu is it...did you bring your medicine? It's almost dawn; maybe you should get some rest."

Shen Yi only realized what was going on when he heard the word "medicine." He felt something about this was rather odd. It was as if

Chang Geng's eyes were constantly glued to Gu Yun, always alert to the slightest sign of trouble.

Gu Yun opened his mouth to deny it out of habit, but Chang Geng spoke first. "I still haven't tried the acupuncture pattern Miss Chen gave me back at the inn. This incident may not be over yet. Yifu, you should let me help, in case more trouble should arise."

Only then did Gu Yun recall that Chang Geng already knew; there was no point in hiding it from him anymore. He muttered, "I'm going to lie down in the back for a bit," and allowed Chang Geng to follow him.

Chang Geng kept an acupuncture instrument set, some common medical ingredients, a small quantity of silver pieces, and a few books in his travel bag. By now, Gu Yun had discovered that however polished he looked on the surface, he in truth only had a few changes of clothes and simply alternated between them. Gu Yun couldn't figure this kid out. As a child, he had hated going outside so much that Gu Yun had to deploy eighteen different types of martial arts just to drag him to the market. Why did he now refuse to stay put in the capital, and instead insist on experiencing every kind of suffering the jianghu had to offer?

A month or two could be excused by novelty. But was it still a novelty after four years?

Chang Geng had performed acupuncture on many people, but now that he was alone with Gu Yun, he began to feel nervous. Not even when he had first learned acupuncture from Miss Chen by placing the needles in his own skin had he been so anxious. He washed his hands over and over, nearly scrubbing off a layer of skin, until Gu Yun finally couldn't stand it anymore. "After all this time, did Miss Chen only teach you how to wash your hands?"

Chang Geng swallowed, his voice slightly strained as he asked, careful, "Yifu, do you mind lying on my lap?"

What was there to mind? It wasn't as if it were a girl's lap; so what if Gu Yun lay on it? Gu Yun very much wanted to ask, *Are you sure you can do this?*

He swallowed those words back down before they could leave his mouth, afraid to put any more pressure on his amateur physician. Adopting a carefree attitude, he thought to himself, *Here goes nothing. It's not like he can stab me to death.*

He had steeled himself to suffer a few jabs, but Chang Geng turned out to be far more competent than he'd imagined. He hardly registered the fine needles as they entered his acupoints. Soon enough, the familiar headache reared its head...but, perhaps due more to psychology than physiology, it really did feel much better with the needles in place.

Once Gu Yun relaxed, he couldn't resist the urge to start rambling. "You keep following the Linyuan Pavilion out here into the wind and rain. What are you after?"

If Chang Geng wished to serve his nation, he ought to return to the capital and enter the court as a commandery prince. Why was an imperial scion running about investigating violet gold with the reckless jianghu denizens of the Linyuan Pavilion?

Chang Geng paused before replying, though his hands continued to move, unfaltering, behind Gu Yun. Finally, he chose a tactful way to decline the question, and said, "I've never asked how Yifu got poisoned."

Gu Yun went silent.

Chang Geng laughed, thinking he had managed to terminate that line of inquiry. But after a moment, Gu Yun said evenly, "When I was young, the marquis took me to the battlefield on the northern border. I was nicked by a barbarian's poisoned arrow."

Chang Geng was stuck dumb.

"There you have it. Now it's your turn."

Gu Yun was an accomplished actor, whether he was acting tough, acting incompetent, or acting ignorant. He would say his piece with a straight face, truths and falsehoods intermixed according to his mood, and as for which was which, it was anyone's guess. Chang Geng could only rely on his intuition to warn him that Gu Yun wasn't telling the whole truth.

"I...I wanted to venture out and see the world for myself," Chang Geng began. He hesitated, then continued. "Great Master Liao Ran once told me that if my heart was as large as the world, worries the size of a mountain would be no more than a drop in the ocean. If I traverse the mountains, rivers, and oceans, see the great profusion of living things, and look often at other people, I will be able to look down and see myself. One who has never treated the dying with their own hands will see their own superficial scrapes as mortal wounds; one who has never eaten a mouthful of yellow sand will see only the brilliant gleam of spears and armored horses when they think of battle; and one who has never gnawed on empty husks complains of an imagined illness when they discuss the suffering of the common people."

Gu Yun opened his eyes and looked up at him.

As the medicine took effect, his eyes gradually recovered their focus. Chang Geng's first instinct was to duck away. When he managed to compose himself and meet Gu Yun's gaze, he still found himself unable to hold it for long. If he looked too much, an overheating gold tank would appear in his chest to bake and scorch him, sending a prickling warmth down his spine. He shifted his legs, struggling to sit still.

"Your teacher's surname is Zhong—Zhong Chan, right?" Gu Yun suddenly asked.

Chang Geng started slightly.

"The General of Flying Cavalry, whose horseback archery skills are unparalleled throughout the land. A dozen or so years ago, he was accused of defying the late emperor, but after civil and military officials up and down the court spoke on his behalf, he was spared the dungeons and merely dismissed from office. He disappeared without a trace. When the Western Regions rose in rebellion, the late emperor tried to restore him to his post in a panic. But he couldn't find him." Gu Yun sighed. "The instant that arrow left your bowstring, I knew he had taught you—no wonder you lost every person I sent to tail you. Is the old general still in good health?"

Chang Geng murmured in assent.

Gu Yun didn't speak for a long time.

He didn't tell Chang Geng that long ago, Zhong Chan had been his teacher too. When the Linyuan Pavilion introduced Chang Geng to General Zhong, had it been a coincidence or intentional? Gu Yun couldn't help but feel a stir of anticipation—could this little prince he had stumblingly raised from a child of scarce more than ten truly grow into a pillar of the state?

Gu Yun drifted off to sleep amid his idle musings. On the foggy edge of consciousness, he seemed to feel someone gently touch his face.

The next time he awoke, it was already bright out. He pushed aside the light blanket someone had draped over him and asked in a low voice, "What's going on?"

"Sir," the Black Hawk standing by at the door replied, "overnight, the three great bandit chiefs gathered their forces and formed a rebel army at the mouth of the Nandu River..."

Gu Yun frowned.

"They have about a dozen parhelion bows and several score of heavy armor infantrymen. If this subordinate's eyes can be trusted— and I believe they can—the rebels even have hawks."

44

A CONTEST OF WILLS

Now Gu Yun was fully alert.

"Hawks?" Gu Yun asked softly. "You're sure there's no mistake?"

"This subordinate is willing to swear it on his own head."

Hawks were unique among the eight military branches. Although they didn't burn the most fuel, the maintenance and upkeep of their armor was extremely demanding. The Black Hawk Division required annual maintenance from a dedicated group of specialists within the Lingshu Institute, and when this was counted in the total, their equipment was no less expensive than heavy armor. In comparison, heavy armor was much more common. Each of the regional armies, and even Kuai Lantu's not-so-legal guard force, possessed a few suits. But across all of Great Liang, the only complete hawk division was the Black Iron Battalion's Black Hawks.

Where had these bandits gotten their hawks?

Did they steal them from the Black Iron Battalion?!

Gu Yun rose and strode outside. The bandit nest at Apricot Grove was abuzz with anxiety, and Fu Zhicheng, stripped of his armor and trussed up like a chicken, knelt in its center. As soon as he spied Gu Yun, he began to proclaim his own innocence.

"Marshal! Marshal, I've been wrongfully accused!"

Gu Yun kicked him square in the chest. The burly Fu Zhicheng flew backward and spewed out a mouthful of blood, then tumbled to the ground coughing, unable to get another word out.

"Wrongfully accused?" Gu Yun asked, voice chilly. "You bastard, you've been raising a rebel army right under our noses. You've got the whole gamut: heavy armor and light pelts, a line of parhelion bows two kilometers long—you even have hawks to deploy. You're a bigger spender than our Great Liang's Jiangnan Navy. Impressive work, Fu Zhicheng!"

Fu Zhicheng was in a sorry state sprawled out on the ground, but the shocked expression on his face looked genuine. He continued to plead his case. "Marshal, I swear to the heavens; I have no idea where the iron hawks came from—even my Southern Border Army doesn't have hawks. Marshal, I'm telling the truth!"

"Sir," Shen Yi said quietly, "I spent all night interrogating him. General Fu can't fully explain the origins of the violet gold, either. He only confessed to having Jing Xu make the connections."

"You fool, you were doing business with a tiger and thought you were raising a housecat." Gu Yun glared at Fu Zhicheng. "Continue the surveillance and bring me the map—order all troops to get into formation and prepare to engage the rebel army. The Southern Border Army is temporarily under my command. Any who disobey orders will face a court martial!"

He made to don his light pelt armor, but when he reached for his bow, his hand grasped empty air. Only then did he recall he had handed it over to the young prince. Gu Yun was still for a beat, then asked, "Where is Chang Geng?"

At the same time, the great bandit chief Jing Xu was racing through the winding mountain tunnels.

Someone was waiting for him.

The man was tall, with sharp features that looked, beneath the lamplight, as if they had been carved by a knife. Deep creases framed the corners of his mouth, but both his age and his nationality were difficult to judge from appearance alone. In any case, he wasn't from the Central Plains. His face was deeply tanned, every inch of his exposed skin weathered by the elements, and his eyes were faintly blue. At this moment, he was staring at an enormous tactical sand table.

Jing Xu was supremely cautious in his interactions with this man. "Mister Ja. Will Gu Yun fall for it?"

This "Mister Ja" looked up at Jing Xu. "You may be able to lure him here, but you won't be able to truly hinder him. The Marquis of Anding has been living rough on the battlefield since he was a child. He'll be able to tell that all your iron machines are far from capable of matching the Black Iron Battalion the instant he gets a good look at them."

Jing Xu froze. "Then..."

Mister Ja lifted a finger to silence him. "Remember what I told you. The Black Iron Battalion was forged over three generations by exhausting the strength of your nation. It is one of the most advanced military forces in the world, a lethal weapon ahead of its time. Don't delude yourself into thinking you can fight them head-on. That is as futile as an infant attempting to challenge a giant. What we are doing here is only temporarily luring the tiger away from its mountain lair and keeping it occupied elsewhere."

As he spoke, he tapped a finger lightly against the sand table. "The hawks and heavy armor units we've waved in front of him will lure Gu Yun to us. It may not stall him for long. But I just received a piece of news—Fu Zhicheng did you a favor. He brought the majority of his army to Apricot Grove, so defenses at the Southern

Border Garrison are weak. The ones left behind to guard it don't yet know you've fallen out with him."

Jing Xu's eyes gleamed.

"Act like you are transporting violet gold for Fu Zhicheng as usual but conceal your men inside the violet gold shipping crates. The guards at the Southwest Supply Depot won't stop you, and they'll be discreet about your arrival. We coordinate our attack from within and without," Mister Ja made a chopping motion with his hand, "and we will have seized the Southwest Supply Depot in less time than it takes to finish a cup of tea."

The Southwest Supply Depot held large amounts of violet gold for military use. If one person with a torch could manage to slip inside, never mind the Black Iron Battalion, even a deity descended from heaven wouldn't dare advance a step.

"Millions of kilograms of violet gold are stored there. If the warehouses should go up in flames, even the Marquis of Anding would be doomed by this crime of negligence." Mister Ja lightly toyed with the gas lamp hanging above the sand table, and the reflection of its flame flickered in his eyes in the darkness. An unreadable smile crooked the corners of his mouth. "You will have plenty of room to negotiate with the imperial court."

Their plans were well laid—how could they know that another force, entirely outside their calculations, lay in wait within the mountainous terrain of the southwest? Before the Black Iron Battalion could mobilize, a second wooden bird found Chang Geng within Apricot Grove.

Chang Geng had released the first bird back to its sender soon after its arrival, and Shen Yi had failed to get his hands on even a single feather. Seeing a second one flutter inside, General Shen nearly drooled all over his clothes. He bounded eagerly up to Chang Geng, rubbing his hands together, and asked, "Your Highness, you see... how about I open this one for you?"

Chang Geng readily handed it over. The craftsmanship of the little creature was so lifelike one might confuse it for the genuine article. Even when he held it in his hands, the hardness of its wooden surface was all that differentiated it from a real animal. Shen Yi cupped this exquisite creation in his palms and felt that his heart was on the verge of melting. "It can even nod and peck!"

Gu Yun looked at him, incredulous. "Old maid, can you stop making a fool of yourself?"

With the miraculous bird in hand, what was the Marquis of Anding? Shen Yi paid him no mind. He stroked the wooden bird's back with a drunken look of bliss on his face, then carefully felt for the catch on its belly.

"All right, I'm opening it."

"Wait, you have to shake—"

Before Chang Geng could finish, Shen Yi had already flicked open the latch on the wooden bird's underside. This delicate little creature was, in fact, booby-trapped, as everyone found when a wad of paper shot out with the force of a cannon the instant it was opened. The projectile struck General Shen right on the high bridge of his nose, nearly giving him a nosebleed, then proceeded to unfurl and plaster itself all over his face.

Shen Yi couldn't get a word out.

A sheet of paper large enough to cover an entire wall had been stuffed into the belly of this bird, which wasn't even the size of a person's palm.

"You have to shake it first," Chang Geng was finally able to say, "the space inside the bird's belly is limited, so sometimes they use billow paper..."

"Oh, *billow paper*!" Shen Yi completely forgot the tears of pain still pooling in his eyes and embarked on a droning lecture, voice somewhat more muffled than before. "I know it. It's a type of paper made using a special technique—no matter how large the sheet, it can be compressed into a ball the size of a large pill without smearing the ink. It will even smooth itself back out after a time!"

There was not a thing in the world that could get between General Shen and his incorrigible addiction to lecturing, not injury nor nosebleed.

Why didn't it smash his mouth instead? Gu Yun thought to himself without a lick of empathy. He snatched the lethal sheet of billow paper from Shen Yi.

It was the schematic for a suit of hawk armor. Every part was depicted in fine and accurate detail, from the wings to the gold tank, and even the visor and cuirass. The drawing was untidily signed with the character *Ge*.

"These are the bandits' hawks?" Gu Yun was no artificer, but he had used all manner of battle armor as an extension of his own body and was intimately familiar with each of them. He could see the difference between the hawk armor in this diagram and the suits used by the Black Hawks at a glance. "A shoddy imitation at best."

Hand cupped protectively over his nose, Shen Yi leaned over to look. "Compared to Black Hawks, they must have cut the weight equivalent of an entire suit of light pelt armor. It's probably to save fuel."

"Flying bamboo kites would save even more..." Gu Yun muttered. But before he finished this thought, a change came over his expression. "Wait!"

This kind of hawk armor was no more than a useless shell, but its designer clearly understood the ins and outs of hawk armor. How could they not know this design was unfit for battle? Flashing hawk armor about so blatantly was clearly an attempt to lure a tiger away from its lair.

But in that case, what exactly was the "lair"?

When hunting a snake, one must strike seven inches below the head to hit its weak point. But what was the Southern Border Army—or even Gu Yun's—weak point?

Gu Yun spun around and stalked toward Fu Zhicheng. "Where do you have those bandits deliver the violet gold?"

Face covered in blood, Fu Zhicheng stared blankly at Gu Yun for several seconds. He seemed to come to some realization, and a hesitant look stole over his face, as if he wasn't sure whether he ought to answer. Wouldn't confessing to smuggling violet gold cement his crime of treason?

Chang Geng spoke up softly from behind Gu Yun. "General Fu, think carefully. Inspector General Kuai is already dead by your hand. With Assistant Minister Sun of the Ministry of War to provide testimony, there is no question you will be condemned for armed rebellion. You're a dead man—is there any difference whether you die in the capital or die here today on this mountain?"

Fu Zhicheng had never met the fourth prince. His glancing impression of the young man was that he was elegant, refined, and noble in manner, like someone who had never done a day of hard work in his life. But at this moment, he had not a sliver of doubt that if he did not cooperate, true to his word, this scholarly fourth prince would strike him down on the spot.

Gu Yun cut in smoothly. "If you do the sensible thing now, you still have a chance to atone for your crimes with a good deed."

Fu Zhicheng's lips trembled. After a long interval, he began to speak in an unsteady voice. "The Southwest Supply Depot. There was no secondary location; I always had Jing Xu deliver the violet gold directly to the Southwest Supply Depot. I never brought a drop to my own estate."

Gu Yun's back shot up straight at once.

"Marshal!" Fu Zhicheng shouted after him, "I may have committed murder, arson, grave robbery, every despicable deed under the sun, but I have always dedicated myself to my duty of guarding the southern border. I have never strayed in my loyalty! As far as I'm concerned, I've never done wrong by His Majesty...but this is how I am repaid. Who knows what my brothers and comrades will think when they hear the news—or what you think, Marshal!"

Gu Yun leveled him with a penetrating look.

For a second, Fu Zhicheng thought he had gotten through to him. But Gu Yun was not moved by compassion, nor was he angered. It was as if his face was an impenetrable mask, impervious to howling wind and torrential rain. As he turned and walked away, he left only a few words behind. "Is it any of your business what I think? Jiping, go ahead with the Black Hawks; you must take control of the Southwest Supply Depot before the enemy arrives. Xiao-An—"

The young Black Iron Battalion soldier who had tailed Chang Geng through Central Shu stepped out of the ranks at his call.

Gu Yun gave him his orders without a backward glance. "Take a contingent of the Southern Border Army and feign an attack on the peak where the bandits are gathering."

"Yes, sir!"

"Wait," Gu Yun continued. "Paint their armor black. You can just splash it with some ink. It doesn't need to be wholly realistic, but be smart about it."

He had learned this trick from Liao Ran, of all people. Xiao-An blinked in surprise. He swiftly caught the meaning behind Gu Yun's order and happily ran off to comply.

Elsewhere, the three great bandit chiefs of the southern border had just completed a head count of their subordinates. Jing Xu looked at the silent mass of assembled bandits and felt a brief surge of pride, as if he were looking out over a proud army of thousands. He cupped his fists toward the sky and called out, "The garrison armies of each region are glutted with iron armor and eminent in their prestige and power. The Black Iron Battalion descends from the skies like demon crows, and their incredible might is spoken of even across the seas. The strength of the Great Liang military is tremendous—yet in the space of less than a decade, Fujian and the Jiangnan Navy have both rebelled, one after the other. Why is this so?

"A fumbling ruler stands at the head of the nation and sycophants run amok. If not for this, why would common people like us need to fight with our lives on the line, to court disaster like a moth flying into a flame? Today, we brothers have been forced into a corner. Our lives and livelihoods are as precarious as a thousand-pound burden carried across thin ice. To retreat is certain death. Unless we fight for our very lives, we have no chance of survival. I call on everyone here today to swear a blood oath—to join together in our common cause, to share joys and sorrows as one. Are you willing?"

The bandits had spent their lives thieving and looting; they could count the number of characters they could read on one hand. Thus, they were stirred up by Jing Xu's impassioned speech, as if they could already see themselves standing among those nobles and ministers.

Jing Xu accepted a cup of wine from a subordinate at his side and drained it in one draft. He threw the cup down, where it shattered against the floor. "Win or lose, it all ends here!"

The bandits swallowed their liquid courage, then smashed their cups on the floor in a resounding avalanche of crashes. As they streamed into the sprawling network of secret chambers, Jing Xu looked back at Mister Ja. This mysterious outsider had been his contact representing the nations to the south when he smuggled violet gold for Fu Zhicheng. He was a shrewd man, and though of foreign origin, had resided in the Central Plains for an unknown number of years.

Not a single ripple of emotion crossed Mister Ja's face as he listened to Jing Xu's rousing speech. The lamplight extended and deepened the creases framing his mouth, and as he stood half ensconced in shadow, he seemed to wear a subtle mocking smirk.

The first time Jing Xu had skimmed his tenth off the top of Fu Zhicheng's violet gold, he had intended to sell it back through Mister Ja in exchange for a pile of solid gold and silver he could sleep on top of every night. But since that first time, Mister Ja had earnestly admonished him to keep the violet gold and transfer it to a safe location in small batches. Then, Mister Ja told him, he could gradually amass armor and weaponry. Mister Ja had even cautioned him not to store his armaments and money in the same place.

Looking back now, it was as if this enigmatic foreigner had predicted the events of today long ago.

The paranoid bandit chief Jing Xu suddenly felt a niggle of doubt. *Is this Mister Ja really just a violet gold smuggler?*

Just then, a subordinate ran in with a report. "Dage, we spotted men in black armor heading toward the area where the hawks are stored!"

The tendril of suspicion sprouting in Jing Xu's heart was instantly drowned by a surge of glee. "Mister Ja had it right; they fell for it! Load the parhelion bows—every minute we can stall them is a minute more! Follow the plan; all troops move out at full speed! Quickly!"

Several kilometers away, a caravan transporting violet gold approached the Southwest Supply Depot, discreet and unnoticed. When it arrived at the gate, the man leading the caravan pushed up his bamboo hat to reveal his face to the captain of the Supply Corps. "It's me."

The fewer people who knew about the violet gold smuggling, the better, so the men sent by both sides were always staunch confidantes of their leaders. The captain of the Supply Corps was the Southern Border Army contact for the bandits. Fu Zhicheng had given him strict orders to keep the violet gold deliveries he received a secret, and to pull them off without a trace.

As usual, the captain said nothing in front of his subordinates and waved them through with a neutral expression. He led the way to the violet gold storehouse as he had done many times before—but for some reason, after walking a few steps, the captain asked an unexpected question. "Didn't you deliver a batch a few days ago? Why is there another one so soon?"

Face hidden under his bamboo hat, the bandit escorting the violet gold delivery replied huffily, "That's the general and Dage's business, how should I know?"

The captain still felt uneasy. He dug for his keys and said, "I'll be honest; our general left with over half our men yesterday. No one knows what's going on."

The bandit with the bamboo hat watched impatiently as the captain moved to unlock the warehouse. He licked his lips and said, now brusque, "We're all just following orders; we don't know, either. Hurry up and open the door!"

The captain paused with the key in the lock. He frowned and turned back. "Why are you being so..."

His voice died out—one of the bandits was pointing a small crossbow at his throat from three steps away. The captain took a breath of cold air and prepared to shout. The game was up; the bandits decided to go all in. At a wave of their leader's hand, the bolt leapt from the crossbow like the flick of a snake's tongue and buried itself in the captain's throat. The breath he sucked in never left his lungs.

The bandit with the bamboo hat lunged forward, catching the captain's toppling body against his shoulder, and reached for the key still stuck in the lock of the warehouse door. His heart thudded as if about to beat out of his chest—open this door, and he would hold tens of thousands of Southern Border Army soldiers and three thousand Black Iron demon crows by the throat.

Something screeched past his ear. Still caught up in the thrill of his imminent victory, the bamboo-hat-wearing bandit turned to look yet saw only the horrified faces of his subordinates. His arm felt a little off. He looked down. The hand that had closed around the key seconds ago had been shot through by an iron arrow striking like a bolt from clear skies, leaving only a flap of tattered flesh hanging from his arm!

The bandit's severed hand remained clenched around the storehouse key, unable to turn it, yet blocking the way.

An inhuman scream finally escaped his throat.

Within this brief interval, the Black Hawks who had rushed to the scene dropped from the air. Shen Yi, still holding his loaded bow, alighted on the roof of the violet gold warehouse and pulled out a Black Iron Tiger Tally. Dangling from a string below it, in a two-in-one deal, hung Great Liang's very first marching orders decree.

Shen Yi stood tall and graceful, the black wings of his hawk armor outspread behind him like storm clouds. He looked down on the dumbstruck garrison soldiers of the Southwest Supply Depot and called out, "The Black Iron Tiger Tally and the marching orders decree are here. I come on the orders of the Marquis of Anding to take command of the Southwest Supply Depot and arrest these insolent bandits. The Supply Depot is now under lockdown. Execute these bandits at once!"

The three bandit chiefs had no idea that, elsewhere, their plan had gone awry. They had split their forces in three, and each led their own subordinates to burrow up from underground, rubbing their hands together in anticipation as they converged on the Southwest Supply Depot.

Suddenly, Jing Xu heard a crisp *clack* of metal on stone, as if some heavy object was rolling down the mountain, bouncing off the boulders as it went. He instinctively looked up.

A human head, still clad in heavy armor, tumbled down the mountain slope.

It was the very same suit of heavy armor they had hidden in the violet gold transport caravan to sneak into the Southwest Supply Depot.

Jing Xu froze. At some point, the Southern Border Army had emerged from the mountains to surround them on all sides, their numbers dotted here and there with the dark silhouettes of Black Iron armor. Before half of Jing Xu's forces could emerge from the underground tunnels, a dense thicket of arrows had taken aim at them from the mountain peak.

45

FUSE

GU YUN GRANTED Jing Xu only the briefest glance before
determining there was nothing much to see. He directly discarded this big bandit chief along with all the others—right
now, he was too busy fretting over what to do about Chang Geng.

Fortunately for Gu Yun, Chang Geng had mentioned his plans
to meet up with his companions who had gone to investigate the
bandits' secret tunnels at just the right time. He had privately
heaved a sigh of relief. Gu Yun had maintained a stern expression
as he assigned a team of Black Iron Battalion soldiers to guard him
and exhorted him to be cautious of straggling bandits. Only after
personally seeing him off did Gu Yun give an order to the Black
Steed next to him. "Get some men to keep an eye on things. If His
Highness comes back too early, find something for him to do; don't
let him come over here."

The Black Steed left to execute his orders, and Gu Yun turned
back to the matter at hand.

He swept a look over the captured bandit forces, an uncharac-
teristic gloom settling deep in his eyes. "I have just one question.
Where are the entrances to your rat's nest? I'd like everyone to think
carefully before you respond. How about this, let's start with the
person furthest to the west, and each of you can tell me the ones you
know. Anyone who remains silent will be beheaded where he stands.

Those who come later can add to what was said before—if you have nothing to add, then I'm sorry, the ones at the front of the line are getting off easy. So, let's begin! I'll count to three. Anyone who doesn't talk loses his head; anyone who babbles nonsense loses his head too."

The captives were shocked stupid by this Marquis of Order who acted even more bandit-like than the bandits themselves.

The Black Steed who had been ordered to conduct the interrogation stepped expressionlessly up to the westernmost bandit. The man instinctively looked left and right, reluctant to speak. Without the slightest hesitation, Gu Yun made a chopping motion with his hand, and the Black Steed's windslasher swung on his command.

The Black Steed's usual job was killing on the battlefield. He'd never kept monkeys for slaughter, so he'd never really studied beheading techniques.[12] The windslasher cut though the bandit's neck, but unluckily got lodged in the man's spine. The bandit's head was only half-severed, and his throat had yet to be slit. His blood-curdling screams caused every bird in the surrounding mountains to startle in fright.

The Black Steed narrowed his eyes. With a second forceful tug of his wrist, he finally finished off that unfortunate soul. Blood poured from the bandit's neck like a groundwater spring, splashing all over the next man in line. The second bandit shook like an overloaded gold tank, his mind going blank. He lifted a trembling finger to point at the exit behind him. "Th-there's one right there..."

Gu Yun sneered. "No shit. Do you think I'm blind?"

A second head hit the ground.

---

12 Monkey brain was a historical delicacy, notably served as part of the Manchu-Han Imperial banquet of the Qing Empire.

The third bandit had pissed himself in fright after seeing that half-severed head. He collapsed with a *thud*, clutching his head with both hands in case that black-armored butcher lost his patience and chopped without giving him a chance to speak. He proceeded to rattle off a dozen locations in a single breath as the captives lined up behind him all but snapped his spine with the force of their glares.

Now that someone had gotten the ball rolling, the rest was almost too easy. One choice spelled life or death, and there was no point in keeping secrets—any information one guarded to their death, someone later in line would spill. Talking while one had the chance to cling to life was the sensible path.

Gu Yun's expression remained stoic, but he was inwardly stunned by the extent of the southern border bandits' network. Some of the entrances and exits the bandits revealed had been found by the Linyuan Pavilion—if they hadn't, even the Black Iron Battalion couldn't have ambushed these groundhogs so neatly. But the vast majority of them were unknown even to the experts from the jianghu.

The Black Iron soldiers behind him slipped away one by one to confirm the veracity of the bandits' information, leaving guards at each hidden entrance. In less time than it took to burn a stick of incense, the bandits had covered the entirety of this vast network of subterranean tunnels like passing a hot potato. Not a pebble of the mountain was left unturned.

In the blink of an eye, this deadly hot potato had reached the instigator himself—the bandit chief Jing Xu.

Over the course of his lifetime, Jing Xu had carved a bloody swath through his enemies, standing on a pile of corpses to declare himself king of his mountain. He had no extraordinary talents, but he had guts and ruthlessness aplenty. The tip of the soldier's windslasher swung toward his face as blood flowed in rivers over the ground. He sucked in a deep breath, straightened his back, and gathered every ounce of the fury that had brewed inside him for so many years, lashing it into a skeleton to support his body. He raised his ferocious triangular eyes and stared at Gu Yun, who had strolled up to him with his hands behind his back.

"I've heard it said that Marshal Gu is unmatched in elegance. I never imagined that you would also be adept at torture and interrogation. I see you've no lack of talents."

"There's no need for flattery." An empty smile spread over Gu Yun's face. "At its heart, the business of war is nothing more than chopping people down. I have neither shut you in a dark room nor laid you over a bed of nails, nor have I offered you a torture rack for your seat. I can hardly claim any talents in 'torture and interrogation.' If you have nothing to add, please be my guest in joining your comrades."

Jing Xu's eyelid began to jump. "There are sixty-four entrances to our tunnels in total. They have already listed all of them, and the last few useless fools before me were clearly beginning to speak gibberish. Forgive my ignorance, Marshal Gu, but I don't understand your intentions."

"I have no intentions. I'm just asking for a little insurance." Gu Yun smiled. "What if they missed something? Are you trying to convince me to chop heads more sparingly? You have plenty of people; don't worry, I won't run out."

Jing Xu stared.

After a moment's consideration, Gu Yun continued. "But since they take you as their leader, perhaps you have more to share with us. Why don't you tell me something I haven't heard before? I'll count it as a pass."

Jing Xu clenched his jaw. He thought of that bastard Fu Zhicheng who had started all of this, and wished he could flay the man alive. "Marshal, have you any interest in hearing how Fu Zhicheng has been smuggling violet gold and plotting rebellion?"

The icy smile slipped from Gu Yun's face. "If I didn't know that much, how could I have guessed you would have the guts to show up to the Southwest Supply Depot like lambs to the slaughter? I'll give you one more chance; tell me something I don't know."

The black-iron windslasher was right beside Jing Xu's ear. He could feel the pitiless chill of the metal with the slightest twitch of his head. With a faint puff of steam, this windslasher would lop off his head as effortlessly as a chef's knife sliced through a melon. Gu Yun was cold and emotionless, utterly unaffected. Jing Xu's head would roll to the ground with the unremarkable masses, coated in a layer of dust and indistinguishable from the rest.

Jing Xu finally yielded. "What do you want to know?"

Gu Yun waved his hand, and the windslasher drew back a few centimeters. "Who is your contact for the acquisition of foreign violet gold after it crosses Great Liang's southern border, who told you to hoard violet gold and stockpile armor and weaponry, and who advised you on tactics and told you to hoodwink me with those bamboo kites so you could seize the Southwest Supply Depot?"

Jing Xu ground his teeth together.

"If I were you, I wouldn't give my life to protect that person." Gu Yun took a step forward and lowered his voice. "Just look at the web of secret tunnels behind you with its sixty-four entrances, Daozhang.[13] If you people had nothing better to do than hole up inside them, even your Daoist deities from the highest order of heaven couldn't dig you out...so who was it that encouraged you to

---

13   道长, daozhang, is a respectful form of address for Daoist cultivators.

assemble the forces of all three peaks just so we could sweep you all up in a single move, hm?"

Gu Yun was an expert at passing black off as white. He'd developed three special skills over the course of his life: warfare, calligraphy, and prevarication. His tongue could turn a castle in the air into something far too real. And on second thought, his words made far too much sense. Jing Xu broke out in a cold sweat.

It took Gu Yun longer to interrogate this bandit chief than it took Chang Geng to find his companions. He returned with them in tow straightaway but was stopped by a dutiful Black Iron Battalion soldier before he rounded the last peak. The young soldier wasn't much good at lying, so he simply repeated what Gu Yun had said. "Your Highness, the marshal would like you to rest here for a while."

Chang Geng was unsurprised. He obediently hunkered down to wait without inquiring further.

Chang Geng hadn't seen Gu Yun in person for the past four years. But under old General Zhong's instruction, he had studied every battle Gu Yun had ever fought, every change in his political stance since he had been bequeathed the title of marquis during the late emperor's reign, and even the development of his calligraphy. If Chang Geng were to walk into Gu Yun's study today and pull an old document at random, he would be able to guess the approximate age Gu Yun had been when he penned it.

This was a far more effective method of understanding Gu Yun than hanging around him every day just to listen to him brag about being the "Flower of the Northwest."

The instant Gu Yun had flicked him that first hesitant look, Chang Geng knew he was planning to force a confession and didn't wish Chang Geng to see. After all this time, Gu Yun still instinctively tried to preserve his precarious image as a compassionate father before Chang Geng. Chang Geng himself had no objections; he treasured this bit of unspoken care his young godfather afforded him.

Two figures followed close behind Chang Geng. These were the two snot-nosed kids who had left Yanhui Town with him for the capital so many years ago, Ge Pangxiao and Cao Niangzi—though they were now called Ge Chen and Cao Chunhua.

In his youth, Ge Chen had been an endearing and chubby little kid. Now grown, he was no longer chubby but tall and sturdy, fit to be called a burly giant on account of his frame alone. Unfortunately, the head that sat atop his broad shoulders looked as if it had come from the wrong set. He had a fair and round little face: two trembling mounds of tender flesh piled up on his cheeks like soft tofu, framing his small nose, mouth, and eyes. The whole picture gave him an air of harmless honesty.

Cao Chunhua had experienced an even more drastic transformation. Whether he willed it or no, his body had grown into an adult man's frame, and it was no longer so easy for him to pull off the seamless androgyny of his youth. He had no choice but to reluctantly admit he really was an icky man and start wearing men's clothes again. However, he insisted on giving himself the name "Cao Chunhua." No one aside from him could explain how "spring flower" was any better of a name than "lady."

"Why do we have to wait here?" Cao Chunhua asked, craning his neck. "It's been years since I've seen my dear marquis. I've been looking forward to it so much I haven't slept in days."

Chang Geng shot Cao Chunhua a cryptic glance and marked a strike against him on his mental tally. Once he had marked down fifty such incidents of infatuated nonsense along the lines of *my dear marquis* from this person, he'd find some plausible reason to give him a sound beating.

Blissfully ignorant, Cao Chunhua asked another question. "Dage, once you get back to the capital, you'll receive your title of nobility, right? I heard the late emperor had the Prince Yanbei Estate prepared for you long ago. Are you planning to move there or stay in the Marquis Estate?"

Chang Geng flinched in surprise. He smiled with some effort and said, "That depends on whether the marquis is willing to keep me or not."

Thinking back now, Chang Geng could no longer recall how he'd screwed up the courage to drop everything—to leave the Marquis Estate and Gu Yun. It was easier before their reunion, but their unexpected encounter in Central Shu felt like a head-on collision with fate. He'd struggle to gather the same resolution a second time, even on pain of death.

Chen Qingxu always told him, "Compose yourself; curb your delusions." This advice was fairly effective in preventing the wu'ergu from flaring...but a person's emotions were all interconnected. Suppress fury and resentment, and joy would also fade into a shadow of itself. As time went on, an individual who continued to smother their strongest feelings would pale like a plant grown away from the sun—able to survive and make do, but at the cost of nearly all its color and vibrancy.

Chang Geng had thought he was on the verge of attaining Buddhahood.

Until he reunited with Gu Yun.

Chang Geng spent his days with Gu Yun hard at work, fighting rebels one day and bandits the next. Yet he was suffused with a baseless and irrational happiness—an effervescent, anticipatory, and ardent sort of happiness, as if he opened his eyes every morning knowing something he'd been looking forward to was about to happen. He felt this way even though he knew there was no such thing; the wu'ergu still visited him in his dreams every night.

If he received his princely title...would Gu Yun let him stay?

Rationally speaking, Gu Yun would of course allow him to stay. The Marquis Estate would be willing to keep him at least until he officially settled down and married. And if he never married, perhaps he could be a bit shameless and freeload indefinitely. Now that was too beautiful a fantasy—it took all Chang Geng's strength to prevent a dopey smile from breaking across his face.

After about thirty minutes of waiting, Gu Yun showed up in person.

The secret tunnels were like an enormous spiderweb spreading in all directions, bound by an intricate geometry of interconnections. Gu Yun had chopped over forty heads in all. Excluding the rambling drivel of the ones who had been frightened to tears, he had uncovered sixty-four entrances.

Ge Chen was shocked to hear this. "What? The two of us brothers roughed it in the mountains for half a year and only found thirty-some entrances. How did you get over sixty in one go?!"

"Without the intel you provided, I couldn't have ambushed them, much less interrogated them." Gu Yun gave Ge Chen a look. He resisted the urge for several seconds but, in the end, fell to temptation and beckoned him over. "Come here."

Thinking the marshal had some important instructions to impart, Ge Chen bounded directly over to Gu Yun. The Marshal Gu who had been so serious just a minute ago thrust out his hand and pinched Ge Chen's chubby cheek. This man suffered from a chronic and terminal case of itchy hands—whenever he saw something with an appealing texture, he couldn't help but grab a handful of it. He had been wanting to do this for ages.

This is the best. Gu Yun squished Ge Chen's face for a while, then thought to himself, his cravings still unsatisfied, *How did he cultivate these?*

Ge Chen didn't know what to say.

Cao Chunhua stared with such envy his gaze could practically pierce through stone. Emotion flowed from his covetous, tiger-like eyes, and he whined softly, "The marquis is playing favorites. Why doesn't he pinch *my* cheeks?"

He was too afraid to say this to Gu Yun's face, so Chang Geng was the only one who heard him. *Strike number forty-eight.*

Cao Chunhua shuddered. He glanced around, suddenly feeling an ominous premonition of danger.

Gu Yun drew a map of the secret tunnels through the mountains according to Jing Xu's testimony and ordered his men to fan smoke into every entrance. They smoked the tunnels out for three days, turning the mountain into a chimney, until every bat, rat, and poisonous insect had packed their bags and fled—but still, the man Gu Yun wanted to capture did not appear.

Several soldiers bravely volunteered to enter the tunnels carrying ropes to aid their way back. They searched the sixty-four entrances from dawn till dusk, but found neither hide nor hair of the man. Their only reward for their exploits was the sand table Jing Xu had mentioned.

On the fourth day, one of Gu Yun's subordinates reported that, in the course of their investigation into Kuai Lantu's associates, they had indeed found a suspicious figure. The man was a visiting dignitary under Kuai Lantu's employ who went by the name of

Wang Bufan, or "Wang the Extraordinary"—clearly an alias. This person rarely showed himself in public, but Kuai Lantu's close confidantes all understood that Kuai Lantu admired and trusted him greatly. He even provided the man a courtyard in his own estate and sent some of his most valued servants and prettiest maids to serve him.

"And where is this 'extraordinary' one now?" Gu Yun asked.

"He ran. All the servants in his courtyard were found dead—poisoned. By the time the other members of the estate discovered them, the bodies had already grown cold."

"Sir." Another cavalryman arrived with a report. "We searched the hideouts Jing Xu confessed to using to transport violet gold. They were all cleared out. Whoever did it didn't leave behind even a single sheet of paper."

Gu Yun silently turned his worn prayer beads in his hand. These incidents—Kuai Lantu's mysterious visiting dignitary, Jing Xu's "Mister Ja"—looked like coincidences, but Gu Yun's intuition told him there was something more here, in a way he couldn't quite explain. He had a nagging feeling that there was some grand plot unfolding just out of sight. These shadowy figures who had ignited the volatile situation on the southern border worked from behind the scenes. They had appeared out of nowhere and disappeared without a trace, and both their identities and goals were a mystery. They seemed to be an enemy, yet via a series of even more coincidences, they had helped him deal, in short order, with quite a number of the people standing in his way.

Gu Yun wasn't entirely sure whether he had thwarted their schemes or fallen right into their trap.

The individual Gu Yun was digging up every centimeter of mountainous terrain to find was currently standing on the deck of an unremarkable little cargo ship sailing the South Sea.

Mister Ja had changed back into his intricate western clothes and was at this moment looking down at a small scrap of sheepskin. Across it spread a map of the vast terrain of Great Liang. He raised a pen dipped in red cinnabar ink and drew a small red circle in the area that represented the southern border.

Including this mark, the map contained three red circles in total. The other two lay upon the northern border and the East Sea. Mister Ja's pen hovered over the map and landed at the entrance to the Silk Road in the west.

"Now, the stage is set." Mister Ja began to chuckle. "All that's missing is a fuse. Once the fuse is lit, with a roar—"

Wang Bufan, who might have passed for a person of the Central Plains in appearance, finished for him. "A great inferno will consume the Central Plains."

The two looked at each other and laughed, then clinked their wine glasses in a toast.

When news of the crisis on the southern border made its way back to the Son of Heaven, he was naturally enraged. He ordered Gu Yun to escort the bandit chiefs and traitor general back to the capital without delay. Thus Gu Yun was forced to set aside his suspicions for the time being and speed north. However, when he thought about how his darling godson was finally willing to go home with him, and how the Marquis Estate would become lively once again, he began to look toward his return to the capital with some anticipation.

"He's much more charming now that he's grown up," Gu Yun whispered to Shen Yi like a proud old father. "But he's gotten so mature and sensible all of a sudden; I can't quite get used to it."

"How shameless," Shen Yi succinctly assessed, and got swatted, as expected. "Speaking of which," he continued, "you've arrested Fu Zhicheng, so what do you plan to do now?"

The playfulness slid from Gu Yun's face. He was quiet for a time, and when he spoke again, it was with a serious expression. "Jiping, there's something I've often thought these last few years. Isn't it a waste of talent for you to follow me around all the time?"

Shen Yi glanced at him in silence.

"You are learned in both ancient history and current affairs, with literary talent enough to enter the Hanlin Academy and martial talent enough to pacify a region. You've spent so many years submerged in the Lingshu Institute and the Black Iron Battalion. It's about time you stepped out of my shadow..."

Even though Chang Geng had analyzed the situation for him, Shen Yi was still moved by these words from Gu Yun. The two were comrades as well as friends, and although theirs was a life-and-death bond such that they would entrust their widows and orphans to each other, Gu Yun had a dog's mouth that could never manage a sincere word. He had not once straightforwardly commended Shen Yi to his face.

Shen Yi's eyes stung. "Zixi, honestly, you don't have to..."

"Besides, I owe you an apology," Gu Yun added, earnest. "With a natural beauty like me hanging around, your chances at romance have been thwarted. After all these years, you're still single. Truly... *tsk*, I can't be sorry enough."

Shen Yi was speechless.

His tiny quota of serious words for the day fulfilled, the self-styled natural beauty had returned to spouting absurdities. Shen Yi hastily shoved the heartfelt reply still stuck in his throat back down into his gut and spurred his horse forward with a scoff.

Chang Geng watched him depart from a short distance away.

He promptly took the opportunity to gallop over and fill Shen Yi's vacant spot, riding shoulder to shoulder with Gu Yun. "What did you do to make General Shen lose his temper again?"

Gu Yun rubbed his nose with a faint smile.

Seeing that a leaf had become stuck to Gu Yun's light pelt armor, Chang Geng reached out and plucked it off. Ever attentive, he said, "Yifu, even the lightest armor weighs over twenty kilograms. Why don't you take it off and give yourself a break?"

Gu Yun had no objections. He allowed Chang Geng to help him unbuckle the light pelt armor and remove the pieces one by one. Perhaps they were riding too close; for some reason, their horses decided they liked the look of each other, and the two began to nuzzle amorously together.

Gu Yun spared a hand to tug his horse's head away. "Don't be such a scoundrel."

The vambrace on his arm was half removed, and with this flick of his hand, the whole piece nearly went flying off his wrist, dragging something out of his sleeve along with it. Chang Geng was quick to react and caught the falling object. It was a crude wooden flute.

At first, neither realized what had happened.

Chang Geng wondered, *Why is he carrying around a shabby little flute?*

Gu Yun was still confused. *What was it that just flew out?*

Their gazes landed simultaneously on that weathered bamboo flute with a cracked foot. Chang Geng suddenly felt that this flute was a bit familiar. Gu Yun, meanwhile, reacted as if he'd been struck by lightning. He remembered now—this item had been acquired through dishonorable means!

They moved at the same instant. Gu Yun's hand shot out to snatch it, while Chang Geng instinctively tightened his grip. Their hands, both clenched around the bamboo flute, froze in midair.

"Can't I see it?" Chang Geng asked innocently.

"What's there to see?"

Gu Yun yanked the small bamboo flute from Chang Geng's grip and shoved it back up his sleeve, which only served to call more attention to himself. Chang Geng had rarely seen Gu Yun act so guilty. He unexpectedly recalled that day in Jiangnan four years ago, and Commissioner Yao's little daughter sobbing with heartache. A vague understanding dawned on him, yet he didn't quite dare to believe it. He asked, obliquely, "Did someone give it to you?"

"I carved it myself." Gu Yun lied without a hint of embarrassed blush or nervous breath.

"Oh." Chang Geng blinked. After a beat, he remarked casually, "I didn't know bamboo grew in Loulan."

Gu Yun did not reply.

Chang Geng blinked slowly once again; his gaze appeared to flicker. He said with a low laugh, "Yifu's craftsmanship is rather crude. Why don't I carve you a better one sometime?"

Gu Yun was utterly unable to defend himself, fatally embarrassed, and absolutely certain the kid had seen through him and was having a laugh at his expense. But his theft of the flute had been too egregious; he had no way to exonerate himself. His only option was to take his loss like a defeated hero, tuck his fluffy cotton tail between his legs, and make a run for it.

Chang Geng didn't chase after him. He stayed in place and savored the aftertaste of this incident for a long time, rather tempted to laugh again. He mentally staged the scene from beginning to end once more: Gu Yun sneaking into a little child's courtyard at the break of dawn to steal a bamboo flute... His heart burst with blossoms of joy that stayed vibrant the rest of the day, their color only fading when the sun tilted toward the west.

The lingering fragrance of those blooms shoved the wu'ergu into a tiny corner of his heart. As their falling petals dyed the river below red, the seed of an idea sprouted into a winding network of branches.

Why did he keep it all these years?

Since he had it with him, did he take it out to look at it from time to time?

When his little yifu looked at this flute, would he think of Chang Geng?

Did this mean that Gu Yun was…more fond of him than he thought?

And in that case…how far could he push his luck? Could he get even closer to him?

The faint scent of Miss Chen's pacifying fragrance drifted from his sachet. Chang Geng stared after Gu Yun, Chen Qingxu's *let nature take its course* echoing through his head. He was on the verge of being incinerated by those words. He didn't dare allow his fantasies to get too out of hand—but as he clung uneasily to that tiny possibility, it clawed at his heart and insides, gnawing him down to his core.

The journey to escort prisoners up north should have been bitter and long. But perhaps because of the Black Iron Battalion's rapid pace, or perhaps because Chang Geng desired so much to delay their arrival, they came to the capital before midwinter.

By now, the southern border rebellion, which had stunned both court and commons, had touched off a seismic explosion in the depths of the capital.

Sun Jiao returned to the capital half dead. After suffering shock after shock, he had fallen ill, and wound up confined to his bed.

Even the Longan Emperor never expected that his maneuver to push through the Marching Orders Decree would actually incite the commander in chief of the Southern Border Army to rebel. Stunned and furious, he ordered a thorough investigation. The implications of this case were widespread, and the Ministries of Personnel, Justice, and War, the Imperial Court of Judicial Review, and even the Supervisory Commission were all on high alert. Gu Yun got no rest during his rare return to the capital. Instead of enjoying a break from military duties, he was summoned into the palace every few days for questioning.

The evidence was clear: Fu Zhicheng, Governor of the Southwest, had colluded with bandits, murdered an appointed official of the court, smuggled violet gold, and plotted rebellion. Every bandit chief and the leader of the rebel faction was sentenced to capital punishment in quick succession, and their families went to the execution block with them.

The merciless and iron-blooded Longan Emperor refused to stop there. Just as an uprooted radish brings up the dirt it grows in, the investigation soon implicated all around the accused, even members of the central Six Ministries. The situation quickly spiraled out of control. Any who had close personal ties with Fu Zhicheng; any who had accepted bribes to open back doors on Fu Zhicheng's behalf; and even the old ministers who had recommended Fu Zhicheng for his position long ago were all guilty by association. Not a one escaped punishment.

Some were imprisoned. Others were dismissed from their positions. A terror settled over the imperial court, and the entire capital city was engulfed in the oppressive gloom of paranoia and suspicion.

The skies remained overcast until the turn of the year, when a great snowstorm finally blew down from the heavens.

*Wind and rain sweep
across a gloomy sky*

ARC 6
THE FROST
ENDURED

46

DRUNK

THAT YEAR, the nation ushered out the old and welcomed the new. The Marquis of Anding handed over his Black Iron Tiger Tally, and the implementation of the Marching Orders Decree was a foregone conclusion. The Ministry of War rapidly dispatched specially appointed officers throughout the nation to supervise the troops.

With this, the Longan Emperor tightened the reins on the military to an unprecedented extreme that surpassed even Emperor Wu.

Perhaps the only thing that didn't cause Li Feng undue frustration as the year drew to a close was the ease with which Gu Yun adapted to his present circumstances. And just as Chang Geng had predicted, having achieved the results he wanted, the emperor showed ample regard for Gu Yun's station, promoting Shen Yi two ranks and issuing an imperial decree appointing him commander in chief of the Southwest Army. At the same time, he conferred the title of Prince Yanbei on the Fourth Imperial Prince Li Min.

On the sixteenth day of the first month, in the name of celebrating the Marquis of Anding's birthday, Old Mister Shen dragged over two giant carts full of gifts and completely blocked the front gate of the Marquis Estate.

Old Mister Shen had retired from his post many years ago, and his only child, Shen Yi, was an unambitious idler. Shen Yi had been peculiar since he was a child. He was decent at both the literary and martial arts yet refused to focus on either. Instead, he preferred to sit in his courtyard and mess around with steam engines. Every single mechanical device in the Shen family home—from great machines like the iron puppet that guarded the property to the gas lamps of all shapes and sizes that hung within the house—had been picked to pieces by Shen Yi. Old Mister Shen was a devout Daoist and believed in following one's natural inclinations in all things. Yet perhaps the strength of his faith was somewhat lacking, for he still clung to certain hopes and aspirations for his son.

Gu Yun had been called to the palace to discuss business first thing in the morning and had already left the estate. Although he spent most of the year away from the capital, he was nevertheless a powerful individual of high status, so there was no shortage of people who sent gifts. Since the Marquis Estate had no mistress to manage the house, the responsibility for sorting out New Year's gift registries fell to the old housekeeper. Hearing that Old Mister Shen had come to add to the pile, Chang Geng followed the old housekeeper to the gate to greet him and peered at him in curiosity.

Old Mister Shen was quite the eccentric himself. He had spent his youth indulging in pleasure and carried on in that vein into midlife before eventually tiring of it all in his old age. It was at that point that he began to fixate on Daoist theories of transcendence and immortality. These days, he concerned himself little with the ways of the human world, and instead spent his time pursuing his twin passions: alchemy and winemaking. Among his gifts to Gu Yun, there were no precious metals or gemstones, no bolts of fine silk or satin, and no rare antiques or curious treasures. Instead, he had come bearing two cartloads of wine, all of which he had vinted himself.

Torn between laughter and tears, Chang Geng glanced up to see the newly minted Southwest Army Commander hurtling over on horseback looking frazzled beyond belief.

Old Mister Shen had acted completely on his own, and by the time Shen Yi caught on and chased him down, it was too late. As he took in the sight of the wine carts barricading the Marquis Estate's front gates, Shen Yi couldn't find the tears to cry. He buried his face in his horse's mane and thought, *This is way too embarrassing!*

When Gu Yun returned that evening, it was to the sight of his household unloading the wine carts while Shen Yi stood to the side, whey-faced. Who knew what the emperor had said to him, but Gu Yun was unusually subdued. He was ordinarily ecstatic to return to the Marquis Estate. Yet today, when he passed through the gate, he neither smiled nor cracked his usual joke with the guard on duty. It seemed he was well and truly unhappy.

"What are you doing here?" Gu Yun asked.

Shen Yi nodded toward the ridiculous wine cart. "A bribe from my old man to thank you for supporting my promotion."

Gu Yun inhaled deeply through his nose and stepped forward to pick up one of the jars. There by the front gate, he broke the clay seal and sniffed the contents, then swallowed a mouthful.

"Excellent timing. Your dad made this himself, didn't he? I can tell just from the smell," Gu Yun sighed happily. "This works out well. Since you're here already, you might as well stay. We'll go our separate ways before the end of the month, and with the two of us on opposite ends of the country, who knows when we'll meet again. Stay and drink with me tonight."

This was precisely Shen Yi's intention, so he gladly agreed.

"Where's Chang Geng?" Gu Yun asked.

"In the kitchen."

Gu Yun's footsteps paused. "What?"

"He insisted on making the noodles himself," Shen Yi laughed. "Uncle Wang really did try, but he couldn't be stopped. That commandery prince of ours is quite the character. He holds the line when facing enemies on the battlefield and performs acupuncture when off it. He filigrees leather sachets in his spare time and is a deft hand even in the holy ground of the kitchen... If he were a young lady, even the Black Iron Battalion couldn't fight off the suitors swarming your door."

Gu Yun knit his brows. "A gentleman stays clear of the kitchen.[14] This is absurd."

Noticing the odd expression lingering on Gu Yun's face, Shen Yi asked, "What's wrong? Why did His Majesty summon you to the palace?"

Gu Yun paused, then lowered his voice. "His Majesty wishes to punish Master Fenghan."

"What?!" Shen Yi was stunned.

Master Fenghan was surnamed Zhang and bore the courtesy name Fenghan. He had been head of the Lingshu Institute for eighteen years. During Shen Yi's days there, he had worked directly under Master Fenghan's supervision. The man was already over the age of sixty and had spent his entire life at the Lingshu Institute. He never married and had neither wife nor children, nor did he have any fondness for those of his own sex.

Rumor had it that even the servants in his residence were made of iron. Aside from himself, the only living creature on the premises was an old dog on death's door. Yet this was only gossip—no one, not even Shen Yi, had ever visited Master Fenghan's estate.

---

14   An idiom derived from the quotation, "A gentleman who has seen a living animal cannot bear to see it die, hence he keeps away from the kitchen," which originates from the eponymous philosophical text Mencius.

The old gentleman had a rather odd personality. He was reluctant to entertain guests and had dedicated his life to the world of steam engines and steel armor. He had taken a clear stand when Gu Yun had rebuilt the Black Iron Battalion, but aside from that instance, he barely acknowledged other people, much less concerned himself with governance. How could someone so indifferent toward worldly affairs anger the emperor?

"But why?" asked Shen Yi.

"The old fellow submitted a memorial expressing his opposition to the Token of Mastery Law. His Majesty is furious."

Shen Yi frowned. "But he's always been opposed to it. He hasn't stopped protesting since the Token of Mastery Law was announced. One of my old classmates told me he submits a memorial every three days, rain or shine. His Majesty never paid him any attention before—why would he suddenly..."

The Token of Mastery Law was the ordinance that restricted the activities of civilian artificers. It had been subject to a period of intense debate when first unveiled, but the discussion had soon been drowned out by the tidal wave of controversy raised by the Marching Orders Decree.

"Master Fenghan's temper really is..." Gu Yun sighed. "You didn't see what he wrote in his memorial the other day. He said the Token of Mastery Law restrains not just the artificers, but the wisdom and intellect of the people, and that, in the long term, implementing the policy would imperil the nation. While we sit twiddling our thumbs, the Far Westerners will come flying in on their steam-powered machines like immortals rising through mist to knock on Great Liang's doors. The way I see it, he came just short of pointing a finger at His Majesty and calling him a traitor to the nation. Honestly, His Majesty ordinarily wouldn't have stooped to his level...but ever since the disturbance on the southern border, the emperor's mind has been in a knot over these matters. Winter is nearly over, but this knot has yet to be untied. The old man ran right into the cannon's muzzle."

Gu Yun shook his head. "His Majesty stopped me today as I was leaving. He said, 'We have asked ourselves and searched our soul. Ever since we ascended the throne, we have been so diligent in our duties that we frequently lose sleep. Why is it, then, that the nation is not at peace?'—You tell me what I could possibly say to that."

It had only been a few short years since the Longan Emperor's ascension. Yet first his own blood brother had been caught plotting rebellion with the Dongying people, then a regional commander had colluded with mountain bandits in an armed insurrection. To the emperor, each of these incidents was the greatest of mockeries. Meanwhile, the violet gold black market, which continued unabated despite repeated prohibitions, had become a major source of anxiety.

Shen Yi fell silent as the two walked side by side into the Marquis Estate's inner courtyard. Although Master Fenghan was undoubtedly courting trouble by speaking out, they both knew what he said made perfect sense. If the civilian artificers were banned from practicing their trade and everyone had to rely on the Lingshu Institute, how would the Institute's artificers have time to innovate? Furthermore, the priority of the Lingshu Institute had always been military armor—how much room was there for growth and development of technologies used by civilians?

"Is there anything you can do to save him?" Shen Yi asked quietly.

Gu Yun glanced up at the twilit sky stretching over the outermost reaches of the capital and exhaled a white cloud into the cold air. "I don't know. I'll do what I can."

Shen Yi nodded. After a beat, he said, "Sir, I grew up in the capital, but there are times I can't even breathe when I'm here."

Gu Yun passed over the jug of wine without a word, and Shen Yi took a swig of his family vintage. The wine was so strong he could barely choke it down. He clapped Gu Yun on the back. "Everyone's waiting to celebrate your birthday. Make sure to do something about that sour face when we head in there."

The two of them stood in that sheltered walkway, taking turns sipping from the earthenware jar until they'd polished off the contents.

Wine had the power to relieve anxieties and warm the blood. It could add a rosy flush to one's cheeks and allow one to set the concerns of the present and future aside and relax, at least for a while.

However, when Gu Yun stepped into the inner courtyard, he was nevertheless rather stunned.

By the looks of it, Ge Chen had dug out a number of the Marquis Estate's old iron puppets that had been relegated to scrap. Who knew how much time it had taken him to fix them all. The giant, pitch-black machines moved as fluidly as the day they were made as they lined up in a ragged row. Relieved of their armor and weaponry, each puppet had instead been equipped with a pair of silk fans, and the whole troupe was now performing a joyful but disorganized folk dance in the middle of the courtyard. The principal dancer and only flesh-and-blood body in the group was the gaily dressed Cao Niangzi.

Gu Yun was at a loss for words.

Shaking his head, Shen Yi sighed deeply. "What a genius."

"...Come again?"

Shen Yi slung an arm over his shoulders. "That kid Ge Chen is a real prodigy. Whenever I remember that the first steam-powered armor he ever touched came from me, I honestly...*tsk*, I wish I could steal him away to the southern border."

Gu Yun held his tongue. Something about General Shen's words seemed a bit off.

As promised, Chang Geng had prepared Gu Yun a bowl of longevity noodles. Last time, he had cracked in an egg and ended up serving him the shell as well. When he stepped into the estate kitchen today, this young man seemed to be an entirely different person. His present cooking skills could hardly be compared with his past efforts. The noodles were mouthwateringly good. After finishing the food, Gu Yun practically inhaled the bowl with it, and never uttered such discouraging words as "a gentleman stays clear of the kitchen" ever again.

Three bowls of wine later, everyone in the courtyard was behaving outlandishly.

"All these years, from the capital to the Western Regions, from the northern border to Loulan, everywhere I went, you were always by my side." Shen Yi sighed. "It's going to feel strange now without you."

"Enough with the chitchat," Gu Yun said. "Drink!"

Ge Chen scurried over. "General Shen," he said earnestly. "I have some friends from the jianghu in the southwest. If you run into any trouble, ask them for help!"

Shen Yi was so moved that tears welled in his eyes. "Never mind your jianghu friends. Will you give me one of your wooden birds?"

The two beheld each other tearfully, feeling as though they had found a long-lost friend, before running off to engage in a heated discussion on improving the lifespan of steam engines. They were punished by Gu Yun with three bowls of wine apiece.

After downing his penalty, Ge Chen rolled under the table and disappeared. Exhausted by his stint in the spotlight, Cao Chunhua too finally collapsed in a tangled heap among the iron puppets in the courtyard. Chang Geng was stretched in four directions at once, taking care of one person after another.

In the end, everyone was plastered.

Yanking on Gu Yun, Shen Yi rambled through the thick slur mangling his words. "Zixi...oh, Zixi. The Gu family stands where the winds and waves are the fiercest—*hic*...it's always stood where the winds and waves are the fiercest. You must...you must be careful..."

Gu Yun lay collapsed against a jug of wine. He had no desire to move, nor did he wish to speak, so he only laughed. Once he started, it was difficult to stop, and he laughed until tears streamed down his face. He thought, *I'm the only member of the Gu family left.*

Shen Yi staggered to his feet, swayed two steps to the side, and fell over with a loud *thud*, mumbling all the while, "His Majesty... His Majesty is scared of you."

It was hard to say who His Majesty was or wasn't scared of, but Chang Geng was certainly a bit scared of both of them right now. He hastily beckoned the estate's guards over and directed them to help Shen Yi up. "Hurry and carry General Shen to one of the spare rooms."

Gu Yun leaned against the table with his head propped in one hand, an inscrutable smile on his face. If not for the slackness of his gaze, one might think he was cold sober.

Through the efforts of the diligent, if somewhat clumsy, estate guards, Shen Yi was pulled upright, but still refused to behave. Struggling against the guards' supporting hands, he slurred, "You... Gu Zixi... You might have...have gotten over it, but His M-Majesty hasn't. He's scared of you, just like the late emperor. How can he not be scared? They wounded you so grievously back then...they tried to destroy you...but you survived. And the Black Iron Battalion is still so...so powerful. These people think to themselves, if the situation were reversed, how would they retaliate? They judge others by their own measure, Zixi... Everyone in this world judges others by their own measure..."

Chang Geng's ability to hold his liquor was no better than average. At Gu Yun's insistence, he had already drunk plenty and was barely holding onto a sliver of clarity. Yet at Shen Yi's words, a chill slid down his spine, sobering him instantly.

What did "they tried to destroy you" mean?

Were Shen Yi's words merely the ramblings of a drunk man? Chang Geng couldn't help but step forward in an attempt to hear more clearly.

Yet after howling a little longer, Shen Yi turned to clutch the pillar behind him and hurled. Once he was done making a mess, he collapsed weakly, like a pile of wet mud, and passed out, drunk.

Chang Geng was at his wit's end. He had no choice but to ask the still-sober members of the household to carry away the sloppy drunks slumped around the courtyard one by one.

Finally, all that remained were a handful of iron puppets still dutifully swinging their limbs as tendrils of white steam emanated from their heads. The sounds of laughter and cheer in the capital slowly faded away.

Gu Yun was half lying on the table. He seemed disoriented, and mumbled in a voice that was barely discernible, "Not so tough after all, huh? These losers can't even walk on their own two legs; they had to be carried out."

The nerve of this man. Sighing, Chang Geng played along, coaxing him in a low voice. "That's right, and you're the toughest of them all. Since you're so tough, let's walk back to your room. I'll help you, okay?"

Gu Yun looked up at him, his eyes so deep and dark that the reeling sensation of drunkenness Chang Geng had just suppressed reared its head once again.

"A-Yan..." Gu Yun called out quietly.

Chang Geng frowned.

"A-Yan." Gu Yun giggled, and said with a mix of helpless exasperation and his usual acerbic irreverence, "I'll tell you a secret, but you mustn't tell anyone else... Your dad...is a real *bastard*."

Chang Geng stared.

What kind of nonsense was this?!

Gu Yun chuckled softly under his breath and whispered incoherently, "Who knows what frost endures this heart of mine, who'll share with me this cup of bitter wine..."

Chang Geng had no intention of having a staring contest with a drunkard. He helped Gu Yun up and dragged him to his bedroom. Who would've expected that Gu Yun was such a clingy drunk? He groped at Chang Geng like an incorrigible old lecher. With Gu Yun's hands all over him, Chang Geng was so agitated he had a mind to fling him directly onto the bed. Yet when he looked down at Marshal Gu's hard, wooden bed with its thin, cotton-padded mattress, he didn't have the heart to drop him.

And who could have known that Gu Yun would abruptly twist around and grasp at the sensitive nerve at Chang Geng's elbow? Chang Geng was caught by surprise; he felt his arm go weak and nearly dropped Gu Yun. In his haste to catch him, Chang Geng lost his balance as well and found himself dragged down on top of him. The sudden weight of Chang Geng crashing into his chest knocked the air from Gu Yun's lungs. After panting a while, Gu Yun patted Chang Geng on the back and said nonsensically, "Aiyo, darling, you're crushing me to death."

As Chang Geng lay against Gu Yun's body, a quiet shoot unfurled from the seed he had struggled to bury deep in the darkness of his heart. Staring closely at the pale lines of Gu Yun's jaw, he suddenly asked in a low voice, "Who are you calling out to?"

Gu Yun made no sound.

Chang Geng was drunk. How else could he act so fearlessly? He pressed closer, taking hold of Gu Yun's chin. "Yifu, who are you calling?"

The word *yifu* seemed to jog Gu Yun's memory. "Chang Geng," he mumbled.

Those two syllables were like a blunt piece of iron brushing past Chang Geng's ears. A rumbling explosion went off in his head, and the words *let nature take its course* propelled him forward as he leaned down and kissed Gu Yun as though possessed. Gu Yun started in surprise. After several long moments, he slowly reacted. He clung clumsily to Chang Geng's collar, then abruptly shoved him away.

Chang Geng's back slammed against Gu Yun's rock-hard bed. His mind cleared; the color drained from his face. *What am I doing?* he thought in a panic.

Gu Yun gazed down at him from above. Chang Geng opened his mouth to call out, "Yifu," and found himself unable to speak.

Suddenly Gu Yun smiled. The drunkard no longer seemed to recognize him and reached out to stroke his cheek. He slurred in a nasal voice, "Now, behave."

He took Chang Geng, who was stiff as a board from head to toe, into his arms and earnestly pressed a line of kisses from his brow to his lips. He licked open the seam of Chang Geng's mouth with utmost tenderness, treating him to a lingering yet fervent bout of sweet torture. His hands weren't idle either as they fumbled with Chang Geng's lapels.

Chang Geng felt like he was about to explode. His hand shook as he held Gu Yun's waist, yet he resisted tightening his grip.

Gu Yun seemed to sense the trembling of his body. He was surprisingly poised in bed, as one would expect from an elegant young master of an aristocratic family. As he groped at Chang Geng's belt, he flashed him a smile overflowing with intoxication, "Don't be scared," he coaxed, gentle. "Stay with me and I'll treat you well."

Chang Geng lowered his voice to the barest whisper and asked hoarsely, "Who am I?"

Gu Yun stared blankly, then paused to ponder his answer. Alas, his sodden brain was incapable of such mental exercise. Not only did he fail to reach a definitive conclusion, he also managed to tangle himself in Chang Geng's belt. He fussed with it for half an age, but the more he tried to loosen it, the tighter the knot became. In the end, exhausted from trying to unfasten Chang Geng's robes, Gu Yun flopped to the side and fell asleep.

In the depth of the stillness that followed, Chang Geng gritted his teeth and painstakingly counted his long, shuddering breaths. By the time he got to sixty, he had scraped together the strength to push Gu Yun aside and climb to his feet.

He yanked his belt from Gu Yun's grip, laid him flat on the bed, and pulled a blanket haphazardly over his body. Unable to stay for a second more, he turned around and fled.

47

MUDDY WATERS

WHEN GU YUN AWOKE, the sun was high in the sky.

He had been upset the night before, so he had drunk to drown his sorrows and gotten successfully sloshed. When he managed to drag himself out of bed, his body was so stiff he felt more exhausted than if he'd gone the entire night without sleep.

Someone had set out a bowl of hangover remedy on the little table in his room. Gu Yun carried it over and, pinching his nose, drained it in a single gulp. Only then did he crack open his crusty eyes. He sat on his bed in a daze and conducted an impromptu round of self-reflection. In his half-awake state, he found that he had been unreasonably anxious lately.

Are things really as bad as all that? Gu Yun asked himself honestly with a yawn.

Upon careful consideration, of course they weren't. The national treasury was more strapped for cash in recent years, so it was natural that military funding had tightened up. Even so, things hadn't gotten to the point where people were going hungry.

The heavens had also been relatively kind. There had been a handful of floods and earthquakes, as well as the drought a couple years back, but nothing severe. The Central Plains were so vast that the imperial court had to fret over disaster relief whenever any random cloud presided over by an errant dragon god so much as convulsed.

Yet since the first year of the Longan Emperor's reign, the nation had been remarkably peaceful.

There were the two incidents in Jiangnan and the southwest, but although they had raised quite a furor and been a source of great alarm for the emperor, to Gu Yun, these were minor scuffles. Regarding the East Sea, Prince Wei had clearly been still in the midst of preparations when his tracks were revealed thanks to leaks from his violet gold smuggling operation. Meanwhile, the situation on the southern border had been an inopportune collision of multiple forces. Fu Zhicheng had likely never intended to rebel in the first place. In short, these incidents were hardly as dangerous as hunting down raiders in the desert.

What were today's troubles compared to when he had led the military campaign against the six nations of the Western Regions? Back then, the country had lacked strong soldiers, and the responsibility for holding up the vast nation of Great Liang had fallen on his own shoulders.

In those days, he had spent each day wondering whether he would see the sun the next morning, but his mind had been free from distractions. Yet now, despite wielding great power and having the leisure to watch iron puppets perform a folk dance in his courtyard, he felt the need to drown his sorrows. Some hero he was!

And then, after soaking himself in wine, he'd gone and done something else...

What was it again?

That's right, Gu Yun thought, rubbing his temples in bewilderment. *I harassed a servant girl and scared her half to death.*

"How disgraceful," Gu Yun muttered as he washed up and began to change his clothes.

Halfway through changing, he froze. *That's not right. This estate doesn't even have a female horse in the stables—where did a servant girl come from?!*

Gu Yun finally woke up completely. He mulled things over, his face ashen, then turned back to lift the blanket—only to see something roll out from a corner of the bed. It was Chang Geng's filigree sachet.

Gu Yun stared at it in silence.

Shen Yi couldn't hold his liquor, so he had been even drunker than Gu Yun. He hadn't even opened his eyes yet that morning when Gu Yun burst into the guest room and dragged him out of bed.

"I need to talk to you." Gu Yun looked like he had seen a ghost.

Shen Yi didn't dare ignore him. A jumble of wild guesses ran through his head: *Fu Zhicheng broke out of prison? The emperor convicted Master Fenghan of a crime? The northern barbarians invaded? Or could it be that the backbone of Great Liang's military, the Central Plains Garrison, launched an armed rebellion?*

Indisposed as he was, Shen Yi did his best to compose himself and waited for Gu Yun to speak. However, after he'd hemmed and hawed for several minutes, his gaze flitting up to the roof beams and down to his own shoes, that Gu bastard didn't issue so much as a fart.

"What's wrong?" Shen Yi asked cautiously, heart in his mouth.

A pause. "Forget it. I don't feel like talking anymore."

Shen Yi lost it, so angry he nearly blew a fuse. With the way this man spoke in halves, it was a wonder no one had yet stabbed him to death.

"Wait." Shen Yi lurched forward and grabbed Gu Yun. "What exactly is going on?!" he demanded furiously.

After his discovery of the evidence left on his bed, Gu Yun had slowly unearthed the memories from the night before. The things he said, the things he did—everything flashed before his eyes in lurid color. He had been so embarrassing, so sleazy, so despicable!

Gu Yun covered his face with his hands. *What have I done?*

He could feel acid lapping up from his stomach. "Do I go crazy when I get drunk?" he asked Shen Yi miserably.

"You've never really gotten that drunk before, have you?" Shen Yi hugged his blankets to himself and curled up by the head of the bed. These two soldiers lived on the frontiers year-round. Even when they drank, they never risked getting drunk, lest some emergency arise and they botch a military operation.

"What?" Shen Yi examined Gu Yun's complexion, then asked with great interest, "Did you do something embarrassing yesterday?"

Gu Yun reached over and shoved that face so eager to feast on his misfortune back into the blankets. He drifted out of the room in a daze, thinking perhaps he ought to find a belt with which to hang himself.

At first, Gu Yun thought optimistically, *Little Chang Geng wouldn't hold a grudge against a drunk, right? I certainly wouldn't take it seriously if I were him.*

At most, he'd use it to tease the boy for about a year.

But soon, that small spot of optimism faded away. Last night, when he had pressed Chang Geng down on the bed, Chang Geng had been shaking the entire time. Not only had Chang Geng taken it seriously—he'd also been mad as hell. Gu Yun's expression was woeful as he held Chang Geng's sachet. He felt as though he were carrying a bomb that might explode in his face at any moment.

The faint, refreshing scent of pacifying fragrance saturated the air, filling Gu Yun's nose as he schemed in silence. *Do I feign confusion? Ignorance? Should I act like nothing happened?*

Before he could decide, he ran into the old housekeeper. Gu Yun promptly assumed the honorable mien of an upright gentleman and asked, "Uncle Wang, where is His Highness?"

"I was just about to come tell you, my lord," said the old house-keeper. "His Highness left for the National Temple first thing this morning."

Gu Yun was stunned. Chang Geng was so angry he ran away from home!

The marquis looked like he had swallowed a mouthful of bitter medicine, but the old housekeeper didn't notice. "One more thing," he continued. "Justice Jiang of the Imperial Court of Judicial Review sent over a painting in celebration of my lord's birthday. There was a letter enclosed with the gift. Would you like to read it now?"

Gu Yun blinked in surprise. "Yes, give it here."

Shen Yi had somehow managed to become a general by following Gu Yun, but, in truth, he had a scholarly background. Back in the day, he had risen through the imperial examination system. Chief Justice Jiang Chong of the Imperial Court of Judicial Review was his shixiong, and it was through this connection that the justice had become acquainted with Gu Yun. The two discovered that they got along very well and had gradually struck up a friendship; however, to avoid arousing any suspicions, they rarely sought out each other's company.

After unfolding the letter and skimming its contents, Gu Yun found he had more pressing matters to attend to than Chang Geng's tantrum. After observing the usual niceties, Jiang Chong's letter succinctly divulged a piece of news to Gu Yun: the emperor intended to take decisive action to dismantle the violet gold black market once and for all.

Such a simple sentence. Yet its implications were enormous.

That evening, Kite's Flight Pavilion was as noisy and bustling as ever. Within the Empyrean Room, the newly appointed Southwest

Army Commander Shen Yi was hosting a banquet. He had invited his old classmates from the capital as well as his former peers from the Lingshu Institute. Shen Yi would soon travel to the southwest to take up a new post. Although this post was far from the capital,[15] it was nevertheless a grand promotion, and all his old friends had clamored for him to treat them to dinner.

Toward the end of the feast, after three rounds of toasts had come and gone, the Marquis of Anding made an appearance. He stayed for a brief time, then excused himself once again to attend to matters at home. Shortly after he left, Jiang Chong, the sitting Chief Justice of the Imperial Court of Judicial Review, also said his goodbyes and took his leave.

Jiang Chong exited Kite's Flight Pavilion but did not climb into his carriage. Instead, he dismissed his attendants so he might take a stroll to sober up, leaving only a young servant boy to follow in his wake. He walked along the icy river, down a small side road lined with frosted willows, and turned a corner. There he saw an inconspicuous old carriage waiting for him. The carriage's hanging screen lifted, revealing Gu Yun's shadowed profile. "It's bitterly cold tonight. Please allow me to give you a lift home, Hanshi-xiong."

"Then I'll thank you for your trouble," Jiang Chong responded. A silent understanding flowed between them, and he climbed into Gu Yun's carriage.

Justice Jiang was already forty, but his age didn't show on his face. If not for his staid bearing, one might mistake him for a young master from a noble family.

After settling himself in the carriage, Jiang Chong accepted Gu Yun's hand warmer to allay the chill. He got straight to the point.

---

15   Far-off official posts in frontier regions were generally considered a demotion and tantamount to exile.

"After the marquis left the palace the other day, His Majesty summoned the heads of the three judicial offices for a secret meeting. He intends to employ a two-pronged approach: not only will he bring back the Gold-Consolidation Decree, he also plans to use the insurrection on the southern border as an excuse to make some bold moves. He wants a thorough investigation of the domestic violet gold black market—and he's starting with the southwest."

The Gold-Consolidation Decree was a relic from the reign of Gu Yun's maternal grandfather, Emperor Wu of Liang. In those days, maritime trade was still in its infancy and civilian use of violet gold was difficult to control. To strengthen regulations, Emperor Wu issued four harsh decrees, which became known collectively as the Gold-Consolidation Decree.

As civilian use of steam engines and steel armor became increasingly widespread, the Gold-Consolidation Decree eventually became obsolete. All four decrees were ultimately repealed during the Yuanhe Emperor's reign.

"The marquis will be returning to the northwest shortly after the New Year. Even if the imperial court sees a great upheaval, it's unlikely to affect you. But the marquis has been stationed on the border for so long. Should His Majesty follow through with his strict investigation of the black market, I fear that...your position will inevitably invite suspicion. Please be careful."

Jiang Chong couldn't point directly at Gu Yun and say, *I know your hands are dirty too. The crackdowns have been very strict recently, so you'd better clean up your black-market connections and put things on hold for a few days.* Nevertheless, his meaning was quite plain.

"Many thanks for your advice, Hanshi-xiong," said Gu Yun gratefully.

Seeing that Gu Yun had received the message, Jiang Chong didn't belabor the point. He smiled stiffly, and said, "Whenever violet gold is involved, we're forced to deal with diabolical individuals. It's one thing for these nefarious criminals to do as they please in the jianghu, but I'm afraid there are plenty of court officials secretly involved as well. Who should be investigated, and how should the investigation proceed? To be honest, I have no idea either."

Just as water that is too clear has no fish, one who is too self-righteous will have no friends. It was difficult to say whether the Longan Emperor's goal was to bring peace to the land or incite pandemonium.

Gu Yun recognized the difficulty of his position. "Don't worry, Hanshi-xiong. Once this news gets out, anyone with eyes and ears won't need to be told twice to keep a low profile. After all, we'll all be much more anxious than you are. When the time comes, if you encounter any trouble, send a letter to me. I no longer hold the Black Iron Tiger Tally, so I haven't the authorization to deploy the country's armed forces. But His Majesty is still willing to give me some face."

Jiang Chong's smile was strained. "In that case, you have my thanks. First there was the Token of Mastery Law, and now there's the Gold-Consolidation Decree... I rarely leave the capital, so I'm often ignorant of these things. But I have heard that, in the past, white steam filled the streets and the night watch sounded without the aid of a human hand. People used to speak of a magnificent future in which everyone rode flying horses. Yet these days, such dreams have long since faded."

Gu Yun fiddled idly with the worn wooden beads around his wrist and changed the subject. "How is Master Fenghan doing?"

"Still locked up," Jiang Chong answered. "But don't worry, I've made sure he'll be looked after. Do you intend to submit a memorial to clarify the situation on his behalf?"

Gu Yun smiled bitterly. "Me? Any memorial I submit would only hasten his death. Actually, there's no need to clarify anything. Many of the devices in the imperial palace are products of the Lingshu Institute. When His Majesty sees them, he'll naturally recall Master Fenghan's virtues. The master has always been enthralled with steam-powered devices and inept at navigating human relationships. His Majesty also knows the old fellow has a terrible temper. In a few days, His Majesty's anger will wane, and everything will work out."

These words were easily said, but once the imperial temper cooled, the question of how to deftly remind the emperor of Master Fenghan would require careful consideration. How to bring up the master artificer, who treated his dog like his son, in such a way that His Majesty would find the old man fondly exasperating, and thus be incapable of flying into a fury once again? Jiang Chong glanced at Gu Yun. This man had likely already made the necessary arrangements without anyone the wiser.

The Marquis of Anding had grown up in the imperial palace, so it wasn't unusual for him to have some connections there. However...

"The marquis seems to have grown much more diplomatic since your return from the northwest this time," Jiang Chong observed quietly.

"With tigers and wolves prowling at our borders, I must exhaust all my ingenuity and dare not leave a stone unturned," Gu Yun said sagely. "Likewise, with the world in turmoil, I dare not lower myself to engage in petty quarrels for petty reasons. What point is there in throwing tantrums or arguing over such useless things as codes of loyalty?"

The two of them exchanged a few more words of news, and Jiang Chong bid Gu Yun farewell. As he slipped out of the carriage, he stopped and turned back to Gu Yun. "Perhaps this is rather insolent of me to say. In recent years, there have been repeat bumper harvests in the regions that have implemented farming puppets, and now there are even new steam-powered machines capable of weaving cloth and sewing garments. Yet still the national treasury remains empty, as if shackled by the various ordinances that have been passed. Despite the passage of so many years, this humble official cannot help but feel as though Great Liang has reverted to the days of Emperor Wu."

"To be honest, Hanshi-xiong," Gu Yun said, smiling, "I've felt inexplicably anxious these past few years as well. But when I think it through carefully, logic tells me my anxieties are baseless. Perhaps all people are like this. We want our lives to improve day by day, so when we reach a plateau, even if we are already well-off, we feel a sense of restless frustration."

Jiang Chong's expression shifted. He seemed to want to say something, but hesitated.

"What is it?" asked Gu Yun.

"Sometimes, when we investigators are on a case, we're guided by pure intuition," Justice Jiang said in a low voice. "The feeling is baseless, but oftentimes, it turns out to be correct. The more storied the veteran, the sharper their intuition. The marquis is someone who has braved untold dangers on the battlefield—perhaps your intuition is likewise a premonition of things to come. Please take care of yourself."

Gu Yun flinched in surprise but held his tongue. The two bid each other farewell and parted ways, each with a heart laden with anxiety.

By the time Gu Yun returned to the Marquis Estate, the sky had gone dark. When he asked the estate's guards, they informed him that Chang Geng was still out and had only sent a message home saying that, since Great Master Liao Ran had returned to the National Temple, Chang Geng planned on staying a few days.

He may as well stay for a while, Gu Yun thought helplessly. *And if his temper cools before he comes back, all the better.*

Perhaps Chang Geng's temper was particularly volatile, for it seemed he fully intended to settle down at the National Temple. Four or five days passed in the blink of an eye. Gu Yun wasn't staying long in the capital to begin with—when he left this time, who knew how many years it would be before they saw each other again? Unable to stand it any longer, Gu Yun finally held his nose and paid a visit to the National Temple.

Liao Ran was the same as ever. These days around the New Year were the only handful in the entire calendar in which, in order to meet with honored guests, he bathed properly. He scrubbed himself as clean as a freshwater lotus and spent every waking moment peddling mystifying hokum wherever he went. That afternoon, the monk had finally managed to carve out some time to sit with Chang Geng in his room and play weiqi. They communicated completely in sign language, so though they seemed to sit in tranquil silence, the topics of which they spoke were diverse and plentiful.

"There is something I want to ask the great master," Chang Geng signed. "What exactly happened to my yifu's eyes and ears?"

"Those who speak of others behind their backs come to no good end," Liao Ran signed rapidly.

"I need to know," Chang Geng signed, his expression resolute. "And I will track down everything there is to know about this matter until I get to the bottom of it. If you won't tell me, I'll find someone who will."

Liao Ran looked at him for a long while, his gaze unwavering.

With careful deliberation, he signed, "This monk has only heard some baseless gossip. When the marquis was a child, his parents, the former marquis and the princess, took him to the northern border. At the time, the fighting between Great Liang and the northern barbarians had died down, so it should have been reasonably safe. No one expected that, in a desperate attempt to bring their enemy down with them, a northern barbarian suicide squad would storm the encampment. In the ensuing chaos, the young marquis was wounded by a stray arrow. And most unfortunately, this arrow was poisoned."

Surprisingly, this account matched Gu Yun's perfunctory explanation.

"What kind of poison?" Chang Geng pressed.

Liao Ran shook his head. "Your Highness has studied under the tutelage of Miss Chen, so you ought to know—even the Chen family is helpless in the face of the barbarians' poisons. This variety is extremely lethal. Those struck with such a poisoned arrow soon become paralyzed and die within days. Luckily, this poison happens to act more slowly in children. Old Doctor Chen rushed overnight from Shanxi to the encampment on the northern border and spent two sleepless days and nights treating the young marquis with the Chen family's most advanced acupuncture techniques. He saved his life, but the young marquis's sight and hearing were severely damaged."

Chang Geng's brow creased slightly. "The northern border..."

If the northern barbarian suicide squad had been the perpetrators, then what did Shen Yi mean when he said, *they tried to destroy you*?

Was it really just the ramblings of a drunk?

Just then, a young novice monk entered. "Your Highness, Liao Ran-shishu, the Marquis of Anding has come."

48
A STARTLING REALIZATION

LIAO RAN STARED in surprise. He never thought he would see the day when the Marquis of Anding would honor the National Temple with his presence. He hastily signed to Chang Geng, "Doesn't the Marquis of Anding find it inauspicious to touch the barest dab of incense ash? Now he's ventured deep into the tiger's lair; is he going to scrub off a layer of skin with evil-dispelling herbs when he returns home?"

Chang Geng had no attention for his questions. A disconcerted expression flickered over his features. He wasn't ready to face Gu Yun's anger and condemnation.

In an unexpected turn of events, Chang Geng and Gu Yun both thought they had transgressed and molested the other while drunk, and now both were suffering from a guilty conscience.

Liao Ran looked at Chang Geng, baffled. In recent years, in order to suppress the wu'ergu, Chang Geng had cultivated his meditative breathing technique to the pinnacle of perfection. He could sit facing a wall and meditate, unmoving, for days at a time. Even an eminent monk like Liao Ran gracefully conceded to him in this regard.

It wasn't unheard of for agitated people to look into Chang Geng's eyes and find themselves soothed. This incomparably handsome young master sat on the penniless monk's old prayer mat, dressed in white with a weiqi stone in hand. He seemed to have reached a peaceful and profound state of sublimity—only for the words *Marquis of Anding* to shatter his serenity like ripples breaking across a pond's still surface.

Chang Geng shifted restlessly and lifted his hand without purpose, reaching for heavens knew what. Halfway through the motion, he noticed Liao Ran staring steadily. He tamped down his emotions and impassively set his hand on his teacup, then lowered his head and disguised his momentary lapse with a sip of water.

Even Great Master Liao Ran, who was quite practiced at acting mysterious, felt slightly bewildered. *What's this? Is the marquis coming to collect on a debt?*

A few moments later, Gu Yun stepped into the room. A barely contained distaste hovered in the arch of his brows and the corners of his eyes, as if he were sorely tempted to walk in on tiptoe. He glanced at Liao Ran with a sour expression and smiled insincerely. "It's been some years since we last met, Great Master. I see you are more pristine than ever."

Liao Ran assumed the demeanor of a great master and refrained from stooping to Gu Yun's level. He pressed his palms together and rose in greeting, signing, "Amitabha Buddha. This monk's heart is like a mirror, clear and bright—there is no place for dust to alight."[16]

Apparently, it was possible to quote the classics to justify refusing to bathe!

Gu Yun looked as if he had smelled something rancid. Unable to stomach another minute in this dodgy establishment, he turned to Chang Geng. "You've disturbed the great master's spiritual practice for several days already. It's high time you came home."

---

16 Slightly modified from a Buddhist verse by Huineng, the Sixth Patriarch of Southern Chan Buddhism.

Chang Geng had spent all these days and much difficulty calming his mind to stillness, only for it to be stirred up once again by the words *came home*. He knew that even if he were to sit under a bodhi tree, he still wouldn't be able to recite the words, "lust is an unworthy pursuit."[17] Thus he could only gather up his great mess of feelings and rise obediently to his feet. The stifling scent of the sandalwood incense burning inside the National Temple made Gu Yun cough. He quickly withdrew to wait outside the cell and looked on with intense boredom as Chang Geng said farewell to Liao Ran.

When it came to friends and family, once Gu Yun had become accustomed to their face, he didn't much notice whether they were attractive or not. Gu Yun had always thought Chang Geng resembled his northern barbarian mother; it was only now, as he examined him from the doorway, that he realized this wasn't completely true. The young man had grown into his features and was favored with an elegant and handsome face. It was difficult to say at a glance whom he resembled, but like a piece of black jade, there was something about him that was uniquely pleasing to the eye.

Gu Yun started. He suddenly remembered that there were people from all walks of life in the jianghu. Since the establishment of maritime trade, the popular customs in Great Liang had become increasingly liberal. In particular, rumor had it that male homosexuality was prevalent in the coastal areas along the East Sea. As a white dragon who had transformed into a fish to swim amongst commoners in a deep pool, could it be that Chang Geng had been harassed by someone who didn't know their place? Was that why he was so angry the other day?

---

17 Humorous reinterpretation of a line from the Heart Sutra. The full line is 色即是空，空即是色, "Form is emptiness, emptiness is form," but 色, "form," can also mean "lust."

That's right, Gu Yun mused, his mind following the thought to its logical end as his imagination took off on a wild flight of fancy. *If I laid one on Shen Jiping, there's no way he would take it seriously. With that poverty-stricken face of his, he wouldn't think I meant anything by it at all. Honestly, if I kissed him, the one drawing the short straw would be me.*

The more he thought about it, the more sense it made and the more awkward he felt. After a bit of deliberation, he decided he might as well play dumb. As Chang Geng strode over, he said nonchalantly, "Why did you stay for so long? Are the cabbage and tofu at the National Temple that good?"

Seeing Gu Yun's easy manner, Chang Geng relaxed as well. "The voice of the Buddha and vegetarian meals help with meditation."

"Young folks like you ought to wear bright colors and live extravagantly. It's not like you're going to become a monk—what are you meditating for?" Walking beside Chang Geng, Gu Yun was about to sling an arm over his shoulders as usual. But just as he lifted his hand, he was struck by the sudden fear that Chang Geng would misconstrue it. He silently withdrew, tucking his hand behind his back instead.

"I have considered it," Chang Geng said evenly.

He'd thought about it once—breaking his worldly ties and taking refuge in a religious life. Maybe that way, all the untamed fantasies in his heart would be transformed by the boundless teachings of Buddha.

"What?" Gu Yun froze mid-stride. It took several long seconds for him to react as he stared at Chang Geng, stupefied. "You mean become a monk?" he asked in disbelief.

Chang Geng rarely saw such astonishment on his godfather's face. "I only said I thought about it; I didn't have the guts to actually do it," he said with a smile.

Nonsense, Gu Yun thought. *If you did, I'd break your legs.*

But in the end, Gu Yun held his tongue. Chang Geng was no longer the helpless little godson he could shelter beneath the eaves of the Marquis Estate. He had undergone his coming-of-age ceremony and been bestowed the title of commandery prince. He still called Gu Yun "Yifu," but that was purely out of a sense of affection rather than an official status. It was no longer appropriate for Gu Yun to lecture this young man as if he were his real son.

Thus he only asked with a slightly downcast expression, "Why?"

Chang Geng exchanged a polite greeting with the young novice monk who walked past them, then responded, "As a child, I grew up looking at 'The World is Inescapable' calligraphy hanging in Yifu's room. Later, I followed my shifu and traveled the land. I have barely tasted the hardships and perils of the world—how can I withdraw from it? I was born to this world. Although my natural ability is limited and I may not accomplish great feats that stand the test of time like the distinguished sages of the past, the least I can do is be unashamed to face the heavens, the earth, and myself..."

...and you.

Chang Geng did not speak those last words aloud, hiding them away in his heart.

Xiu-niang had once dragged Chang Geng behind her horse, but in the end, she had failed to drag him to death. The wu'ergu tormented him, but so far, it had failed to torment him to madness. At times, Chang Geng thought that only by pushing through the stormiest waves, constantly swimming against the current, would he reach a place where he could finally respect himself. And only then would he deserve to dream, however briefly, about his little yifu in the dead of night.

Gu Yun's expression cleared, but he still asked unhappily, "Then why do you keep running off to surround yourself with a bunch of monks?"

"I come to have tea with Great Master Liao Ran," Chang Geng dodged the question neatly. "Sometimes, I suffer from excess internal heat and have trouble sleeping. Miss Chen gave me a prescription for pacifying fragrance, didn't she? It's in my sachet, but I haven't been able to find it these past few days."

Gu Yun abruptly became mute.

"I don't know where I managed to lose it," Chang Geng continued, perplexed.

At this, Gu Yun's complexion turned pale—some people really were remarkably proficient at hitting right where it hurt.

Marshal Gu wrestled with his conscience in silence for a while, but in the end, he reached into his lapels and pulled out that little leather perfume sachet. He handed it to Chang Geng. "Here."

Now it was Chang Geng's turn to fall silent.

The shocking revelation caught Chang Geng, who had inadvertently been snared in a trap of his own making, so off guard that he almost bit through his tongue. Prince Yanbei, who only moments ago had been the paragon of a worldly and capable savant, felt his palms immediately dampen with cold sweat. "Wh-why does Yifu have this?" he stuttered.

With his thick face, which had been thoroughly tempered by all sorts of awkward predicaments, firmly in place, Gu Yun said without batting an eye, "It fell onto my bed somehow. Perhaps I accidentally yanked it off you that day I got roaring drunk."

Chang Geng examined his expression, petrified.

Gu Yun shamelessly feigned innocence. "What's the matter?"

Chang Geng hurried to shake his head and breathed a sigh of

relief. Somehow, he had managed to muddle his way through this disaster and could once again interact with Gu Yun calmly and intimately, as before.

At the same time, he couldn't help but feel a sliver of disappointment.

Noticing his change in expression, Gu Yun thought Chang Geng was still offended, so he offered an olive branch. "I forgot to mention this the other day, but His Majesty wants you to start listening in on court assemblies," he said. "What kind of position do you want? I'll see if I can put in a word."

Chang Geng's relaxed expression became serious. "Each of the Six Ministries have their own spheres of influence," he said. "It wouldn't do for me to disrupt their work. In all these years, I've accrued no civil or military accomplishments, and am accustomed to idleness. If His Majesty insists I listen in on court assemblies, then it's enough for me to listen. I wouldn't mind helping Justice Jiang of the Imperial Court of Judicial Review with his investigations, either."

Gu Yun wasn't sure if Chang Geng's answer was reflective of his true feelings, but he was certain the emperor would be happy to hear it. He felt a slight ache in his heart. He didn't want to send Chang Geng to the Longan Emperor only for him to be mistreated, his talents to be wasted—but the alternative was an impossibility. Chang Geng's surname was Li. Even if he became an idle prince and succumbed to decadence, there was no way he could spend his whole life hiding away in the Marquis of Anding's estate.

"You can work in the Imperial Court of Judicial Review if you want, but wait a while—don't go just yet," Gu Yun said. "His Majesty intends to investigate the violet gold black market, so Justice Jiang is under a lot of pressure right now. The situation's already messy enough, so stay out of it. Don't get the Linyuan Pavilion involved."

Chang Geng hummed in assent; he didn't seem surprised by this news in the least. "So soon? I see His Majesty really can't wait. Just the other day, I was wondering when he would reinstate the Gold-Consolidation Decree."

"How do *you* know about it?" Gu Yun asked, surprised.

"Just a guess." A light snow had begun to drift through the air. Chang Geng borrowed an oil-paper umbrella from the doorway of a monk's cell. The umbrella was small, and Chang Geng kept tilting it in Gu Yun's direction. In no time at all, his exposed shoulder was covered in a thin layer of snow. He didn't bother to brush it off, but continued to walk at a steady pace, as if relishing the experience. "Actually, it's not really a guess. Think about it, Yifu. His Majesty the Longan Emperor, the Yuanhe Emperor before him, even Emperor Wu—although all extraordinarily wise in different ways, when it comes to violet gold, they've all been exactly the same. They all see it as a source of danger and concern."

Gu Yun had always viewed Chang Geng as a child of the younger generation. This was the first time he had walked with him shoulder to shoulder and listened to his thoughts. He found the experience awfully novel, so he didn't interrupt and only listened to him speak.

"Back when I was young and lived in Yanhui Town, I saw with my own eyes the way the imperial court squandered manpower and resources for the sake of violet gold. These last few years, I've also had the thought—why control its use so strictly? If violet gold were treated like food or textiles, and everyone could buy however much they wanted, wouldn't the black market cease to exist?" Chang Geng shook his head, then continued, "Later on, I realized that such a thing is impossible. Perhaps it is treasonous to say so, but it doesn't matter who the emperor is—whether they're impotent or enlightened, a frail scholar or a hale practitioner of martial arts—no one can allow commoners to trade in violet gold. Otherwise, in the future, powerful merchants, Western foreigners, Eastern barbarians, nefarious criminals, even officials with a few resources...any one of them could hold a blade to the nation's throat."

"Like those bandits on the southern border," Gu Yun said.

"Exactly. That was only the black market, some bandits, and a handful of mountain peaks near the southern border—but what if we broadened the scope to the entire nation of Great Liang? What if everyone held such a 'blade'? It's impossible for the imperial court to please everyone. If such a time were to come, similar cases would spring up like weeds, and there's no way the government could attend to them all. The nation would be controlled by he who wields the largest weapon. Those who wish to vie for power will stop at nothing to obtain that invaluable dragon-slaying blade and fight to conquer each other. Allowing violet gold to be traded freely would be like raising the legendary gu insect—by the time all the other creatures have been devoured and the gu king rears its venomous head, who will reign supreme over the land?"

Gu Yun frowned. "Chang Geng, there's no harm in saying this to me, but don't mention this to anyone else. So then, do you mean that the emperor is right to reinstate the Gold-Consolidation Decree?"

"No, that's not it. Actually, the best solution would be to keep the late emperor's moderate restrictions on violet gold in place until the situation is stable and focus on resolving the most vital issue: money. Ever since the implementation of the farming puppets, a significant portion of the yearly crop yield has been left to rot in granaries. As the price of rice plummets, rather than stocking up on foodstuffs, many have shifted to hoarding gold and silver. There's only so much gold and silver to go around—if all of it has been hoarded away, then it's inevitable that the National Treasury remains empty.

Ingots cannot be created out of thin air, and a distant spring cannot quench present thirst—even if we were to mint more coinage, it would be too little too late. Thus, we must look to foreign trade as a source of gold and silver. Once the Silk Road has been fully established, it will be Yifu's most monumental accomplishment. Even a hundred quelled rebellions won't compare to such a feat.

"As long as there is money," Chang Geng continued, "the house will have its rafters and the people will have their pillar of support. Then, we can slowly address the nation's domestic affairs, like a pot simmering over a low flame. There will still be challenges, but the situation will not escalate. We can look forward to centuries of peace and prosperity. After a few generations of stability, perhaps we will find a way forward." Chang Geng sighed softly. "It's unfortunate that both armed rebellions in the last few years involved the black market. His Majesty's extreme reaction is unsurprising. Truthfully, I suspect that the incidents in the East Sea and on the southern border are no coincidence. I've been borrowing the Linyuan Pavilion's resources to investigate and have only recently come upon a vague lead...but our enemies are truly devious. Yifu, you must be careful."

After listening to Chang Geng's speech, Gu Yun fell silent for a long while, his expression difficult to read. Chang Geng left him to his thoughts and slowly accompanied him out of the National Temple.

The evening drum reverberated from within the temple, echoing into the mountains. In the deep silence that followed, snow drifted down without a sound.

Old General Zhong could raise a military commander capable of bringing peace to the nation through battlefield victories, but he couldn't singlehandedly produce an official talented enough to govern the nation and pacify the land. Not for the first time,

Gu Yun was overcome by intense regret. *Why must this child be surnamed Li?*

If Chang Geng were not the prince Li Min, becoming an official through the imperial examination would be as easy as the flip of the palm. Rather than sharing a few stray thoughts with Gu Yun in this lousy temple while proclaiming that his only desire was to idle his days away as a pretty but useless fixture in court, he could enjoy a meteoric rise, aid the nation in its recovery, become the greatest statesman of his generation... But such was his fate.

"The weather is worsening, and Yifu is much too lightly dressed," Chang Geng said. "Instead of riding back on your horse, why not join me in my carriage?"

Gu Yun was still lost in thought. At the sound of his voice, Gu Yun turned his head and unexpectedly met Chang Geng's eyes. His heart stuttered in his chest. He'd never noticed how Chang Geng looked at him before. His gaze, faintly reflecting the soft white snow, was unwavering in its focus. It was as if he wished to swallow Gu Yun whole within the depths of his eyes.

Startled, Chang Geng swiftly looked away. He dropped his head and flicked his sleeve in an attempt to appear innocuous, but only seemed all the more suspicious. The sleeve was already soaked through, and the fabric stuck to his hand. Only then did Gu Yun realize Chang Geng's shoulder had been covered in a chilly layer of melted snow. He hadn't said a word about it as he accompanied Gu Yun on his unhurried stroll.

Gu Yun reached out and ran his hand over the damp fabric; it was icy to the touch. "You..."

The instant he lifted his hand, Chang Geng's body tensed. It lasted only a fleeting moment—but it did not escape Gu Yun's eyes.

Gu Yun wasn't one to bother with trivialities in his private life;

he was rather indifferent and rarely took note of such minor details. But with the awkwardness from his drunken episode still fresh in his mind, he found himself more sensitive to Chang Geng's reactions than usual.

Am I imagining things? Gu Yun wondered, bewildered, as he climbed into the horse-drawn carriage.

The heater within the carriage had already been lit, so Gu Yun leaned back and closed his eyes to rest. He was half-asleep when he felt someone draw near. He kept his eyes closed, and, after a beat, felt Chang Geng lay a thin blanket over him. His touch was light as a feather, as if afraid of waking him. When it was Shen Yi, the man only ever carelessly tossed a blanket on top of him, and even that made him an exceedingly considerate subordinate. His motions were never so gentle one might mistake them for loving devotion.

Gu Yun's drowsiness evaporated at once. He strained to continue feigning sleep, not moving a millimeter, until his neck was stiff with the effort. The whole time, he felt as if there were a pair of eyes staring unblinkingly at him.

Perhaps there are no secrets in this world that can be perfectly concealed—merely those who fail to observe the subtlest clues.

A cord inside Gu Yun's heart quietly drew taut and he couldn't help but begin to stealthily observe Chang Geng. But rather than dispel those indescribable misgivings, the longer he watched, the more panic-stricken he became.

Along with the internal turmoil caused by Chang Geng, Gu Yun had his hands full worrying about the Gold-Consolidation Decree and the emperor's attempts to crack down on the violet gold black market. On top of that, he needed to formulate a roundabout way to rescue the Lingshu Institute's number one curmudgeon, Master

Fenghan. It was a hellish situation that left Gu Yun mentally and physically wrung out.

On the twenty-third day of the first month, Gu Yun traveled to the outskirts of the capital to see off Shen Yi, who was leaving for his new post in the southwest.

On the twenty-fifth day of the first month, the emperor's imperial dragon carriage broke down in the middle of his tour of the imperial gardens. A chance remark by one of his personal attendants reminded the Longan Emperor that Master Fenghan had once knelt down to help him fix his steam-powered carriage. Much of the anger scorching his heart promptly receded. After further inquiry, he learned just how solitary and impoverished the old man was—namely, that after being imprisoned, aside from his students from the Lingshu Institute who came to see him, he didn't have a single friend or family member to bring him food. The Longan Emperor happened to be in a good mood, and after hearing all this, he found himself pitying the old man. Sighing, he ordered that Zhang Fenghan be released from prison, and only deducted half a year of the man's salary as punishment. Thus this case came to a close.

With these two matters put to bed, Gu Yun couldn't stand to remain in the capital a day longer. He submitted a memorial requesting to return to Loulan.

Indeed, it was about time he was on his way. The emperor had no objection, and approved his request the day it was submitted.

Now it was the evening before Gu Yun was set to pack up and leave. The night had already grown old, and he had just finished taking his medicine. Although Chang Geng had treated him with acupuncture for some time, such means could only dull his symptoms. They couldn't eradicate his headache at its source.

It was then, as he lay struggling to fall asleep, that a messenger arrived with a summons for the Marquis of Anding to enter the imperial palace. Perhaps it was a side effect of the medicine—Gu Yun's eyelid suddenly began to twitch.

49
DEFIANCE

G U YUN ROSE AT ONCE and threw on some clothes. When he stepped out of his room, he was shocked to find Chang Geng waiting in the outer chamber. He had yet to retire and appeared to have just shrugged on his outer robe. A pocket gas lamp gave off a pea-sized halo of light by his hand, and a half-read book lay open on his knees. The outer chamber was usually the territory of nighttime attendants, but Gu Yun was accustomed to living simply. He had no attendants, and only asked the old housekeeper to stop by occasionally in the early evening to load up the coals for the underfloor heating.

"Chang Geng?" Gu Yun asked, stunned. "What are you doing here? I thought it was Uncle Wang..."

"I wanted to wait till you fell asleep before leaving," Chang Geng replied.

"You're a commandery prince." Gu Yun's brow creased in a deep frown, and he hesitated, his words turning on the tip of his tongue. After a beat, he said pointedly, "Lowering yourself to stay in servants' quarters—it's completely inappropriate."

"What do you mean, 'lowering myself'? Must I abide by such superficial courtesies in my own home?" Chang Geng asked mildly. He rose to pick up the little kettle warming on the stove, then poured a bowl of medicinal tea and handed it to Gu Yun. "Is Yifu going to the palace? If you refuse to wear a fur coat, then at least drink something hot before you go."

A strange anxiety seized Gu Yun's heart. Even a duly wedded wife would find herself hard-pressed to match Chang Geng's level of attentiveness. Gu Yun mentally slapped himself the instant that thought unfurled in his mind. *You absolute bastard. Have you lost your mind?*

He drained the medicinal tea in a gulp. As he passed the cup back to Chang Geng, their fingers brushed. Chang Geng flinched back slightly, as if scalded, then turned around to set the little kettle back in its place with an air of nonchalance. Watching his back, Gu Yun's eyes dimmed slightly. *We can't go on like this,* he thought. *When I get back from the palace, I have to have a proper talk with him, no matter what.*

The palace attendant was waiting expectantly at the gate. Gu Yun left in a hurry, unable to linger a moment longer.

The first month of the year was marked by cold frost and heavy dew. After a few gusts of glacial wind, Gu Yun's disordered mind cleared as if pricked by a pin.

The attendant leading the way didn't dare lift his head. As they walked beneath the palace walls, they passed guards every few steps. Qilin-shaped[18] crossbows glared at them from all directions, forming neat arrays of beast heads breathing white steam through their fanged mouths. The gears in their necks turned slowly, emitting low grinding sounds like the roars of wild animals. The combination was so awe-inspiring that the red walls and glazed roof tiles seemed impossible to look at directly.

---

18 A mythical chimerical creature typically represented as a hoofed beast with dragon-like features and horns.

The giant palace lanterns floated in midair, enshrouded in thick mist and giving off a hazy, otherworldly glow. Yet there was nothing ethereal about these lanterns; the light they shed was coldly sinister, almost ghoulish in nature.

The Longan Emperor's personal attendant, Zhu Xiaojiao, was escorting several people out of the Warm Pavilion in the west wing of the palace when he happened to cross paths with Gu Yun. Behind him was a group of Far Westerners led by a tall, thin man with white hair and falcon-like features. He had a pair of menacing eyes, an aquiline nose, and thin, barely visible lips that framed a knife-like gash of a mouth.

Zhu Xiaojiao hurried forward and greeted Gu Yun. "My lord. These are the pope's envoys from the West."

The white-haired man examined Gu Yun. When he spoke, his accent was indistinguishable from the standard speech of Great Liang officials. "Could this be the illustrious Marquis of Anding?" he asked.

Gu Yun's lashes were dusted with a fine layer of snow, his whole person shrouded in an icy chill. He cupped his hands in greeting, face a mask of cool indifference.

In contrast, the white-haired man pressed a hand to his chest with utmost solemnity and bowed. "I didn't expect the Marquis of Order to be such a young and handsome man. It is an honor to make your acquaintance."

Gu Yun nodded slightly. "You flatter me."

The two groups passed each other. When the Westerners were some way off, Gu Yun shot a glance at Zhu Xiaojiao. He winked at Gu Yun, then stepped forward to whisper into his ear: "I don't know what those hairy Westerners said, but His Majesty is in an incredibly good mood right now. He kept saying they ought to send for the marquis. So you can relax, my lord. It's not bad news."

This old eunuch's depravity was known to all under heaven and, true to his awful reputation, he was the emperor's most accomplished bootlicker. However, he had a decent relationship with Gu Yun; one might say he had watched Gu Yun grow up within the palace. Once, Zhu Xiaojiao had accidentally angered the late emperor, and Gu Yun happened to witness the incident. The young marquis had casually offered a few words on his behalf, thereby saving his life. Zhu Xiaojiao might have been a moral degenerate, but he was conscientious when it came to repaying debts of gratitude, and always remembered the kindness Gu Yun had shown him. The rescue of Zhang Fenghan the other day had been thanks to his efforts in orchestrating events from behind the scenes.

Despite his reassuring words, unease rose in Gu Yun's heart. Honestly, he would have felt more prepared if the emperor had been unhappy. In that case, he could have been almost certain that someone had impeached him for buying violet gold on the black market. It didn't matter if someone accused him—Gu Yun had already instructed his subordinates to tie up loose ends. With no proof, at worst, he and the emperor might get into a heated argument...but "His Majesty is in an incredibly good mood"?

Gu Yun's eyes twitched even more sharply.

When he stepped into the Warm Pavilion, he saw Li Feng with his head bent over a memorial. The Longan Emperor didn't seem particularly joyful in the lamplight. In fact, he seemed even more haggard than Gu Yun, whose own vicious headache had only just receded. Before Gu Yun could perform his customary greeting, Li Feng waved a hand and said pleasantly, "There's no one else here; there's no need for Uncle to be so courteous."

Li Feng turned to Zhu Xiaojiao. "Go ask if there's any ginseng soup left from the evening meal," he said. "Bring a bowl for my imperial uncle so he may warm his hands."

Gu Yun sighed and thought to himself, *He who offers unsolicited hospitality must be harboring evil intentions.*

Blissfully unaware of Gu Yun's uncharitable thoughts, Li Feng asked blithely, "I recall the last time we spoke, Uncle mentioned that a portion of the violet gold obtained by the traitor Fu Zhicheng came from the south?"

"That's correct. Please forgive my incompetence. I could not track down the source of this violet gold."

Li Feng didn't seem to mind. "No matter. These traitors are all wickedly cunning, and you were unfamiliar with the terrain. The fact that Uncle managed to uncover the bandits' secret passages and apprehend them so rapidly is already a remarkable feat. If even *you* call yourself incompetent, oughtn't we toss out all the civil and military officials in our court?"

Still unable to figure out what he was getting at, Gu Yun hastily assured Li Feng that he wouldn't dare suggest anything of the kind.

"The violet gold black market in Great Liang has gone unchecked for too long." Li Feng's tone shifted as he came to his point. "In recent days, we have dispatched our people to thoroughly investigate the black market. We have discovered that a significant portion of the violet gold originates beyond our nation's boundaries."

At once, Gu Yun understood. Individuals within the country who had been leaking violet gold from government sources had likely caught wind of the crackdown through their own channels and, seeing which way the wind was blowing, had gone to ground. The ones caught by Jiang Chong and his men were small fry who had excavated private mines. Gu Yun listened in silence.

"Uncle spends much of his time traversing the frontiers," Li Feng continued unprompted. "You possess much more experience and insight than those of us who spend all our time viewing the world from the capital like a frog seeing the sky from the bottom of a well. Do you know where most of these private mines are located?"

Gu Yun hesitated slightly. "To answer Your Majesty, many are located in the northern barbarian grasslands."

"Correct." Li Feng smiled. "However, that's not the whole story. Uncle, please come take a look at this."

Gu Yun accepted the confidential memorial from Li Feng and skimmed it rapidly. Suddenly, blood roared in his ears. The confidential memorial cataloged, in fine detail, routes for the sale of violet gold excavated from private mines. None of the names listed were any surprise to Gu Yun, with the sole exception of the last item—written at the very bottom, clear as day, was "Kingdom of Loulan."

How could Loulan be listed here?

Li Feng glanced at him. "Well?"

Gu Yun broke out in a cold sweat, and countless thoughts swirled through his mind in the space of an instant. "Your Majesty, the Black Iron Battalion and the Kingdom of Loulan have lived as neighbors for many years. I have no knowledge of any violet gold mines within Loulan. Please forgive my presumption, but may I ask who submitted this memorial? What evidence do they have of this?"

"Ay, Uncle, why are you acting so paranoid?" Li Feng asked, laughing. "It's not as if we accused you of colluding with these violet-gold-excavating scoundrels. It's no surprise that you didn't know about this."

Gu Yun took a deep breath and assumed an expectant expression, waiting to be enlightened.

"This is a rather long and convoluted tale," Li Feng began. "During the ninth month last year, Uncle led a detachment of soldiers to the southern border. While you were away, Loulan asked the remaining Black Iron Battalion troops for help surrounding and annihilating a group of desert raiders. Assistant Regional Commander Qiu Wenshan sent a team and seized a decisive victory. Not only did they hunt down and kill over a hundred desert raiders, they also managed to rescue a group of captured Sindhu merchants. These merchants carried travel documents allowing them to enter Great Liang, so Commander Qiu followed protocol and escorted them to the western relay station. However, when they arrived there, they were shocked to discover that these merchants' documents were fake."

Li Feng was in high spirits. He paused dramatically, as if deliberately keeping his listener in suspense. Yet when he turned back, he found Gu Yun's expression inexplicably grave, lacking any intention of asking him eagerly to continue.

The emperor couldn't help but feel slightly vexed. He carried on dully, "By law, those who forge travel documents are handed over to the Protectorate of the Northwest to be investigated and punished. Yet when the protector-general looked into their backgrounds, he discovered these Sindhu folk weren't merchants at all, but a group of gold scuttles from the black market!"

These so-called "gold scuttles" were desperados who smuggled violet gold.

"As it happened, our secret envoy had just reached the Western Regions. He hadn't even put down his bags before he ran into these gold scuttles. According to these traitorous rogues' confessions, they were working in a private mine beyond the Great Northern Pass until they obtained a treasure map, which marks several locations in Loulan with huge violet gold reserves. Thus, they came to try their luck. It's funny, isn't it? The fact that we are more familiar with what's buried under Loulan than the Loulan people themselves."

A chill ran down Gu Yun's spine. He suddenly remembered four years ago when the Black Iron Battalion had captured that group of desert raiders. The raiders had long been silenced by him and Shen Yi. Afterward, Gu Yun had dispatched his subordinates on secret investigations within Loulan more than once. Yet he had never found any of these elusive violet gold mines, nor had he come across any similar cases.

And now, years later, just as this incident had almost completely faded to the back of his mind, it had been dug up once again!

Also...why was the commanding officer who sent the troops Qiu Wenshan? Qiu Wenshan was the Assistant Regional Commander of the Black Iron Battalion, responsible for laying out the battalion's defense. He rarely handled any matters concerning trade routes. Had someone more experienced been in command, they would have never handed the merchants over to the protector-general before authenticating the travel documents. The protector-general's office was directly subordinate to the central government. Once they had custody of the prisoners, the Black Iron Battalion lost any authority it might have to follow up on the case.

Gu Yun had taken Shen Yi with him, but the Black Iron Battalion's three division commanders had all remained in Loulan—where was everybody?

Gu Yun's thoughts took a sharp turn. "If I may be so bold as to ask Your Majesty, when did this desert raider attack occur?"

"The end of last year," Li Feng responded. "Why do you ask?"

Gu Yun summoned up a smile with difficulty. "It's nothing. This subject just finds it a bit strange. The desert raiders of the Western

Regions were purged long ago—why did they appear again with no warning?"

His headache was worsening, the pain that had been suppressed by Chang Geng's acupuncture surging forth once more. Now he recalled—at the end of the year, there was a great market, and people of all nations gathered at the entrance of the Silk Road. The Black Iron Battalion always dispatched additional personnel to guard the area. What's more, the protective escort bringing the annual tributes from the northern border passed through the northwest at the same time, and a number of Black Steeds were usually reassigned to assist with transport. Everyone had been sent away.

Why did the desert raiders happen to attack at precisely this time?

Why did the Longan Emperor's secret envoy arrive just as the protector-general discovered the identities of the gold scuttles, thus leaving no chance for intervention?

And finally, why had he received no word about any of these matters before or after they happened?!

Gu Yun's heart seemed to tighten like a string pulled taut, and his mind twisted into a knotted mess. Standing inside the Warm Pavilion, temperate as spring all seasons of the year, he suddenly found it difficult to breathe.

"The desert raiders of the Western Regions tend to skulk beyond the bounds of Great Liang's borders," Li Feng went on. "Absent a request for aid, it would be inappropriate to send troops outside our territory, so of course it's difficult to track their movements or numbers. The reason we called Uncle here today is not to ask how many desert raiders lurk in the wastes, but because we wish to entrust you with an important matter."

Gu Yun lifted his head and gazed at him.

Under the lamplight, Li Feng's eyes blazed with fire. "Our secret envoy is currently deep undercover in Loulan territory. There's a good chance that there really is a rare vein of violet gold concealed beneath the lands of Loulan... Does Uncle take our meaning?"

Gu Yun's heart sank in his chest. Slowly, emphasizing every word, he said, "I beg forgiveness for my ignorance. Please enlighten me, Your Majesty."

Li Feng's hand pressed down on his shoulder. Gu Yun's body never seemed to warm up. No matter where or when, he was like a boulder that had spent three days frozen in ice.

"Uncle, if I may speak plainly: You know well the difficulties that plague Great Liang both at home and abroad," Li Feng said with a sigh. "Our mind is so deeply troubled by these problems that we struggle to sleep at night. We have no one we can confide in. It is wearying, bearing the burdens of such a nation."

Gu Yun considered his next words for a beat, then said tactfully, "Your Majesty attends to myriad state affairs every day. You are the hope of the people. Please take care of your health. I am unversed in government affairs, but I have overseen the establishment of the Silk Road these past few years. The region becomes livelier with each passing day, and wealthy merchants of the northwest have begun to venture abroad. The people of the Central Plains have always been conscientious and hardworking. I believe that in just a few more years, the prosperity we now see on the Silk Road will spread throughout the entirety of Great Liang. When that time comes..."

His evasive flattery was like a bucket of cold water splashed in the face of the fervent Li Feng.

"Marquis Gu," Li Feng interjected, curt. "You are indeed unversed in government affairs. It's true that the nation has profited from trade routes these past few years—but can you guarantee that they will continue to prosper in the future? How well do you know these businessmen and their affairs? We certainly had no idea that, in addition to slaughtering enemies on the battlefield, the Marquis of Order was also an expert in the ways of commerce."

The emperor's mood had soured.

Gu Yun knew the second he heard "Marquis Gu" that he ought to shut his mouth, accept his orders, and do his job as commanded. He fell silent. Behind the emperor, a gas lamp in the pavilion began to flicker unsteadily with a soft hiss. Only a short while ago, Gu Yun mused, he had solemnly vowed to Justice Jiang that he dared not "lower himself to engage in petty quarrels for petty reasons."

Rubbing the space between his brows, Li Feng broke the impasse between them. "Forget it," he said with a stiff wave of his hand. "Go back and rest for now. We have briefed you on this matter, so go home and think it over carefully. Spring has yet to come, and the northwest is still bitterly cold—there is no need for my dear subject to hurry back."

"Your Majesty." Gu Yun closed his eyes briefly, then swiftly lifted the hem of his robes to kneel before Li Feng. He had said he wouldn't throw tantrums or argue over useless codes of loyalty—but how could this possibly compare to such insignificant trifles?

"Please forgive me, Your Majesty," Gu Yun said. "Violet gold is certainly a matter of great importance, but please pardon my dull wit and inability to understand the deeper significance of Your Majesty's decision. The peace and prosperity of the Silk Road has not come easily. Does Your Majesty truly wish to cast it aside for the sake of some unsubstantiated rumors?"

"It's impossible to ignore Marquis Gu's contributions to the Silk Road's current affluence. We understand that you hate to see it destroyed, given how many years of heart's blood you have poured into its development... How could our heart not ache as well?" Li Feng replied, patiently curbing his temper. "But this great nation of ours is like a dilapidated house filled with drafty windows—the slightest rain shower gusts in and we must frantically tear down the eastern wall to repair the western wall. We lack resources in every area."

Gu Yun sneered internally, but it wouldn't do to reveal his true feelings. His countenance remained indifferent.

"It is cold on the floor. Uncle's complexion looks rather poor, and I can still smell the scent of your medicine; please, stop kneeling like this." Li Feng's expression warmed as he tried again to reason with Gu Yun. "When we were young, Grand Tutor Lin once told us that two arms form the strength of the nation: heavenly blessings and manmade creations. Does Uncle remember?"

"I do. The Grand Tutor said, 'The heavenly blessings are the mountains and rivers, the trees and vegetation, the types of soil, the variety of fauna, and the violet gold flowing beneath the earth. The manmade creations are the aphorisms of sages, the techniques of construction, and inventions such as steam engines and steel armor.' These two entities are like unto the pillar and rafter of a house. You can rely solely on one of the two, but if both are broken, the structure will crumble. This is something a sovereign must bear in mind."

"Uncle's memory is impressive." Li Feng gazed down at him. "Today, the pillar and rafter of our nation have been hollowed out by termites. What can we do?"

In all honesty, Gu Yun wanted to say, *If you didn't enact that ridiculous Token of Mastery Law, perhaps there would be fewer termites eating our house.* But he thought of Master Fenghan, currently shut away in his home reflecting on his mistakes in the company of his canine son. Even if he did say it aloud, there would be no use.

Perhaps remembering their childhood days, when they studied side by side as fellow students, the anger on Li Feng's face gradually receded.

"Please rise. Uncle is the sharp blade of our nation. We must still rely on you to maintain order throughout the land."

Gu Yun bowed low, lightly touching his forehead to his fingertips.

Li Feng breathed a sigh of relief, feeling as though he had finally gotten through to his stubborn subject. Gu Yun had grown increasingly moderate in recent years, adapting smoothly to his new circumstances. He no longer exploded at the slightest provocation the way he did back when Li Feng first ascended the throne. His mild defiance today was likely only due to alarm at hearing the word Loulan... And well, it was Loulan. Gu Yun had been stationed there for over five years. It was understandable that he would develop an attachment toward the place.

At this thought, Li Feng's expression softened once more. He resolved to personally help Gu Yun to his feet.

But before he could reach out, Gu Yun had already straightened his back. "Your Majesty," he said, voice quiet. "Although Loulan is small, it has always been a friend to our nation. Back when so many countries in the Western Regions rose in armed rebellion, our troops were besieged in those barren, yellow sand dunes for more than twenty days. It was the citizens of Loulan who secretly relayed information to us and supplied us with food and medicine. Later, when the Far West, Sindhu, and the kingdoms of the Western Regions signed the new agreement to expand the Silk Road, Loulan joined the accord as well—"

Caught off guard, Li Feng stared blankly in shock for a beat, then exploded in uncontrollable rage. "Enough!" he shouted.

"Sending troops to invade another sovereign nation because

you covet their riches would be inhumane. Turning your back on past kindnesses, breaking promises, and betraying trust would be immoral!" Gu Yun hadn't said enough at all, and his every word was like a knife crashing decisively to the floor of the gilded Warm Pavilion.

Li Feng shook with anger. "Silence!"

He swept his hand through the brushes and ink on the table, picked up the inkstone, and flung it at the kneeling man. Gu Yun made no attempt to dodge; the inkstone knocked harshly against his armor-encased shoulder with a bright, resounding *clack*, and wet ink dripped down the front of the Marquis of Anding's cloud brocade court robes.

Li Feng glared with such ferocity his eyes were nearly torn from their sockets. "Gu Yun, what are you trying to do?"

Slow and deliberate, Gu Yun spoke. "An army that is inhumane and immoral is inauspicious. Although the fifty thousand soldiers of the Black Iron Battalion do not fear death, I dare not accept this mission. Please rescind your orders, Your Majesty."

50

KILLING INTENT

THE UNDERFLOOR HEATING SYSTEM of the Warm Pavilion automatically added coal at regular intervals. Its rice-bowl-sized gears interlocked smoothly. Whether it was adding coal or blowing away the smoke, everything moved in mechanical harmony. Tendrils of white steam streamed in spirals from the back of the machinery, which occasionally emitted murmuring noises like soft sighs.

On the floor above, ruler and subject—one standing, one kneeling—faced each other in opposition. Li Feng clutched the edge of the dragon-engraved writing desk, veins bulging. Displeasure clear in every word, he replied, "*Say that again.*"

Gu Yun had already said his piece; he knew he shouldn't go too far in defying the emperor. He promptly conceded ground. "This subject deserves a thousand deaths."

Face ashen, Li Feng compulsively turned the white jade ring adorning his finger over and over.

"However," Gu Yun continued in a low voice, "when it comes to the Silk Road, pull one thread and the whole will unravel. I beg Your Majesty to please consider this decision more carefully."

"Is the Marquis of Anding under the impression that, aside from you, we have no other capable generals at our disposal?" Li Feng asked, a terrible chill in his voice.

Their conversation had already reached a tipping point. If it continued, it would only devolve into a full-blown row. Gu Yun pressed his lips together and did his best to play dead.

It was at that moment that Zhu Xiaojiao bustled into the Warm Pavilion. "Your Majesty," he announced in a high-pitched voice, as if he were singing the part of an old woman in an opera, "Imperial Uncle Wang has arrived. He is outside, awaiting your permission to enter..."

Usually, if other senior ministers came to call on the emperor while he was in a black rage, the palace attendants would advise them to wait outside the hall. In stepping forward like this, Zhu Xiaojiao was deliberately helping Gu Yun out of his predicament. Casting the old eunuch a glance, Gu Yun blinked once to indicate his gratitude.

The corner of Li Feng's eye twitched several times as the lines of his face drew taut. He glanced haughtily down at Gu Yun. "I see the heat from the coals has muddled the Marquis of Anding's head," he said coldly. "In that case, perhaps you ought to go cool down outside, lest you forget what can and cannot be said!"

Gu Yun kowtowed deeply, his forehead touching the ground. "Please take care, Your Majesty."

He withdrew from the Warm Pavilion with his head bowed. When he reached the snow outside the hall, he dropped easily back onto his knees, cooling down as ordered.

Li Feng watched Gu Yun's departing figure, his eyes flashing with menace. Imperial Uncle Wang entered shortly thereafter. He was afraid to even breathe too heavily, and remained standing to the side, waiting. An oblivious young palace attendant stepped forward to tidy up the inkstone that had broken over the Marquis of Anding's armor, then froze in place at a pointed look from Zhu Xiaojiao.

Petrified, the attendant stood in panicked silence for several seconds before shrinking back against the wall and making his escape.

Studying the emperor's countenance, Wang Guo soothed him in a low voice. "Your Majesty, the Marquis of Anding is yet young and impetuous. He is accustomed to serving alongside the bloodthirsty ruffians in the border garrisons. If he sometimes lacks a sense of propriety, it's only to be expected. It's not worth Your Majesty's ire."

Li Feng was silent for a long while.

Years ago, the Yuanhe Emperor had set his heart on naming Li Feng the crown prince precisely because he was diligent yet astute, and had the bearing of a wise sovereign. He should have been more than capable of building upon the strong foundation laid down by his predecessors—and it was true that, for a short time after Li Feng had succeeded the throne, he had lived up to the late emperor's expectations. However, it was also true that the Yuanhe Emperor had left his successor with an awful mess. As it stood, Great Liang needed an emperor blessed with both daring resolve and great foresight; a ruler capable of restoring the nation. A sovereign who could only build on the foundation of his predecessors no longer sufficed.

Since his ascension to the throne, the Longan Emperor had encountered adversity at every turn. Lying awake at night, he often asked himself with bleak honesty, *Can we take responsibility for this nation?*

But the more a person doubts themselves, the less they can tolerate others questioning them in the same way. This holds especially true for those in positions of great power.

Wang Guo's smile had nearly frozen into a rictus. "Your Majesty—"

"Uncle," Li Feng cut him off. "There has been a question on our mind recently. The Black Iron Tiger Tally was bestowed by Emperor Wu. Why would Gu Yun return it to us of his own accord?"

Wang Guo blinked in surprise, then mustered up the courage to sneak a glance at the Longan Emperor's face. This seemed like a completely superfluous question. Did the emperor really expect Gu Yun to throw a fit, or worse, rebel outright?

"That's because..." Imperial Uncle Wang's mind raced. He didn't know what he ought to say and fell back on his tried-and-true method of dealing with the emperor's fickle moods through resolute ass-kissing. "Your Majesty is a wise sovereign, a ruler seen once in a thousand years. As your subjects, we spare no effort in performing our duties and attending to Your Majesty's needs. The Black Iron Tiger Tally is a trifling matter. Even if Your Majesty asked for our family's lives and all our worldly possessions, who would utter a word of complaint?"

Li Feng chuckled softly. "We fear that's not necessarily the case, Uncle. We realized this only today: in reality, it does not matter whether Gu Yun returns the Black Iron Tiger Tally. If it came down to it, how many high-ranking military officers occupying key positions throughout the nation would march under the Gu family's banner? When it comes to military affairs, the marquis's words carry more weight than ours. The Tiger Tally is nothing more than a meaningless chunk of iron. What use does he have for it?"

Li Feng's voice was low and very gentle. Although he spoke as if they were having an amiable afternoon chat, Wang Guo couldn't help but shiver at the sound—to his ears, the murderous undercurrent in the emperor's words was a hairsbreadth away from breaking the surface.

"We summoned Uncle here today because we wanted to speak to you about the Loulan issue...but forget it." Li Feng waved a hand in extreme exhaustion. "You may leave, my dear subject. We are tired."

Wang Guo nodded his assent at once, and obligingly withdrew from the west wing's Warm Pavilion.

It was a peculiar year. The time for snow to give way to rain had clearly passed, yet the capital remained afflicted with round after round of snowfall, as if the stubborn skies had yet to exhaust themselves. Before he had knelt a full hour, Gu Yun's court robes had frosted over with a thin layer of ice. Covered in fine snow, the black-iron pauldrons on his shoulders grew bitterly cold.

As Wang Guo brushed past him in his haste, he caught a glimpse of the illustrious Marquis of Order's pale but handsome face. *What a pity*, he sighed. Yet that was all he thought. Wang Guo was a sensible man; just as he knew to whom he owed his current lofty position, standing second only to the emperor himself, he also knew the appropriate course of action in this matter.

The sky grew steadily darker above the capital.

It was only after helping Li Feng settle down for the night that Zhu Xiaojiao dared to slip out of the palace, trembling with cold and apprehension as he tottered out with an umbrella in hand to see Gu Yun.

Gu Yun had practically become one with the snow. Zhu Xiaojiao, gesturing theatrically, proceeded to chew out the young, gray-robed palace attendant standing in the open-air corridor. "Wretched servant! It's snowing so hard, yet you don't even know to fetch an umbrella for the marquis? Are those eyes in your head for decoration?"

Though Zhu Xiaojiao was mocked by one and all, to this young attendant, he was a high official of colossal importance. The young man quaked in fear, and his complexion instantly went ashen.

Blinking away the snowflakes clinging to his lashes, Gu Yun said mildly, "Please stop scaring the kid, gonggong. His Majesty told me to cool down outside. How can I do that if I cover myself with an umbrella?"

Zhu Xiaojiao scuttled over to where he knelt on the ground. He tried to brush away the snow blanketing Gu Yun's shoulders, but the instant he reached out, he yelped "Aiyo!" and flinched back. Gu Yun's black pauldrons were so cold, they nearly peeled a layer of skin off the tender flesh of Zhu Xiaojiao's palm. The old eunuch shivered uncontrollably and grumbled, "My dear marquis, why would you go and pick a quarrel with His Majesty? You're sure to injure your legs if you spend the night kneeling like this. Aren't you just inviting hardship on yourself? Why do such a thing?"

Gu Yun smiled. "It's fine. Us military men are all tough as nails. I got a little hotheaded back there, lost control of my tongue, and said too much. Thank you kindly for your concern, Zhu-gonggong."

Zhu Xiaojiao thought for a second, then lowered his voice. "What if I sent someone to summon Prince Yanbei to the palace first thing tomorrow morning so he can say some kind words on your behalf?"

Gu Yun shook his head once again. "Please don't involve him. I'll be fine."

Zhu Xiaojiao turned things this way and that in his head, but in the end, there was nothing he could do. He couldn't risk leaving His Majesty's side for too long, as he feared the Longan Emperor would wake in the middle of the night and call for him. Before he left, he set the umbrella down next to Gu Yun.

"Zhu-gonggong," Gu Yun called out to him, low-voiced. "Thank you very much, but you'd better take the umbrella with you."

Zhu Xiaojiao started in surprise.

"I just have to kneel for a while. Once His Majesty's temper cools, everything will be fine. You are one of His Majesty's personal attendants...you mustn't give him cause to doubt you."

His words were vague, but Zhu Xiaojiao understood at once. The old eunuch sighed. "If the marquis spoke and acted this cautiously before with His Majesty, what need would there be for you to suffer in the cold like this?"

Once Zhu Xiaojiao was gone, Gu Yun exhaled a cloud of white mist. Bored stiff and with nothing to do but think, he carefully mulled over what Chang Geng had said to him at the National Temple—that the dragon threat in the East Sea and the armed rebellion in the southwest were likely no coincidence.

Slowly, Gu Yun began to tease out the thin thread of a lead.

When Prince Wei had amassed an army in the East Sea, he had planned to use his naval power to breach Great Liang's defenses. Gu Yun had defeated the East Sea rebel army with few casualties, but because of the ensuing political tidal wave raised by this incident, the reaction had been disproportionate to the threat. The whole imperial court had fallen into an uproar, and the Jiangnan Navy had been purged from top to bottom. For a time, the emperor had even ordered the Lingshu Institute to focus their resources on creating a fleet of sea dragon warships. Military funding for the four border garrisons had tightened up all the more as a result.

But the greatest consequence of the dragon threat in the East Sea had been the institution of two imperial edicts: the Token of Mastery Law, which restricted the activities of civilian artificers, and the Marching Orders Decree, which centralized the nation's military power. The latter directly targeted Gu Yun, and now that he thought about it, the Longan Emperor hadn't been making things difficult for him for no reason. Chances were the actions he took in Jiangnan had not gone unnoticed.

The pronouncement of the Marching Orders Decree had intensified the conflict between the border garrisons and the imperial court as quickly as the sun casts a shadow. It was also the root cause of the Fu Zhicheng case. Gu Yun had himself been a player in the incident in the southwest, so it was easier for him to sense the invisible hand manipulating pieces on the board. Someone had intentionally fomented conflict between Fu Zhicheng and the mountain bandits, then used that idiot Kuai Lantu to exacerbate the situation and timed the eruption precisely to Gu Yun's arrival. They had gift-wrapped Fu Zhicheng and the mountain bandits of the southern border and used the Black Iron Battalion's hands to present both as an offering to the emperor in the distant capital.

What would the Longan Emperor think?

He would be horrified to discover that, although he had restricted the flow of violet gold within his own nation, the precious fuel continued spilling into the country from abroad.

Gu Yun suddenly had another thought: He and Shen Yi had spent so much time both openly and secretly searching within Loulan yet had never found this fabled "Loulan Treasure Trove." But the emperor sends a single secret envoy—one unfamiliar with the area at that—to look into things, and mere days later, this envoy submits a memorial report stating that there was a "good chance" such a vein existed?

Was this secret envoy preternaturally skilled, or had someone deliberately guided them?

The snow grew heavier and heavier. Gu Yun shivered violently.

Behind him, the branch of a plum tree in full bloom succumbed to its burden of snow and broke with a crisp *snap*, the lovely blossoms dying a premature death.

Chang Geng was startled awake by the sound of branches splintering under fallen snow.

Gu Yun had yet to return. Chang Geng had waited up for him half the night and was still in his clothes from the day before. Just now, he had leaned against the head of the bed in a light doze, but his dreams had been filled with all manner of grotesque nightmares. The sky was dimly lit—there were still many hours left before dawn— but the window lattices already glowed deathly pale, bright with the reflection of light off the falling snow. Chang Geng rose to his feet and opened the door just in time to see Uncle Wang hurrying toward him.

"Uncle Wang, please slow down," Chang Geng called out to him. "What's the matter?"

Despite the cold north wind blowing through the estate, the old housekeeper's forehead was drenched in sweat from running here. "Your Highness, there's news from the palace: last night, for some reason, the marquis defied the emperor, causing His Majesty to explode with rage..."

Chang Geng's pupils contracted.

Shortly thereafter, a fine steed dashed out from the Marquis Estate's rear courtyard under the cover of night. It galloped toward the National Temple, buffeted by the wind and snow.

There was no grand assembly the next day, so there was no need for the Longan Emperor to rise early. Yet due to excess internal heat in his liver, he slept poorly and awoke in a groggy daze. Seeing his state, Zhu Xiaojiao astutely stepped closer and began massaging the Longan Emperor's temples. He carried on with his ministrations as he said, "Your Majesty, the Sindhu incense that Great Master Liao Chi gifted you the other day is remarkably effective at soothing the body and mind. Your Majesty said it was excellent when you tried it, didn't you? How about I light some for you now?"

Li Feng muttered his approval. After a pause, he asked, "Is the great master still in the palace?"

Liao Chi, the abbot of the National Temple, was staying in the imperial palace for the entire first month of the year to pray for blessings for the nation of Great Liang. While here, he expounded on the classics of Buddhism and provided spiritual guidance to the deeply devout Longan Emperor.

"He is," Zhu Xiaojiao rushed to answer. "I hear that the great master got up early to give the morning recitation as he always does, rain or shine. This old servant sees that Your Majesty's eyes are a bit red. Perhaps it is due to internal heat. Why not summon the great master here to recite some Buddhist scriptures and aid Your Majesty's meditation?"

Li Feng snorted disdainfully. "What impudence. Great Master Liao Chi is one of the most eminent monks of our age. What are you doing, treating him like some lowly busker?"

Zhu Xiaojiao promptly slapped himself across the face with an apologetic smile. "Ay, this accursed mouth of mine. Once again, I've made a fool of myself due to my lack of insight—but even though this old servant does not understand it, whenever I listen to Great Master Liao Chi strike his wooden fish,[19] all the troubles in my heart seem to melt away."

---

19   A type of woodblock used by Buddhist monks during the ritual chanting of sutras, mantras, or other Buddhist texts.

Li Feng was moved by this suggestion. After a moment's consideration, he said, "In that case, we will trouble the great master to come."

Zhu Xiaojiao made a noise of assent and passed on his instructions, then returned to silently help the emperor wash up and change into a fresh set of robes.

"Where is Gu Yun?" Li Feng suddenly asked.

Zhu Xiaojiao had wanted to mention him all this while but was too afraid to broach the subject. He replied hastily, "To answer Your Majesty, the marquis is still kneeling outside the Warm Pavilion."

Li Feng scoffed softly, unmoved. Zhu Xiaojiao didn't dare mention Gu Yun again. He could only hope that old monk, unreliable savior that he was, would be of some use.

Soon thereafter, Great Master Liao Chi arrived at the Warm Pavilion in the west wing. He made his way in on slow, measured steps with his head bowed, as if he didn't see the snowman kneeling outside the palace at all.

Who knows what kind of magical Amitabha-Buddha-infused potion the old monk poured down the Longan Emperor's throat, but shortly after his arrival, Zhu Xiaojiao came scurrying out. "His Majesty has decreed that for his breach of etiquette and insolence toward His Majesty, the Marquis of Anding's seal of command is temporarily revoked," he declared loftily. "He will forfeit three months' salary, return to the Marquis Estate, and reflect on his transgressions in isolation."

Gu Yun started in surprise, and Zhu Xiaojiao shot him a meaningful glance.

"...This humble servant accepts this decree and thanks His Majesty for his favor."

The instant he finished speaking, Zhu Xiaojiao raised his voice and berated the attendants standing to the side. "Look at all these useless monkeys loitering about! Hurry and help the marquis up!"

But before he could finish relaying his instructions, Gu Yun had already staggered to his feet. All four of his limbs felt like they were shot through with sharp pins. The melted snow had soaked through his court robes and steel armor long ago, drenching him completely, and a dreadful chill lanced through his bones. Gu Yun cupped his hands at Zhu Xiaojiao, then turned to take his leave of the palace, his heart heavy with worry. *Has that old bald donkey been possessed? Why would he come help me?* He was thoroughly bewildered.

That is, until he caught sight of Chang Geng waiting for him beyond the palace gates.

Understanding dawned on Gu Yun. "So it was you who brought in the National Temple," he said with a smile. "I was wondering why that old bald donkey was being so kind."

Chang Geng didn't have the wherewithal to respond. He wrapped a thick fox fur coat around Gu Yun without waiting for permission, then reached out to touch his face. No matter how tough he was, Gu Yun's reactions were sluggish after spending a night freezing in the cold. Before he could so much as flinch, Chang Geng's hand landed right on target.

This touch was way too suggestive. It would have been awkward whether Gu Yun shied away or not, so he could only crack a joke. "Are you going to gaze into my eyes and tell my fortune or something?"

Who knew whether this person was unusually tolerant of his circumstances or if he truly was without a care in the world. He was half frozen to death, yet he was still messing around!

Chang Geng dragged Gu Yun into his carriage without another word. His heart ached so badly that the rims of his eyes were slightly red.

A wave of warmth enveloped Gu Yun the second he entered the carriage. Rubbing his hands together, he turned to Chang Geng. "Is there any wine?" he asked. "Pour me a cup."

Chang Geng didn't respond. Gu Yun glanced at him, taking in his eyes, which were now so red they looked as if they were about to drip blood. He couldn't help but laugh. "My goodness, I never saw you cry even as a child. I've certainly witnessed something novel today. Hurry and get Uncle Wang to fetch a basin to catch these tears. His Majesty's docked three months of my salary, but thanks to these pearls you've shed, we'll still be able to eat."

Of course, Chang Geng wasn't on the verge of tears—he was trying to suppress a wu'ergu attack. Since the moment he'd heard that Gu Yun had spent the night kneeling in the snow, his mind had been beset by wave after intensifying wave of hallucinations and killing intent.

Gu Yun finally sensed something was wrong with the look in his eyes. "Chang Geng?"

Chang Geng forced himself to breathe. "Yifu, let's get you changed first," he squeezed out from the back of his throat.

His voice was hoarse, like two rusted pieces of iron scraping against one another. Gu Yun frowned at the sound, watching him carefully as he untied the dripping wet knot of his hair and quickly changed into the dry clothes set out in the carriage. Chang Geng didn't dare look at him. He sat to the side with his eyes lowered, doing the breathing exercises Miss Chen had taught him, slowly calming his mind. But though the rustling of fabric was soft as a sigh and should have been easily drowned out by the rumbling of the carriage, at that moment, it was as if the sound had gained a life of its own. It burrowed its way into his ears, and instead of calming down, Chang Geng's heart grew more restless with each breath taken.

It was only when Gu Yun set his crown atop the tiny desk inside the carriage with a clatter that Chang Geng jerked out of his trance. "I decocted a warming tonic to help drive the chill from your body," he said. "You should—"

His words came to an abrupt stop as Gu Yun's ice-cold fingers caught his wrist.

Chang Geng shivered. He wanted to pull away, but Gu Yun's grip was tight as he checked his pulse. He called out quietly, "Yifu..."

"I've no great skill at reading pulses," Gu Yun said, face grim, "but I know what qi deviation[20] caused by improper martial training looks like."

Chang Geng avoided Gu Yun's eyes with a look of abject misery.

"Chang Geng, tell me the truth. Is there..." Gu Yun paused awkwardly. Even though his skin was as thick as a city wall, he still found his next words rather difficult to say.

As if he sensed what was coming, Chang Geng gradually lifted his reddened eyes. After a beat of silence, Gu Yun steeled his heart. Gathering even more courage than he'd needed to defy the emperor, he forced the words out. "Is there something you're not telling me? Some unspeakable secret?"

Chang Geng gulped down several anxious breaths, then asked in a low voice, "A secret of what kind?"

"...Of the romantic kind."

---

20 A physiological and psychological disorder believed to result from improper spiritual or martial training. Symptoms of qi deviation in fiction include panic, paranoia, sensory hallucinations, and death.

51

ROMANCE

THE INSTANT Gu Yun spoke these words, he felt Chang Geng's pulse begin to race. At this rate, it could barely be considered a pulse. The skin Gu Yun held pressed in his palm was searing, as if there were an unseen volcano beneath the surface of Chang Geng's inner wrist, and the slightest disturbance would cause an eruption so violent it would burn all the meridians in Chang Geng's body to ash.

Gu Yun hadn't expected this—even though he had spoken as tactfully as possible, Chang Geng still had such an explosive reaction. Worried that he'd crossed a line, he touched his hand lightly to Chang Geng's chest. "Focus. Get ahold of yourself!"

Chang Geng yanked Gu Yun's hand away, gripping it so tightly Gu Yun's knuckles cracked. Gu Yun's eye twitched slightly. Chang Geng's complexion was as pale as joss paper, his eyes blood red. Countless phantasms flashed across his vision, and the clamor of a thousand-strong army seemed to reverberate in his ears like a great iron bell. The flickering shadows of demons tormented him; the wu'ergu drank his heart's blood through its grasping roots and swelled to a monstrous size with a roar; its dense branches were covered in thorns, choking him with a heartrending agony—

And there, beyond the wu'ergu, stood Gu Yun.

The two of them may as well have been separated by perilous mountains and fast-flowing rivers.

Gu Yun was scared witless. His lips moved imperceptibly, but he had no idea what to say.

Chang Geng took Gu Yun's hand, clasped tightly between his own, and lifted it to his chest. With a muffled sob, he closed his eyes and pressed his trembling lips to the back of Gu Yun's cold-chapped hand like a brand. For all Gu Yun's uneasy suspicions, he'd never anticipated *this*. As Chang Geng's scorching breaths seared their way up his sleeve, Gu Yun began to bristle with anxious indignation. He nearly blurted out, *Have you gone mad?*

Without warning, Chang Geng shoved him away. Retreating as far as he could in the small carriage, he curled in on himself, bowed his head, and threw up a mouthful of purple-black blood.

Gu Yun was stunned into silence.

Everything had happened in an instant. Before Gu Yun's temper had a chance to flare, he was overcome with alarm. Dumbstruck, he remained frozen in place, choking back his words so hard his throat hurt.

The anguish in Chang Geng's eyes was replaced with a bleak desolation. But after spitting out that mouthful of curdled blood, his heart seemed to calm, and his mind slowly regathered his scattered consciousness. When Gu Yun reached out to help him up, he turned his head and shied away. "I've offended Yifu," he muttered. "Whether you beat me or scold me...*cough*, please do as you see fit."

Gu Yun sucked in a sharp breath. Countless feelings twisted themselves into knots within his chest, culminating in a lengthy treatise that wouldn't have been out of place in a collection of General Shen Jiping's greatest quotes. Yet he didn't dare utter a word of it. He felt suffocated, and thought to himself, *I haven't even berated him and he's already spitting blood. How the hell can I say anything now!*

Bending down, he scooped Chang Geng off the floor and set him on the spacious couch inside the carriage. He pushed aside the whirlwind of confused thoughts obscuring his mind and said sharply, "Shut up. Regulate your breathing and take care of your internal injuries first."

Chang Geng obediently closed his eyes and fell silent. Gu Yun watched over him for a while, then turned away to rummage through the carriage. All his ransacking didn't turn up a single drop of wine, so he had no choice but to pick up the warming tonic sitting on the little stove and toss it back, the fresh ginger in the decoction so strong it made his brain ache. He had thought that, perhaps, Chang Geng was just a bit confused—that perhaps he had been affected by the shameful things Gu Yun did while drunk and developed some inappropriate notions. He had thought that, given the boy's exceptional intelligence, he'd need only give him a nudge and he'd see reason. He'd never expected that, before he could even begin to nudge, Chang Geng would spill it all on the first experimental poke!

How did this happen?

Gu Yun glanced morosely at Chang Geng, who was currently modulating his breathing with his eyes shut tight. He took a seat off to the side and, with a mind as clear as mud, began to fret with earnest devotion. The ancients said, "Cultivate thyself and thy house shall be managed, manage thy house and thy state shall be governed."[21] Gu Yun wondered whether it was because he failed to cultivate himself properly that both his house and state were in turmoil. He felt bruised and battered, agitated to the extreme.

The Marquis Estate was only a few steps away from the imperial palace. Even if the carriage were pulled by tortoises, the journey would be a swift one.

---

21 A line from the Book of Rites.

The moment Gu Yun stepped down from the carriage, he was greeted by a wooden bird. It alighted unerringly on his shoulder and cocked its head to stare at him with lifelike vitality. Without warning, a hand reached out from behind Gu Yun—Chang Geng had at some point quietly emerged from the carriage—and caught the bird.

His complexion was no less ghastly than before, but he seemed to have recovered some of his usual serenity. Chang Geng held the wooden bird but didn't immediately open it to check the sender. While the old housekeeper took care of the horse-drawn carriage, Chang Geng stepped up beside Gu Yun. "If Yifu is uncomfortable, I will move out," he said quietly. "I'll never offend your eyes with my presence again, nor will I overstep the bounds of propriety."

Now that the bloody glint had faded from his eyes, Chang Geng's expression was cold and desolate, and when he lowered his gaze, his demeanor was one of resigned attentiveness. Gu Yun stood in a stupor for several seconds. Finding that he had nothing to say, he turned on his heel and left without a word.

Ge Chen and Cao Chunhua had learned of the events of the night before when they woke up early that morning and had long been waiting by the front gate. Before they could rush up and welcome them back, a grim-faced Gu Yun swept past them without so much as a hello. Chang Geng watched his departing figure. The corner of his mouth was stained with what looked like blood, and his complexion was somehow even more pallid than Gu Yun's, who had spent the entire night kneeling in the snow.

"Dage, what happened?" Ge Chen asked, perplexed.

Chang Geng merely shook his head. Only when Gu Yun's figure had disappeared completely did he finally tear his gaze away.

He turned to the little wooden bird in his hand and, opening its belly, removed a slip of paper bearing a message.

The beginning of the first year of the current emperor's reign, when Marshal Gu escorted the northern barbarian crown prince beyond the pass, he fell gravely ill. My erge[22] left Taiyuan Prefecture and specially rushed over, returning a month later.

The letter was signed *Chen*.

There were clear signs of wear on the bird's wooden wings—who knew how far it had flown with this note.

Chen Qingxu's message had neither beginning nor end; it was utterly incomprehensible. As he finished reading it, Chang Geng's eyes flashed slightly. He knocked on the back of the wooden bird's head, and the creature opened its iron beak and belched out a tiny spark, burning the slip of paper to ash in the blink of an eye.

"Dage," Cao Chunhua began cautiously, "Recently, I've noticed wooden birds coming and going from the Marquis Estate at all hours. Are you investigating something?"

"An old case," Chang Geng said softly. "I've always felt that, though his nature remained the same, his mindset changed significantly after he arrived in the northwest. I had thought it was due to the gradual influence of Loulan and the Silk Road, but it seems this is not the case."

Ge Chen and Cao Chunhua glanced at one another but failed to grasp his point.

Chang Geng seemed to briefly recover from his despondency of just minutes ago. "What happened when he traveled beyond the pass on the northern border?" he murmured.

---

22   二哥, erge, is a word meaning "second eldest brother."

Gu Yun was the type, who, if the sky was falling, would wrap its broken fragments around himself as a blanket. How had this great marshal become so grievously ill on his way to deployment that the Chen family of Taiyuan were alarmed enough to send one of their own?

Did he encounter someone...or learn something...beyond the pass?

"Xiao-Cao," Chang Geng broke the silence. "Can you run an errand for me?"

After Cao Chunhua's discreet departure from the Marquis Estate, Chang Geng emerged from his rooms furtively, if at all, appearing one moment and disappearing the next.

Gu Yun, meanwhile, spent his nights tossing and turning. He'd planned to sit down with Chang Geng for a proper chat but was stunned to find that he couldn't catch him—Chang Geng was purposely avoiding him! With nothing better to do than let his mind spiral into wild imaginings, he decided he might as well stop taking his medicine. Though he could neither see nor hear, he felt surprisingly at peace.

Yet soon, the imperial court began to roil once more.

First, there was the Longan Emperor's motion to reinstate the Gold-Consolidation Decree. As soon as this intention was announced, it was met with a joint memorial of protest submitted by the Ministries of Works and Revenue. Even the Ministry of War, which had been purged of all detractors and was now the Longan Emperor's most obedient child, produced a few voices of dissent. But, like a tortoise that had swallowed a steelyard weight, Li Feng could not be moved. Determined to cling to his course, he soon returned fire.

On the second day of the second month, the Censorate impeached the Assistant Minister of Revenue for the crime of accepting bribes from foreign powers. In the extensive investigation that followed, a laundry list of rotten incidents involving various regional officials who had accepted kickbacks and committed other infractions was dragged into the light of day. It quickly evolved into the greatest government corruption case of the Longan Era.

The Minister of Works was much like Imperial Uncle Wang— though he wished to serve the nation and its people, he lacked the courage to follow through and cowered at the first sign of danger. When he saw the emperor's attitude, he tactfully clamped his mouth shut, buried his head in the sand, and went back to his job building houses. He never dared defy the imperial dragon or provoke his sovereign's wrath by mentioning the Gold-Consolidation Decree again.

On the tenth day of the second month, after Gu Yun had been confined to the Marquis Estate for several weeks, a Black Hawk quietly landed at the Northern Camp on the outskirts of the capital. There, the soldier removed his Black Hawk armor and changed into civilian clothes. He entered the capital by night and proceeded to slip surreptitiously into the Marquis Estate.

Thanks to this, Gu Yun finally had the opportunity to meet with Chang Geng, who had been avoiding him like the plague.

When Chang Geng arrived at his room with a bowl of medicinal soup, the silence between them was deep and awkward. "There's a Black Hawk here to see you," Chang Geng said tonelessly.

Nodding, Gu Yun picked up the bowl of medicine and drained it. Chang Geng had already prepared his silver needles. After watching Gu Yun set the bowl down, he spread the implements out before him and asked with his eyes, *Is this okay?*

His distant courtesy left Gu Yun all the more at a loss.

Chang Geng no longer had the audacity to ask Gu Yun to lie across his legs. He was like an unfamiliar doctor, only speaking to him in sign language or clinically repositioning his limbs. It was as if he didn't want to touch Gu Yun at all.

Gu Yun closed his eyes and allowed the medicine to take effect. His hearing slowly returned, and his surroundings gradually swelled with noise. The low murmurs of the servants sweeping the snow outside, the sound of the estate guards' armor and weaponry chafing against each other...even the soft rustling of Chang Geng's clothes as he moved to and fro—all of it stabbed into his ears. After over ten days of silence, Gu Yun felt incredibly unused to it.

Despite his discomfort, Gu Yun seized his opportunity and said, "Chang Geng, can we talk?"

Of course Chang Geng knew what he wanted to ask. He didn't make a sound.

"Is it because..." Gu Yun began hesitantly, "I got drunk that day and did...uhh...something...to you..."

Chang Geng's hand trembled slightly, and the needle he held hovered in midair for several seconds.

It hardly needed to be said how uncomfortable Gu Yun felt at Chang Geng's extended silence. No matter what mistreatment he suffered from Li Feng, he felt neither shame nor regret, and could face heaven and earth with a clear conscience. But with Chang Geng, Gu Yun couldn't make sense of things. He felt that, just as one palm cannot clap alone, romantic attachment must grow between two people. If he hadn't done something untoward in the first place, how could Chang Geng possibly...

"No," Chang Geng replied, serene. "That day, it was I who took liberties with Yifu first."

Gu Yun didn't know what to say.

"There is no reason." Chang Geng pressed gently on Gu Yun's head to prevent him from making any sudden movements. When he continued, his voice was extraordinarily detached. "When it comes to these sorts of things, what reason can there possibly be? If I had to say, it's likely because I grew up with no mother or father to care for me. Aside from Yifu, no one loved me, so over time, I developed this inappropriate attachment. You never noticed, and I had no intention of mentioning it to anyone either. But that day, for a moment, my emotions got the better of me, and I accidentally let slip a hint of my feelings."

Gu Yun felt as if a boulder the size of a man's head had fallen from the sky and bludgeoned him in the chest. For a second, he could barely breathe. Originally, he had thought Chang Geng's sorry state that day was merely a breath of vital qi going down the wrong way—but it turned out it was actually a symptom of a chronic illness that had been festering for years!

"You don't have to take this to heart, Yifu. You can just act like nothing happened," Chang Geng said, indifferent.

His hands as he placed the needles were steady. If not for the fact that Chang Geng had admitted it himself just now, Gu Yun might have wondered whether, in his shamelessness, he had forgotten to act his age and was flattering himself with his disgraceful presumptions. But how could he possibly act like nothing happened? Gu Yun was about to go mad. Suddenly he felt old beyond his years; for the first time, he realized that the Flower of the Northwest was no longer in the springtime of life. He couldn't understand what young people were thinking these days!

"Recently, His Majesty has been asking me to attend court." Chang Geng rather stiffly changed the subject. "I hear the court

222 ✺ STARS OF CHAOS

officials have been quarreling all day, and that they've managed to unearth a major case of corruption. I have a fairly good idea of His Majesty's intentions. What does Yifu plan to do?"

Gu Yun looked at him with a deadpan expression. He was in no mood to discuss court politics.

Chang Geng sighed softly, then reached out to remove Gu Yun's glass monocle and set it aside. "For you, I am willing to do anything. If you find me an eyesore, I will stay out of sight. If you want only a filial and well-behaved godson, I promise never to step over this line. Yifu, I'm already so ashamed I can't bear to show my face. Can you please stop asking me about this?"

Gu Yun's refusal was written clearly on his face.

Chang Geng began removing the silver needles from Gu Yun's body. "Then what would you have me do?" he asked evenly. Before Gu Yun could respond, he added, "Anything is fine."

If Chang Geng really had been so lacking in respect as to disregard his wishes and hound him, Gu Yun likely would have called upon the three hundred guards of the Marquis Estate long ago and had him packed off to the Prince Yanbei Estate. Then, like a sharp sword cutting through a tangled rope, he would have taken decisive action and ruthlessly ignored Chang Geng for a year or so, until everything went back to normal. But Chang Geng had gone and launched this kind of, *Even if you were to exile me to the ends of the earth, I would endure it willingly*, countermeasure.

Gu Yun's headache was excruciating. He felt like a dog trying to bite into a tortoise—he had nowhere to bury his fangs. After trying and failing to speak several times, he finally asked, "Have you recovered from your internal injuries?"

Chang Geng nodded and made a hum of assent, as if reluctant to utter so much as a single extraneous word.

"What happened?"

Chang Geng answered easily. "After spending so many years indulging in foolish hopes and wild fantasies, I accidentally underwent qi deviation."

Hearing this, Gu Yun only felt all the more vexed.

After gathering his silver needles, Chang Geng made his way to a corner of the room and lit a bit of pacifying fragrance. "Shall I invite that Black Hawk brother in?" he asked with a bland expression.

"Your Highness," Gu Yun called out to him, now solemn. "You are a noble descendant of the imperial family. In the future, your status may become yet more invaluable. Others treat you like a priceless pearl or precious jade; this humble servant hopes that Your Highness will likewise treat yourself with care regardless of time or place. So please do not speak of yourself with such disdain."

Face half hidden in shadow, Chang Geng responded, utterly unmoved, "Mm, you can rest assured, my lord."

He stood there for a while, as if awaiting further instruction. Seeing that Gu Yun had no more to say, he turned and left without a sound.

Gu Yun leaned back heavily on the bed and heaved a sigh. He would much rather Chang Geng act as he did as a child, ignoring his explanations and starting a huge row. He had soon realized that once this bastard started up with his "I desire nothing" routine, he became practically invincible. The overwrought Gu Yun paced up and down his room a few times before resolving that he would never again fantasize about fragrant beauties attending to his needs or other such nonsense. Enough was enough.

Finally, the long-awaited Black Hawk knocked on the door and entered.

This Black Hawk seemed to have rushed the entire way here.

Though he had washed up, his face remained haggard, and his jaw was covered in stubble he hadn't had time to shave.

"Sir." The Black Hawk fell to his knees.

"No need for hollow courtesies." Gu Yun forced himself to focus. "What happened? Did He Ronghui send you?"

"Yes, sir!"

"Give me his report."

He unfolded the letter with a flick of his wrist and skimmed its contents. Black Hawk Commander He Ronghui's chicken scratch was hideous, but his words were brief and to the point:

At the end of last month, Qiemo and Qiuci, two tiny countries in the Western Regions, came into conflict over border trade. Disputes between nations of the Western Regions had always been settled autonomously by the nations themselves. It would have been inappropriate for the Great Liang troops stationed there to intervene, so initially, they did not follow the situation closely. Along with Loulan, these two nations formed a triad of power and influence in the Western Regions; thus, the king of Loulan sent his younger brother as a peace envoy to mediate the conflict. However, the diplomatic mission was ambushed at the border of Qiuci and completely wiped out.

At first, the slaughter of the envoy was blamed on desert raiders. But when the king of Loulan sent a party to investigate, they discovered a sword bearing the emblem of the Qiuci royal guards. The Loulan king at once called on Qiuci for a proper account of what had transpired. However, not only did Qiuci categorically deny any involvement in the attack, they accused Loulan of siding with Qiemo and proceeded to humiliate the Loulan envoy. In response, Loulan dispatched their royal prince to lead three thousand light cavalry to advance on Qiuci and demand an explanation. At first,

Qiuci shut their doors, refusing to receive him. When they at last opened their gates, it was to reveal several hundred sand tigers.

This so-called "sand tiger" was a type of war chariot used in the desert. It was extremely heavy, and the cost of the violet gold required to operate it was exorbitant. The construction process of these machines was also exceptionally complex.

Gu Yun had encountered such war chariots when he had put down the revolt in the Western Regions ten years ago. Back then, the enemy had only three enormous sand tigers, yet they had come close to entrapping half of Gu Yun's still-immature Black Steed Division. Yet as far as he was aware, fielding even three sand tigers had required the revolting nations of the Western Regions to pool all their resources.

When he finished reading the letter, Gu Yun rose to his feet. He furrowed his brow as he pinched involuntarily at the prayer beads on his wrist. This situation bore a remarkable resemblance to the armed rebellion in the southwest. Lowering his voice, he asked, "These were real sand tigers, not hollow shells?"

The Black Hawk was quick on the uptake and responded without hesitation. "Yes, sir, they were real sand tigers. The Loulan light cavalry were defeated in less time than it takes to finish a cup of tea. The little prince was nearly killed in action; he only survived thanks to his soldiers laying their lives on the line to protect him. That very same day, the king of Loulan sent an envoy to our garrison requesting aid. But before we could so much as break the wax seal on his letter, the news had already spread to the other nations encamped along the Silk Road, throwing everyone into a state of alarm. And now, the other nations of the Western Regions, Sindhu, the Far Westerners—all of them—have begun to gather their armed forces in their respective garrisons. Protector-General Meng of the

Protectorate of the Northwest personally came to our garrison and ordered us to lie low and wait for a marching orders decree."

Gu Yun slapped his hand sharply against the table. "Absurd."

Thinking he was referring to the marching orders decree, the Black Hawk added, "General He of the Black Hawk Division said the same; the Black Iron Battalion isn't bound by the Marching Orders Decree in the first place. But that Protector-General Meng said His Majesty had placed the marquis under house arrest with orders to reflect on his transgressions, and commanded the three divisions to wait for an imperial edict to arrive."

52

NO BOUNDARIES

G U YUN'S MIND RACED. Everything was happening much faster—and far more chaotically—than he had imagined. The Western Regions were a small pond full of big fish. Tiny nations dotted the area like sheep droppings—a clump here, a clump there—and new tensions arose between them every other day. Everyone wanted to annex everyone else. But with the Black Iron Battalion standing guard at the entrance to the Silk Road the past few years, no one had made any trouble for a very long time. Even if they sold everything they owned, there was no way a lousy little country like Qiuci could afford a hundred-odd sand tigers. The one responsible for this improbable development was a far more ruthless and fearsome enemy—that much was obvious.

The question was not whether there was a power standing behind the kingdom of Qiuci, but rather what was the objective of that power?

Gu Yun doubted this plan could be laid at the feet of a certain someone in the imperial court. Li Feng was too much of a control freak. He preferred to use tried-and-true methods that allowed him to call the shots—there was no way he would commit to such a rash operation on such a short timeline, especially without all the necessary arrangements in place. It was likely that Li Feng had been caught off guard by this as well. On one hand, the emperor had no idea what was going on in the northwest; on the other, he feared the Black Iron Battalion would act without authorization and throw the court into disorder. Thus, in order to restrain them, he took advantage of Gu Yun's revoked seal of command and also refused to issue a marching orders decree.

"What is the strength of each country's garrison?" Gu Yun asked.

"The Far Westerners' diplomatic corps have two to three thousand men encamped. The Sindhu force is somewhat smaller, with only about a thousand soldiers laying out their defense. The rest are all from various nations of the Western Regions."

"That's impossible." Gu Yun bit down on his tongue, swallowing the words *go check again* back down into his throat. He remembered that he wasn't presently deployed—he was stuck in this capital city the size of a manhole, much too far away to help.

"If the enemy has truly unleashed over a hundred sand tigers, they're determined to win this war. They should have tens of thousands of elite troops standing by for a second wave of attack—if not, this opening move is merely a waste of violet gold. Even if they appear to lack numbers, that doesn't mean they don't have more forces in hiding." Gu Yun closed his eyes briefly, his fingers tapping lightly against the table. "A single team of heavy armor infantry would be sufficient to handle Loulan's useless cavalry. There's no way they're gathering an army of tens of thousands and driving so many sand tigers along our border just to end a petty squabble between Western Regions nations."

Stunned, the Black Hawk stammered, "In...in that case, this subordinate will hurry back at once..."

"Not necessary." Gu Yun cut him off. "Besides, you wouldn't make it in time."

The Black Hawk had shot back from the Silk Road to the capital at top speed, but despite his incredible pace, it had still taken him almost two days to make the trip. The airspace above the capital was a no-fly zone, so he'd had to first land at the Northern Camp, and though he had entered the capital that very same night, by the time he met Gu Yun, it was already the third day. If he were to return to the front line with Gu Yun's instructions, even if he ran himself to death on this round trip, the orders would still arrive with a delay of five to six days.

The battlefield could change in the blink of an eye. Five or six days was time enough for a nation to fall. Gu Yun gritted his teeth. Of all times for him to be detained in the capital!

"Go get some rest first," Gu Yun said in a low voice. "Let me think."

The Black Hawk didn't dare say another word and left after being dismissed.

Gu Yun warmed himself a pot of wine, then paced a few circles around the room. Within a few steps, he had calmed down and put the main threads of the situation in order. *Perhaps the worst hasn't yet come*, he reflected.

He was detained and Shen Yi was gone, so the Black Iron Battalion troops stationed in the northwest were currently headed by Black Hawk Commander He Ronghui. Gu Yun knew his subordinate's temper. He Ronghui was a notorious pain in the ass—he listened to Gu Yun, but as for anyone else, even Shen Yi might not be able to tame him. There was no way he would take the Protectorate of the Northwest seriously. If Protector-General Meng Pengfei tried to throw his weight around with a marching orders decree, He Ronghui would be the first to revolt. And if he did, chances were... Protector-General Meng would be the first problem he took care of.

And then what?

There was a knock at the door. Gu Yun pulled it open and was greeted by the sight of Chang Geng standing outside.

Gu Yun clutched the doorjamb. He took one look at Chang Geng and his heart, which had only just settled, began to kick up a fuss once more. He felt an ache developing in his stomach as he asked, "What did you come back for?"

"I thought Yifu might need me."

Gu Yun didn't know what to say.

Chang Geng stood before the door, the picture of obedient propriety. "May I come in?"

After making his request, he turned slightly to the side and stood attentively awaiting orders, as if all Gu Yun had to say was "fuck off" and he would vanish in a puff of smoke.

I must have owed this bastard a fortune in a past life, Gu Yun thought to himself.

Resigned to his fate, he stepped aside to allow said bastard to enter the room.

Gu Yun had been lost in thought, and his lapse in attention had allowed the wine warming on the stove to bubble and boil. The scent of alcohol wafted through the room. Searching for something to say, Gu Yun picked up the pot of wine. "Drink?"

Chang Geng pulled out a flask of plain water in answer. He took a seat next to the weiqi board set up in the room, posture perfectly upright. If he had shaved his head, he would have looked exactly like an ethereal monk.

"A Black Hawk wouldn't come rushing from the Northwestern Camp overnight for no good reason. Has something happened on the border?"

Gu Yun didn't particularly want to talk to him about this matter. "Just a spot of trouble," he answered vaguely. "It's nothing serious."

Gu Yun was a highly respected authority within the military. No one ever questioned his orders, and this allowed him to effortlessly assume control of situations and operate with great efficiency. Yet it was possible to have too much of a good thing. Gu Yun couldn't help but wish to preserve his respected image; even when he encountered something beyond his comprehension, it never occurred to him to ask others for help. Over time, it was all too easy for him to become entrenched in old patterns of thought.

Chang Geng glanced up at him, then quickly dropped his eyes. He bowed his head, as though afraid he'd become entranced if he looked too long. Chang Geng plucked a weiqi stone out of its bowl and fiddled with it between his fingers. The stone was so black it looked almost green, and it gleamed with a soft fluorescence in the light of the gas lamp. Seeing that Gu Yun was reluctant to speak, Chang Geng continued, "All commanding officers of the Black Iron Battalion are capable of leading independently. They wouldn't bother you over minor border conflicts when you're so far away. My guess is an unusual number of foreign troops—ten thousand or more—have gathered. It must be something of that magnitude for that Black Hawk brother to rush back to the capital like this."

Gu Yun turned the hot cup of wine in his hands and narrowed his eyes. The scent of alcohol pervaded the room. "Old General Zhong has taught you much."

"There is also still much old General Zhong hasn't taught me. Yifu, what are you thinking?"

"The soldiers of the Black Iron Battalion have always made the protection of the homeland their bottom line," Gu Yun murmured. "In a sudden, unexpected situation with many unknowns, Old He will treat the border as the battlefield's front line. He will seal off the Silk Road and cut off all routes into the country, and will execute without exception any who cross the border illegally. Even if an ally seeks help, without the commander in chief present, the most the Black Iron Battalion will do is provide asylum. They absolutely will not abandon their post by deploying troops. The Black Iron Battalion stands fifty-thousand strong—short of a heavenly army storming down from the sky, it doesn't matter who comes knocking—none will find it easy to break our border defenses in the northwest. So I'm not worried about that for the time being. But I do wonder what our adversary's next move will be."

His voice was deep and mild, even richer than the fragrance of the wine. The base of Chang Geng's ears tingled hearing it, and he lowered his head further, doing his utmost to maintain composure and rid himself of distracting thoughts. "If it were me," he said, "I wouldn't try to attack Great Liang right now."

Gu Yun's eyes lingered on the black weiqi stone, stark against Chang Geng's pale fingers. "Why?"

Chang Geng placed the weiqi stone on the board with a bright *clack*.

"Because the situation has not yet reached a tipping point," he said. "The conflict between Yifu and His Majesty is not yet as irreconcilable as fire and water. He has temporarily detained you in the capital, but the Black Iron Battalion has not been dissolved. It remains an iron wall. Should foreign powers invade now, His Majesty would not hesitate to rely on your expertise. The intensifying clash between political and military power would be resolved overnight, and plans carefully laid for years would be spoiled in a single day."

Ever since the episode in the carriage, Chang Geng had become shrewd and incisive before Gu Yun. Whether he spoke of family matters or national affairs, he struck the bullseye with each word out of his mouth. Gu Yun flinched, stung by the words *clash between political and military power*. His fingers, seared red by the heat of his wine cup, froze in midair.

This was the secret wound buried beneath Great Liang's prosperous and peaceful façade.

Emperor Wu had no male heirs, so the crown prince had been adopted from a collateral branch. No matter what the legends said of his peerless wisdom and fearsome abilities, Emperor Wu was still no more than a man. As he lay on his deathbed, a wisp of selfishness uncurled in this venerable elder's heart: he passed his military power, capable of forcing the Son of Heaven and his vassals to their knees, to his beloved daughter. Henceforth, the military and political powers of Great Liang were unnaturally divided.

This was likely the greatest mistake Emperor Wu made in his life. Provided that the commander of Great Liang's armed forces was content with his lot, and the emperor was exceedingly broad of mind, perhaps ruler and subject might peacefully coexist for a generation. But what about two generations? Three?

Gu Yun was acutely aware that there would come a day when the conflict between the Black Iron Tiger Tally and the jade seal of the Son of Heaven would indeed become irreconcilable. At that point, there would be only two possible outcomes: either the traitor to the nation usurps the throne, or the sovereign casts his general aside like a bow once the birds have gone to roost.

"Rather, this is a good opportunity for our enemy to try killing two birds with one stone." Chang Geng placed several more pieces onto the weiqi board. "If the foreigners have learned that the Black Iron Battalion becomes a listing bale of hay shoved this way or that by the Marching Orders Decree whenever Yifu is away, then the great army eyeing our borders so covetously was raised with us in mind. Aside from the Western Regions, the barbarians on the northern border who have been a constant threat and the wokou pirates who have lain dormant for years in the East Sea may also be waiting to attack us. However, the chances of such an attack are very small. Right now, the most likely scenario is that the border defenses on the northwestern front will remain impregnable, and that General He will seize the bearer of the marching orders decree, the Protector-General of the Northwest, and toss him into the nearest military prison—"

Gu Yun's eyes widened with surprise.

Chang Geng met his gaze with a thin smile. "You needn't be so shocked, Yifu. When it comes to matters that concern you, there's no one who knows better in all Great Liang."

Gu Yun didn't know how to respond.

This troublesome youth was truly difficult to handle. Chang Geng was unmoved by force or persuasion; Gu Yun couldn't strike him or yell at him, nor could he cajole or advise him. But after choking on his words for several seconds, Gu Yun hit upon a bright idea. He turned to Chang Geng with a serious expression, then whipped out his ultimate technique: carefree shamelessness. "What, are you flirting with your yifu now?"

As expected, his response took Chang Geng completely by surprise. The boy's long white sleeves caught on his cup, spilling clear water across the table.

The invincible Marshal Gu revealed no hint of satisfaction at claiming this small victory. He waved a graceful hand. "Go on."

Chang Geng quickly composed himself. He had been startled by Gu Yun, but he also felt a bit relieved. Even if the sky were to fall on his head, this person would spring right back up again.

"If it were me," Chang Geng continued, "I would apply pressure at the entrance of the Silk Road with massive forces and put the heavy armor and war chariots front and center. Give the Black Iron Battalion the impression an invasion might come at any moment.

With Yifu away, General He will at most bar the gates. He won't be so rash as to send troops to engage the enemy without your orders. Instead, he will dispatch a messenger to report the situation to you while he calls for reinforcements from nearby—perhaps from the Northern Border Defense Corps or the main force stationed at the Central Plains Garrison."

Gu Yun's brow twitched.

"For the Black Iron Battalion to request reinforcements, the border must be in a state of emergency. No one would disregard their call. Though the Marching Orders Decree was applied successfully on the southern border, it has only been a few months since its implementation. Its power of command has not yet been acknowledged by the rest of the nation's military leaders. The generals defending the borders will almost certainly defy the Ministry of War and deploy reinforcements on their own."

Chang Geng looked down at the weiqi board mottled with black and white stones, eyes grim. "But if I remember correctly... back when the northern barbarian prince infiltrated Yanhui Town, Yifu personally purged the Northern Border Defense Corps. While *you* might say you didn't use the opportunity to plant your own people there, those who judge others by their own measure will see it differently.

"What's more, Old General Cai Bin, the commander in chief of the force stationed in the Central Plains, happens to have been a direct subordinate of the former marquis. Now, consider the leadership of the five great military districts of Great Liang: The southwest goes without saying—General Shen is your own trusted subordinate. The Western Regions are the Black Iron Battalion's home turf—the soldiers there heed not law and order, and dare openly detain the Protector-General of the Northwest. The Northern Border and

Central Plains Garrisons turn their nose up at the Ministry of War's Marching Orders Decree and deploy troops without authorization the second the Black Iron Battalion whistles for them."

Chang Geng grabbed a palmful of weiqi stones and cast them onto the board with a flick of his sleeve. They landed in a haphazard pile with a cascade of bright clattering sounds, like pearls striking jade.

There was no need to say more. In this scenario, Emperor Li Feng would surely assume that Gu Yun's concession on the Marching Orders Decree was nothing more than false pretense. He would view Gu Yun through the lens of his own suspicions and fear that half the country lay in the Marquis of Anding's hands.

The emperor would find it difficult to breathe.

Chang Geng's eyes were dark and unfathomable. "Yifu, will you hear me out?"

"Speak," Gu Yun said quietly.

"First, send that Black Hawk to General Cai tonight with a message. He mustn't transfer troops without proper authorization under any circumstances. Even if General Cai has already decided to send reinforcements, he'll need to organize his forces and ready his supplies before he can set out. We can likely still catch him."

"Why not send word to the Northern Border Defense Corps?"

Chang Geng didn't bat an eye. "Because Yifu only has one Black Hawk, so we can only place a single bet. If even I have recognized the possibility that the northern barbarians may take advantage of this crisis to fish in muddy waters, there's no way General He won't see the danger as well. He will most likely pass over his nearest allies and seek help from the faraway Central Plains Garrison.

"Second, once the Black Hawk returns to the Northwestern Camp, he must instruct General He to remain calm. He doesn't have to heed the Marching Orders Decree if ordered to deploy troops against his judgment, but he mustn't offend the Protectorate of the Northwest too severely."

Gu Yun nodded. "And third?"

"Third." Chang Geng began slowly, "Before the news from the Silk Road reaches the capital, I would ask Yifu to submit a memorial to His Majesty. Find some reason to permanently turn over your seal of command and declare that you will never again partake in military affairs. You must clearly hand the reins to His Majesty. Tell him the security of the northwest is of critical importance, and that, before leaving, you placed your subordinates under strict orders: come hell or high water, the commanders of the three divisions are forbidden from lifting a finger without the seal of command. Say that the northwest cannot go a day without a leader—it is imperative His Majesty select someone to take over your position at once."

By stepping back now, not only would Gu Yun avoid a fatal strike, he might even save the insubordinate He Ronghui.

Gu Yun remained silent for a long while, mind drifting. He suddenly found himself remembering that heavy snowstorm beyond the pass, and the child he snatched from the jaws of wolves many years ago.

Shen Yi had once fobbed Chang Geng off, saying they had found him that day by coincidence.

But it wasn't true.

Back then, Gu Yun had his own informants on the northern border. After accepting the imperial decree from the Yuanhe Emperor, the first person Gu Yun found was Xiu-niang. He soon discovered that she was in contact with the northern barbarians and chose to observe the enemy without revealing his presence.

Gu Yun was still young himself back then, no more than an unreliable upstart. His eyes were fixed on the barbarian threat; he'd long forgotten that the late emperor had charged him to bring the little prince back to the capital with all speed. That day, while Gu Yun's attention was elsewhere, Chang Geng somehow managed to run off alone beyond the pass. Only then had he panicked and chased after the boy with Shen Yi in tow.

Even now, Gu Yun only had to close his eyes to see Chang Geng as he was back then: curled up in an emaciated little ball, body covered with injuries. Although battered by the wind and snow and savaged by the wolves' vicious fangs, the child had miraculously survived while they rushed to the scene. When Gu Yun wrapped him in his large overcoat, he was so light Gu Yun could have lifted him with one hand. He felt as if he were cradling a baby bird on the brink of death; as if he would smother the helpless creature if he held him too tightly.

Time passed like the ebb and flow of water—somehow, in the blink of an eye, that boy had already grown so much.

Noticing his long silence, Chang Geng couldn't help but ask, "Yifu?"

Gu Yun turned slightly. For a moment, his expression was almost tender under the lamplight. Chang Geng's heart tripped over in his chest with a violent *thud*.

Perhaps it was because just when Gu Yun should have been shocked and angered, Chang Geng had thrown up that timely mouthful of blood. Or perhaps it was because of all the harried activity of the days that followed. It was clear that Gu Yun found the situation absurd and was helplessly vexed. And yet...he wasn't as furious as Chang Geng had imagined.

Gu Yun finally broke the silence. "I understand. You should get some rest."

Chang Geng recognized the dismissal for what it was and tactfully rose to leave.

"...Wait," Gu Yun called out. He seemed to hesitate, then continued. "Last time, you told me you would be fine with anything I asked you to do."

Chang Geng paused, hand outstretched to open the door. His fingers curled slightly in midair.

"I don't want you to leave; I don't want you to force yourself to do anything. All I want is for you to be well."

Chang Geng stood frozen in place for a long interval, face blank. Then, he turned and made his escape without a sound.

Gu Yun calmly picked up the half-full pot of wine. He tested its temperature, then took a swig directly from the spout. *Little brat,* he thought. *As if I can't handle you.*

53

DÉTENTE

WHEN CHANG GENG had arrived at Gu Yun's room, he had been perfectly self-possessed, as if the entire world lay in the palm of his hand. By the time he left, he had become a puddle of human-shaped goo. He had no idea how he managed to put one foot in front of the other on his way out.

After an unexpected thaw, the temperature had plunged once again. Yet in the chilly night air, his breath felt like a raging ball of fire burning in his chest.

Chang Geng fled back to his own courtyard, heart racing. He exhaled heavily as he pressed his forehead against the sword-training puppet standing by the courtyard's entrance. After so many years, this iron puppet was already very old. Chang Geng couldn't bear to continue using it as a sparring partner, so he had the servants leave it in his courtyard as a rather incongruous lantern stand.

The frigid chill of the iron soon cooled Chang Geng's burning flesh. He tilted his head back to look up at the big fellow, and childhood memories washed over him. He remembered giving it a box full of pastries to carry every morning before the sky had lightened, the two of them—a boy and his automaton—bounding off to Gu Yun's courtyard to listen to his godfather's rambling lectures.

Then there was the time they celebrated Gu Yun's birthday. They had trussed it up in a ridiculous outfit of silk and made it deliver an unappetizing bowl of noodles to Gu Yun... A smile spread across Chang Geng's face unbidden as his mind wandered through the past. It seemed every one of his happy and warm memories had to do with Gu Yun.

Chang Geng hung the lamp he carried on the iron puppet's outspread arm and gave the exposed gear protruding from the back of its neck a familiar pat. He thought back on Gu Yun's words just now and sighed, his eyes growing dim. He had imagined Gu Yun would either fly into a rage or persist in his efforts to counsel him. He'd never expected Gu Yun to take this approach.

Like the verdurous spring breeze and rain, Gu Yun had gently made his position clear: *I am still your yifu. I am still the person who cares for you the most. No matter what you think, I will remain as before. I will forgive your transgressions and will not take your foolish words to heart. Though I cannot indulge your wild fantasies that run contrary to the social order, I believe there will come a day when you will find your way back to the correct path.*

Chang Geng had emblazoned the words, "I want for nothing, thus I am strong,"[23] onto himself, only for Gu Yun to counter with, "I stand steadfast and unmoved."[24]

He shows me so much consideration, Chang Geng thought, torn between laughter and tears. *Why doesn't he spare a little for himself when facing that man in the imperial palace?*

Chang Geng knew why Gu Yun had so abruptly dismissed him. It wasn't because he found him an eyesore. Rather, it was because he had more or less surmised what Chang Geng was about to say, and tactfully hinted for him to leave it unsaid. Certainly, in Gu Yun's position, stepping back to avoid a fatal strike was the inferior course

---

23 A line from The Analects of Confucius.
24 A line from the Huainanzi.

of action. It would be far simpler to rebel outright, force the Son of Heaven and his vassals to their knees, and consolidate military and political power in his own hands.

On the surface, Gu Yun was a scoundrel. But beneath this skin, steeped within the deadly resolve of his iron blood, lay a dignified and upright gentleman's bones. He was simply not capable of overthrowing his sovereign and usurping the throne.

As Chang Geng stepped slowly into his room, the air was filled with the familiar flapping of birds' wings. He reached out and caught a battered wooden bird. Its open belly revealed a letter from Chen Qingxu, her handwriting so crabbed that Chang Geng struggled to decipher the words.

I've tracked down the origin of the poison on the arrow that struck the marshal that year. If I can find the secret formula, I may be able to create an antidote.

Chang Geng froze where he stood. Before triumphant exultation could surge through his heart, he saw there was more to Chen Qingxu's message.

However, the marquis's eyes and ears have suffered years of damage. He has also been treating poison with poison, and this, too, has accumulated over time. Poison can be neutralized, but grave illness is difficult to cure. Please prepare yourself, Your Highness.

Finally, there was an even messier line scrawled at the bottom.

I suspect this poison is one of the most closely guarded secrets of the barbarian goddess. The last goddess of the tribe married into the imperial harem; tracking down more information beyond the border will be difficult. If convenient, you can try investigating in the palace.

Chang Geng read the letter in full, then burned the scrap of paper to ash. His heart sank.

The family of the Marquis of Anding had served in the army for generations and enjoyed the great favor of the emperor. The Marquis Estate had likewise been specially bestowed. From within Chang Geng's little courtyard, one had only to lift their head to see the magnificent eaves of the imperial palace gleaming in the moonlight. Chang Geng glanced, perhaps unintentionally, in the direction of the palace, a tempest brewing in his eyes.

That hair-raising glare lingered for but a flash, then disappeared without a trace.

Bright and early the next morning, Gu Yun dispatched a messenger to the palace to deliver a memorial bearing his plea for forgiveness—just as Chang Geng had suggested.

First, he systematically delineated the results of his self-reflection and sincerely admitted his wrongs. Then, he declared that due to a flare-up of an old injury, it would be difficult for him to continue to bear such heavy responsibilities and requested that His Majesty permanently revoke his seal of command. Claiming illness was a common pretext for evading one's duties, but the Marquis of Anding's memorial seemed more credible than most—he followed it up with a long note written in that famous calligraphic script of his, in which he laid out, in minute detail, all military affairs that needed to be handed over. Finally, he signed off with the bluntness of a cudgel by requesting His Majesty allow him to move the site of his confinement to the capital's outskirts.

The most elegant brushstrokes in the world couldn't mask the meaning between these lines: *I've done enough self-reflection, now let me go out to play.*

The memorial brimmed with the Marquis of Anding's insouciant style and impudent practicality. It was obvious that it hadn't flowed from the pen of a ghostwriting advisor. The Longan Emperor held onto the memorial for a full day. The following morning, he bestowed on his subject a considerable quantity of rare and precious medicinal ingredients to express his special favor and repealed the decree imprisoning Gu Yun to his residence—thereby tacitly accepting Gu Yun's resignation. In order to maintain some semblance of harmony between ruler and subject, he did not appoint a new commander. He left the seal of command unassigned and offered warm words of solace, proclaiming his intention to return it once the Marquis of Anding recovered from illness and came back to court.

That day, after his afternoon nap, Li Feng chanced upon a book he once read as a child. When he lifted it, a calligraphy sample note fluttered out from between its pages. Compared to the memorial sitting on his writing desk, the penmanship on the note was childish and clumsy, the turns of each stroke somewhat lacking in power. Yet one could already see the vigorous style into which it would one day develop.

After examining the note for a long time, Li Feng sighed. "Do you know the author of this note?" he asked Zhu Xiaojiao.

Zhu Xiaojiao feigned ignorance. "This...this old servant does not know what constitutes good or poor calligraphy, but since Your Majesty kept it, it must be the work of some renowned master."

"What a glib tongue you have—but we suppose he can indeed be considered a renowned master. This was written by Imperial

Uncle Shiliu." Li Feng placed the note carefully on the desk and smoothed it out with a paperweight. His eyes grew distant with thought. "When we were young, we lacked the patience to practice calligraphy and were often scolded by our imperial father. When Uncle found out, he went home and stayed up the entire night. The next day, he gave us a stack of calligraphy sample notes he had written himself..."

Back then, Gu Yun's eyesight was already poor during the day, and it was even more difficult for him during the hours of darkness. To see at all, he had to wear his glass monocle. After staying up all night, his eyes became so bloodshot he looked like a rabbit the next day, yet he insisted on feigning nonchalance before others.

As Li Feng spoke, he remembered those happy days of youth. He murmured, nostalgic, "Uncle was so withdrawn as a child, he didn't like people getting close to him at all. He was the polar opposite of the way he is now—ay, that's right, where is he now?"

Zhu Xiaojiao responded respectfully, "I hear that he is convalescing at the hot spring villa in the northern outskirts."

Li Feng was torn between laughter and tears. "He really went out to play? He truly is carefree. Forget it... The spring tea from Jiangnan has just arrived. Have someone deliver him some to try. We'll ask him to inscribe a horizontal plaque[25] for the northern imperial residence later."

Zhu Xiaojiao accepted the order and said no more. A light touch, he felt, was sufficient.

That very afternoon, the Protectorate of the Northwest sent an urgent missive to the emperor. It reported the unusual movements of foreign forces beyond the pass, then detailed the Black Iron

---

25 *Being asked to inscribe a horizontal plaque is an honor typically reserved for individuals of high learning and great prestige.*

Battalion's refusal to heed the Marching Orders Decree, their outrageous subsequent detention of Protector-General Meng, and various other offenses.

The Longan Emperor was still steeped in nostalgia over his childhood with Gu Yun. He made a grand show of displeasure, but the consequences he meted out were light. He instructed someone to reprimand He Ronghui for lack of regard for the nation's laws and docked his salary. He then ordered the Black Iron Battalion to rigorously defend against any suspicious movements on the border.

When Chang Geng finally eked out some free time, he made his way to the hot spring villa in the northern outskirts of the capital to inform Gu Yun of these developments. Upon arrival, he was greeted by the sight of that Gu bastard wrapped in a bathrobe with his feet soaking in a hot spring. With a wine glass in hand and a pair of lovely female attendants rubbing his shoulders and massaging his back, he looked so content he was on the verge of transcending the mortal plane.

To think when Gu Yun said he was planning to "convalesce" he'd actually go and do just that!

The half-deaf man failed to hear Chang Geng's approach. He turned his head and said something to the girl beside him, and she smiled, her face reddening.

Chang Geng was beyond words.

Gu Yun found the attendant's blush quite cute and moved to touch her rosy cheeks. But just as he lifted his hand, he saw the girls hastily greet someone and spring up to withdraw.

Gu Yun turned back and groped for his glass monocle, which he set on the bridge of his nose. When he saw Chang Geng, this old reprobate wasn't ashamed in the slightest. He gleefully called Chang

Geng over and pushed himself languidly into a sitting position. "It's been ages since I relaxed like this. My bones are about to melt from lying around so much."

"...You sure they're not melting for some other reason?"

Chang Geng regretted these words the instant they left his mouth.

"Hm?" Gu Yun didn't seem to hear him, his face perplexed. "What was that?"

Chang Geng at once remembered how, back when Gu Yun and Shen Yi had disguised themselves as impoverished hermits in Yanhui Town, Gu the Deaf and Blind would wield his extraordinary talent of failing to hear anything that didn't please him. He was already an expert at playing the fool, so once he started up with his deafness, he was like a tiger that had sprouted wings—more powerful than ever before.

The Marquis of Order, greatest fool in the land, asked with great eagerness, "Oh, did you bring my medicine? I'll take you to the Snowy Plum Blossom Pavilion in the rear courtyard tonight. They've hired a few new songstresses over there. Apparently, they're all competing for the opening spot at the New Year's Eve perfor-mance at Kite's Flight Pavilion. We can get a sneak peek."

Chang Geng had thought Gu Yun wanted him to bring the med-icine because of some emergency he needed to attend to. After all this fuss, it turned out it was because he couldn't enjoy the company of beautiful women to the fullest if he couldn't hear. Chang Geng pasted an insincere smile on his face. "Every medicine is three parts poison. Seeing as Yifu has no urgent business at hand, you ought to take it less."

"Mm, wonderful," Gu Yun responded nonsensically, "I'm glad you brought it. The water here is superb; you should come in and relax awhile."

Chang Geng was speechless. He gave up on trying to reason with Gu Yun. He sat solemnly beside the hot spring and didn't even look up as he lifted his hands and signed, "His Majesty has received a report from the northwestern front. You can rest assured—all is well."

Gu Yun nodded slowly. "Mm. Seeing as you're here already, why not join me for a soak?"

"I'll pass," said Chang Geng, face blank. "You can enjoy it by yourself, Yifu."

Tsk. Gu Yun clicked his tongue. He made no attempt to avoid Chang Geng's eyes as he calmly stripped out of his robe and slid into the water. Chang Geng, flustered, averted his gaze. With nowhere to rest his eyes, he haphazardly snatched up a wine glass and took a sip, as if trying to hide something. Only when the wine moistened his lips did he remember he was holding Gu Yun's cup. He jerked to his feet so abruptly he nearly upended Gu Yun's little table and said hoarsely, "I just came to tell Yifu the news. Now that you know, I...I have to go back, I still have some business to attend to, so..."

"Little Chang Geng," Gu Yun called him to a stop. He removed the glass monocle, which had fogged in the steam, and set it aside. He could only see a dozen centimeters past his nose and his eyes were unfocused—yet he stood as regal as a flood-wielding dragon king. "We're all men here," Gu Yun said, careless. "You have everything I have, and I don't have anything you lack. There's absolutely nothing to write home about."

Chang Geng held his breath and finally lifted his gaze. Even with the mist of the spring blurring the lines of Gu Yun's figure, the scars covering his body were shocking to behold. One slash began at his throat and sliced diagonally across his chest, as if his torso had been cleaved in two and sewn back together.

Gu Yun was an expert in human nature. He knew that with some things, the greater the taboo, the more intoxicating they became, and the more forbidden they seemed, the more difficult they were to give up. Thus, he might as well be magnanimous and allow Chang Geng to look as he pleased. Besides, it wasn't as if there was anything worth seeing.

"Everyone feels very deeply for their parents. You're not alone; I was like that too," Gu Yun said. "My father was a brute who sent iron puppets to chase and hack at me. The first person who held my hand and taught me to write was the late emperor. The first person who coaxed me to take my medicine and rewarded me with candied fruit was also the late emperor. As a child, I thought he was the only person who ever cared for me. Sometimes, when this kind of feeling grows too strong, it may lead to certain misconceptions. It's okay; it will fade with time. The more you dwell on these feelings, the more you will buckle under their weight, and the more they will plague you."

Chang Geng opened his mouth to reply, but Gu Yun made the most of his weak hearing. Unconcerned whether Chang Geng responded or not, he forged ahead on his own: "Yifu knows you're a good kid. But you've got a bad habit of taking on too many mental burdens. Lay them down and stay here with me for a few days. What are you doing rubbing elbows with old monks all the time? There are so many marvelous sights in this world, and plenty of pleasurable diversions. Why stick to the same old beaten track?"

54

A SUDDEN DISTURBANCE

CHANG GENG STOOD FROZEN for several seconds before walking over to the hot spring. He dropped slowly to his knees and stared at the ropes of scar tissue covering Gu Yun's body. After so many years, he had grown accustomed to being startled awake by the wu'ergu in the middle of the night. He would jerk back to consciousness, and then he would toss and turn, thinking of Gu Yun. Chang Geng had preferred peace and quiet since childhood. He had often felt, in those days, that his overly energetic godfather defied reason. Later, after pondering it over many sleepless nights, he was struck by a curious question: How did Gu Yun grow into the person he was now?

As the only child of the former Marquis of Anding and the eldest princess, he must have been an incomparably precious, insufferably arrogant noble young master. Yet after losing his sight and hearing at such a young age, he had been driven forward under his own father's whip, beaten and reshaped like wrought iron, his unfledged wings riddled with scars. He lost two parents in rapid succession and, as the past glories of the Black Iron Battalion faded with time, was confined deep within the interior of the imperial palace. A person who has experienced so much pain as a child, even if they don't become withdrawn or volatile, at least oughtn't become someone so playful and mischievous—Chang Geng felt sure of this.

He couldn't imagine how many layers of overlapping wounds it took to temper a person like Gu Yun.

Chang Geng suddenly hated that he was born ten years too late to hold this person's young and clumsy hands amid a thicket of brambles and thorns. For that reason alone, he would envy Shen Yi all his life. He reached forward, as if possessed, and brushed aside Gu Yun's long hair, which draped over his shoulders and into the water. Then, he carefully touched the scar that stretched across Gu Yun's chest.

"*Sss*...how impudent." A prickling sensation shivered across Gu Yun's scalp at the touch, and he hastily stepped back. "I'm trying to reason with you here—what are you pawing at me for?"

"How did you get this?" Chang Geng asked, his voice hoarse.

The deaf man didn't hear him. Chang Geng caught Gu Yun's hand and wrote his question, word by word, into his palm.

Gu Yun blinked in surprise. His memory momentarily failed him.

Chang Geng wiped away the condensation on Gu Yun's glass monocle and set it back on his nose. He gazed deeply at Gu Yun and signed, "Yifu, let's take turns coming clean, okay?"

Gu Yun had an ill-fated relationship with the words *coming clean*, so naturally, he wasn't okay with this at all.

Chang Geng didn't give him a chance to demur. "You cared deeply for the late emperor. But did you want to kiss him, embrace him, and entangle intimately with him your entire life?"

"What?" Gu Yun blurted.

He couldn't help but recall the late emperor's withered face, which always seemed to overflow with misery. He promptly broke out in gooseflesh.

"Very well. You've answered, so now it's my turn," Chang Geng said, his face ascetic as a monk's. "I do."

It was several seconds before Gu Yun managed to digest the meaning of Chang Geng's *I do*. His previous wave of gooseflesh had barely subsided before a second wave was upon him, all his hair standing on end like a hedgehog.

"I want it—at all hours of the day, even in my dreams. And I especially want it now... I also want other things. I'm afraid I'll sully Yifu's ears if I say them aloud, so I won't." Chang Geng closed his eyes and turned his face away from Gu Yun. "How could I have experienced a qi deviation if I weren't deeply and irrevocably entrenched in these feelings?"

After a lengthy silence, Gu Yun finally said, rather stiffly, "Perhaps you should go back to reading scripture with those monks."

"If only you had said that to me five years ago," Chang Geng said. "Maybe if I'd let go then, we wouldn't have gotten to this point today."

But so many days and nights had come and gone. So many nightmares and tribulations he had only endured by invoking Gu Yun's name. He had been quenching his thirst with poison all this time, and it was far too late.

The Marquis of Anding was struggling to keep up. After staring at Chang Geng in stupefaction for a good while, he thought to himself in consternation, *Five years ago, I still thought of you as a nursing infant!*

"Next question." Chang Geng squeezed his eyes shut. "Does Yifu find me disgusting?"

Gu Yun once again fell silent. Chang Geng's lashes quivered violently, and his hands involuntarily balled into fists within his sleeves. Gu Yun's physical reaction just now couldn't deceive him. His obvious discomfort was clear from the gooseflesh breaking out over his body.

Perhaps Gu Yun could understand his affection, but he would never understand his desire.

Chang Geng heard the splashing of water as Gu Yun climbed ashore and draped his robe back over his body. Sighing, Gu Yun reached out and patted Chang Geng on the shoulder. "You know that's not possible," he said, calmly skirting the question.

The corner of Chang Geng's mouth curled slightly, as if he were about to smile. But in the end, he failed. In a barely audible whisper, he said, "I know. I won't make things difficult for Yifu."

Gu Yun sat down beside him. It was a long time before he finally found his composure. Just as he was about to open his mouth to speak, a fierce blast of wind lanced toward his back. The glass of wine that Chang Geng had set aside shone with a sharp light. Before Gu Yun could react, Chang Geng had already lunged toward him.

Pulling Gu Yun into his embrace, Chang Geng rolled to the side, his arms tightening around the other man. At the same time, Gu Yun's doglike nose caught a whiff of blood.

An arrow trailing white steam grazed Chang Geng, tearing through his long sleeve and lacerating the skin beneath. Chang Geng lifted his head and glimpsed the cold gleam of metal darting past the tranquil little courtyard outside—it was a figure in light pelt armor!

The distance between the hot spring villa and the Northern Camp was less than three kilometers. Even without spurring a horse to full speed, it was possible to ride from one to the other in no time at all. Where did this assassin come from?

The assassin's first strike failed to kill its target—but the danger wasn't over yet.

As the sun sank heavily over the horizon, the man in light pelt armor leapt out from behind the courtyard wall on the other side. A blast of steam jetted from the armor's soles, and the assassin moved like a flash of lightning to arrive before them in an instant. Gu Yun shoved Chang Geng aside and pulled an iron sword from beneath the little table on which they had set out their wine. With a flip of his wrist, he exchanged several rapid blows with the assassin.

Gu Yun's martial skills had been honed sparring barehanded with iron puppets in his childhood. He thought nothing of engaging a light armor burning violet gold. Yet after a brief clash with the enemy, Gu Yun retreated several steps. He was alarmed to find that his hands were shaking, and he struggled to lift the weight of his iron sword.

One glance was all it took for Chang Geng to realize something was amiss and reach out to catch him. Grabbing Gu Yun's wrist, Chang Geng guided his hands to viciously thrust the blade up through the assassin's throat with pinpoint accuracy. The tip of the sword pierced all the way through the assassin's head and struck the top of his iron helmet. There was a sharp *clang* followed by a fine spray of bloody mist.

Chang Geng spared not a single look toward the dead man, but immediately slid his fingers over Gu Yun's inner wrist to check his pulse. "You've been drugged," he said in a low voice.

Gu Yun's chest felt numb, and his heart pounded erratically. He grunted in acknowledgement, struggling to catch his breath. As the numbness spread through the rest of his limbs, the deaf and blind Gu Yun became tense with unease.

"I'm fine." Gu Yun sucked in several quick breaths. "The attack might not be over yet. You..."

Gu Yun's crow's beak hadn't even completed its premonition before a dozen light pelts vaulted over the courtyard walls. At the same time, startled by the disturbance, the marquis's guards standing watch outside rose in response. Perhaps there was something wrong with these assassins' heads—their assassination attempt had failed, yet they refused to back down. They swarmed forward to engage the guards, as if eager to die.

The household retainers of the Marquis Estate were all former soldiers who had retired from the battlefield. They were a different breed from the hired thugs usually employed to protect the homes of wealthy families. These guards were highly disciplined and mobilized with speed and efficiency. Seeing that the fight was now overwhelmingly one-sided, Chang Geng helped Gu Yun to the sidelines.

"Yifu..."

Gu Yun raised a finger to his lips. He patted Chang Geng on the shoulder and gently lifted Chang Geng's wounded arm, indicating that he should take care of himself first. Chang Geng ignored him. He knelt beside Gu Yun and took him by the wrist; his pulse was already steadier than before. Chang Geng struggled to stay calm. He remembered that Gu Yun had been abusing medicine for years, so he was more resistant to drugs than the average person. It wasn't so easy to knock him out—in all likelihood, the reason the drug had such a precipitous effect was because he'd been soaking in the hot water.

An explosion suddenly reverberated across the courtyard, the whole villa trembling in its wake. Even the half-deaf Gu Yun heard it. After a brief scuffle, the assassins had been subdued by the capable estate guards. Yet before the captain of the guard could apprehend them, every assassin ruptured the gold tanks on their armor and self-destructed!

Gu Yun narrowed his rather useless eyes and murmured under his breath, "A suicide attack..."

The captain of the guard ordered his men to put out the fire and hurried over to Gu Yun. "Forgive this subordinate's incompetence. I ask that the marquis and His Highness please evacuate first."

Gu Yun made no response. He seemed to be caught up in his own thoughts.

Faded memories were dragged brutally to the surface of his heart. They bared their fangs viciously before his eyes, and brandished claws made only sharper by time. The winds whipping beyond the pass that year had been filled with killing intent. Everywhere he looked there was black iron, and boundless, bleak grasslands stretched into the distance. A huge flock of vultures circled overhead, and horses cantered through the tall grass, every few steps kicking up chunks of white bone scored by the teeth of wild beasts.

Little Gu Yun, whose head barely cleared the top of a writing desk, was currently being disciplined by the old marquis for some minor infraction. He'd been forbidden from eating breakfast and was now holding a horse stance in the middle of the camp as punishment. The soldiers that walked by couldn't help but snicker when they saw him. The boy had been excessively proud since he was very young, and the soldiers' laughter made his eyes swim with tears, but he stubbornly refused to let them fall.

By then, the fighting on the border had abated. The eighteen tribes' tribute of violet gold had been delivered to the national treasury, and their goddess had been conferred the title of noble consort. Everything had been peaceful.

Without warning, a heavy-armored soldier on patrol collapsed next to Gu Yun. Every guard in his courtyard followed suit, crumpling one by one where they stood. The sound of thunderous battle cries reached him from outside the walls. Little Gu Yun had never seen combat before. Petrified, he instinctively cast about for a weapon.

But he was only a child. Even if he used both hands, he couldn't lift even the lightest of swords.

The attackers who stormed the camp that day had also been a suicide squad, their movements swift as the wind as they rushed forth like demons or deities. Gu Yun had watched as a soldier who had laughed at him only minutes ago began to struggle like a dying bird, resolutely shielding the young Gu Yun beneath his body.

Even now Gu Yun remembered that sea of carnage; how he had looked on helplessly as those soldiers were cut down one by one in their own camp like livestock awaiting slaughter. Something had struck him in the back, and the pain was unbearable—but the pain was soon replaced by numbness. Little by little, his body began to feel like it had been severed from his mind. The din around him faded, and what little consciousness he retained seemed to be trapped alongside his heart as it nearly beat through his chest. He couldn't breathe...

In this half-conscious daze, he had heard such an earth-shattering explosion—this was the moment the princess arrived with reinforcements and those intruders self-destructed their light armor.

Chang Geng pressed down on his shoulder. "Yifu!"

Gu Yun's glassy eyes finally refocused. "Is there a wolf head tattoo on the unburnt corpses?" he murmured.

"What?" Chang Geng asked.

The captain of the guard flinched in surprise, then jerked his head up—the Gu estate's guards remembered that incident even more clearly than their master, who had still been so young back then. "The marquis is saying..."

"Check after you extinguish the fire," Gu Yun said, expressionless. "And find the person who drugged me."

Gu Yun could feel the drug's effect fading as he spoke. He walked forward in a daze. His glass monocle had shattered when it tumbled to the ground in the earlier chaos; he could barely see where he was going, and almost stepped right into the hot spring. Chang Geng lurched to his feet, uncharacteristically clumsy. He wrapped his arm protectively around Gu Yun's back without so much as a by-your-leave and led him all the way across the courtyard.

So lost was Gu Yun in his thoughts that he didn't even push him away.

Chang Geng helped him into his room and laid a thin blanket over his shoulders. He was about to check his pulse when Gu Yun finally spoke. "Bring me my medicine."

Chang Geng frowned. "No, you're still..."

Gu Yun's face went blank. "I said, bring me my medicine," he repeated, more insistent this time.

Chang Geng stared at him in surprise. He could sense that Gu Yun's temper had begun to spark. Although his face remained impassive, a viciousness slowly revealed itself as the brutality of a million suits of iron armor coalesced in his unseeing eyes. For an instant, that delicately handsome man seemed like a demonic fiend roused from slumber—but it was only for an instant.

Gu Yun soon came to his senses, and his expression softened. He fumbled about slightly for Chang Geng's arm, then patted him on the hand. "Go get your wound treated first. When you're done, help me prepare a dose of my medicine—what happened to listening to me, hm?"

Chang Geng fell silent for a spell. Then he turned to leave, slamming his fist against the pillar by the door on his way out.

At that moment, a still more violent storm was sweeping toward the capital city's sea of lights.

That night, in a house off a narrow lane in the Legation Quarter, a beardless old man with thinning hair took one last look at the blood letter[26] sitting on the table. He hung himself from the rafters, ending his ailing life as the first glimmers of dawn stole over the capital.

---

26 A letter written in one's own blood, expressing unvoiced grievances, determination, or last dying wishes.

In his agitated state, Gu Yun had forgotten to instruct the captain of the guard to keep the attack under wraps. The hot spring villa and the Northern Camp were practically neighbors; word of this incident flew from one to the other as swiftly as if it had sprouted wings. Tan Hongfei, the commander of the Northern Camp, was a former member of the Black Iron Battalion who had campaigned with the old marquis in the north. When he received word that his own commanding officer had met with an assassination attempt in the heart of the empire—right under his nose—he flew into a rage. He personally led a contingent of soldiers to investigate the incident.

It was impossible to conceal such a dramatic move, and in no time at all, news of the attempt on Gu Yun's life in the capital outskirts had spread like wildfire. But this was only the beginning.

By the time Gu Yun recovered the use of his eyes and ears the next day and remembered his oversight, it was too late; Tan Hongfei had already led his troops into the capital to browbeat the harried capital magistrate into investigating suspicious out-of-towners. As for the herald sent to chase down Tan Hongfei with Gu Yun's orders, he had hardly dismounted from his horse when an unknown individual carrying a blood letter arrived to strike the drum.[27]

Gu Yun's herald didn't dare barge into the capital magistrate's office without permission. He hastily sent someone to bring word of his arrival, unaware that the place had already become as chaotic as a bubbling pot of porridge. He waited long enough to burn through a full stick of incense before someone from the magistrate's office finally led him inside to deliver his message.

Before he could make a sound, Tan Hongfei, commander of the Northern Camp, had risen to his feet with a ferocious glare and

---

27   In ancient China, court officials were equipped with a 鸣冤鼓, or "grievance-voicing drum," that people seeking justice would beat in order to summon the presiding magistrate.

slapped the writing table before him with such force that it cracked. Magistrate Zhu, the capital magistrate, was frightened so badly, his black gauze official's hat slipped and hung crookedly from his head.

"Who the hell are you? Say that again!" Tan Hongfei barked at the man before them.

The middle-aged man holding the letter spoke slowly and distinctly. "This lowly subject is the owner of a pastry shop located just outside the Eastern Legation Quarter. My adoptive father was once known as Wu He-gonggong, imperial eunuch and Keeper of Seals of the late Yuanhe Emperor. Many years ago, to avoid prosecution, he faked his death and was lucky enough to escape the imperial palace. He has been living in secret among the common people all this time. He never expected, after more than a dozen years, to be discovered by treacherous individuals. Last night, he committed suicide to avoid implicating his family.

"This lowly subject's life is as brief as a firefly's glow and as insignificant as decaying grass—so lacking in value that it is not worth mentioning. However, in light of my late father's death, I feel compelled to expose this great injustice to the world."

Capital Magistrate Zhu Heng immediately sensed the profound ramifications of the case before them. He promptly cried, "Impudent miscreant, what nonsense! The imperial eunuch Wu He was imprisoned and sentenced to death by waist chop for his crime of conspiring to murder an imperial prince. Are you accusing the Imperial Court of Judicial Review of mishandling this case?"

The man fell to his knees and knocked his head against the ground. "This lowly subject holds a blood letter written by my father minutes before his death. Today, I lay my neck on the line for this audience with you, Your Honor. How would I dare speak a single word of falsehood?"

Back then, the imperial eunuch Wu He seemed to have been taken by a fit of madness. He had accepted bribes and conspired with a disfavored imperial concubine to murder the third prince. The uproar that followed this scandal had touched even the young Gu Yun, who had still resided within the imperial palace at the time. Because of this, former members of the Black Iron Battalion had dearly wished to chop that ignorant eunuch to pieces with their own hands.

Tan Hongfei's expression was dark. "Magistrate Zhu, there's no harm in hearing him out."

Gu Yun's instructions had been clear: do not, under any circumstances, allow Tan Hongfei to cause trouble. Sensing the situation was taking a dangerous turn, the herald made a quick decision. "General Tan," he interjected, "the marquis asks that you return to the Northern Camp at once."

"That's right," Zhu Heng said hastily. "General Tan, please return to the Northern Camp. If there is any news regarding those foreign scoundrels, this lowly official will send someone to notify you at once..."

The complainant kneeling below the dais raised his voice. "This lowly subject brings suit against the late Yuanhe Emperor for the crimes of falling for the barbarian enchantress's deceptions and conspiring to poison his loyal subject!"

55

CONFLAGRATION

EVERYONE WAS STUNNED.

Only after a long silence did the herald once again recall the purpose of his visit. "General Tan," he said hoarsely, "the marquis—"

"Shut up!" Tan Hongfei thundered. His glaring bull's eyes gleamed like bronze bells as he turned toward the man kneeling in the center of the hall. Tan Hongfei's throat felt tight, and the hair on his body seemed to shudder and stand on end. "What did you say? Speak clearly—which loyal subject?"

The man straightened up. His complexion was sallow; he seemed rather pitiful. Yet as he spoke, his face was filled with an indescribable conviction.

"Twenty years ago, the grasslands of the northern barbarians were beset by natural disasters, and the ambitious Wolf King raised troops and invaded our nation. The former Marquis of Order led the Black Iron Battalion to pacify the northern border and forced the wolf pack's surrender. In addition to the annual tributes, the barbarian goddess and her younger sister were sent to our imperial court as a peace offering. The Yuanhe Emperor took the elder sister as his consort. As for the younger sister, he bestowed upon her the title of commandery princess and brought her into the palace as an attendant, no doubt intending to marry her off to a member of the imperial family.

"No one expected that pair of wicked enchantresses to harbor malice in their hearts and conspire against the nation. These sisters fabricated correspondence between the former marquis and the Wolf King. They framed the former marquis, making it look like he'd threatened the eighteen tribes after the treaty was signed, extorting violet gold for his own private use. They then used their sorcery to bewitch the emperor, driving the wedge between sovereign and subject deeper with each passing day..."

Before he could say another word, Magistrate Zhu exploded with fury. "Guards! This lying scoundrel is slandering His Majesty— arrest him!"

Tan Hongfei's eyes were about to burst from their sockets with the intensity of his glare. "Any who try will answer to me!"

At his roar, the Northern Camp soldiers at his side drew their weapons. Silver armor flashed as they lined up behind their commander in a neat row, swords gleaming bright as snow. The ferocious beasts engraved on their blade hilts snarled as if about to spring forward and tear into their enemies.

The color drained from Zhu Heng's face. He was a scholar, not a soldier; he braced himself with what little courage he had. Voice trembling, he asked, "Tan Hongfei, are you trying to start an insurrection?"

Tan Hongfei sneered. He strode down the stone steps toward the man, stood before him, and thrust his saber into the ground, where his blade stood like a great iron tower. "Go on," he demanded. "What happened next?"

"I wonder whether the general remembers," the man said. "Back then, the young marquis was only a child. No one in the Marquis Estate could control him, so once the fighting in the border regions subsided, the marquis and the princess brought him to the military encampment."

Tan Hongfei's eyes flickered; he was swept up in old memories by this handful of words. He remembered—the glorious Marshal Gu had once been a hellion of a child. He feared no one and got himself into all manner of mischief. Neither the former marquis nor the princess had parents or elders who could look after or discipline him in their stead. Seeing that the child would become absolutely lawless if no one took him in hand, they had no choice but to bring the boy with them.

Tan Hongfei nodded slowly. "Yes, it's as you say."

"The enchantress exploited this situation," the man continued. "She insinuated that the former marquis took his only son from the capital because he was plotting treason. Perhaps he was planning to rend a great tract of land from the body of Great Liang and found his own nation in the west. Spellbound, His Majesty the Yuanhe Emperor grew increasingly acrimonious toward the former marquis. At the same time, he feared the Black Iron Battalion—a force capable of annihilating the barbarians with only thirty armored cavalry. He didn't know what to do."

"Preposterous!" Tan Hongfei exclaimed.

The man's face remained unmoved, his voice steady. "The enchantress devised a vicious plot with the help of another villain. They tasked my late father, Wu-gonggong, with leading thirty suicide fighters and two individuals with unusual talents to the northern border. Their ostensible purpose was to reward the troops stationed on the front line, but their true mission was to infiltrate the garrison and carry out the assassination. To prevent the plot from being exposed in the event of failure, the suicide fighters tattooed wolf heads on their chests to disguise themselves as barbarians."

Tan Hongfei's breathing grew heavy.

He had been there—back then, thirty barbarian suicide fighters had snuck into the Northern Border Garrison. Their attack had come without warning, as if the warriors fell from the sky. The enemy used an underhanded tactic and dosed the soldiers' food and drink with paralytic powder. Then, they donned black-iron light pelt armor and rose from inside the soldiers' own ranks. The garrison soldiers were accustomed to seeing light pelt armor going to and fro every day while on patrol—when it happened, they were completely defenseless...

"That's right," Tan Hongfei mumbled. "Everything you've said matches what happened that day. I was just a lowly squadron commander back then. There were indeed only thirty light pelt suicide fighters."

The former marquis had used thirty suits of heavy armor to decimate the eighteen tribes. Thus the enchantress sent him thirty light pelts to turn the invincible Black Iron Battalion upside down and wound the Marquis of Anding's sole heir.

A low chuckle escaped Tan Hongfei's throat. "That was the Black Iron Battalion's greatest and most humiliating shame. The former marquis happened to be out on patrol at the time, and Her Highness the princess woke up that morning feeling indisposed and couldn't keep anything down. Otherwise, the young marquis wouldn't have been the only one wounded that day. Isn't that right?"

The commander of the Northern Camp had stabbed his great saber into the ground so violently that a crack had formed in the thick stone flooring. "In her fury, the princess became convinced that there were enemies within our ranks. There were a dozen or so of us brothers responsible for the Northern Border Garrison's defense. Our position was suspicious; we could not absolve ourselves of blame. We had no choice but to shed our armor, step down from our posts, and return to the capital one by one to accept punishment.

All these years, I've privately resented Her Highness. I thought she had lost her mind from distress for her beloved son...when in reality, she was right..."

Tears streamed from Tan Hongfei's eyes. He didn't bother to wipe them, nor did he sob aloud. He remained standing, as rigid as his towering iron sword, gasping as if he was in excruciating pain.

Zhu Heng was stunned by the sight; it was like seeing tears on the grim face of the king of hell. For a moment, the swollen anger in his heart was punctured by Tan Hongfei's tears and released a thin stream of air. The capital magistrate couldn't help but soften his voice as he addressed him. "This is a very serious matter. It would be unjust to rely solely on this man's one-sided testimony. General Tan, please proceed with caution."

Tan Hongfei came back to his senses, but truthfully, he already believed most of the man's tale. As the one in command of the Northern Border Garrison's defenses at the time, no one knew better than he how impregnable the Black Iron Battalion had been. Over the years, Gu Yun had always treated the former members of the Black Iron Battalion with kindness and generosity. He had even supported Tan Hongfei's promotion to commander of the Northern Camp. But Tan Hongfei never forgot that on his back, he carried the wrongful conviction of dereliction of duty, which he had no way to appeal.

Tan Hongfei shot Zhu Heng a glance. He gritted his teeth and leaned down to question the complainant before him. "Indeed. What evidence do you have?"

The man pulled the blood letter from his lapels, then prostrated himself again. "This letter was written by my late father's own hand. His body lies outside the door as we speak. If the general examines him, he will recognize him as Wu He and know that all I have said is true."

Zhu Heng frowned, but Tan Hongfei had already ordered his men to bring in the corpse. A few minutes later, a dried-up husk of a man was carried in. This hanged ghost was not at all resting in peace—its cheeks were swollen, and its tongue protruded from its mouth, its throat bruised as purple as a malevolent spirit. Tan Hongfei took only one look before diverting his gaze as if unable to bear such a burden. "I remember there was a triangular scar at the corner of the old eunuch's eye..." he said, voice rough.

The middle-aged man crawled forward on his knees. He carefully turned the corpse's face upward and pushed aside its withered white hair. There, covered in wrinkles and age spots, yet clearly visible at the corner of the dead man's eye, was an old, triangular scar.

Silence descended upon the room. Zhu Heng's face drained of all blood, and he inhaled sharply. His shaking, scholarly hands reached up to straighten the official's hat that had been knocked askew by Tan Hongfei's earlier slap. "And then what happened?"

"Luckily, the heavens help those who are worthy," the man below the dais responded. "The young marquis escaped calamity. As time passed, the late emperor awakened from the enchantress's sorcery. He deeply regretted what happened and secretly punished the barbarian enchantress and her sister. At the same time, he treated the young marquis with greater favor than ever before, bringing him into the imperial palace and personally taking charge of his care. But although the enchantress was executed, the villain who first presented that vicious plot to His Majesty remained at large.

"A few years later, fearing that the Gu family was once again growing in influence, this person colluded with Wu He-gonggong and set his sights on the young marquis once again."

Zhu Heng's face was dark as an overcast sky. "Matters concerning the imperial harem are not to be discussed in public. Think carefully before you speak."

The middle-aged man's laughter rang loudly through the hall. "Many thanks, Your Honor. This lowly subject grew up in a farming family on the northern border. For generations, my family suffered at the hands of the barbarians. My father, mother, and brothers all died under the swords of those fiends and their phony sorcery. It was the former marquis who saved our lives and gave us satisfaction for our anger. I am but a commoner, a lowly man of ignoble status who has endured in silence for many years. I waited upon that old eunuch all this time, not for the sake of any inheritance or privileges, but for the arrival of this day!"

Tan Hongfei was nearly numb, without even the energy to cry anymore. "But I remember...the one who died that year was His Highness the Third Prince."

"That's right," the man agreed. "Wu He employed a poison that dispersed through the air when heated and applied it to the gas lamp the young marquis used to study. Wu He said that as a child, the young marquis liked to crank the gas lamp up to its brightest setting, and he would often leave it lit even when he retired to bed. After burning all night, the lamp would be hot enough to fry an egg. Naturally, the poison would vaporize and diffuse through the air and be inhaled. The young marquis would first be afflicted with a lingering cough and persistent low fevers—ailments common in young children, nothing that would arouse suspicion. But over time, his body would gradually weaken until the poison reached his vital organs, at which point it would be too late for any treatment to save him."

Tan Hongfei's eyes were so red they were on the verge of dripping blood.

"The young marquis's gas lamp was a special tribute from the Far West. It had a lampshade fashioned from colored glass and was terribly precious. The lamps were presented only to the imperial princes and the young marquis; not even the empress received one. However, the third prince accidentally broke his gas lamp. He feared he would be scolded and didn't dare ask anyone else for help, so the young marquis exchanged lamps with him. The marquis secretly glued the shattered pieces of the prince's broken lamp back together and covered it with a book every day, pretending to use it as usual.

"We all know the rest of the story: the third prince was poisoned and died young; the late emperor was furious and turned the imperial harem inside out; and Wu He was imprisoned for plotting against the life of an imperial prince. Thus the eunuch became a scapegoat for that crafty man in the shadows." The man prostrated himself on the ground once more with a flip of his sleeves. "Now, the entire sequence of events has been laid before you," he said in a ringing voice. "My sincere thanks to all the lords and generals present. As for that crafty and fawning villain who walks free to this day—he is none other than the Imperial Uncle, Wang Guo!"

"Insolence... H-how dare you!" Zhu Heng stammered, dumbstruck.

"I've no attachment to this insignificant body of flesh—I dare to be insolent!" the man cried.

"What evidence do you have?" Zhu Heng pressed.

The man pulled out a tattered letter, so old its edges had begun to curl. "Your Honor, this is a letter that Imperial Uncle Wang penned with his own hand as he conducted his secret dealings with the imperial eunuch. As for its authenticity, you will know at a glance."

The man set the letter on the ground. He tilted his head back slightly and seemed to sigh.

"With this, the grievances of the past have been settled."

By the time Tan Hongfei noticed the queerness of his expression, it was too late. The man rose swiftly to his feet and, before anyone could react, turned and slammed his head into a pillar.

Blood and brain matter splattered the ground. The man died on the spot—clearly a suicide fighter of a different kind.

Back in the hot spring villa, Gu Yun's eyelid inexplicably began to twitch.

Huo Dan, the captain of the Marquis Estate's guards, burst into his room, his whole body heaving for breath. "M-my lord..."

Gu Yun's head whipped around. "What is it?"

Captain Huo's heart had been pounding wildly since the moment he received word of the disturbance in the capital. But before he could open his mouth to report, the door was flung open once more.

In the doorway stood Chang Geng, a wooden bird—beak open wide and wings outstretched—clutched in his hand. The little creature's head had been unceremoniously detached; Chang Geng had crushed its solid wooden body in his grip. The jagged edges of the exposed gears stabbed into his palms and left a bloody mess behind, but he seemed not to register the pain. He was like a fish ripped from the water, gasping for air, yet his chest couldn't hold even a single breath.

Clenched in his other hand was a bloodstained piece of billow paper. A wooden bird was faster than a carriage or horse, after all—someone had already sent him news of the farce in the capital. Chang Geng felt as though there were a blade pressed to his sternum, as if blood would seep out with every rise and fall of his chest. He stumbled over to Gu Yun and enfolded him in his arms.

Captain Huo, who had been standing to the side, started in surprise. "My lord..."

Gu Yun waved him toward the door. "Old Huo, step out for a minute."

Captain Huo's throat bobbed slightly. He seemed to want to say something, but in the end, he quietly withdrew.

This unfortunate child was surprisingly strong. Gu Yun felt as if his waist was about to snap in two from the force of his embrace. Once Captain Huo was gone, he freed one of his hands and patted Chang Geng on the back. "What's wrong?"

Chang Geng dropped his head and buried his face in Gu Yun's shoulder. The medicinal fragrance that clung to Gu Yun's body lingered all around him. Chang Geng used to find the scent soothing—even in his dreams, it had the power to dispel the shadowy haze of his nightmares. Yet at this moment, he never wanted to smell the fragrance of medicine on Gu Yun's body again. Chang Geng closed his eyes. His ears roared, and a single thought was stark in his mind: *I'm going to slaughter every last member of the Li family.*

Gu Yun extracted the crumpled piece of billow paper from his hand and skimmed it from top to bottom. He inhaled sharply and shoved Chang Geng away. "Huo Dan!" he shouted as he stood, furious.

Captain Huo had been waiting by the door and promptly re-entered at his call.

Gu Yun felt like he was going mad. He'd risen too quickly to his feet, and for a second, his vision darkened at the edges. He hastily leaned against the table, his arms shaking nonstop.

"Ready my horse. I'm returning to the capital." Gu Yun sucked in a deep breath. "Take...*cough*..."

His voice cracked, but he harshly cleared his throat and continued, "Take a few light pelts and move out first. You must stop Tan Hongfei at all costs."

Captain Huo shot him a searching look. "Yes, sir!"

Gu Yun had already turned to fetch his court robes and light armor when his wrist was caught by Chang Geng.

"Is it true?" Chang Geng asked, his voice trembling.

Gu Yun dipped his head and gazed at him, his eyes filled with a roiling tempest of emotions. After a brief pause, he said in a low voice, "Of course not. There's no such thing as sorcery, and Imperial Uncle Wang is merely a..."

Merely a subservient dog of the imperial throne who attacked where he was pointed. As for the two barbarian women, they were pitiful figures who had been surrendered to a far and foreign land in the wake of their nation's defeat.

Everyone knew the truth, but no one dared to say it aloud.

Gu Yun yanked his hand out of Chang Geng's grasp. "The situation is tumultuous right now. Keep away from the capital for the time being and stay here for a few days..."

But Chang Geng would not be put off. "So aside from the sorcery and Wang Guo, everything else is true? You know? You've always known?"

Gu Yun was out of patience. "This isn't the time. Don't stir up any more trouble—step aside!"

Chang Geng spoke over him: "Why do you still exhaust yourself for him to protect this rotten nation? Why do you concede so much ground? Why...did you take me in and care for me for so many years?" he finally asked quietly.

Chang Geng's voice was soft as fallen snow, so weak it was barely audible over Gu Yun's furious shout. Yet somehow, the instant these words escaped him, they flew unerringly to the ears of the one who needed to hear them.

Gu Yun's heart constricted.

Chang Geng's lips were bloodless. His eyes bored into Gu Yun and he asked again, "Yifu, why?"

Gu Yun's throat bobbed. He didn't know where to begin—what should he say?

Should he say that, back then, he had no idea? That for years, he assumed his wound had been nothing more than an accident? That he thought it had been he who failed to protect A-Yan; that he had looked on helplessly as the little prince died, a victim of vicious struggles within the imperial harem? That...not until he was ordered to escort Crown Prince Jialai Yinghuo beyond the pass did he learn from the barbarian's own malicious mouth that the poison of the grasslands' goddess was a closely guarded secret. That it had remained the sole knowledge of the goddess for generations—that even members of the same tribe could not reproduce it—and so, the thirty light cavalrymen who carried that poison and inflicted such heavy casualties on the Black Iron Battalion twenty years ago absolutely could not have been sent by any barbarians in the north?

Home and country, enmity and resentment. The road of life was wide enough that anyone could make their own way without impeding others' paths. But no matter what direction one chose, the moment they took that very first step, they would never be able to turn back.

These affairs encompassed so many things that weren't fit to be spoken. In the end, Gu Yun said nothing. He pried open Chang Geng's hand, donned his armor, and tied up his hair.

The general had a heart—what a pity it was cast from iron.

Gu Yun's reaction was hardly slow, and the hundred Marquis Estate guards could hardly be considered ineffective. But they were still too late.

By the time Huo Dan, drenched in cold sweat, reached the capital's city walls, the Northern Camp had risen in mutiny. The Imperial Guard had mobilized to deal with the crisis, the nine city gates were sealed, and the capital descended into chaos.

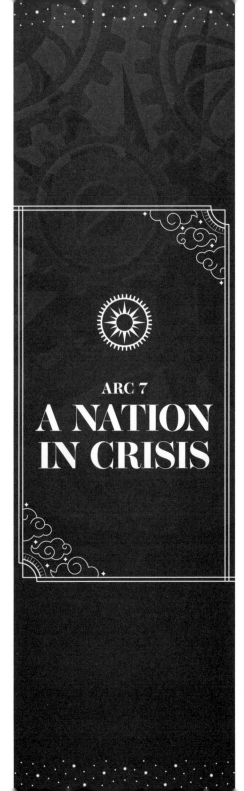

ARC 7

A NATION
IN CRISIS

56

MUTED THUNDER

CHANG GENG chased after Gu Yun. "Yifu, wait!"

Gu Yun, already astride his horse, glanced down from his high perch. His warhorse was as anxious as its rider, and though Gu Yun kept a firm grip on the reins, it paced impatiently in place. All the blood in Chang Geng's face seemed to have migrated to the palms of his injured hands and the crimson edges of his sleeves, as if he were an ink portrait drawn on paper. His expression, however, was almost apathetic, as if he had pasted a mask over that face that had been so pained just seconds ago.

Chang Geng said, every word deliberate, "If Uncle Huo fails to keep General Tan in check, Yifu, you will invite disaster upon yourself by returning to the capital now."

Gu Yun's graceful eyebrow jumped slightly. He opened his mouth to speak, but Chang Geng cut him off.

"I know. Even if you invite disaster upon yourself, you will return to the capital, because the Imperial Guard is no match for the Northern Camp. Aside from Yifu, there isn't a single other person who can keep General Tan in check. If a rebellion were to rock the capital, the consequences would be unimaginable." Chang Geng sucked in a deep breath, then stretched a bloody hand toward Gu Yun. "But if His Majesty detains you, the generals on all four borders will doubtless become uneasy; that, too, may lead to disaster. Yifu, give me a token that will reassure the hearts of the people."

Shock flickered across Gu Yun's face. This child who had just been vexing him so thoroughly felt suddenly unfamiliar.

Everyone wears many faces. Some wield authority with legendary might in public yet transform into a small child around their closest family: forgetful, fickle, and ignorant of the ways of the world.

Chang Geng was growing further and further from that boy who had rebelliously called his young godfather Shiliu but relied on him at every turn. Yet still, the admiration and reliance he felt toward Gu Yun lingered in his heart. Even if his affections stirred in more passionate directions in the middle of the night, this paternal or fraternal facet of their relationship gave the whole affair a touch of taboo.

And so it would, until the easterly winds of change scattered the last remaining fragments of his youthful sentiments.

Chang Geng was rapidly realizing that he was on the verge of stepping alone onto a road where no one would understand him, and no one would accompany him.

From now on, he was no longer anyone's son, nor a child of anyone's younger generation.

Gu Yun took out his personal seal and tossed it to Chang Geng. "This doesn't carry the same weight as the Black Iron Tiger Tally," he said, "but all veterans of my command will recognize it. It may be of some use. If it comes down to it...think of some way to contact Old General Zhong."

Chang Geng didn't even look at the seal before tucking it away within his sleeve. "I understand. Yifu needn't worry," he said with a slow nod.

He had hardly finished speaking before Gu Yun dug his heels into his horse's flanks and galloped off into the distance. Chang

Geng stared at his retreating back until it disappeared from sight. He suddenly squeezed his eyes shut and murmured, "Zixi…"

The Marquis Estate guard standing beside him didn't hear him clearly. He asked in confusion, "Your Highness, what did you say?"

Chang Geng spun around. "Prepare a brush and paper."

"Your Highness, your hands…" The guard chased after him.

Chang Geng paused, picked up Gu Yun's abandoned jar of wine, and, with no change in expression, poured the whole jar of strong liquor over the wounds on his hands. The cuts, which had already begun to scab over, bled again with the rush of liquid. Chang Geng carelessly retrieved a handkerchief from his lapels and wrapped them tight.

In the capital, no one expected that an old eunuch's death would raise such a storm of controversy.

The resentment Tan Hongfei had suppressed for twenty years erupted—he had very likely already lost his mind. He first sent soldiers to surround Imperial Uncle Wang's estate. Upon learning that the old bastard had abandoned his wife and children to cower within the palace, he did an about-face and brazenly turned his blade on the Imperial Guard who had rushed to the scene.

The Imperial Guard and the Northern Camp had always been the last lines of defense for the capital, one within and one without, and the two constantly crossed paths. The Imperial Guard was by and large made up of two groups: young-master soldiers benefitting from nepotism and living off the imperial coffers, and elite soldiers selected from the Northern Camp. The former had already pissed their pants in terror and could not be relied on. The latter were skilled, but, stuck in the impossible position of drawing blades against their maiden family, quickly crumpled. Just as

Chang Geng had predicted, in no time at all, the Imperial Guard was defeated.

Music and song from Kite's Flight Pavilion still echoed through the halls, and white steam from heated jars of flower wine had yet to disperse, but the capital city had erupted into pandemonium.

Tan Hongfei and his men advanced right up to the restricted area of the imperial palace. The general plucked off his helmet, as if he were holding his own head in his arms, and performed three bows and nine kowtows in the direction of the great hall. He bellowed at the Imperial Guard blocking his way, "This guilty subject Tan Hongfei requests an audience with His Majesty! May His Majesty hand over the conniving traitor taking shelter within the palace walls and offer a proper explanation to all my comrades who fight in defense of our nation, and to all under heaven! This guilty subject is willing to die a thousand deaths for the crime of forcing his sovereign's hand!"

When his words were relayed to Li Feng inside the palace, the emperor, who hadn't even gotten around to blaming Wang Guo, flew instantly into a rage. Wang Guo had fled with his tail between his legs, but the Son of Heaven was made of much sterner stuff. Li Feng almost smashed the imperial jade seal in his fury. Brushing off all his attendants' counsel, he tossed a robe over himself and turned to leave, striding through the doors of the great hall to face Tan Hongfei in person.

The massive forces of the nation's capital and the imperial bodyguards of the emperor's palace gazed at each other across dozens of meters of white marble steps. Even the sparrows perched on the palace walls began to sweat with nerves.

Gu Yun arrived on the scene just in time to witness this dangerous standoff.

Gu Yun had brought only twenty-some men with him. They had carved a path through the Northern Camp troops encircling the imperial palace and charged straight in. At the sight of this confrontation, the enraged Marquis of Anding nearly spat up a mouthful of heart's blood. He strode forward and lashed his whip across Tan Hongfei's face, leaving a bloody gash. "Are you looking to die?" he roared.

The rims of Tan Hongfei's eyes reddened at the sight of Gu Yun. "Marshal..."

"Shut up. What are you trying to do, force His Majesty to abdicate?" Gu Yun kicked Tan Hongfei in the shoulder, practically stomping him into the ground. "Do you still have any deference in your heart? Any loyalty? Do you understand the hierarchy between lord and subject? What about the rule that the soldiers of the Northern Camp are not to enter the capital city without a summons? Who gave you the guts to rebel against your superiors?"

Tan Hongfei sprawled on the ground, sobbing through his words. "Sir, it's been twenty years. Our brothers who died in vain, our brothers who have yet to be avenged..."

Gu Yun looked down at him, eyes cold as ice and just as unmoved. "Order all members of the Northern Camp to withdraw beyond the nine gates within the hour. If you are late by a second, I'll cut you down myself. Scram!"

"Marshal!"

"Get out!" The corner of Gu Yun's eye throbbed incessantly. Kicking Tan Hongfei away, he stepped forward, flipped up the hem of his robes, and knelt before the stone steps of the great hall. "Peace, Your Majesty. General Tan acquired injuries in his youth and has long suffered from bouts of insanity. He was instigated by malicious parties and must have been momentarily possessed, causing his illness to flare. On account of his many years of meritorious and tireless service, please spare this lunatic and send him home to recuperate."

Zhu Xiaojiao took the chance to whisper into Li Feng's ear. "Your Majesty, you see, the marshal is here too. You mustn't take any risks with your venerated body; why don't you step away and head inside for now?"

Li Feng laughed in fury and turned to look at Zhu Xiaojiao. When he spoke, his voice was frosty. "What, he's your 'marshal' now too?"

Zhu Xiaojiao's face went deathly pale, and he dropped to his knees with a thud.

Li Feng stood on the white marble steps with his hands behind his back, gazing down at the Marquis of Anding in his black-iron light pelt armor. He finally understood one thing: why it was that, before the late emperor passed, he had grabbed Li Feng's hand and exhorted him to beware a certain individual—not the ambitious Prince Wei, nor the covetous foreigners, but his very own right hand, Gu Yun.

An hour later, the Northern Camp had retreated beyond the nine gates. Including Tan Hongfei, nine senior officers involved in the incident were thrown behind bars, along with the Marquis of Anding.

At the same time, countless wooden birds rose from the hot spring villa in the northern outskirts. Light cavalrymen galloped along two different routes, each carrying a letter stamped with Gu Yun's personal seal. Dressed in civilian clothes, they rushed toward the northwest and the East Sea coast in Jiangnan, two vital regions along the border.

If Chang Geng had even one or two Black Hawks on hand, perhaps he would have stood a chance. But when the Longan Emperor confiscated Gu Yun's seal of command, he had sent every last one of his Black Iron Battalion soldiers back to the Northwest Garrison.

Once again, they were too late.

At the jewel that was the entrance to the Silk Road in the Western Regions, currently abloom with the beautiful flush of spring—

The flourishing scene of several months ago was no more. Every border pass was barred; the Black Iron Battalion stood by in full battle array, lethal black crows as far as the eye could see. He Ronghui was under orders to stand as acting commander of the three divisions, and the marching orders decree gathered dust on his desk.

It was a thickly overcast day, and black clouds loomed low over the city. Each nation's garrison had their gates sealed, and all was silent. It was as if this field of yellow sand was waiting for a single spark to set it aflame.

Perhaps General He was overthinking. He was struck with a sense of foreboding: something was about to happen.

A Black Hawk suddenly dropped from the sky. The man missed his footing on the landing and tumbled into the Western Regions' sandy dust. A Black Iron light pelt cavalryman who happened to be passing on patrol saw and hurried to investigate. That aerial assassin, lord of the skies, seemed to buckle under the weight of his Black Hawk armor. He knelt on the ground, clutching his comrade's hand in a vise grip. Beneath his visor, his youthful face was terrifyingly wan.

The captain of the patrol hurried over. "Didn't General He order you to the capital to inquire when the marshal would recover his seal of command? What is it? What exactly is going on?" he asked, rapid-fire.

The Black Hawk clenched his jaw; blood oozed from between his teeth. His handsome face twisted as he tugged the hawk armor off his body. Hoarsely, he said. "I need to speak with General He..."

With the Northern Camp incident barely ended and Tan Hongfei imprisoned, the Nine Gates Infantry Commander feared news of the Marquis of Anding's detainment would incite still greater turmoil. After taking over the Northern Camp's defensive duties, the first thing he did was send his men to seal every entrance to the capital and its surroundings. The Black Hawk sent by He Ronghui was still airborne when he was met with a volley of parhelion arrows. After a harrowing struggle to shake off the barrage, he landed in disguise and finally gleaned the shape of the situation from rumors bubbling among the common people.

Infuriated, the Black Hawk had turned around and winged straight back to the northwest, passing the light cavalryman Chang Geng had dispatched to He Ronghui on his way. A Black Hawk was much faster than a horse; he arrived at the Black Iron Battalion's garrison several days ahead of the rider.

The powder keg called He Ronghui exploded on the spot. That very night, he led his men to storm the Protectorate of the Northwest. At the same time, the sand tigers that had assembled in Qiuci slowly rolled out of their encampment and raised their heads, turning their pitch-black muzzles to the east.

Every party had done all that was humanly possible. The rest was up to fate.

How unfortunate that fate had utterly abandoned the House of Li, whose destined years were running out.

In the wastelands of the northern frontier, where a second chill had descended after a sudden warm spring—

The ridge of a winding mountain range curved in a gentle arc, and eager wildflowers pushed up wave upon wave of buds. A pack of gray wolves stood high on a hill. Hunting hawks screeched as they wheeled through the air, and a dusty, oil-stained flag whipped in the wind beside flapping animal skins. The endless sky was azure above, the vast earth was black and yellow below, and deep within the thick grasses stood an army of thousands.

Amid the cold iron and the roar of machinery, a voice was raised in a hoarse yet tender song.

"The purest spirit of the grasslands, even the heavenly winds seek to kiss the hem of her skirt. All living creatures sing along, all living creatures bow their heads, they kneel on the land where she sings and dances. These lands in the coming year will flock with cattle and sheep, they will flourish with lush vegetation, they will bloom with a carpet of flowers that stretches to the edge of the Mountains of Heaven. In the coming year, there shall be eternal sky and evergreen grass, wild hares shall creep out from their burrows, wild horses shall return—"

In the blink of an eye, it had already been five, nearly six, years. Jialai Yinghuo, the northern barbarian crown prince who, spurred by rage, had brashly launched a head-on attack on Yanhui Town, had now inherited the eighteen tribes and become the true Wolf King. The northwest winds beyond the pass had etched his face with lines deep as if cut by a blade, and thousands of days and nights had fallen like carving knives upon his visage, his very bones steeped in hatred and resentment.

Now the hair at his temples was streaked with white, and the murderous gleam in his eyes had been neatly stored away in his heart, not a hint discernible on his face. The expansive reaches of his song had also gathered dust. He only crooned a couple of verses—familiar lyrics from that familiar song—but his voice had already grown rough.

He raised the wine flask at his waist and swallowed a mouthful of unfiltered liquor from the lip, tasting rust. His eyes were turned to the sky, locked on a soaring figure approaching from a distance, and his face was tense. Flying wing to wing with the hunting hawks, the black figure swiftly closed in—it was a suit of hawk armor, larger than that of the Black Hawks and far more ferocious in appearance. The soldier careened in with a shrill screech, alighted before the Wolf King, and presented with both hands a small golden arrow fashioned of some unknown material.

Jialai Yinghuo picked up that small arrow and poured his wine over its surface. A line of text in the eighteen tribes' script gradually appeared on the once-glossy shaft. Those slender and arching characters spread beneath the strong liquor, forming words: *May the Wolf King take the first step.*

Jialai Yinghuo sucked in a breath. He once thought that when this day finally arrived, he would be overcome with a wild glee.

But it was not so. Only now did he discover that, after so many years, hatred had left him hollow. His chance to turn the tables was close at hand, but he had forgotten how to laugh with joy. The reigning Wolf King looked up at the boundless sky and was rendered dizzy by the light of the sun. It was as if the eyes of the dead in their countless pairs were staring straight at him.

"It's time," he murmured, and raised a hand. His army of thousands fell silent.

He swung his hand violently down.

The gray wolves howled at the skies. They charged down from the hills, turning their claws toward the south.

On the archipelagos of the south, where warm winds wailed through evergreen foliage—

A large ship, black from prow to stern, sailed into a tranquil, rough-hewn harbor. Before the ship was solidly moored, a crowd of warriors bearing armor and weapons had already opened the doors and poured from the cabin. The uninhabited little island was instantly awash with light. Row upon row of battle armor was arrayed amid the colossal rock formations like an ominous army of ghostly soldiers, visors sinister in the faint glow of fire. Amid the ranks of heavy armor, an enormous military map was displayed, delineating every last secret tunnel within the southern border's mountain ranges. The sixty-four Gu Yun had dug up were merely the tip of the iceberg.

Finally, in the once-peaceful East Sea—

Snakelike ninja and Dongying warriors wielding long sabers disguised themselves as coastal wokou pirates and furtively rowed across the ocean in tiny boats, undetected, communicating with each other using strange gestures. They streamed in from all directions and slowly gathered like teeming ants. The cargo ships that ordinarily flowed in and out like water slid out of Great Liang's harbor one by one, then silently turned toward the islands of Dongying.

A long and piercing blast from a steam whistle sounded over the boundless ocean, and the merchant ships gathered in neat formation, their movements orderly and severe. As they cleared the cruising range of the Jiangnan Navy, the ship at the head of the formation struck its merchant flag. In its place, the Western pope's austere and heavy battle flag ran up, towering above the ocean's surface and casting a long shadow in its wake.

The swapping of the flag was some sort of frightful cue: each of the enormous merchant ships began to disassemble themselves. Their outer layers, used to affect an illusion of peace, sloughed off into the sea, revealing row after row of pitch-black cannon muzzles beneath. These were dragon ships such as the world had never seen. They were small and peculiar in their construction; they could be wrapped in the shell of an ordinary merchant ship, but they sailed as fast as lightning and moved like sea monsters, leaving gales in their wake as they cut through the surf.

Signal flags conveyed orders, and this swarm of monsters dispersed. A giant black shadow rose inexorably from beneath the water.

A wave like a small mountain surged from the once-still surface of the sea. What emerged was an enormous beast, unparalleled in size. It broke the surface, revealing a grotesque head and countless suckers, to which thousands of armed and ready sea dragons and warships were attached. Vertical columns atop the great beast were filled with violet gold, and its thick iron shell yawned open with the turning of countless interlocked gears to reveal rows of cannons in every size, their gaping muzzles like so many malevolent eyes swiveling without pause.

This enormous sea monster could carry over a dozen of Great Liang's dragon ships on its deck.

The cabin door slowly swung open. An inky black staircase seemed to unfurl from nowhere like a great tongue, and two ranks of Western sailors in curious little hats walked out single file. A black umbrella opened from within the black doorway and lifted to block the seawater streaming down from above. A man ducked his head and stepped serenely into its shelter—he was none other than the white-haired Westerner whom Gu Yun had once encountered in the imperial palace.

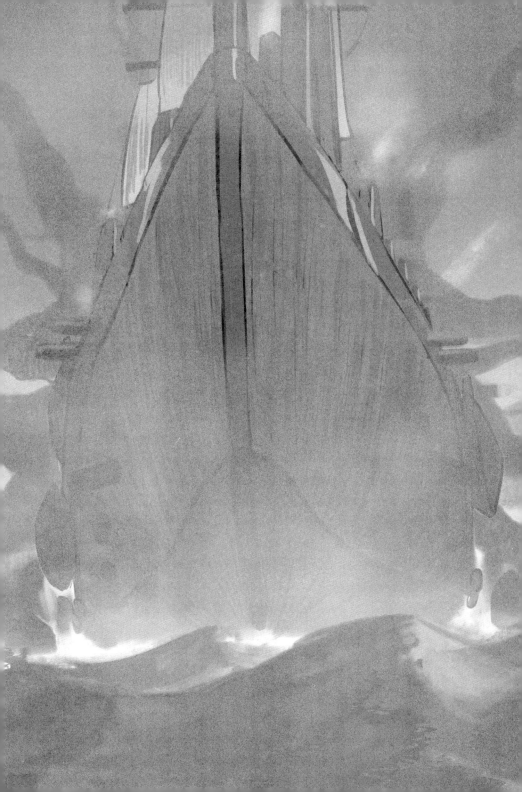

The figure holding the umbrella walked out a half-step behind. This was the very same "Mister Ja" who had hung the southern border's bandits out to dry all those months ago.

57

A NATION IN CRISIS

"Y OUR HOLINESS, our preparations are now complete." Mister Ja reached out to assist the white-haired man. This person who had visited Great Liang numerous times, claiming to be an envoy, was in truth the pope himself.

"Despite so many deviations from the plan along the way, with this result, your painstaking efforts have not been wasted here," said Mister Ja.

The pope stared at the malevolent swarm of sea beasts floating on the ocean's surface, face placid. He did not look pleased at the sight; rather, an indescribable trace of compassionate melancholy seemed to color his expression.

"It's early yet to discuss results," said the pope. "Fate is a mysterious thing. The fate of one person is already unpredictable—never mind that of a nation. This, perhaps, is something only God knows."

Mister Ja laughed. "Like when that idiot Jialai Yinghuo couldn't resist temptation and revealed the truth of that incident to Gu Yun ahead of schedule?"

Jialai Yinghuo hated Gu Yun, the last remaining member of the Gu family, too much. Other than this bit of hatred, he had practically nothing left in his life. He had long cast aside the dignity of the Wolf King and transformed into a mad dog with his sights locked only on his prize. In his eyes, so long as he could land a blow on Gu Yun, he cared not a whit whose plans he spoiled.

Unfortunately, they had no choice but to cooperate with this mad dog. The grudge between the eighteen tribes and the Central Plains, built up through generations of conflict, ran too deep, and the forces the goddess had buried within the capital city were too crucial to their plans.

"I truly admire Gu Yun," Mister Ja sighed. "If I were him, I might have done nothing—but he actually dealt with it in absolute secrecy. If he hadn't, the situation would have spiraled even further out of control when we exposed the truth today. Perhaps the regional garrisons would have already...what do they call it again? 'Rid the emperor of treacherous ministers'?"[28]

The pope chuckled. "The effect may not be ideal, but we've done all we can. The window of opportunity was brief, and we had little choice. Ja, every one of us is a trapped beast clawing toward survival. If we don't devour others, others will devour us. Countless pairs of eyes are watching the enormous, plump herbivore that is Great Liang. We *must* make the first move. Otherwise, in three to five years, we may no longer have the strength for this battle."

Mister Ja looked out over the boundless ocean. All within view was water, and sea and sky blurred into one. "Your Holiness," he asked, still confused, "if it is only an herbivore, why must we go to such effort to extract its claws and teeth?"

"Herbivore or carnivore isn't determined by the shape of its body or its teeth and claws," the pope muttered. "The question is whether it feels greed, whether its heart hungers to gnaw, tear, and devour... have you ever smelled this scent?"

---

28   "Ridding the emperor of treacherous ministers" was historically used as an excuse to stage a coup d'état.

Mister Ja started in surprise. Violet gold of sufficient purity was practically odorless when it burned; dogs and Gu Yun were probably the only ones who could detect it. "Your Holiness, do you mean... the scent of the ocean?" he ventured.

"It's a stench, child," the pope said quietly. "If the devil exists, then he is undoubtedly this tiny little ore. Since the day it broke through the earth, those violet flames have ignited this damned era. It has turned the children of God into the hearts of iron beasts."

But weren't the machines that burned violet gold created by humans? Mister Ja shrugged. He didn't reply, but neither did he quite take these words to heart.

The pope spoke no further. He merely lowered his head and kissed the ring on his hand, which was carved with the image of his staff. He spoke under his breath, murmuring a simple prayer.

"Forgive me," he whispered. "Please forgive me."

An azure blue signal flare rose from the dragon ship at the vanguard and shot into the sky. Its reflected fire seemed to burn in Mister Ja's eyes. He made a great effort to remain calm but could not completely suppress his surging excitement. "Your Holiness, it's beginning!"

It was the seventh year of Longan, the eighth day of the fourth month—and the third day after the Marquis of Anding, Gu Yun, had relocated from the hot spring villa to the imperial dungeons.

The imperial dungeons were dark and gloomy, but fortunately, the capital was quite warm, the chill of winter having retreated after the onset of spring. The hay piled inside Gu Yun's prison cell was softer than an army cot, so it was no trial to stay there for a few days. Gu Yun viewed it as a holiday. Unbroken silence ruled his surroundings; he didn't have so much as a single cellmate with whom he could chat and brag about his achievements, and the prison guards were iron puppets who obviously couldn't speak. This was the innermost chamber of the imperial dungeons—only members of the imperial family or their in-laws, high nobility, and eminent ministers and generals could enter. Someone like Tan Hongfei, the commander of the Northern Camp, hadn't even the right to be imprisoned there.

The last person who had been qualified to grace these cells with his presence was the emperor's own brother, Prince Wei. Gu Yun had the pleasure of being treated to his own private room, so alone he stayed.

Had there been someone with whom he could converse, he wouldn't have been able to hear them anyway—the medicine he had hastily taken before his departure had long worn off, and the moles at the corner of his eye and on his earlobe had faded to near invisibility. He hadn't brought his glass monocle either, so his vision was barely sufficient to count the fingers on his own hand. Even the footfalls of the iron puppets clanking in and out sounded muffled to his ears.

To pass the time, Gu Yun caught a little rat to keep as a pet. He fed it a few bites from each of his meals and played with it when he was bored.

Someone had dug up that incident on purpose. Gu Yun was well aware of this. Five years ago, when he had quietly looked into the matter, he had destroyed some of the most damning evidence—but he hadn't touched Wu He. First of all, the man was merely an old dog on his last legs, and second...perhaps Gu Yun wasn't entirely unselfish, and was reluctant to scrub every trace of the heartrending truth from this world.

Gu Yun had to admit this was a misstep on his part. If, back then, he had been even half so steady and astute as he was now, he would have understood that his choices were to either gather up the evidence, wait until the time was ripe, and present it all at once as he rebelled outright, or to steel his resolve and burn every last trace of it to ash, bury the past in the past, and never allow a hint of this matter to see the light of day again.

An absolute blunder. He had hesitated at a time when he should have been resolute.

The Yuanhe Emperor had been the same. If he hadn't been so indecisive, Gu Yun would have long passed from this world. That would have resulted in a different kind of peace.

As for what awaited in the aftermath of this incident, Gu Yun didn't know—nor did he know whether Chang Geng, a boy still wet behind the ears, really had the ability to reassure the nation's generals. But he was deep in the imperial dungeons; worrying about it would do no good. Gu Yun had little choice but to try to relax and conserve his energy.

The rat, meanwhile, discovered that this person had annoyingly mischievous hands. Unable to escape, it decided to play dead and ignore him henceforth. The little marquis, beloathed of all animals, could only go sit listlessly against the cell wall and meditate. In fact, he found this rat's attitude rather like Chang Geng's when he was younger.

As his mind wandered toward Chang Geng, Gu Yun couldn't resist heaving a sigh. "With the way he is now, I think I preferred it when he was little and always acted like I was getting on his nerves," he lamented to the rat.

The rat showed him its round little rump.

Gu Yun sucked in a deep breath and shoved this momentary distraction from his mind. Uncaring of the filth, he dragged the

moldering blanket from the hay pile and draped it over himself, then leaned back to rest his eyes. He would need all his strength to face the difficulties to come.

No clamor in the world could be loud enough to disturb a half-deaf man in the depths of the imperial dungeons, and Gu Yun soon fell asleep. Wreathed in the gloomy scent of mildew, he had a dream:

Gu Yun dreamed that he was lying beneath a giant guillotine. The thousand-kilogram blade pressed into his chest, biting into flesh and sinking into bone bit by bit as it cut him in two. He lost all connection with his body and limbs; only the wound on his chest was left, burning with pain down to his core. His ears echoed with a cacophony of sounds: sobs, cannon fire, wails, and, nearly inaudible, the halting and dissonant trill of a barbarian flute...he was split open by that heavy blade, but no blood seeped from the wound. Instead, a signal arrow tumbled out and screeched into the sky, shaking the earth with the force of its explosion.

Gu Yun started awake with a muffled groan. The old wound across his chest ached without reason, and the piercing shriek of the signal arrow in his dream echoed in his ears, stretching into a peculiar ringing hum.

Perhaps he indeed had some mysterious connection with his Black Iron Battalion. For that very night, from within the Silk Road garrison in the Western Regions, the first ominous signal arrow burst into a vibrant explosion in the night sky.

The emergency dispatch didn't reach the capital until the next day. The Black Hawk bearing the message arrived with only one leg remaining. He had endured, on his last breath, in order to reach the anxiety-stricken Northern Camp, but failed to utter a single word before he died, perishing almost the instant he landed.

Four hours later, news of an attack on the Black Iron Battalion in the Western Regions shook the court and commons.

Several days ago, when news of the incident in the capital had leaked, He Ronghui had rallied his men to surround the Protectorate of the Northwest. No one expected that the instant he left the garrison, Qiuci would strike: one hundred and sixty sand tigers blasted through the Black Steeds encamped at the entrance to the Western Regions. War chariots like sand tigers were the greatest nemesis of the light-pelt armored cavalry. For a terrible moment, smoke and dust billowed through the air, lit by a veritable curtain of fire. Warhorses died with drawn-out screams, and armored cavalrymen fell in swathes.

But the Black Iron Battalion was still the Black Iron Battalion. After a brief interval of disordered scrambling, they swiftly found their bearings. Black Carapaces pushed the enemy back without the slightest hesitation, and once He Ronghui got the news, he immediately led the Black Hawk Division back the way they came and decisively cut off the sand tigers' supply lines from the air. Such giant war chariots burned enormous quantities of violet gold; with their supply lines cut, they became no more than piles of scrap metal.

But this initial wave of sand tigers was no empty threat. Behind them was everyone's worst nightmare come true: an army tens of thousands strong, brandishing their banners toward the sky.

Coming from their various garrisons, the Far Westerners, the kingdoms of the Western Regions that had once rebelled, and even the Sindhu people who had long taken advantage of regional turmoil to skim off the top...the numbers were even greater than imagined. They may have been a motley horde, but they were a horde nevertheless. With sand tigers on the enemy's side, the Black Iron Battalion had no choice but to face them head-on with heavy armor. Victory soon became a matter of who had the larger stockpiles of violet gold.

He Ronghui authorized the emergency use of the Western Regions Camp's violet gold stores, but upon opening them, he stood in shock: the stores were already depleted. When the Longan Emperor cracked down on violet gold smuggling, Gu Yun had been forced to pause his own secret operations; in the meantime, the amount of violet gold allocated to the Black Iron Battalion by the court was only enough to sustain regular patrols. It couldn't possibly see them through a sudden outbreak of war.

He Ronghui sent his men to procure more, but they encountered yet more obstacles on their way. News of the Marquis of Anding's imprisonment had spread throughout the nation, but no one knew the details of the situation. Times were uncertain and all sorts of rumors were in circulation. Who would be brave enough to supply violet gold to the Black Iron Battalion without a marching orders decree? What if their next step was to slay their way to the capital and start a rebellion?

He Ronghui had no choice but to send Black Hawks to the capital while requesting backup from their closest allies in the Northern Border Defense Corps. But before the messengers could depart, the eighteen tribes launched a surprise attack from beyond the pass. The news that the Wolf King Jialai Yinghuo was personally leading an expedition south crashed down on the nation with a resounding bang.

After five years of peace, the situation beyond the iron wall had undergone a complete transformation.

Jialai Yinghuo had assembled an army of tens of thousands of elite soldiers, almost a thousand suits of heavy armor, and an unstoppable new hawk armor that was larger and more lethal than Black Hawks. This great beast opened its maw and tore into the northern border defenses of Great Liang, which were stretched thin over a vast length of thousands of kilometers.

The northwest descended into chaos. Without orders from the Marquis of Anding, their commander in chief, the Black Iron Battalion wouldn't dare retreat a single step, even if they were down to the last man. He Ronghui held the line for three bitter days and two nights, emptying their munitions, as the miraculous army forged over three generations was bled of almost half its men.

It was then that Chang Geng's messenger arrived at last.

With Gu Yun's personal seal in hand, this mysterious commandery prince far off in the capital city had mimicked Gu Yun's handwriting with flawless perfection. He gave the messenger two letters—if all was well on the border, the man was to deliver the first letter. The contents would order He Ronghui to ignore matters of the court, fill the violet gold stores in the Western Regions to full capacity immediately and by any means necessary—whether from the black market or elsewhere—tune up the garrison's armor, and be prepared for battle at any second.

If fighting had already broken out on the border, the messenger was to deliver the second letter. The contents therein would instruct He Ronghui to avoid fighting to the death or drawing out the engagement, and to retreat to Jiayu Pass some hundred kilometers to the east at full speed and await reinforcements.

Their hidden enemies had already made their move. It was undoubtedly too late to initiate an attack now—Chang Geng had no Black Hawks, and there were an extremely limited number of people whom he could contact using the Linyuan Pavilion's wooden birds. Whether the sky should fall or the earth should collapse, it was unlikely that his messenger could arrive in time to stop it. Thus, he thought of the worst-case scenario and focused his efforts on repairing the pen after the sheep had escaped in hopes of preserving the rest of the flock.

If fighting broke out in the Western Regions, it was unlikely the northern border would escape unscathed. Thus, while the Black Iron Battalion retreated to focus on defense, General Cai Bin received yet another letter from Chang Geng asking that he send reinforcements north and transport as much of the violet gold stored by his enormous army as he could to Jiayu Pass and thereby resolve their most pressing emergency.

Chang Geng was well aware that if the worst were to happen, these few strategic moves were far from enough.

He had no influence over the vast mountain ranges of the southwest. Shen Yi was there, but Shen Yi was a commander who had practically dropped from the sky with no connections or support to speak of. There was no way he could mobilize the army without a marching orders decree. Meanwhile, the Jiangnan Navy operating along the coast of the East Sea was even more of a headache: Zhao Youfang was Li Feng's man and would never respond to the summons of Gu Yun's personal seal. Furthermore...Chang Geng had a certain premonition that even if he managed to run himself ragged putting out fires everywhere else, a fatal blow was lurking within the vast expanses of the East Sea.

The grievous news carried by the Black Hawk confirmed his worst suspicions. Chang Geng took a deep breath, released the last wooden bird, and turned to Huo Dan, who had developed a bloody blister at the corner of his mouth from stress. "Prepare the horses. I'm going to the imperial palace."

Chang Geng was stopped by Liao Ran right at the palace gates. The monk was dusty and travel-worn, but his visage exhibited his usual unruffled calm, as if even the most urgent emergency would melt within the neat rows of his incense scars.[29]

Liao Ran pressed his hands together and bowed in greeting, then signed, "Amitabha Buddha, Your Highness..."

Chang Geng interrupted him, his voice indifferent. "Great Master, say no more. I'm going to plead on another's behalf, not force the emperor's abdication."

Liao Ran's expression shifted slightly. "This humble monk trusts that Your Highness knows what lines should not be crossed."

"It's not that I wouldn't cross the line." The silver-tongued fourth prince tore off his refined mask and spoke bluntly for once. "The Qinling mountain range splits the nation north and south; the territories of the southeast and southwest are not under our control. Even if I cut Li Feng down where he stood, I would be unable to ameliorate this crisis. On top of that, there is no one who can ascend the throne. The eldest prince is nine years old, and the crown prince is younger still. The empress is a beautiful but useless invalid, and Zixi has no rightful claim. As for me..." He scoffed. "I am the son of a barbarian enchantress."

Liao Ran looked at him, worry written plainly on his face.

"Great Master, fret not; I was always a poisonous creature. If I was the slightest bit more capricious, I would in all likelihood have already brought disaster upon the nation and its people. But I haven't done anything at all yet, have I?" Chang Geng's expression smoothed, returning to its usual placidity. "Now isn't the time to speak of such things. Foreign enemies breach our borders as we speak, and theirs must be a plan long in the making. This isn't over yet. However—they reacted far too quickly. I suspect that someone

---

29 香疤, xiangba, or incense scars, are ritual burn scars received by Buddhist monks as an ordination practice. The ritual involves burning incense atop the head to create the burn scars, which motivates the name.

in the palace...perhaps even someone attending Li Feng himself, has been liaising with our enemies. Does the Linyuan Pavilion have anyone we can call upon in the palace?"

Liao Ran's expression became grave. He signed, "Your Highness means..."

"This involves an old case from twenty years ago and is most certainly connected to the northern barbarians. Investigate everyone the two barbarian women had contact with inside the palace—every single person. The barbarian shamaness was a skilled wielder of poisons and had countless tricks up her sleeve. Leave no stone unturned."

His voice was perfectly steady as he spoke of these "two barbarian women," as if they had nothing to do with him.

"I should have found it strange a long time ago," Chang Geng said quietly. "There must have been an extraordinary reason for Li Feng to so easily allow a tiger like Jialai Yinghuo to return to his lair. Unfortunately..."

Unfortunately, he had been too young, and his fist-sized heart could then only hold a handful of youthful worries about leaving his home behind.

"If I were born ten years earlier..." Chang Geng suddenly began.

Liao Ran's eyelid twitched.

Chang Geng continued, word by word, "This world would not be as we see today."

Nor would he have ever let go of Gu Yun.

"Zixi once said that our dragon warships are ten years behind our other military branches. I worry that war will break out in the East Sea. General Zhao is talented enough to build on the accomplishments of his predecessors, but he may not be capable of overseeing a great battle," Chang Geng explained briskly. "I have already written a letter to Shifu. The Linyuan Pavilion's roots in Jiangnan run deep;

Great Master, please take care of things on that end. I'll be taking my leave." With that, he urged his horse forward and disappeared into the palace grounds.

A rare frown creased Liao Ran's brow. For some reason, hearing that *Zixi* from Chang Geng made his heart pound in terror. But there were more pressing matters at hand, and it wasn't the time to make a fuss over a simple name. The monk draped a rough linen robe over himself and melted into the light of dawn, racing off into the distance.

The moment Chang Geng stepped into the palace, he was met with a flurry of bad news. Reports from the front lines, each more urgent than the last, caught the Longan Emperor and the officials of the court utterly unprepared—

The Black Iron Battalion had retreated to Jiayu Pass.

The northern border had lost seven cities overnight…before Cai Bin's reinforcements could even set foot on the scene.

As if the angry mobs on the southern border had been waiting for this day, they had coordinated with roving foreign bandits, who had appeared out of nowhere, and blown up the Southwest Supply Depot…

"Report—"

Everyone in the great hall turned toward the door, faces ashen. Li Feng hadn't even had the chance to allow Chang Geng to make his formal greeting.

"Urgent report, Your Majesty: a Far Western navy a hundred thousand strong has invaded from the Dongying archipelago—"

Li Feng's eyes nearly popped out of his head with fury. "Where is Zhao Youfang?"

The messenger knocked his head against the floor. He spoke, voice choking with sobs. "General Zhao has given his life for the nation."

58

A BLADE SUSPENDED

I FENG SWAYED where he stood. Chang Geng watched expressionlessly as the emperor collapsed back onto the throne in his magnificent palace—yet from some part of his mind outside his rational control, a sudden wave of malicious glee rose within him. Of course, he was extremely disciplined and allowed it to persist for no more than a split second; he discreetly pinched himself on the palm and shoved that burst of bloodthirsty elation back down. He knew it was the wu'ergu's meddling and not his true feelings.

"Take care, Your Majesty," Chang Geng said, not entirely sincerely.

Now that Prince Yanbei had spoken, the dumbstruck officials in the great hall came to their senses and echoed, "Take care, Your Majesty."

Li Feng's gaze slowly shifted to consider Chang Geng. Nominally, Chang Geng was his only remaining brother, but Li Feng rarely took notice of him. Though His Highness the Fourth Prince Li Min had received his title of nobility and started attending court, he rarely spoke up during court sessions, nor did he go out of his way to establish connections with other officials. He didn't even avail himself of Gu Yun's influence to converse with the military generals, and only occasionally made idle conversation about classic literature with a few poor and humble Hanlin scholars.

Chang Geng seemed not to notice the emperor's attention as he continued steadily, "Since General Zhao has given his life for the nation, we are now defenseless along the East Sea. If the Westerners turn their ships north, they'll be upon Dagu Harbor in an instant. Now that the situation has deteriorated to this point, it is too late for mere commentary to turn the tide. Your Majesty, please put aside distractions and make a decision on this matter with all haste."

Naturally Li Feng was aware of this; but with his mind an awful mess, he couldn't get a word out of his mouth.

At this point, Imperial Uncle Wang, who had been so thoroughly disgraced by the rampant rumors, snuck a glance at the emperor's expression, then plucked up his courage to offer a suggestion. "Your Majesty, the only troops available to us in the area around the capital are those in the Northern Camp. We are surrounded by boundless inland plains easily traversed on horseback. If we make our stand here, our military forces will no doubt be insufficient. Moreover, the case of Tan Hongfei's rebellion remains open, and the Northern Camp has no leadership to speak of. If even the dragon navy in Jiangnan has been wiped out, is the disordered Northern Camp up to the task? Who has the capability to protect the safety of the Imperial City? When it comes to our best way forward, why not...um..."

Wang Guo trailed off as every general in the great hall nailed their gazes into him like a volley of parhelion arrows. This old bastard hadn't even finished wiping his own ass—how dare he have the nerve to urge the emperor to move the capital at the slightest whiff of trouble. If not for the fact that they were at present plagued by threats both within and without, everyone in the room probably would have wanted to chop him up and eat him.

Wang Guo gulped, defeated, then bent over in a bow and did not straighten up again.

Li Feng's expression went gloomy and unreadable. After a few beats of silence, he ignored Imperial Uncle Wang and spoke. "Restore Tan Hongfei to his position and give him a chance to redeem himself with meritorious service... We summoned you here to discuss business. Anyone who spouts any more bullshit can fuck off!"

In his rage, a street curse slipped from the emperor's mouth. The great hall went wholly silent, and Wang Guo's face flashed red and pale in turns.

Li Feng turned irritably toward the Minister of War. "My dear subject Hu, you oversee the Ministry of War and wield authority over the Marching Orders Decree. What are your thoughts?"

The Minister of War was born with a sickly, greenish complexion and a long face. His name, Hu Guang, was pronounced somewhat like hugua, or calabash gourd. Thus people called him "Minister Calabash" in private. Upon hearing Li Feng call on him, Minister Calabash strained his mind so hard, bumps appeared all over his face and turned him into a bitter gourd. In theory, marching orders decrees were issued by the Ministry of War, but did they dare hand them out left and right? In practice, he was but a brush in the emperor's hand. Since when did a brush have the audacity to harbor its own opinions?

Hu Guang wiped at the sweat on his brow and began diffidently, "Um...Your Majesty is quite correct. The capital is the foundation of the fate of our Great Liang; it is the guiding light upon which all the people of the nation gaze. How can we allow those hairy foreigners to barge in at will? Absurd! So long as one soldier remains, we must fight to the bitter end. If we sound the drums of retreat now, would the hearts of our soldiers not falter?"

Li Feng had no patience for his prattle and cut him off there. "I'm asking you to give us a battle plan!"

Hu Guang fell silent.

Everyone had glowered at Wang Guo, but Wang Guo was right. If the commander in chief of the Jiangnan Navy had already given his life for the nation, who would direct the battle along the coast of the East Sea? With their dragon navy scattered, how would they deploy troops? If the Westerners turned their sights on the north, how many rounds of cannon fire could the Northern Camp and the Imperial Guard repel?

On some level, Wang Guo could be considered courageous. At the very least, he had spoken a truth no one else dared voice. Hu Guang was rapidly turning into a rotten bitter gourd as sweat rolled down his face like rancid fluid leaking from spoiled produce.

It was then that Chang Geng stepped forward. "Your Majesty, may I speak?" asked the youthful Prince Yanbei.

Hu Guang cast Chang Geng a look of gratitude. Chang Geng offered him an elegant smile, and his tone softened slightly. "Your Majesty, spilt water cannot be recovered, and the dead cannot return to life. The sorry state of our four borders is established fact, and arguments and anger will do nothing to change our circumstances. Instead of sowing chaos within our own house, we ought to consider which of our weaknesses can yet be addressed."

This young man must have spent too long a time in the company of monks; not a trace of earthly mundanity lingered in his aura. He stood at the front of the hall like a jade tree in the wind, emanating a steady calm that could soothe a person down to the bone. Just the sight of him was enough to snuff out any roaring flame of fury.

Li Feng sighed quietly and waved for him to continue. "Speak."

"Fires blaze at all four corners of our nation. Our military forces have already mobilized but have yet to be properly provisioned. To avoid further delay in supplying our troops, this subject requests

Your Majesty open the national treasury and distribute all the violet gold therein. This is my first request."

"That's right, you've reminded us." Li Feng turned to the representatives of the Ministry of Revenue. "Give the orders to do as he says."

"Your Majesty," Chang Geng continued, unhurried, "This subject said to distribute *all* of it—this is a national emergency, and the Marching Orders Decree has become a hindrance, shackling our generals' claws and teeth. Does Your Majesty truly wish to order them to the battlefield in chains?"

If anyone else had uttered these words, it would have been a profound offense. But for some reason, it was impossible to grow angry when they came from Prince Yanbei's mouth.

Hu Guang, who had been abandoned to the side, hastened to add, "This subject agrees."

Before Li Feng could agree or dissent, the Ministry of Revenue exploded. The Assistant Minister of Revenue called out, "Your Majesty, you mustn't! Distributing violet gold now will indeed address the most urgent of our problems—but if you'll permit this subject to speak an unpleasant truth, if we get through today, what will we do in the future? Eat next year's food?"

Han Qi, the captain of the Imperial Guard, likely very much wanted to twist off the assistant minister's head so he could dump out the cotton wool inside. He shot back, "The bandits are at our doorstep, yet you ministers are still fiddling with your abacuses, wondering how we'll make a living. This lowly general has truly seen something novel today. Your Majesty, if we don't address our most pressing issue now, what *future* will there be to speak of? If enemies hem us in on all sides, even digging up every centimeter of the meager violet gold veins within our borders won't be enough for our needs!"

As if afraid he wouldn't get a chance to talk, Hu Guang cut in once again, face flushed and neck bulging with fury. "This subject agrees!"

Chang Geng hadn't yet said a word about how to fend off their enemies, and already he had incited a fierce quarrel. He, however, spoke no further, but stood patiently to the side and waited for their argument to reach a conclusion.

Li Feng's head was about to crack open. He suddenly felt that all the so-called pillars of his court were entirely fixated on the tiny patches of grass in their own backyards, and that the long-term pictures they were considering, when pieced together, created a tableau smaller than the size of a bowl. If their squabbling grew any more heated, he might as well send them to the imperial kitchens and dispense with the stoves—maybe there they could fry up an impressive table of dazzling new dishes from a hitherto unknown cuisine.

"Enough!" Li Feng roared.

Everyone in the hall fell silent—other than Chang Geng, who now slipped back in to continue his speech. "This subject is not finished. My second request is that Your Majesty be prepared to order a retreat."

At this, the officials exploded once more. Even the Son of Heaven's rage couldn't stop this pot from boiling over, and some of the older ministers looked to be on the verge of bashing their heads into the pillars to demonstrate their resolve.

The corner of Li Feng's eye twitched. Fury surged up into his throat, and he barely managed to suppress it in time to avoid lashing out at Chang Geng. He grimaced like he was choking on his anger and issued a soft warning. "A-Min, there are certain things you should not say without thought. Our ancestors did not pass the nation into our hands to have us cede territory to tigers' jaws."

Chang Geng's composure didn't flicker a mote. "This subject asks Your Majesty to feel the fullness of his own purse. Even if we exhaust the strength of our nation, how large a territory can our court support? This is not a ceding of our land to tigers' jaws, but a brave warrior severing his own hand at the wrist to avoid dying from snake venom. If we are not decisive, if we do not make this sacrifice of our own volition, we will be forced to make it when the venom has sunk to the marrow and the nation has been overtaken by the Westerners."

His voice, which was as serene as if he were merely reciting *The Analects*, was like a merciless bowl of ice water dumped over Li Feng's head.

Chang Geng didn't look up to read the emperor's expression. He pressed on, "As for my third request, Imperial Uncle Wang is correct. The northwest is under the aegis of the Black Iron Battalion; even if their losses are heavy, they will hold. The most urgent front is the coast of the East Sea. Once the Westerners advance north, they will meet the Northern Camp, whose battle capabilities are cause for concern. All possible reinforcements, near and far, are tied up elsewhere, and may not arrive in time. Your Majesty, what are your plans when that time comes?"

These words aged Li Feng ten years in an instant. He sat slumped in defeat for a long interval before he finally spoke again. "We proclaim an imperial edict... Bring Uncle to us."

Chang Geng didn't so much as blink at this edict. He showed neither joy nor resentment, as if this was both wholly expected and well within reason. Afraid to even breathe too loud, Zhu Xiaojiao accepted the edict and turned to leave when Chang Geng spoke up again with a reminder. "Your Majesty, isn't it rather belittling to have Zhu-gonggong declare an imperial edict to summon a prisoner from the imperial dungeons without an official of the court present?"

He had begun to distrust every one of Li Feng's attendants out of instinct—including this person who had nominally been helping Gu Yun from the shadows all this time.

Li Feng was exhausted. "What times are these for you to care so much for hollow rules of etiquette? My dear subject Jiang, please make the trip on our behalf."

Zhu Xiaojiao tottered after Jiang Chong on tiny steps. He unconsciously snuck a glance back at Chang Geng from afar. The eunuch was a veteran of the palace and was familiar with every noble and minister active in Great Liang's court. This Prince Yanbei was the lone exception. Gu Yun had kept him sealed up tight in the Marquis Estate since youth, and after he grew up, he ignored his proper duties to travel all over the nation and rarely showed his face. He stood amid the crowd to attend court and listen to the proceedings, but rarely entered the palace on his own. He only accompanied Gu Yun to pay his respects during the year-end holidays...no one knew anything about him.

They knew nothing about him—and thus he was an unknown variable.

Jiang Chong and Zhu Xiaojiao exited the palace and rode for the imperial dungeons with all speed. Just as they were practically upon them, Zhu Xiaojiao had a sudden thought and spoke up in his pinched voice. "Wait, Justice Jiang, how improper would it be for the marquis to have an audience with the emperor in a prisoner's uniform? Why don't I send someone to look through the newly made court uniforms for marquises of the first rank and bring one over?"

Jiang Chong's mind was filled with grief and indignation for the catastrophes devastating his nation. When his soul was summoned back to his body by the old eunuch's words, he was so flabbergasted he didn't know whether to laugh or cry. "Zhu-gonggong, you're still worrying about such trifles at a time like this? I..."

Before he could finish, he spied a rider galloping in their direction. The newcomer soon arrived before them and dismounted to offer a formal salute to a superior—it was the captain of the Marquis Estate's guard, Huo Dan. Huo Dan quickly cupped his fist in his hand. "Justice Jiang, Zhu-gonggong, I am a servant of the Marquis of Anding's estate. Our prince ordered me to bring these for the marquis."

He offered up a set of court robes and armor with both hands.

Jiang Chong's heart stirred. Prince Yanbei was clearly a meticulous person—but what reason was there for him to mind the fine details to this extent?

Whom was this prince guarding against?

In the imperial dungeons, Gu Yun was dangling that plump rat by the tail out of sheer boredom, making it swing around in midair. Sensing a shift in the flow of air behind him, he turned, a bit shocked, and saw the vague silhouettes of three people charge in from outside. The first person swept forward like the wind and seemed to be wearing court robes. Seconds later, the lock on the cell door swung open, and the unique scent of court incense entered Gu Yun's nose along with a hint of Li Feng's personal sandalwood fragrance.

Squinting, Gu Yun managed to recognize the thick-waisted man as Zhu Xiaojiao. If these people were here to interrogate him, there was no reason to send Zhu Xiaojiao. But Li Feng wasn't the type to make a fool of himself by declaring two contradictory edicts in such quick succession, locking Gu Yun up only to let him go the next moment. In that case, the only remaining possibility...

The smile slid off Gu Yun's face. *What now?*

Jiang Chong uttered a stream of rapid syllables. Gu Yun could barely hear him, and only vaguely caught the words "Enemy invasion...Zhao..." and nothing else. Hopelessly confused, he could only affect a visage of impenetrable calm and nod, the picture of an immovable object meeting an unstoppable force. Infected by his stoic mien, Jiang Chong was at once greatly reassured. His emotions that had swung drastically between anxiety and sorrow finally settled back within his stomach, and he well-nigh burst into tears on the spot. "Having a pillar like the marquis is truly a blessing upon Great Liang and its people."

Gu Yun was baffled. *Shit, what's he saying now?*

But on the surface, he only gave Justice Jiang a brief pat on the shoulder and a terse instruction: "Lead the way."

Fortunately, at this point, Huo Dan stepped forward. As he presented Gu Yun with his court robes, he retrieved a wine flask from his hip. "His Highness requested I bring this to my lord to relieve the chill."

Gu Yun opened the lid; one sniff was all he needed to tell it was medicine. He exhaled a sigh of relief, as if an enormous weight had been lifted from his shoulders, and drained the flask in a single draft.

With Huo Dan's help, he changed with great efficiency. At least now he looked more or less presentable. Their party raced straight to the palace. The deaf-blind Marquis of Anding fumbled his way along in their midst, wishing more than ever that the medicine would take effect quickly. Gu Yun's hearing finally began to improve with needle-like stabs of pain as they reached the palace walls.

He gave Huo Dan a discreet hand signal. Immediately taking his meaning, Huo Dan stepped forward, leaned into his ear, and repeated every word Jiang Chong had said to him in the imperial dungeons.

As Gu Yun listened to his account, something seemed to snap inside his head, which was already close to bursting with headache. An explosion of golden sparks swirled before his eyes, and he stumbled before Huo Dan caught him by the arm. "Sir!"

Jiang Chong jumped in alarm. The Marquis of Anding had been a model of near inhuman calm moments ago—what had happened? Seeing Gu Yun as pale as the dead, he asked anxiously, "My lord, what's wrong?"

"The Black Iron Battalion suffered casualties of more than half their number...Passes along the northern border fell into enemy hands in quick succession...General Zhao has given his life for the nation...The Southwest Supply Depot was bombed..." Each of these brief reports became a lethal blade that twisted its way into Gu Yun's flesh and bone. Pain pierced his chest, and the taste of iron flooded his throat.

Veins popped from Gu Yun's forehead and sweat trickled down his temples; his eyes seemed to lose focus. Jiang Chong knew no one would dare torture the Marquis of Anding even if he were in the imperial dungeons, but he was still profoundly frightened. "What's wrong with the marquis? Should I summon a sedan? The imperial doctors?"

Gu Yun's body swayed slightly.

"My lord, the safety of Great Liang rests on your shoulders. We can't afford to lose you now!" Jiang Chong cried out.

His words were like a crack of thunder in Gu Yun's ear. The scattered pieces of his soul shuddered, then wrenched themselves back into that extraordinarily resilient iron spine. Gu Yun closed his eyes and determinedly swallowed a mouthful of blood. After a beat, he laughed hoarsely under Jiang Chong's trepidatious gaze as if nothing were wrong. "I haven't seen the sun in a few days, so I have a slight headache—it's no matter, a long-standing affliction."

As Gu Yun spoke, he bowed his head and straightened the light armor on his body. He tugged his arm out of Huo Dan's grasp and tossed him the gray rat that had been curled in his palm since they left the prison. "This is my rat brother and closest confidante. Get him something to eat; don't let him starve."

With that, he turned and strode into the palace.

In the great audience hall, those few words from Chang Geng had sparked a verbal brawl. But when Zhu Xiaojiao's ringing voice called out the words, "The Marquis of Anding has arrived at the palace for an audience with the emperor," everyone held their fire, and a deathly silence settled over the hall.

As soon as Gu Yun lifted his head, he met Chang Geng's gaze. They locked eyes only briefly before glancing away, but Gu Yun did not miss the storm of unspeakable words swirling in Chang Geng's eyes.

Gu Yun stepped forward to bow in greeting to the emperor as if they were the only two in the room, so indifferent he might have just woken from a nap in the Marquis Estate rather than been pulled from the imperial dungeons.

Li Feng at once declared an end to the court session and kicked out every mouthy debater and useless sponge, leaving only Gu Yun, Chang Geng, and the senior military officials to discuss adjustments to the capital city's defenses through the night. Master Fenghan, who had been reflecting on his behavior at home, was called forth from his hermitage once again, and the Lingshu Institute was soon awash in lamplight, working overtime to tune up every piece of the capital's available equipment.

Li Feng, dark smudges beneath his eyes, kept them hopping for a whole day and night, all through the fourth night watch[30] until the sky began to pale along the horizon.

---

30   The fourth night watch period (of a total of five) is from 1:00 to 3:00 a.m.

On their way out, Li Feng called for Gu Yun alone to stay behind.

All others had been dismissed from the great hall, leaving only one lord and one subject, face to face. Li Feng was silent for a long while, until the palace lamps sensed the sunlight and extinguished themselves with a *click*, startling him back to his senses. He regarded Gu Yun with a complicated expression, then said vaguely, "Uncle has suffered a grievance."

Gu Yun had a bellyful of well-worn niceties that he could spout without a second thought. "Furious thunder and gentle rain are both an honor coming from my sovereign," "There is no reason to feel aggrieved over dying for the nation," and other nonsense of that type had already strung itself seamlessly together beneath his silver tongue.

But all of a sudden, it was as if that silver tongue had rusted over; no matter how he tried, he couldn't utter a word. He could only smile in the Longan Emperor's direction.

It was a peculiarly stiff smile, a bit awkward in its presentation.

The two of them really had nothing to say to each other. Li Feng sighed and waved him off.

Head bowed deferentially, Gu Yun took his leave.

59

ENTERING BATTLE

WHEN GU YUN exited the great hall, his vision was beginning to blur. He let nothing of it show as he stood and gasped in a few breaths. For the first time in his life, he felt crushed under the weight of the paltry few dozen kilograms of light armor he wore.

In times of emergency, a person's latent potential seemed infinite. In the palace, Gu Yun had worked straight through the headache that was usually unbearable even with acupuncture and a bed to lie on for an entire day and night without thinking twice. But as soon as he stepped outside, he discovered that his body was on the verge of collapse, his clothes practically plastered to his skin. The faint breeze carried a trace of morning dew, and he shivered with cold as it blew past, his head spinning.

Earlier there had been a glimmer of sunlight, but dark clouds had covered it in the blink of an eye, leaving the dawn weak and pale.

Chang Geng was waiting for him at the door, facing away from the endless layers of the palace, laid out building upon building like the realm of immortals. The hem of Prince Yanbei's court robes fluttered in the wind as he stared in the direction of Kite's Flight Pavilion, lost in thought. Chang Geng only turned when he heard the pad of footsteps behind him. As soon as he saw Gu Yun's complexion, he frowned. "The carriage is waiting outside; you can rest on the way."

Deeply exhausted in both body and mind, Gu Yun mumbled a thoughtless hum of assent.

"What did that guy keep you behind to discuss?"

"Idle chatter...nonsense," Gu Yun replied woodenly.

Chang Geng saw he hadn't the energy to talk, so he held his tongue the whole way back to the Marquis Estate. Countless arrow tokens of command had been distributed that morning, and all Six Ministries would have to dance to their tune. They both understood this might be their only opportunity to rest for some time.

Gu Yun's knees went weak the instant he stepped into his room, and he stumbled over to collapse on his couch. He had yet to remove his armor, and as he crashed down with a *clang*, half of his body went numb and the ceiling spun above his head. Gu Yun suspected he might never be able to get up again.

Chang Geng pressed his fingers to Gu Yun's wrist and took his pulse. Those hands which had been icy cold some minutes ago were now frightfully hot, as if they had been freshly fished from a brazier. "Yifu, when did you get a fever?"

Gu Yun let out a quiet groan. Aches seeped from every joint, and his eyelids were so heavy he could no longer lift them. He struggled to find his voice. "Is my little brother still in good health?"

"...Who?" asked Chang Geng.

Huo Dan, who was following them closely, made a prompt sound of assent and produced that little gray rat, which was indeed still alive and kicking. "Sir, he's doing perfectly well."

"Then I should be fine too," said Gu Yun, lethargic with illness, and lurched back to his feet under the power of his own strength. He allowed those around him to remove his armor in a flurry of limbs, then roughly swept his sweat-soaked hair out of his face.

"I either have a cold or an excess of internal heat; it'll pass. I only need to take some medicine and sweat it out."

Huo Dan stood to the side in befuddlement, unsure when his marquis had tied his life to that of a common gray rat. Chang Geng, however, understood at once, and his gaze flickered slightly. He pressed Gu Yun down on the couch to stop his fidgeting. "Leave it to me."

Chang Geng dismissed Huo Dan and personally peeled Gu Yun out of his clothes, which were so wet one could wring water from them. Gu Yun's entire body was limp, and simply opening his eyes made him dizzy, so he could do nothing but keep them closed, slump over, and let Chang Geng manhandle him as he pleased. Gu Yun's breathing was unusually fast, and for some reason, he looked rather frail. Once his outer and middle layers had been removed, Chang Geng's hands inadvertently trembled. Gu Yun's thin inner robe was soaked through with sweat; it concealed about as much of what lay beneath as a layer of garlic skin. Just enough of his chest and waistline showed through that it would have been less suggestive had he been completely naked. Somehow, Chang Geng found this sight even more lethal than the time Gu Yun had jumped into the hot spring before his very eyes.

Chang Geng's heart pounded like thunder in his chest. He didn't dare remove more of Gu Yun's clothes, so he dragged the blankets over from the bed and hastily wrapped them around Gu Yun's body. He dug out a set of clean clothing and placed it beside him, then said, a note of pleading in his voice, "Yifu, do the rest yourself, okay?"

Gu Yun had seldom fallen sick after reaching adulthood, which made this rare exception seem all the more serious. He was so hot it felt as if smoke were pouring from his seven orifices, and his ears rang without cease. At these words, he gestured weakly at Chang Geng and grumbled. "Of all the times to...you're really something else."

Chang Geng stood to the side, head bowed. Infected by his embarrassment, Gu Yun too began to feel self-conscious, and neither of them spoke for a long interval.

Chang Geng finally, awkwardly, broke the silence. "I'll go prepare your medicine."

He turned on his heel and left, allowing both to let out a sigh of relief.

Gu Yun lay still for a while, thoughts melting into a pot of congee under the heat of his fever, everything mixed together. First it was, *What exactly am I to do with this little brat?*

Then it was, *The Black Iron Battalion has retreated to Jiayu Pass. No one will retrieve the bodies of our fallen brothers, even if only to bring them back wrapped in horsehide.*

As his thoughts ran on in this manner, a cavernous hole yawned in his heart, leaving him vulnerable to every gust of bleak wind and wretched rain. All the heartbreak that had been shoved down by a few alarmed words from Jiang Chong as they rode toward the palace came roaring back with a vengeance, leaving him in such anguish he wished he were dead.

Half of a force of fifty thousand iron-armored soldiers, lost in one night...

In the end, Gu Yun's consciousness faded. Rather than fall asleep, it was more like he fainted dead away. His thoughts were murky; they drifted between dream and waking, segments from the past and present knotting together in an inextricable tangle. As his consciousness slid down these threads, memories from the long-ago past flashed before his eyes one by one. He recalled that when he was still young, in those years when he was neither blind nor deaf, he was like a jumping flea that couldn't be beaten into submission—whenever the old marquis laid eyes on him, he would huff and glare in fury.

But once, there was a day when the old marquis discovered a rare reservoir of patience and took his son to see the sunset beyond the pass.

The old marquis was tall and broad and strict in conduct, and treated his young son who was still the size of a dumpling just the same. He refused to pick him up; reluctantly leading him by the hand was the extent of the old marquis's limited parental affection. This arrangement forced the adult to bend at the waist and lean to the side, and the child to stretch his arm up as high as he could. It was uncomfortable for all involved.

But Gu Yun didn't complain. It was the first time he had seen the setting sun paint the desert beyond this border town the color of blood. The figure of a Black Hawk swept across the sky like a golden crow[31] dragging a parhelion tail behind it, and yellow sands and silent flatland groves spread as far as the eye could see. The young Gu Yun was awed by the sight. They watched until the great red disk of the sun sank below the horizon, and Gu Yun heard the old marquis say to his deputy general, who was standing beside him, "As a soldier, becoming a sacrifice of the nation can also be a lifetime's greatest fortune."

Back then, he hadn't understood.

But twenty years had passed.

Marshal, Gu Yun thought though the haze, *looks like...I really will become a sacrifice of this nation.*

...Like a swift steed galloping past a crack in the wall, a spark from a stone, a figure within a dream.[32]

Not long after, someone stepped through the door. He raised Gu Yun to a seated position and held a bowl of water to his lips.

31   Also known as a three-legged crow, a mythological creature that represents the sun.
32   Lines from the lyric poem 行香子 · 述怀, "An Expression of Emotion, to the tune of 'Ritual Offering of Incense'" by Su Shi, a Song dynasty poet.

That person was surpassingly gentle, as if he were long accustomed to taking care of others, and didn't spill so much as a drop. After he finished helping Gu Yun drink, he murmured coaxingly into his ear: "Zixi, take your medicine before you sleep."

Gu Yun mumbled without opening his eyes. "One hour...wake me up in one hour; pour cold water on my face if I don't get up."

Chang Geng sighed, fed him the medicine without a word, then took a seat at the side to watch over him.

Gu Yun appeared to be uncomfortable; he tossed and turned, nearly kicking off all his blankets. Chang Geng replaced the covers a few times, then gave up and wrapped Gu Yun in the blankets completely before pulling him into his arms.

Perhaps it was because Gu Yun hadn't been especially intimate with anyone since childhood, but strangely, he settled down as soon as he felt another pressed up behind him. The person holding him even considerately arranged him in the most comfortable position. Miss Chen's pacifying fragrance filled his nose, and a hand stroked his forehead with the perfect amount of pressure, then massaged his forehead, shoulders, and neck.

Gu Yun had never slept on such a comfortable "bed" in his life. He quickly drifted off, content as could be.

The quiet minutes swept by like fast-flowing water, and an hour passed in the blink of an eye. Chang Geng glanced at the nearby table clock, truly reluctant to do as Gu Yun asked—both reluctant to let go of Gu Yun, and reluctant to wake him.

But there was nothing to be done; this disastrous battle was already upon them. In all the world, was there a single place Gu Yun could sleep in peace?

Chang Geng steeled himself and lightly flicked one of Gu Yun's acupoints, waking him right on schedule. As Gu Yun's consciousness returned, Chang Geng rose and headed to the kitchen.

Gu Yun's mind had remained on high alert this whole time. With a bowl of medicine and some time to sweat it out, he managed to fend off his illness by sheer willpower. After an hour of rest, his fever had mostly receded. He lay on the bed for some minutes, then got up and put on his clean clothes. He felt like he had come back to life. With his body on the mend, his mind was also much more at ease.

They're just a bunch of foreigners, aren't they? If they were really so omnipotent, would they need all these plots and schemes?

No matter how dire the present circumstances, he was still alive. As long as the Gu family had a member remaining, the Black Iron Battalion had not fallen.

At this thought, Gu Yun let out a long sigh. Only then did he realize he was so hungry that his belly was practically flat against his back. He rubbed his stomach in misery and thought to himself, *If someone brought me a couple of shaobing flatbreads right now, I swear to heaven, I'd marry them on the spot.*

Chang Geng entered just then bearing a bowl of hot noodle soup. The steamy aroma slapped Gu Yun in the face without a trace of politeness. He was so hungry, his innards were twisting themselves into a knot.

Gu Yun could only gloomily eat his words. *This is an exception, this doesn't count...*

The moment he thought this, there came a timely clap of muffled thunder in the distance.

Gu Yun remained silent.

Chang Geng reached out and checked his temperature. "Your fever's gone. Yifu, come eat something first."

Gu Yun accepted the chopsticks wordlessly. When he heard the word *yifu*, something stirred in his heart. He felt that something was off, but before he could grasp what it was, the thought vanished, flitting away in an instant.

"You made this?" Gu Yun asked.

"I was a little short on time, so I only tossed some noodles in a pot," Chang Geng said, his face unchanging. "You'll have to make do."

Gu Yun suddenly felt rather uncomfortable. He had no idea why the illustrious Prince Yanbei was acting like some virtuous wife.

Chang Geng seemed to sense his thoughts. "If the country falls, I'll off Li Feng and open a noodle house in the northwest. It'll be enough to live on," he said evenly.

Gu Yun choked on a mouthful of soup, coughing so hard he nearly keeled over.

Laughing, Chang Geng said, "I'm joking."

Gu Yun picked up a cup of herbal tea and gulped it down. "What a good child you are. You've learned to play me for laughs, I see. You're getting more and more out of hand."

Chang Geng's expression turned solemn. "Back in Yanhui Town, when you told me you were going to bring me back to the capital, I had actually planned to run away. I thought I'd either head deep into the mountain forests and become a hunter or find some tiny border town and open a barely profitable shop, just enough to scrape by. But in the end, I figured I probably wouldn't be able to slip away under your nose, so I settled down."

Gu Yun pushed the vegetables to the side and scooped up the ham from the bottom of the bowl to eat first. He was still chewing when Chang Geng suddenly leaned back in his chair and took a deep breath. "Yifu, you don't know this, but every day you fail to appear before me safe and sound is a day I dare not close my eyes in sleep. At last—"

"I'm far from safe and sound right now," Gu Yun cut in tonelessly. "Give me an update on the current state of affairs."

Chang Geng understood at once that he meant the things Chang Geng couldn't mention in Li Feng's presence.

"You're the one who called for the Black Iron Battalion to retreat," Gu Yun said. "Otherwise, He Ronghui and the others might very well have fought to the last man."

"I forged your handwriting," Chang Geng said. "I ordered the Black Iron Battalion to retreat to Jiayu Pass. Then I asked General Cai Bin to lead reinforcements north to assist along the border. Considering how much time has passed, the emergency stores of violet gold in General He's hands have likely already been depleted— but Li Feng doesn't need to know about any of these matters. In any case, he's already abolished the Marching Orders Decree."

Gu Yun blinked. "You know how to forge…"

"It's just a bit of trickery." Chang Geng shook his head. "As for Jiangnan, I sent a letter to Shifu, but I was too late. I also suspect that the northern barbarians' operatives from twenty years ago are still within the palace. I've entrusted an ally with the investigation. As for General Shen, there's been no word from him yet, but I'm afraid that when it comes, it won't be good news."

"No news is good news." Gu Yun fell silent for a short while, then continued, "That old maid was born under a lucky star. There's no way he'll die."

"Yifu, although the assault on the northwestern front came in a furious rush, the situation there appears to be stable for now. Do you think we'll be able to hold the capital after the disaster in the East Sea?"

Gu Yun glanced up at him, his eyes like flint—cold and unspeakably hard, yet capable of producing sparks at the slightest contact. He and Chang Geng were the only two people in the room, a bowl of noodles between them. Gu Yun didn't bother equivocating and answered him honestly. "That will depend on whether we can hold out until reinforcements arrive. After traveling all this way, the foreigners want to end this quickly too. Otherwise, they wouldn't have opened with such a spectacle. The longer we drag this out, the greater our advantage. However..."

However, Great Liang did not have the strength to wage a war of attrition.

Li Feng lost his mind trying to obtain Loulan's violet gold reservoirs because, despite being the most bountiful nation with the richest resources in the world, there was very little violet gold to be excavated in Great Liang. Supply failed to meet demand. Nearly forty percent of the violet gold in Great Liang came in the form of tributes from the eighteen tribes. Another large portion came from assorted purchases from foreign nations. It was in this way that the money flowing in from maritime trade flowed right back out. Now, with the eighteen tribes rebelling and all four borders under siege, they could only make use of the violet gold they already had in reserve. Before long, they would struggle to make ends meet.

And that was only violet gold. What about supplies? Provisions? Where could the impoverished National Treasury, which was presently leaner than a daylily, possibly find that much cash?

Gu Yun continued in a low voice. "Just as you said, if we run out of options, we can pull back every military force in the country and hunker down while we formulate a plan. That would certainly be the most rational way to proceed. But such a thing may not be possible. The Black Iron Battalion's retreat to Jiayu Pass is already water under the bridge—though the region beyond the western pass is usually incredibly lively, most of those who frequent the area are itinerant merchants. The Silk Road has only been open a few years; not enough time for people to settle down. After tensions rose around the new year and the passes were closed, most of these people likely saw there was no business to conduct and moved on. But the same cannot be said of the region inside the pass. There are thousands of villages, tens of thousands of families, and millions upon millions of people living there. He Ronghui cannot retreat any farther even if his body is hacked into ten thousand pieces."

The Black Iron Battalion held the people of Great Liang's faith in their keeping. They were the backbone of the nation. If that backbone were to snap, what point was there in fighting on? They may as well change the nation's name and be done with it.

After a beat, Chang Geng said, "I meant as a last resort."

"There is no last resort." Gu Yun shook his head. "You are far-sighted and astute; you know how to govern a country, but you have never fought a war. I'm telling you, when it comes to war, aside from temporal and topographical considerations, two factors remain: One is equipment such as steam engines and steel armor. The other is courage in the hearts of soldiers who have no fear of death. With regard to our equipment, it is what it is; there's nothing we can do at this point. But it is my belief that even if the foreigners are strong, they're not so much stronger than we are—and that's not even getting into those barbarian bumpkins who use cannons like cudgels. My subordinates are people, not chess pieces. They are brave, but they also fear death. Do you remember what I told you back when we were fighting bandits in the southwest?"

"I do," Chang Geng said. "You told me, 'On the battlefield, whoever clings to life is the first to die.'"

Gu Yun hummed in muffled agreement. Even seeing their nation riddled with holes couldn't deter him from eating his fill. Over the course of their brief conversation, he had polished off the whole bowl of noodles. Finally, he held his nose and slurped those hateful leafy greens down alongside the last of the soup in one gulp—he didn't even bother to chew. Meal demolished, he set the bowl on the table. "Is there more?"

"No, I only made one bowl. You were just ill; your stomach and spleen are still weak. Sixty to seventy percent full is just right for you," Chang Geng said. "As for how we fight, you're in charge. You don't have to worry about any future consequences, nor about the opinions of others. How to make money, how to obtain violet gold, how to coordinate and distribute resources—leave it all up to me."

Gu Yun was slightly startled and laughed in spite of himself. "I'm in charge of everything? What if I lose?"

Chang Geng smiled without a word, his eyes fixed intently on Gu Yun like a pool of still water suddenly broken by a ripple. If eyes could speak, his would have clearly announced to the world, *If you lose, I will share your burden of infamy for all eternity. If you die, I will accompany you in death.*

It was then that Huo Dan rapped lightly on the door. "Sir, Master Fenghan and General Tan have arrived. They've brought the second military dispatch from the East Sea."

Gu Yun called out at once. "Send them in!"

Chang Geng tucked away his gaze and tidied up the bowl and chopsticks. With his head lowered, he said, "Just now, there was one thing I said that was complete nonsense."

Gu Yun started in surprise.

"I said the reason I didn't run away was because I thought I wouldn't be able to slip away under your nose." Chang Geng smiled without lifting his head. "Back then, I was nothing more than a country boy from a tiny border town; I didn't think that far ahead at all..."

Gu Yun had already astutely parsed his unspoken implication. "Chang Geng, that's enough," he said, stern.

Chang Geng obediently closed his mouth, swallowing the rest. At the time, he hadn't thought that far ahead at all. There was only one reason he didn't run away: there was one person whom he couldn't bear to let go.

Tan Hongfei and Zhang Fenghan were soon led in, and the wax-sealed report from the frontlines was presented to Gu Yun. As he handed it over, Tan Hongfei's hands trembled faintly. Gu Yun's heart sank.

"Sir, the report from Jiangnan says that our navy was routed and has been forced to retreat some five hundred kilometers. The Westerners have already begun to sail north. The foreigners have some sort of new dragon warship; it's fast as lightning and two to three times larger than our naval dragons. And they're said to be escorted by a giant sea monster," Tan Hongfei said. "If this report isn't unfounded nonsense, they'll reach Dagu Harbor in two or three days!"

60

CANNON FIRE

CHANG GENG TOOK HOLD of the military report. "What of the Jiangnan Navy remains?" Gu Yun asked.

"Hard to say." Chang Geng skimmed the missive. "Our dragon warships have never gone out to sea, much less engaged in true naval battles. When Zhao Youfang fell, the troops under his command panicked and scattered in all directions—Yifu, do you remember back when Prince Wei attempted his armed rebellion?"

Gu Yun pinched the bridge of his nose, understanding at once what he was getting at. Back then, Prince Wei had bribed the Jiangnan Army and Navy Commander along with half his forces and amassed an army in the islets near Dongying. From this foothold, he greedily eyed the capital. But to his surprise, before he could complete preparations, his plans were scuttled by the joint efforts of Gu Yun and the Linyuan Pavilion. Or rather—on paper it was a joint effort between Gu Yun and the Linyuan Pavilion, but in reality, Gu Yun had been accompanied by only a handful of Black Hawks and a couple of half-grown children at the time. Likewise, the Linyuan Pavilion had merely dispatched thirty-odd members of the jianghu, including that useless monk Liao Ran who, after climbing into a suit of heavy armor, didn't even know how to climb back out again.

Gu Yun was highly respected in the military, so the case might be made that his sudden appearance, which cowed the rebel forces into submission, had been a major factor in that mission's success. Yet this case only further proved that Great Liang's navy was its greatest handicap—it couldn't even pull off a proper rebellion with ease.

If such an incident had occurred during the late Yuanhe Emperor's reign, Gu Yun might have seized the opportunity to do as he did with the Northern Border Defense Corps and involve himself in the reorganization of the naval troops. Unfortunately, Li Feng was nothing like the soft, tender-hearted late emperor who wavered irresolutely when it came to killing anyone. Such unilateral action was no longer possible under the Longan Emperor's reign.

"What about Yao Chongze? Is he dead too?" Gu Yun asked.

"There's no mention of him," Chang Geng responded. "There were too many killed in action for a full accounting."

Gu Yun sighed. "So, what exactly is this 'sea monster'?"

Chang Geng scanned the report. "Apparently, it looks like a giant octopus and has the ability to hide underwater. When it surfaces, it towers over the ocean like a mountain and possesses overwhelming power. Compared to the giant kite, the latter looks like a pigeon sitting on the shoulder of a brawny man. It's equipped with countless iron tentacles covered in thousands upon thousands of small dragon warships, and when the tips open, they release huge flocks of armored hawks..."

At this point, Chang Geng paused and tapped lightly on the report with a slender finger. "If this is true, they're burning through at least two or three hundred kilograms of violet gold a day..."

Gu Yun shot him a look, but Chang Geng shook his head slightly. Having made his point, he went no further, his voice petering out as he elided the rest—the fact that the Westerners had invested such a huge quantity of violet gold meant they likely wanted to end this as swiftly as possible.

CANNON FIRE ☼ 339

"They've dealt with Jiangnan, so there's no need for them to worry about an enemy attacking from the rear by sea as they advance. The fleet at Dagu Harbor is no match for them, so their next move will be to make landfall and press on toward the capital." Gu Yun pulled down a map from where it hung on the wall. "Old Tan, how many deployable troops are there in the capital?"

Tan Hongfei licked cracked lips. "The Northern Camp has two thousand suits of heavy armor and sixteen thousand light cavalry-men. There's also two thousand charioteers and eighty war chariots. Each chariot is outfitted with three parhelion bows, plus a cannon on each end."

This level of firepower was sufficient to force an abdication, but in the face of the Westerners' long-planned all-out assault, it was a cup of water to a raging fire. Gu Yun furrowed his brow. "What about the Imperial Guard?"

"The Imperial Guard is no good. They have less than six thousand men in total, and over half of them are feckless noble sons who only know how to wave their weapons about and have never seen bloodshed." Tan Hongfei paused as he remembered something. He pulled an object from his lapels and, with both hands, held it out solemnly to Gu Yun. "Right; His Majesty asked me to give this to the marshal."

Wrapped in fine plain-weave silk, it was presented like some precious gemstone of enormous value. When the package was unfolded, however, the ferocious-looking Black Iron Tiger Tally lay within.

Gu Yun glanced at the tiger tally, a thin smile bowing his lips. "What's the point in returning this to me now? That ship has sailed."

Tan Hongfei didn't know what to say.

Gu Yun carelessly tossed the Black Iron Tiger Tally back to Tan Hongfei. "Very well. I see that His Majesty has made up his mind;

go ahead and write up mobilization orders in accordance with his wishes. Summon the troops garrisoned in Shandong and Zhili back to defend the capital against imminent siege. Send word to Cai Bin and instruct him to send reinforcements...hm. Dispatch the mobilization orders first. If that fails—well, we'll cross that bridge when we come to it."

The wizened old Zhang Fenghan wasn't at all so iron-hearted as these beasts of burden. After spending this whole time terrified out of his wits, he at once recognized the unspoken implication within Gu Yun's words. The blood drained from the old Lingshu scholar's face, and he couldn't help but ask, "Does the marquis mean that... the reinforcements may fail to arrive?"

Chang Geng spoke up from the side. "If the information in these military reports can be trusted, it's impossible for the Westerners to have brought much in the way of supplies. They cannot afford to prolong this war. If they think to deal us a killing blow by making landfall in Jiangnan, they must split their forces in two, sending one contingent to advance on the capital by sea while leaving the other to blockade us and cut off communication between the capital and the rest of the country by land... I'm afraid at this stage, we'll be lucky to get any of our military dispatches through the siege."

Master Fenghan almost fainted on the spot, collapsing into a chair and hyperventilating. Chang Geng hadn't expected his words to affect the man so gravely. He hastened to pour Master Fenghan a glass of water, then skillfully tapped a handful of acupoints on his back. "Please take it easy, sir. The older you get, the more careful you must be to avoid sudden fluctuations of extreme emotion. Otherwise, you could easily suffer a stroke..."

Zhang Fenghan grasped his hand, close to tears. "My dear Highness, do you naturally lack a sense of crisis?"

"Master Fenghan, please calm down. I haven't finished yet," Chang Geng continued hurriedly. "Back when Yifu was thrown in prison, I was worried something like this might happen on the borders. I've already gotten in touch with a few of my friends."

So saying, he produced a wooden bird from within his sleeve.

"These wooden birds utilize a special kind of magnet to direct their flight and can carry messages between holders of said magnets. My friends received my earlier messages, so they've doubtless already set out for each of the nation's major garrisons by now. Hopefully, there's still time—if the capital should really be besieged, I can use these wooden birds to send word and pass on information outside military channels. The Black Iron Tiger Tally and my yifu's personal seal ought to lend our letters sufficient credibility."

Chang Geng had realized that without the Black Hawks, the delay in long-distance communication would hamper military operations. Thus he turned to the Linyuan Pavilion to preemptively organize a giant communications network in hopes of avoiding future disaster.

Tan Hongfei and Zhang Fenghan gaped at Chang Geng in amazement.

"It's just a trifling little trick. I couldn't come up with anything else on such short notice," Chang Geng said. "This plan is feasible as long as it remains a secret, but it's not sustainable in the long term. The minute our enemies catch on, these birds will no longer be a secure mode of communication; they can be knocked out of the sky with a mere pebble."

At that moment, Gu Yun couldn't quite describe what he was feeling. He'd had his worries about Chang Geng when he was in prison, but it seemed even if Gu Yun had been free to handle matters, he couldn't have done much better himself. Not only had this child's timely action saved half of the Black Iron Battalion, he'd also managed to preserve some room for them to maneuver.

Gu Yun sighed in appreciation. He was overwhelmed with pride. Yet he also felt that the young boy who only knew to close his eyes and flee when faced with a sword-training puppet should not have grown up so quickly, and that it was all because he'd failed to look after him properly.

With so many others present, open sentimentality wasn't appropriate, so Gu Yun merely offered nonchalantly, "Your Highness's actions have certainly been thorough and well-considered."

Gu Yun plucked a wine jar from where it hung behind the door and, without bothering to don any armor, draped a straw raincoat casually over his shoulders. "Come on," he said to Tan Hongfei. "Let's head to the Northern Camp."

Chang Geng rose as well. "I'll accompany Master Fenghan back to the Lingshu Institute. Then I'll stop by the Ministry of Revenue and see how things are going over there."

The two rushed off on their separate ways. The ceaseless rolls of muted thunder on the horizon suddenly changed their tune. A dazzling flash of cold lightning split the dreary firmament in twain, and a torrential downpour seldom seen in spring relentlessly pounded the earth.

The deluge fell in buckets as wind and rain swept across a gloomy sky.

Braving the pelting tempest, Gu Yun and Tan Hongfei sped out of the city toward the Northern Camp with a detachment of guards. Tan Hongfei fiercely shook off a face full of water droplets and at once remembered Huo Dan, back at the Marquis Estate, saying that the marquis was ill. He couldn't help but spur his horse forward until he was abreast of Gu Yun and bellow, "Sir, this rain is too heavy and you've yet to recover from your cold. Why don't we find some-where to take shelter? Once this storm passes, we'll still have time to hurry on our way…"

Gu Yun shook his head. For some reason, perhaps because this storm had rolled in too rapidly, he had a sudden and ominous premonition.

Foreigners called the Black Iron Battalion "black crows," and sure enough, as the leader of these black-winged harbingers, Gu Yun was possessed of an unmatched crow's beak. A frightening number of his ominous premonitions seemed to come true with unfailing accuracy.

Gu Yun assumed control of the Northern Camp with grim efficiency. Meanwhile, Chang Geng hurried over with the precious steel armor and steam engines he had unearthed from the Lingshu Institute overnight. There were even numerous suits of heavy and hawk armor among his haul.

Tan Hongfei had reckoned that the Westerners would begin their march north within a few days' time. He was too optimistic.

That night, on a watchtower over Dagu Harbor, a long and cylindrical field scope peered out over the water. It was equipped with two palm-sized lens wipers that were scrubbing up and down—a futile effort, as a blast of wind soon forced the little things to bow their heads. The soldier standing watch in the tower reached out the window and groped around for a rust-mottled handle on the field scope's side—the steam engine inside had broken down long ago and never been repaired, so the device had to be turned manually. The soldier flicked away a handful of raindrops and began to crank the long arm of the handle, cursing all the while. The chipped gears let out an exhausted shriek as a tiny metal umbrella spread unsteadily open, shielding the field scope from the bleak wind and icy rain.

The soldier wiped away the film of water covering the scope's lens and grumbled to his companion, "We all serve in the army, but others fly through the sky shaking heaven and earth, while here we are spending our days in this tower sweeping the floor and playing dominoes. We don't even get any perks. Nothing ever happens, yet we waste our time here all year round. My woman barely even recognizes me anymore... Seriously, what the devil is going on with this rain? Was there a miscarriage of justice somewhere or what?"[33]

His companion didn't lift his head from where he was sweeping the floor. "You'd better keep praying nothing happens. Didn't you hear the squad leader say the Westerners are coming?"

"The squad leader harps on about the Westerners a couple days a month," the soldier responded. "Isn't the Marquis of Anding still keeping an eye on things in the capital next door?"

"The Marquis of Anding got thrown in prison."

"But they let him back out again, didn't they?" Here, the soldier seemed to realize something. "Wait, wasn't the rumor that the Marquis of Anding tried to force the emperor to abdicate? Why would they let him out so soon? Unless..."

"Shh!" His companion's head snapped up. "Do you hear that?"

A faint rumble like the roll of thunder shook the air. The watchtower began to tremble, as if it too sensed something coming.

Was it the storm?

No—thunder came in intermittent crashes. It wouldn't linger on like this, drawing closer and closer.

The old soldier lurched over to the field scope and swung its barrel up. Through the ink-black curtain of rain, the soldier's searching eyes crashed into an enormous shadow on the water.

33　A riff on 六月飞雪，必有冤情, "If it's snowing in June, then there's definitely been a great injustice." The expression ties into the traditional Chinese belief that abnormal natural phenomena are linked to present or future catastrophe.

Such a terrifying monster was beyond the stuff of nightmares. Extending its tentacles to the sky, it emitted a deafening roar. The old soldier doubted his own vision; he rubbed fiercely at his eyes. Yet this "sea monster" moved with such swiftness, it seemed to fly. By the time the soldier looked again, it was no longer the blurry shadow from a moment ago. In the blink of an eye, it had traversed untold kilometers and could now be seen in clear detail through the field scope. Dense masses of sea dragons slipped through the darkness with a cold and murderous aura, and battle flags billowed in the wind and rain, viciously revealing their razor-sharp claws and fangs.

"Enemy attack..." the old soldier choked out.

"What?"

"Enemy attack! The Westerners are here—sound the alarm! What are you doing standing there? *Hurry*—"

An urgent drumbeat punctured the furious downpour as the watchtower's steady, rotating light began to swivel like mad. The news spread from two men to ten and from ten to a hundred, like wildfire. Within the span of a few breaths, every watchtower in Dagu Harbor reverberated with the pounding of war drums. Lian Wei, commander in chief of the Beihai Army and Navy, hadn't dared sleep a wink since receiving reports of the defeat in Jiangnan. With his heart beating so madly it was on the verge of crashing through his chest, he snatched the field scope from his personal guard's hands.

A single glance, and a chill lanced from his chest all the way through to his back. *Heaven help us.*

"Sir!"

"Deploy..." Lian Wei licked his lips. "Deploy all dragon warships to the vanguard. No warning shots necessary. Bombard the enemy with cannon fire...no, wait—iron chains. Lash the dragons together with iron chains and form a boom across the mouth of the harbor."

"Ready the parhelions—"

"Notify any fishing and merchant boats in the harbor to evacuate immediately!"

Lian Wei glanced down at his desk and the war beacon decree that he had yet to put away. This was the highest state of alert for Great Liang's military. The instant a war beacon decree came down, it meant that the entire nation had entered a state of imminent war.

The war beacon decree was inscribed with the character *Gu*—it had been personally signed by the Marquis of Anding.

Years ago, when the Black Iron Battalion had suffered the suicide attack on the northern border, over a dozen wrongfully accused junior and senior officers were forced to cast off their black-iron armor, lay down their windslashers, and scatter to the far reaches of the country. By now, many of them had either withdrawn into obscurity or retired. As for Lian Wei, he'd imagined he would spend the rest of his life stuck in this tiny little harbor. Every day he'd stroll idly along the docks with his men in tow, and occasionally he'd deal with a case of petty gambling or scuffles between fishermen...

"Send word to the Northern Camp." Lian Wei tightened the buckles on his armor and took a deep breath, sucking in his bulging paunch. "Tell them Dagu Harbor is under enemy attack by the Western navy. Go, now!"

As he strode out, he seemed to remember something. He turned on his heel and picked up a windslasher that had been standing in the corner gathering dust all these years. This he slung over his back. The blade, once a seasoned veteran of desert battlefields, was now so badly rusted even the tiny trough that stored violet gold could no longer be pried open. It had been reduced to a heavy black-iron rod that probably couldn't serve much use beyond mugging people in the middle of the night.

Yet when Lian Wei strapped it once more to his back, he seemed to regain the feeling he'd had when he donned black-iron armor and gazed down upon the rest of the world in disdain.

After so many years of wallowing in idleness, and beneath so many layers of fat, the brand left on his blood and bone by cold blade and steel armor hadn't faded in the least.

The iron boom of dragon ships met the rampaging sea monster head-on as the two forces closed in on each other. The Western warships cut through the wind and rain like demonic fiends, faster even than the whipping tempest brewing over the water. The stormy sea raised tidal waves so terrible they seemed capable of swallowing the mainland whole, and the uninterrupted report of cannon fire filled the heavens. Countless warships exploded into splinters in an instant, sinking beneath the roiling crests of the ocean waves.

"Sir, the boom isn't going to hold!"

"Sir, we've lost too many ships on our left flank. The iron chains..."

"The watchtower—look out!"

A cannonball burst forth like a fiery dragon. Even the dense curtain of rain couldn't dim its raging flame as it scored a direct hit on a watchtower with an earthshattering *boom*. The tower staggered for a breathless moment before slowly bending at the waist.

The lantern casting light through the rain from atop the tower went dark.

Shoving his personal guard aside, Lian Wei leapt onto the deck of a warship and bellowed, "Cannons, maintain barrage fire! Parhelions, load firebrand arrows!"

"General Lian, it's impossible for Dagu Harbor to..."

"Out of the way!" Lian Wei shoved the foot soldier standing by the parhelion arrows aside. With a great shout, he hoisted the fifty-some kilogram firebrand arrow and slammed it down on the parhelion bow. Scrubbing the rainwater from his face, he grabbed the parhelion's calibrator.

The first firebrand arrow tore from the parhelion bow and ruthlessly blasted into the sky, shedding the iron shell encasing its tail mid-flight. Violet gold gleamed like impenetrable hellfire spurring it on, and it gathered speed, brushing past the battle flag flying atop the sea monster like a streaking meteor and crashing among the waves.

The force of the impact shredded the fluttering flag of the Holy See into diaper cloth, and the torn-up scraps scattered before the wind in all directions—but the firebrand arrow had yet to reach the end of its flight. It struck a rampaging Western sea dragon, exploding over the ocean in a dazzling display of fireworks.

Absent an order from their commander, members of the Black Iron Battalion dared not retreat a centimeter.

Report of the attack on Dagu Harbor reached the capital in the middle of the night. Sitting in the commander's tent, Gu Yun was in the midst of sorting out the capital's defenses with Tan Hongfei and Han Qi, the captain of the Imperial Guard. Shocked, Han Qi practically sprang to his feet. "How could the attack come so fast?!"

Gu Yun's expression grew overcast. "Who is the commanding officer of the Beihai Army and Navy?"

"Lian Wei." The rims of Tan Hongfei's eyes reddened faintly. After a pause, he couldn't help but add, "He was once this humble general's deputy in the Black Iron Battalion."

Gu Yun's eye twitched slightly. "Captain Han."

Han Qi caught on immediately. "This humble general will return to the capital at once. Please rest assured, Marshal. Even if the Imperial Guard is no more than an assemblage of noble young masters, their final resting place lies before the city walls of the capital."

Gu Yun cast him a searching look before lifting the flap of the commander's tent. "Can those old geezers at the Lingshu Institute please pick up the pace?"

He'd barely finished his grousing when a messenger hurried over. "Sir, Prince Yanbei has arrived!"

Gu Yun jerked his head up, but Chang Geng's horse had already galloped straight in. Pulling back on the reins, Chang Geng said, "Marshal, the Lingshu Institute has completed repairs on the thousand suits of black-iron heavy armor and five hundred suits of hawk armor they have on hand. They've also sent over what light pelts they have in pieces, giving us a total of three thousand sets of iron cuffs and vambraces, four thousand pairs of poleyns and greaves, and a whole batch of pauldrons and visors. They'll be sending everything over shortly."

61

REPORT OF VICTORY

NEVER IN TAN HONGFEI'S wildest dreams had he imagined that he would don black-iron armor again one day. All the sorrow in his heart evaporated; even if he were to lose his life in this upcoming battle, he thought, it would be worth it for this.

Tan Hongfei stepped forward and declared in a ringing voice, "This subordinate is willing to join the marshal's vanguard!"

"Well, we certainly can't do without you. Parhelion bows and war chariots will clear the way, light cavalry and Black Hawk units will follow me, and heavy armor will bring up the rear." Gu Yun quickly passed out his orders. "Someone get me a windslasher. Whatever demon, ghost, or monster we face, we'll only know once we see it for ourselves."

Chang Geng unshouldered the violet-gold-assisted longbow from his back. It was the very same weapon he'd acquired from Gu Yun when they were vanquishing bandits in the southwest. The bow seemed to be the last presentable invention out of the Lingshu Institute before the Longan Emperor began to cut military spending in earnest. The unadorned iron bow was incredibly heavy; it was impossible for those who weren't true masters of archery to draw it. Thus, though it could have seen widespread use in the army after further refinement, this remained the only prototype of its kind in the entirety of the Great Liang military.

Smoothing a hand across the ice-cold iron of the bow, Chang
Geng asked, "Yifu, may I accompany you?"

Gu Yun hesitated. He didn't really want to bring him along—if
for no other reason than that, over the course of this unfolding crisis,
he had developed still greater expectations for this young and inex-
perienced little prince. Perhaps Gu Yun could indeed dig in his heels
before the capital and fight to the bitter end, but what then? Who
would clean up the crumbling remains of the nation? Who would
cut a path across the chaos and help the common people find their
way through?

Chang Geng was far more diplomatic in his personal conduct
than Gu Yun had been in his own youth. Maybe he wouldn't end up
like Gu Yun, caught in such a hopeless and unsalvageable situation
after falling out with the emperor...

Chang Geng seemed to sense the direction of his thoughts. "No
eggs remain whole when the nest overturns. As it stands, there's
no difference between waiting in the palace and joining you on the
front line. If the city falls, would it not merely be a matter of an
earlier or later death?"

Before Gu Yun could respond, Tan Hongfei burst into laughter.
"Well said, Your Highness! The court is filled with pedantic scholars.
Your Highness is the only real man among them!"

Gu Yun could only wave a hand and say, "You've said all there is
to say. If you want to come, then come."

He shot Tan Hongfei a withering glare. Seeing the swollen whip
mark, yet unhealed, on General Tan's face, he had half a mind to
give him another lash on his other cheek and make him symmetrical.

Outside the walls of the capital, black iron formed a dense mass
that curved around the city like the glimmering waters of a desert
oasis.

Looking back from atop their horses, the lights of Kite's Flight Pavilion were bright as ever under the heavy downpour; yet standing opposite the towering Imperial City in the distance, they seemed enshrouded in a gentle luster, like the glow of polished tortoiseshell. The twenty red kites that only ever took flight on New Year's Eve had made an exception today. They floated high in the air like the uneasy eyes of an anxiously awaiting crowd.

Gu Yun raised his hand and gave the signal. The Northern Camp's vanguard had already solemnly moved out. There were no stirring, mournful songs, nor were there any fervent speeches. The soldiers marched through the rain, their faces hidden beneath visored helmets, like a platoon of impassive iron puppets.

In the heavy deluge, the capital looked like it was floating on water, the city's ancient blue flagstones reflective as a mirror.

The previous night, the Western navy had sailed north and launched a surprise attack on Dagu Harbor. Lian Wei, commander in chief of the Beihai Army and Navy, led three hundred dragons and one thousand corvettes in a vigorous defense. They began by chaining their dragons together to form an iron boom across the mouth of the harbor. By eleven forty-five the next evening, every single dragon warship had sunk under the Western sea monster's cannon fire. There were no survivors.

The Beihai Navy had thirty-six thousand firebrand arrows and ten thousand rounds of parhelion iron arrows on hand. By the end of the battle, not a shaft remained—every one had been blasted into the furious waves of the bottomless deep. When they ran out of ammunition, General Lian ordered his captains to power their corvettes to full speed and, using their ships as firebrands and their own bodies as parhelions, ram their vessels into the enemy's ranks.

Raging fire spread over the sea as loyal souls sacrificed themselves in the line of duty.

The Beihai Navy bombed, sank, and smashed to pieces nearly three thousand enemy warships. Ultimately, they forced the Western sea monster to brave the rain and open the hangars at the tips of their iron tentacles to launch the armored hawks hidden within. Only when the bedraggled enemy hawks reached the shore did they discover that Dagu Harbor had but a bare handful of active combatants remaining.

By three in the morning, the Westerners who had breached the shore were profoundly vexed. Eager to make up for the losses sustained in battle, rather than remain longer in the area they chose to advance directly on the capital. On the way, they encountered the Black Iron Battalion—that is, the Black Iron Battalion that Gu Yun had spent a single day and night cobbling together—on the outskirts of Dongan City.

The Western navy forces had yet to recover from their disastrous and casualty-heavy landfall. They were caught completely off guard and were soon driven back by the eighty war chariots leading the charge. The Black Iron Battalion followed their initial onslaught with a second wave: light cavalrymen rode out from their encirclement and hawks soared high overhead, their fearsome cries slicing through the air like swords.

Met suddenly with windslashers in the hands of light cavalry, the pope's personal guard nearly scattered then and there. They made a hasty retreat back to their ships in Dagu Harbor.

It had been years since Great Liang had endured such a harrowing night. Messengers bearing military reports sped in and out of the palace as though they were running to the market, more frequent than the strikes of the night watch. Not a soul in the capital slept soundly until the next morning, when reports of victory arrived alongside the first glimmers of dawn.

It was the first good news in days. When Li Feng heard, he went weak at the knees, momentarily torn between laughter and tears.

Just as the sky cleared after the rain, so too came hope after hardship. The Hai River swelled overnight, and an indescribable smell, mixed with the scent of gunpowder and blood, filled the air. The earth had already thawed, and the humidity lingered heavy on the breeze. Gu Yun had no navy and the Westerners were in a sorry state, so after a night of fierce battle, both forces retreated to their respective fortifications.

Gu Yun sat beside a cannon still emanating residual warmth, his black-iron helmet tossed to the side and a loose lock of messy hair obscuring his face. He accepted a bowl of medicine from Chang Geng and tossed its contents back in one gulp.

"I didn't bring my acupuncture needles, but even if I had, I wouldn't dare stab you with any of them right now," Chang Geng said.

After wielding that iron bow the whole night through, his palms were covered in deep grooves, and his fingers still trembled from fatigue. Gu Yun caught him by the wrist and pulled him over. Only when he confirmed that Chang Geng was exhausted but uninjured did he relax. He waved a hand and said, "Don't worry about me. Go count the casualties. Old Tan has no head for numbers."

With that, he leaned right back against the cannon, making the most of this little downtime to rest his eyes.

Yet moments later, Gu Yun was startled awake by a herald from the Imperial City.

The herald who had rushed to the scene was an imperial guard with a rather youthful face. Under ordinary circumstances, one of his rank would have little opportunity to meet Gu Yun. Seeing the Marquis of Order in the flesh, he was so excited he could barely contain himself. The young soldier galloped straight up to Gu Yun and leapt from his saddle—but his foot must have caught on something, for he lost his balance and face-planted precisely at Gu Yun's feet. "My lord!"

Gu Yun hastily retracted his toes. "Aiyo, no need to be quite *this* courteous."

"My lord," the herald responded eagerly, "His Majesty has tasked me with rewarding the Northern Camp with food and drink. I've brought...I've brought..."

Wonderful. In his excitement, he'd forgotten his lines.

No wonder the Northern Camp had beat the crap out of the Imperial Guard. Exasperated, Gu Yun climbed to his feet and patted the young soldier on the head. "There's no need to tell me—you can let General Tan handle this kind of thing. Go inform His Majesty that it's too early to celebrate. The Northern Camp has a limited number of troops. Even I can't magic more soldiers into existence when we run out of men. If reinforcements don't arrive by then..."

The herald stared at him, taken aback.

As stated in *The Art of War*, "When in battle, lead by convention, win by ingenuity." Most people only remembered "win by ingenuity," thinking that a famous general must be able to fight his way out of any impasse and save a great edifice on the verge of collapse single-handedly—but that wasn't possible, not unless Gu Yun could sculpt out of mud an army of godlike soldiers who neither ate nor drank.

Now that news of Gu Yun's victory in his first battle had spread back to the capital, the court officials were sure to be overjoyed—but what came next? Never mind such long-term goals as competing with the Westerners on the grand scale of national strength, material stockpiles, and available resources. He had only this small portion of military power in his hands right now—what could he possibly do?

Gu Yun knew very well that however impressive this opening match appeared, he was in truth putting up a last-ditch struggle with his back against the wall.

He offered the emperor's herald a grim smile. Then, he left the young man hanging where he stood and strode over to Tan Hongfei. Tan Hongfei was holding a windslasher that had been crushed flat on one end. Through the black scorch marks marring the tip, half the inscription of the character *Lian* was still faintly visible.

Many soldiers carved their names onto their windslashers. That way, even if they handed their blade in for maintenance, they could be reunited with the partner who had accompanied them through so many life-and-death struggles. In the event that the owner of such a weapon should fall in battle and his body be unrecoverable, his brothers-in-arms would bring back his windslasher and pour out a pot of wine in libation before it so their brother's soul could rest in peace.

Tan Hongfei lifted that windslasher with both hands and presented it to Gu Yun. "Sir."

Gu Yun accepted the proffered blade. Suddenly, he felt that despite its many misfortunes, the Black Iron Battalion, which had gathered and separated time and again, had always been supporting the nation, woven deep into its foundation. Its members were like a handful of seeds scattered in all directions—you never knew where a towering tree might unexpectedly sprout up toward the sky.

Chang Geng walked up behind him. "Last night, we lost a total of thirteen war chariots. In addition, five hundred light cavalrymen were killed in action and close to a thousand seriously wounded. Those with minor injuries weren't counted, so I didn't include them in my final tabulation. We also lost twelve armored hawks. Most of their gold tanks exploded in midair, so I'm afraid the bodies..."

Gu Yun nodded; these casualty numbers were acceptable. "This is thanks to General Lian's efforts."

"I fear there will be those who urge us to initiate peace talks during this morning's court session," Chang Geng said quietly.

"It won't work," Gu Yun said with a sigh. "The foreigners suffered a great humiliation yesterday. They won't have the face for peace talks now, and until they've besieged the capital so thoroughly that we couldn't escape even if we sprouted wings, they won't be open to having them."

And that was likely only a matter of time.

Chang Geng fell silent for a spell. "I've heard it said that the last emperor of a previous dynasty dealt with a similar crisis in which the northern barbarians attacked by sneaking out of the city through a secret passageway. If we really can't defend the capital..."

"We defend it to the end, regardless," Gu Yun responded. "Do you know the Sunlight Palace west of the capital?"

Chang Geng started in surprise.

Gu Yun lifted a finger to his lips and spoke no further. The Sunlight Palace on the west side of the capital was built during the Yuanhe Emperor's reign. The late emperor had no tolerance for hot weather and spent every summer at the Sunlight Palace to escape the heat.

After Li Feng ascended, he hewed to simplicity in all things, from food and drink to everyday expenses. Even the empress and the imperial harem's cosmetics allowance was halved. He never indulged in extravagances like hunting or pleasure excursions. Yet despite being such a frugal person, the complete opposite of his father, Li Feng had inherited his habit of removing to the temporary imperial residence every summer. Not that he went there to enjoy himself—due to the speed with which government work piled up, he usually hurried over to the Imperial City so early in the morning that the moon and stars still hung in the sky, only to hurry right back to the summer palace before nightfall, touring the capital city as though he were walking a dog and returning just in time for morning roll call. Forget trying to escape the hot weather—with all this running about, he was lucky if he didn't get heatstroke.

Considering the way Li Feng fussed over this, if there weren't something wrong with his head, it could only mean that...there was something stored within the Sunlight Palace which required frequent and personal monitoring.

Chang Geng's mind was keen as ever, and he was immediately struck with an idea: defending generals on all four of the nation's borders had at one point or another privately hoarded violet gold— then what about the emperor? Chang Geng had only recently joined the imperial court, so he had yet to finish auditing the Ministries of Revenue and War's accounts. But given Li Feng's control-freak personality, it wouldn't be at all strange for him to maintain a private cache of violet gold.

"Your big brother trusts no one," Gu Yun said softly, "so this is merely my own conjecture; don't tell anyone else."

Chang Geng frowned. "Well, that's going to be a bit troublesome... Do you think Li Feng will sue for peace when the time comes?"

Gu Yun couldn't help it; he burst out laughing. Shaking his head, he said, "Maybe if the other party comes to him asking to open peace talks. Oh—but it's unlikely that he'll run, either."

Chang Geng clasped his hands behind his back. He was covered in filth from head to toe. The muddy water that had splashed him the night before had dried, leaving him mottled in a spectacular array of gaudy colors; yet the young Commandery Prince Yanbei donned the colors with leisurely composure and processed through the camp as if he were merely taking a post-meal afternoon stroll through the imperial gardens. After a moment's consideration, he said blandly, "True, Li Feng does not fear death. He fears something else."

Gu Yun couldn't help but shoot him a glance. He realized Master Fenghan was right: Chang Geng really did always seem wholly unperturbed. He suddenly asked, "When exactly did you become so cool and collected?"

"How am I cool and collected? I'm terribly impetuous, honestly," Chang Geng said with a laugh. "Actually, I learned this from you. I noticed that Yifu always pretends to be awfully happy whenever you're upset. If you put on a show of being cheerful, the distress in your heart becomes easier to bear. So whenever I'm feeling particularly restless, I try to slow down a little, and in doing so, I really do find myself becoming more calm. Oh, and also, excess internal heat in the liver is detrimental to maintaining good health and makes it difficult to..."

"...fall asleep." Gu Yun had been exasperated by this line of his on more than one occasion and could at this point finish his sentence. "Just how deeply do you care about sleeping? Also, when do I ever force a smile when I'm unhappy?"

Chang Geng raised an eyebrow, the very image of calm amid chaos as he looked at him. The words *whatever you say* were written plain across his face.

"Assemble the troops for a tactical withdrawal." Gu Yun weakly changed the subject. "Send the wounded back first. It won't be long before the Westerners recover their wits. We're going to lay an ambush."

After walking a few steps, Gu Yun found himself abruptly overcome with intense exhaustion. He couldn't help but think back to Chang Geng's spiel from a minute ago—who knows what fraud of a doctor had taught him such quackery. He untied the wine pot from his waist and took a swig, then strapped General Lian's windslasher to his back and whistled sharply. A warhorse trotted up in response, and the trill of his whistle dipped, capriciously transforming into a self-penned ditty. He bent down to pluck a tiny yellow wildflower from the turf, then vaulted onto his steed and called out, "My light cavalry brothers, mount your horses and follow me!"

Wildflower in hand, Gu Yun had planned to casually tuck it into Chang Geng's hair where he stood closest to him. Just as he raised his hand, however, he found himself ensnared by Chang Geng's gaze. He was surprised to find that Chang Geng's eyes had followed him closely all this time. The expression on his face seemed to declare, *Even if you placed a wedding veil on my head, I wouldn't mind.*

Gu Yun shivered slightly. In the end, he didn't dare follow through with this piece of mischief and stuck the flower in Tan Hongfei's stock-pot-sized helmet instead, providing a vivid enactment of the expression "a fresh flower stuck into a pile of you-know-what." As the wily old veterans of the Northern Camp roared with laughter, the black-armored light cavalry followed in Gu Yun's footsteps and dashed away accompanied by a chorus of shrill whistles as, to a one, they emulated his example. Tunes of all kinds, with origins in all regions of the country, rose and fell in rapid succession. From his position at the front, Gu Yun bellowed furiously, "What are you copying me for?! You're gonna make me pee my pants!"

It was an odd thing—after all the ruckus, he really did feel rather refreshed.

Elsewhere, aboard the Western sea monster—

A battered and exhausted Mister Ja pushed open the cabin door and ran right into the captain of the pope's personal guard.

"How is he?" Mister Ja asked.

"He's awake," answered the captain. "His Holiness was just about to call for you."

During the harried naval battle, the pope's position was grazed by a firebrand arrow, and an artillery battery aboard detonated with such force that the venerated commander lost consciousness on the spot. The pope's incapacitation dealt a devastating blow to the Western navy, which had thereafter suffered a thrashing each time they encountered the Black Iron Battalion.

Mister Ja heaved a sigh of relief and stepped into the cabin. The pope's forehead was slathered in a medicinal poultice, and his limp white hair lay scattered on the pillow, revealing subtle liver spots at the corners of his eyes.

Mister Ja fell to his knees. "Your Holiness," he said, his face full of dismay, "I'm so terribly sorry..."

The elderly man on the bed murmured without opening his eyes, "It's Gu Yun."

"Yes, it's Gu Yun. We planned to pin him down here and even made preparations to engage him in the Beihai region, but yesterday, the black crows appeared out of nowhere." Mister Ja paused, obviously frustrated. "With the Black Iron Battalion held in Jiayu Pass by the allied armies of the Western Regions, I was confident of our success, and yet..."

"You lost control of the front lines."

Mister Ja could not reply.

The pope smiled. "Over the course of our lives, we all encounter enemies who seem invincible. Some are great catastrophes, while others are merely tests of character. Do you know the difference between a catastrophe and a test?"

Mister Ja stared at him uncomprehendingly.

"The difference is this: catastrophes are insurmountable, while tests may be overcome. I believe it is quite easy to distinguish the two. We have already cut the communication lines of the Central Plains people. If their tiny capital truly had so much fighting power at their disposal, would events have so readily spiraled out of control when we incited the Northern Camp to mutiny?"

"You mean..."

"Gu may be young, but he has spent the greater part of his life on the battlefield. Do not allow him to lead you by the nose. Even if he is an insufferably arrogant king of wolves, he has at present been detained and defanged. Go; do not lose confidence so easily."

That day, the Western navy once again rallied their troops and sent a landing party into Dagu Harbor. They were again met with an intense onslaught upon landfall. This time, fighting in the light of day, Mister Ja felt much more assured. Under his steady and methodical command, the Western soldiers made quick work of their beleaguered adversaries and captured every last one of the defending heavy armor units. It was an easy victory—yet before Mister Ja could revel in it, he lifted the visor of one of these newly captured "prisoners of war" and found that these soldiers were not members of Great Liang's armored cavalry at all, but a bunch of iron puppets!

The puppets had plainly been conscripted from the households of high officials and eminent personages of the capital at the eleventh hour. Beneath one puppet's visor, there even lay a deathly pale child's mask: it had a large round face and leered at them with a bloody maw of a grin in unspeakable derision.

One Western soldier, unable to restrain his anger, reached out to yank it off. Mister Ja cried in alarm, "Wait, don't—!"

But his words came too late. The mask was affixed to a thin fuse; at the slightest tug, the iron puppet exploded with a thunderous *boom*, blasting more than a few of the Western soldiers nearby sky-high.

Half of the cracked mask clattered down to rest at Mister Ja's feet, its mouth still drawn in that mocking smile.

By the time these decoys had discharged their mission, the Northern Camp had long finished their general retreat from the harbor. The Western navy furiously charged their way into the city, prepared to quench their anger with blood, but found naught but an empty fort.

When news of enemy attack in Jiangnan had reached the capital, Prince Yanbei had ordered his men to evacuate civilians from the front lines without delay. Of course, there were those who staunchly refused to leave their homes—but after the deafening roars of artillery fire howled in their ears that first night, they too had picked up and fled, and were by now long gone.

In preparation for the Westerners' arrival, Gu Yun had left behind nothing but scorched earth.

62

SIEGE

THE DESERTED CITY was deathly still. The hair-raising silence set the soldiers on edge, one small fright away from panic. Mister Ja waved his hand, and his men scattered in all directions to search civilian homes. The houses and courtyards here were built along the city's winding rivers; twisting and turning through the streets, it was all too easy for outsiders to lose their bearings. Here and there, the soldiers also encountered giant boulders blocking their way. This only served to make the incomprehensible topography even more impossible to unravel.

Mister Ja had an ominous premonition. He suddenly regretted his impulse to advance so quickly.

At that moment, a Western soldier cried out in alarm. Like a flock of birds startled by the twang of a bow, the men around him drew their swords as one. In no time at all, countless suits of steel armor had gathered in a circle, each and every one aiming pitch-black cannon muzzles at a suspicious pagoda tree. It was then that they saw what hung from the branches: the body of a Western soldier, swinging limply. Half the man's face had been blasted away; who could say on which battlefield he had died. Strapped to the bloody wreckage of the man's head was a deathly pale mask—this time, its painted face was weeping!

An explosion rocked the area—one of the Western soldiers had, in his agitation, accidentally fired his cannon. The corpse hanging from the tree exploded in a shower of mangled flesh, and raw meat fell in chunks. Hair-raising laughter filled the air. As if faced with some great enemy, the Western soldiers beneath the tree cautiously retreated in unison. Seconds later, a round-faced owl poked its head out from the tree's canopy. After loftily surveying the two-legged beasts below, it shot straight into the sky with a flap of its wings, leaving that unnerving laughter to drift in all directions.

Though they stood in broad daylight, the sound still made the soldiers break out in a cold sweat.

"Lord Jakobson, should we continue the search?"

Mister Ja swallowed with difficulty. "No...pull back for now. Let's get out of here—immediately!"

He'd barely issued his orders when another sharp explosion went off, this time in the distance. The sound was followed by blood-curdling screams as a number of fireworks whistled through the air and blossomed into a brilliant display in the sky.

"It's an ambush!" someone shouted, their expression twisting in panic.

"Fall back!"

"Retreat!"

The boom of cannon fire and hiss of arrows tangled in a cacophonous racket as several more explosions of unknown origin knocked over a tottering stone house. The shattered rock littered the thoroughfares and, combined with the giant roadblocking boulders from before, turned the deserted city into a giant maze that rendered the Westerners' map a useless scrap of paper. The weakness that was the outsiders' unfamiliarity with the terrain became obvious. Trapped in this labyrinth, the group of heavy armor infantrymen and foot soldiers buzzed aimlessly around like headless flies for a long while, but still could not find their way out.

Mister Ja had little choice but to whistle a summons to the Western hawks so they could lead the ground troops out from the air.

The panic-stricken Western troops beat a hasty retreat to the city gates. Yet someone must have tripped some mechanism as they stumbled out, for all of a sudden, there came the ear-splitting screech of grinding gears from atop the city wall. The Western soldiers instantly drew their bows, their countless arrows trained on the gate tower.

An object floated down from above.

Mister Ja pushed aside his terror-stricken personal guards and stepped forward. When he saw what it was that had fallen, he flew into a rage, his features twisting until they were almost unrecognizable. It was yet another deathly pale mask—this time with a silly, cockeyed grin.

"My lord, perhaps...perhaps we ought to take the long way around."

Mister Ja raised a hand to cut the soldier off. He stood there for a time, his expression sinister. "His Holiness was right. Gu Yun has no cards left, so he must rely on these cheap tricks. Don't tell me you're all scared witless because of a few lousy masks. An ambush... hah!" he scoffed.

He was so angry he could only laugh. "Raze the city to the ground," he said coldly. "Then we shall see where they lay their ambush!"

But more than two hours later, after leveling the entire settlement and searching thrice amid the wreckage, Mister Ja was forced to admit that this shitty hellhole that had wasted so much of his precious time and violet gold really was but an empty shell. The so-called "ambush" had amounted to nothing more than a few white masks and an owl which had long flown away!

Mister Ja ground his teeth so violently his gums nearly began to bleed. "Where are the scout hawks? After them! Give chase at full speed!"

Meanwhile, on the only road leading to the capital from Dongan—

Hidden under a tree, Gu Yun accepted a field scope from Tan Hongfei and raised it to his eye, following the handful of scout hawks hurtling overhead toward the capital. He spat out the stalk of grass he had been worrying between his teeth and patted Lian Wei's windslasher, which still hung on his back. "Old Lian, you've done a great deed."

"What is it?" Tan Hongfei asked quietly.

"Haven't you noticed?" Gu Yun said lazily. "The commander who led the Westerners before is likely dead or wounded; the person presently giving orders is clearly unfamiliar with the capital. Otherwise, he would never so rashly send his scout hawks off in a fit of anger."

The vital region of the capital held the Imperial City nestled within its center, thus it always had extremely tight security against intrusion. Even Black Hawks didn't dare fly through its airspace. No matter how extraordinary the circumstances, Black Hawks still made their landings at the Northern Camp, where they removed their hawk armor before entering the city on horseback.

What most didn't know was the true reason Black Hawks did not fly over the capital: It wasn't because soldiers of the Black Iron Battalion were particularly conscientious and rule-abiding. It was because Gu Yun knew that if a Black Hawk defied these rules, they could easily run into the "aerial exclusion field."

Beyond the nine city gates of the capital lay the invisible aerial exclusion field. Construction on this device had begun during

Emperor Wu's reign and was only completed thirty years later. This was the Lingshu Institute's magnum opus. Beneath the perimeter of the aerial exclusion field lay countless hidden mechanisms, all controlled by a dispatch center at Kite's Flight Pavilion.

The towering Kite's Flight Pavilion was a popular tourist destination where travelers from the world over could eat, drink, and make merry—but this was not the primary reason it was built so tall. It also served a vitally important function: it was the linchpin of the aerial exclusion field. On "Moon-Shot Platform," there was a "Cosmos Pavilion" that kept its heavy doors locked at all times. Who knew how many great masters of the Lingshu Institute had gone bald building this Cosmos Pavilion? The unique network of light it cast from beyond the nine city gates was so fine that even at night, it was easily drowned out by the illumination of the moon and stars and the overflowing lamplight of the city. Unless one possessed extraordinary senses, it was nigh impossible to see with the naked eye.

This network of light hovered a hundred meters above ground; the people and animals moving below were not impeded by it in the slightest. As for any who tried to fly into the capital in hawk armor, at low altitudes of a hundred meters or fewer, they would be spotted by sentries on the nine city gates and welcomed with a volley of parhelion arrows. If they tried their luck above a hundred meters, they would encounter the aerial exclusion field.

As soon as this field was breached, the disturbance in the network of light would reflect back to Cosmos Pavilion, then reflect yet again off a specialized mirror back to its point of origin, where it would trigger hidden mechanisms buried along the perimeter of the net. Once locked onto the invader's position, the field's defenses would shoot the airborne trespasser down from eight different directions at once. If the armored hawk attempted to evade the attack, they would find that no matter where they tried to take cover, within the aerial exclusion field, there would always be hidden ordnance waiting to openly or secretly attack from the shadows.

Only on New Year's Eve did the aerial exclusion field shut down—this was the singular day of the year when Cosmos Pavilion conducted maintenance. On that day, sentries stationed on the red-headed kites took over surveillance of the skies.

"Those scout hawks are taking a one-way trip," said Gu Yun. "The foreign commander will soon recall the legendary aerial exclusion field. With the war beacon decree in effect, the red-headed kites will take flight. The placement of the aerial exclusion field will also be adjusted accordingly. It will take the Westerners some time to figure out its exact coordinates, so the closer they get to the capital, the more reluctant their armored hawks will be to fly too high…"

Gu Yun muttered into Tan Hongfei's ear, "Pass my orders on to our brothers. Tell them to get some rest—we move after nightfall. The Black Hawks will lead the charge and suppress the enemy from above. The light cavalry units will follow, flanking the enemy on both sides and smashing through the enemy's formation. Warn them not to zealously extend the fight. A single strike will do; we don't want to become trapped. As for the charioteers, pretend to cut off their retreat. Batter them with a few rounds of attack, then let them pass. We're not looking to force the enemy into a life-and-death struggle. We don't have the men for that."

"Sir, why didn't we lay an ambush at Dagu Harbor?" Tan Hongfei asked quietly.

"Who on earth would lay an ambush in broad daylight?" Gu Yun rolled his eyes. "Is there something wrong with your head?"

…At that moment, Mister Ja must have sneezed twice in rapid succession.

Tan Hongfei modestly considered this for a while and concluded that what Gu Yun said made great sense. Thus, he asked
a different question: "Sir, how do you know they'll get here by
nightfall?"

"Your darling Prince Yanbei ran the numbers. If he's wrong, I'm
docking his pay. It's not like he needs it—the money in his red
envelope at New Year's is more than half of my annual salary."

Chang Geng was presently sitting off to the side repairing the
grip on his iron bow. After fighting through the night, the leather
had begun to fray. He had produced a tiny file and a scrap of new
leather from who knows where and begun to fix it, his fingers so dex-
terous they dazzled the eyes. Despite being called out so suddenly,
Chang Geng didn't even lift his head as he smiled. "Well, regardless
of what happens, everything's recorded in one ledger at the Marquis
Estate anyway."

Tan Hongfei was a bit of a boor; he lived by the philosophy that
all fellow soldiers were his own brothers. After fighting shoulder to
shoulder, he had long taken Prince Yanbei as one of his own and
cared not a whit about his parentage. Upon hearing Chang Geng's
response, he immediately shot off his mouth and teased him. "Our
Highness shares everything with the marquis. If only you were a
princess. That way, maybe we could add a princess's tent to our camp
again, just like we did back in the day."

Gu Yun was beyond words. He couldn't help but grit his teeth
in irritation.

Chang Geng's hands stilled. After a beat, he picked up the thread
of Tan Hongfei's conversation. "But what a pity. The marquis,
whose beauty drives crowds to fill his carriage with flowers and fruit,
wouldn't want me unless I had a face like flowers blooming under
moonlight."

"Aiyo, but wait, that match wouldn't work," the simple-minded Tan Hongfei said. "His Majesty usually calls our marshal 'Imperial Uncle'—you belong to different generations!"

"Fuck off!" Gu Yun snapped.

Tan Hongfei, who was purely yanking his chain, and Prince Yanbei, who harbored secret intentions, both burst into laughter.

Shortly after nightfall, the call of a cuckoo bird sounded from a short distance away. This was the signal: their enemies had come within range. Tan Hongfei was about to rise when Gu Yun pushed him back down.

"Wait a little longer," Gu Yun murmured. "Until the fourth watch."

His eyes were terrifyingly bright in the black of night, like a pair of divine blades ready to draw blood the instant they were unsheathed.

Tan Hongfei couldn't help but lick his cracked lips. "How exactly did His Highness figure out the timing? Seriously..."

Gu Yun was about to say, *His teacher is old General Zhong*, when Chang Geng, who had at some point walked up behind him, cut in. "Merely a natural consequence of spending all my time sorting out budgets and running calculations."

"What?" Tan Hongfei asked, flummoxed.

Chang Geng shot Gu Yun a glance. "I have to prepare a dowry so I can marry a general."

"You're still going on about that?" Gu Yun hissed irritably.

The idiot Tan Hongfei began to snicker. Gu Yun was completely powerless against bastards like these who specialized in poking people in their sore spots and spared no effort in driving their commanding officer mad. On top of that—when did this little brat Chang Geng become so fearless of him? Back at the hot spring villa,

Gu Yun had advised him to shoulder fewer mental burdens; to his surprise, Chang Geng seemed to have actually taken his advice and moved forward with a lighter heart.

Chang Geng knew when to quit, so after teasing Gu Yun, he made up for it by saying, "Yifu, I'm just joking, don't get mad."

"Our marshal's temper isn't that ferocious," Tan Hongfei said. "All these years, I've only ever seen him blow up that one time at the palace."

Even a man like Tan Hongfei realized he misspoke the instant the words left his mouth. He promptly shut it in embarrassment.

Gu Yun's expression cooled at once.

Unable to contain himself, Tan Hongfei blurted out a short while later, "Sir, about that..."

Gu Yun cut him off. "Tell the Black Hawks to prepare for takeoff!"

Tan Hongfei ground his teeth, but in the end, he could do nothing but sigh.

Chang Geng patted him on the shoulder. "I'll go."

The night gradually deepened as the moon sank below the horizon and Qiming climbed into the sky. The darkest hour had arrived, just before dawn.

Mister Ja had marched through the daylight hours on tenterhooks, worrying again and again that his troops would run into Gu Yun's ambush. Trepidation and anger roiled in his mind, leaving him unable to relax even when they made camp for the night. He feared that, after so many false alarms, Gu Yun would finally follow through with a real attack. Thus Mister Ja spent the night terrified of shutting his eyes. Only when it was nearly dawn, and he saw that his surroundings remained as quiet and peaceful as ever, did Mister Ja finally succumb to his exhaustion and briefly doze.

374 ☼ STARS OF CHAOS

Yet just as he was about to sink into a deeper sleep, the booming sound of an explosion came from outside. Mister Ja woke in a cold sweat and rolled out of bed. He ran from his tent to see the vast night sky ablaze with fire.

"My lord, look out!"

A flaming volley of arrows rained down from the vault of heaven as a soldier shoved Mister Ja aside. As if seared by the conflagration, the night wind itself curled with steam. A chorus of battle cries pierced the air and two squadrons of Black Steeds stormed past like a dark cyclone.

"Heavy armor units, hold your positions!" Mister Ja howled. "Do not panic! The Central Plains troops lack in numbers—"

Before he could finish, a thunderous rumble rose behind him. A line of war chariots seemed to appear from nowhere like an army of ghosts. They charged forward, sand and stone flying in their wake, as mayhem descended on the camp.

Mister Ja was a master at sowing dissent and exercising diplomacy. Yet however he might excel at scheming and intrigue, he wasn't a terribly competent commander in the field. He was overly accustomed to acting only after careful deliberation; once the enemy exceeded his expectations, he struggled to react with speed and easily lost control of his troops.

An indescribable chill crawled up his spine. Mister Ja suddenly felt as if he were a frog paralyzed by the killing intent of a venomous snake. He looked back in terror and spied an iron arrow hurtling across the night sky like a shooting star chasing the moon, heading straight for him. It was too late for Mister Ja to evade. In this moment of imminent peril, a heavy armor infantryman threw himself before his commander with a furious roar. The iron arrow punched through the heavy armor's thick iron plating, its tip peeking viciously from the soldier's back.

Reeling in shock, Mister Ja traced the trajectory of the arrow to its source and saw a young man with a longbow in hand standing atop the back of a Black Hawk.

With a field scope still sitting on the bridge of his nose to help him calibrate his shot, the young man gazed down—or perhaps more accurately, looked askance—at Mister Ja, his eyes filled with poison. Mister Ja's personal guards swung their cannons up toward the Black Hawk hovering in the sky. The youth appeared to smile, then shook his head with a nonchalant expression as if to say, *How unfortunate that I missed my target.* Then, he coolly leapt from low altitude, parting ways with the Black Hawk and perfectly dodging a smoking cannonball.

Gu Yun shot forward on his horse and caught Chang Geng, who had just jumped down almost twenty meters. With a hiss of steam, the blades of the windslasher in his hand spun in an invisible whirlwind of iron. His horse reared, and he swung his windslasher in an arc with a sharp and sustained whistle. A spot of blood—its owner unknown—landed on the cinnabar beauty mark at the corner of his eye. With a squeeze of his legs against the flanks of his steed, the warhorse sprang out of the heart of the fray in the blink of an eye.

Gu Yun smacked Chang Geng harshly on the back. "Asshole. Do you want to die?"

Chang Geng had intended to jump straight down and then activate the steam propulsion of his light pelt armor's greaves to slow his descent as he neared the ground. He hadn't expected Gu Yun to intervene like this and was momentarily speechless. As he stared at Gu Yun's face from mere centimeters away, a violent tremor shuddered through his chest; he nearly lost his seat on the horse and could only clutch at the cold iron gauntlet encasing Gu Yun's wrist.

This gaze tore through his stoic façade in an instant, burning so fiercely it was like a physical touch. Grumpily, Gu Yun asked, "What are you looking at?"

Chang Geng forced himself to calm down, briefly closing his eyes to stifle the flames smoldering therein. He coughed awkwardly. "It's about time to cast the net."

Gu Yun pulled him up against his chest, then wheeled his horse around and let out a shrill whistle. The light cavalry units reformed their ranks to charge the enemy as one, as if they were rolling up a rug. After falling into disarray under the aerial bombardment from the Black Hawks, the Western soldiers finally began to clumsily fall back into formation. Mister Ja bellowed, "Heavy armor, lead the charge! Tear a hole through their rearguard!"

But there was no need to tear a hole through their rearguard; the war chariots of the Northern Camp had deliberately thinned their ranks. They scattered at the slightest touch, as if incapable of withstanding the enemy's assault, and allowed the Western soldiers to retreat.

Gu Yun gave a signal to Tan Hongfei nearby. The Black Iron light cavalry quietly withdrew like a pack of lackadaisical wolves—they ran after taking one bite and quit while ahead. Such a small light cavalry force wouldn't stand a chance if they waited for the Western army to regroup.

By the time the Western army once again got their wits about them, the black cyclone had already blown past and disappeared into the boundless night sky, never to be found.

The seventh year of Longan, the fifteenth day of the fourth month. The Black Iron Battalion ambushed the Western army west of Dongan City under the cover of night.

The seventeenth day of the fourth month. After being led a merry dance for two consecutive days, the Westerners' advance guard could no longer bear the Black Iron Battalion's persistent attacks and paused their advance to request reinforcements from their fleet at Dagu Harbor.

The twenty-third day of the fourth month. The Westerners' reinforcements arrived, forcing the Black Iron light cavalry to withdraw. The Western army pursued their retreating enemy all the way to Wuqing District, where they were lured by Gu Yun into tripping the aerial exclusion field and lost over half of their armored hawks. The Westerners once again had no choice but to retreat.

The twenty-sixth day of the fourth month. The pope's condition slightly improved; he directly took to the field in person.

The twenty-ninth day of the fourth month. Wuqing fell into enemy hands.

The third day of the fifth month. The Western army bombarded Daxing Prefecture with cannon fire. In the face of unrelenting pressure from an army tens of thousands strong, Gu Yun had led the Northern Camp's meager light cavalry and armored hawks against the Westerners' superior force for nearly a month—but in the end, it was impossible to continue.

The seventh. Gu Yun retreated to the capital with his troops and barred the nine city gates. Still, reinforcements had yet to arrive.

By now, all past debts of gratitude, grudges, love, and hatred had retreated behind the city walls. In the capital of Great Liang, summer arrived in the dense shadows of viridescent trees, but there were no longer any pleasure boats wrapped in music and song adrift on its manmade lakes. And so, the Westerners finally sent forth their sanctimonious peace envoy.

THE STORY CONTINUES IN
Stars of Chaos
VOLUME 3

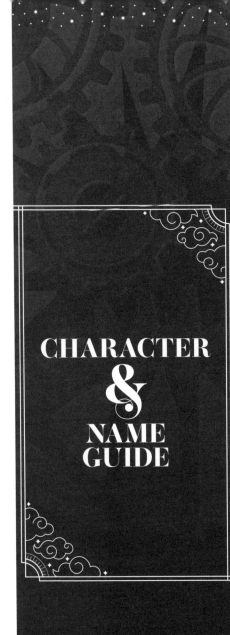

CHARACTER
&
NAME
GUIDE

CHARACTERS

The identity of certain characters may be a spoiler; use this guide with caution on your first read of the novel.

Note on the given name translations: Chinese characters may have many different readings. Each reading here is just one out of several possible readings presented for your reference, and not a definitive translation.

MAIN CHARACTERS

Chang Geng

MILK NAME: Chang Geng (长庚 / "Evening star" or "Evening Venus")

GIVEN NAME: Li Min (李旻 / Surname Li, "Autumn sky")

TITLE: Prince Yanbei (雁北 / "Northern goose")

Chang Geng spent nearly fourteen years living an uneventful life on the Northern Border, only for his world to be turned upside down when he learns he is actually the long-lost fourth prince of Great Liang.

Gu Yun

MILK NAME: Shiliu (十六 / "Sixteen")

GIVEN NAME: Gu Yun (顾昀 / Surname Gu, "Sunlight")

COURTESY NAME: Gu Zixi (顾子熹 / Surname Gu; "Daybreak," literary)

TITLE: Marquis of Anding (安定 / "Order")

RANK: Marshal

Gu Yun begins the story in disguise as the handsome but useless Shen Shiliu, but soon reveals his true identity as the fearsome leader of the Black Iron Battalion.

SUPPORTING CHARACTERS

Shen Yi

GIVEN NAME: Shen Yi (沈易 / Surname Shen, "Change" or "Easy")

COURTESY NAME: Shen Jiping (沈季平 / Surname Shen, "Season," "Even" or "Peaceful")

RANK: Commander in Chief of the Southwest Army

Gu Yun's loyal friend and right-hand man.

Ge Pangxiao

MILK NAME: Ge Pangxiao (葛胖小 / Surname Ge, "Chubby youngster")

GIVEN NAME: Ge Chen (葛晨 / Surname Ge, "Dawn")

Chang Geng's childhood tag-along who leaves Yanhui Town with Chang Geng after becoming orphaned. Ge Pangxiao has a fondness for machines.

Cao Niangzi

MILK NAME: Cao Niangzi (曹娘子 / Surname Cao, "Lady")

GIVEN NAME: Cao Chunhua (曹春花 / Surname Cao, "Spring flower")

Chang Geng's childhood admirer, who leaves Yanhui Town with Chang Geng. Cao Niangzi has a fondness for dressing up as both women and men, and is an expert at taking on different roles.

Chen Qingxu

GIVEN NAME: Chen Qingxu (陈轻絮 / Surname Chen, "Gentle," "Silk floss")

A jianghu physician with a cool demeanor whose family specializes in medicine.

Liao Ran

DHARMA NAME: Liao Ran (了然 / "To understand," "To be so")

TITLE: Great Master

A multi-talented monk from the National Temple and member of the Linyuan Pavilion.

THE EIGHTEEN TRIBES

Xiu-niang

ALIAS: Xiu-niang (秀娘 / "Refined lady")

GIVEN NAME: Huge'er (胡格尔 / "The violet gold at the center of the earth")

Chang Geng's "mother," who turns out to be his aunt. She is a member of the Celestial Wolf Tribe and their agent inside Great Liang.

Jialai Yinghuo

GIVEN NAME: Jialai (加莱)

NAME TRANSLATED INTO CHINESE: Yinghuo (荧惑 / "Glimmering deceiver" or "Mars")

TITLE: Wolf King of the Celestial Wolf Tribe

The crown prince and later king of the Celestial Wolf Tribe. He orchestrates the infiltration and attack on Great Liang at the beginning of the story.

THE CAPITAL

Emperor Wu

The reigning Emperor of Great Liang prior to the Yuanhe Emperor at the start of the story. Gu Yun's maternal grandfather.

Li Feng

GIVEN NAME: Li Feng (李丰 / Surname Li, "Plentiful")
ERA NAME: Longan (隆安 / "Grand Peace")
Chang Geng's elder half-brother, the crown prince, who ascends the throne after the death of his father, the Yuanhe Emperor.

Liao Chi

DHARMA NAME: Liao Chi (了痴, "To understand," "Infatuation")
TITLE: Abbot of the Temple of National Protection
Abbot of the National Temple and Liao Ran's shixiong.

Jiang Chong

GIVEN NAME: Jiang Chong (江充 / Surname Jiang, "Abundance")
COURTESY NAME: Jiang Hanshi (江寒石 / Surname Jiang, "Cold stone")
TITLE: Chief Justice of the Imperial Court of Judicial Review
Shen Yi's senior via the imperial examination system, a friend and ally of Gu Yun, and member of Chang Geng's Grand Council.

The Noble Consort

TITLE: Noble Consort
TITLE: Goddess of the Celestial Wolf Tribe
Chang Geng's birth mother. As the goddess of the Celestial Wolf Tribe, she was gifted to Great Liang after their surrender, and became the sole noble consort within the imperial harem.

Prince Wei

TITLE: Prince Wei (魏 / "Kingdom of Wei")
Chang Geng's elder half-brother, the Second Prince. Son of the Yuanhe Emperor. Colluded with Dongying nationals in an

unsuccessful plan to overthrow the Longan Emperor by striking the capital from the East Sea.

The Yuanhe Emperor

ERA NAME: Yuanhe (元和 / "Primal," "Harmony")
The reigning emperor of Great Liang at the start of the story. Chang Geng's birth father.

Wang Guo

NAME: Wang Guo (王裹 / Surname Wang, "To enfold")
The Longan Emperor's maternal uncle and the most favored official in the imperial court.

OTHER

Fu Zhicheng

GIVEN NAME: Fu Zhicheng (傅志诚 / Surname Fu, "Ambition," "Honesty")
RANK: Commander in Chief (of the Southern Border Army)
TITLE: Governor of the Southwest
A military commander in the south who got his start as a bandit. Gu Yun's father, the former Marquis of Anding, supported his military career after defeating him in battle.

Lord Jakobson

ALIAS: Mister Ja
A mysterious operative from the Far West. He is the right hand of the Western pope, who, in the world of Stars of Chaos, is a military leader as well as a religious one.

Tan Hongfei

GIVEN NAME: Tan Hongfei (谭鸿飞 / Surname Tan, "Swan goose," "To fly")

RANK: Commander (of the Northern Camp)

A former member of the Black Iron Battalion who was forced to leave his position after the attack that injured young Gu Yun.

Yao Zhen

GIVEN NAME: Yao Zhen (姚镇 / Surname Yao, "Town")

COURTESY NAME: Yao Chongze (姚重泽 / Surname Yao, "Great favor")

TITLE: Regional Judiciary Commissioner of Yingtian

Gu Yun's longtime acquaintance and a local official in Jiangnan.

Zhong Chan

GIVEN NAME: Zhong Chan (钟蝉 / Surname Zhong, "Cicada")

RANK: General

A general who was dismissed from his post after defying the emperor, and both Gu Yun and Chang Geng's shifu in martial arts.

INSTITUTIONS

The Government of Great Liang

The emperor is the highest authority in Great Liang, an autocratic monarchy. The top-level administrative bodies of the state include a number of departments and ministries, such as the Ministry of Revenue and Ministry of War.

Years ago, the militant Emperor Wu expanded the borders of Great Liang and built the nation to the height of its power. Due to his lack of male heirs, the more compassionate Yuanhe Emperor was selected as his successor from a different branch of the imperial royal family. The Longan Emperor, the son of Yuanhe Emperor, takes after his father in temperament.

The Military of Great Liang and the Black Iron Battalion

The armed forces of Great Liang consist of eight major military branches—the Kite, Carapace, Steed, Pelt, Hawk, Chariot, Cannon, and Dragon Divisions—each of which specializes in a particular type of warfare. Troops are divided between five major garrisons located in five different regions throughout the country.

Chief among these is the Black Iron Battalion, which is presently stationed in the Western Regions. An elite group of soldiers widely considered to be one of the most powerful military forces in the known world, the Black Iron Battalion is currently under the command of Marshal Gu Yun and comprises the Black Hawk, Black Carapace, and Black Steed Divisions.

The Temple of National Protection

The Temple of National Protection, also known as the National Temple, practices Buddhism, the religion of Great Liang's imperial family.

The Lingshu Institute (灵枢 / "Spiritual pivot")

An academy directly under the emperor's authority that develops the equipment of Great Liang's military, as well as other mechanical inventions.

The Linyuan Pavilion (临渊 / "Approaching the abyss")

A mysterious organization of people from all levels of society that emerges to aid parties they find worthy in times of chaos.

LOCATIONS

GREAT LIANG

The Capital

The capital city of Great Liang.

Dagu Harbor

A naval base in the Beihai region, several days' ride south of Great Liang's capital.

The Southern Border

The mountainous southernmost region of Great Liang, where bandits run rampant.

Yanhui Town (雁回 / "Wild goose's return")

A town on the Northern Border of Great Liang, where Chang Geng grew up.

Yingtian Prefecture

A prefecture in Jiangnan Province near the East Sea.

FOREIGN POWERS

The Eighteen Tianlang (Celestial Wolf) Tribes

A people residing in the grasslands north of Great Liang, where violet gold is plentiful. They pay an annual tribute to Great Liang after being defeated in battle by the Black Iron Battalion.

Loulan

A small but prosperous nation in the Western Regions located at the entrance of the Silk Road. They have a friendly relationship with Great Liang.

Qiuci

A tiny nation in the Western Regions that acquired a suspicious number of sand tiger war chariots.

Qiemo

A tiny nation in the Western Regions that came into conflict with Qiuci.

Dongying

An island nation to the east of Great Liang.

The Far West

A region far to the west beyond the Silk Road that excels in seafaring trade and creating violet-gold-powered devices.

NAME GUIDE

NAMES, HONORIFICS, AND TITLES

Courtesy Names versus Given Names

A courtesy name is given to an individual when they come of age. Traditionally, this was at the age of twenty during one's crowning ceremony, but it can also be presented when an elder or teacher deems the recipient worthy. Though generally a male-only tradition, there is historical precedent for women adopting a courtesy name after marriage. Courtesy names were a tradition reserved for the upper class.

It was considered disrespectful for one's peers of the same generation to address someone by their given name, especially in formal or written communication. Use of one's given name was reserved only for elders, close friends, and spouses.

This practice is no longer used in modern China, but is commonly seen in historically-inspired media. As such, many characters have more than one name. Its implementation in novels is irregular and is often treated malleably for the sake of storytelling.

Milk Names

In China, babies are traditionally given their 大名 (literally "big name," or less literally, "given name") one hundred days after their birth. During those first hundred days, parents would refer to the child by their 小名 (lit. "little name") or 乳名 (lit. "milk name"). Milk names might be childish, employing a diminutive like xiao- or doubling a syllable, but they might also be selected to ward off harm to the child, for example Cao Niangzi's milk name meaning "lady." Many parents might continue referring to their children by their milk name long after they have received their given name.

At the beginning of *Stars of Chaos*, Chang Geng is already thirteen or fourteen years old, but has not been given a "big name." Since Yanhui Town is a backwater border town, this is not terribly strange—historically, many rural families have tended to give their children given names much later in life than the hundredth day. This may be because life in the countryside was harsher and it was more difficult to raise children to adulthood.

Diminutives, Nicknames, and Name Tags

A-: Friendly diminutive. Always a prefix. Usually for monosyllabic names, or one syllable out of a disyllabic name.

XIAO-: A diminutive meaning "little." Always a prefix.

Family

DAGE: A word meaning "eldest brother." It can also be used to address an unrelated male peer that one respects. When added as a suffix, it becomes an affectionate address for any older male. Can also be used by itself to refer to one's true oldest brother.

DAJIE: A word meaning "eldest sister." It can be used as a casual term of address for an older female.

JIEJIE: A word meaning "elder sister." It can be attached as a suffix or used independently to address an unrelated female peer.

NIANG: A word meaning "mother" or "lady."

XIONG: A word meaning "elder brother." It can be attached as a suffix to address an unrelated male peer.

YIFU: A word meaning "godfather" or "adoptive father." (*See Godparentage Relationships for more information*)

Martial Arts and Tutelage

SHIDI: Younger martial brother. For junior male members of one's own school.

SHIFU: Teacher or master. For one's master in one's own school. Gender-neutral.

SHISHU: The younger martial sibling of one's master. Gender-neutral.

SHIXIONG: Older martial brother. For senior male members of one's own school.

XIANSHENG: A respectful suffix with several uses, including for someone with a great deal of expertise in their profession or a teacher. Can be used independently.

PRONUNCIATION GUIDE

Mandarin Chinese is the official state language of mainland China, and pinyin is the official system of romanization in which it is written. As Mandarin is a tonal language, pinyin uses diacritical marks (e.g., ā, á, ǎ, à) to indicate these tonal inflections. Most words use one of four tones, though some are a neutral tone. Furthermore, regional variance can change the way native Chinese speakers pronounce the same word. For those reasons and more, please consider the guide below a simplified introduction to pronunciation of select character names and sounds from the world of *Stars of Chaos*.

More resources are available at sevenseasdanmei.com

Shā pò láng
Shā as in **sho**p
Pò as in **pu**t
Láng as in **long**

Cháng Gēng
Ch as in **ch**ange, áng as in **long**
G as in **goo**se, ēng as in s**ung**

Gù Yún
Gù as in **goo**se
Y as in **you**, ún as in **bin**, but with lips rounded as for **boon**

GENERAL CONSONANTS

Some Mandarin Chinese consonants sound very similar, such as z/c/s and zh/ch/sh. Audio samples will provide the best opportunity to learn the difference between them.

X: somewhere between the **sh** in **sh**eep and **s** in **s**ilk

Q: a very aspirated **ch** as in **ch**arm

C: **ts** as in pan**ts**

Z: **z** as in **z**oom

S: **s** as in **s**ilk

CH: **ch** as in **ch**arm

ZH: **dg** as in do**dg**e

SH: **sh** as in **sh**ave

G: hard **g** as in **g**allant

GENERAL VOWELS

The pronunciation of a vowel may depend on its preceding consonant. For example, the "i" in "shi" is distinct from the "i" in "di." Vowel pronunciation may also change depending on where the vowel appears in a word, for example the "i" in "shi" versus the "i" in "ting." Finally, compound vowels are often—though not always—pronounced as conjoined but separate vowels. You'll find a few of the trickier compounds below.

IU: **y** as in **y**ou plus **ow** as in sh**ow**

IE: **ye** as in **ye**s

UO: **wa** as in **wa**rm

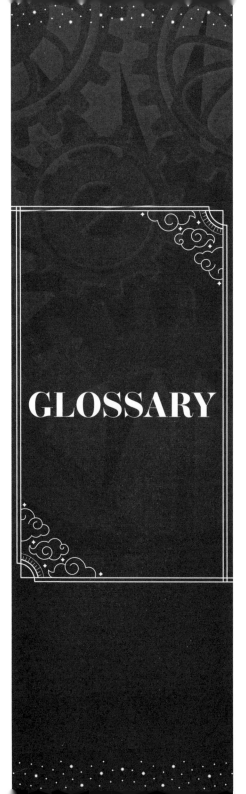

GLOSSARY

GLOSSARY

While not required reading, this glossary is intended to offer further context to the many concepts and terms utilized throughout this novel and provide a starting point for learning more about the rich Chinese culture from which these stories were written.

TERMINOLOGY

BALD DONKEY: A derogatory epithet used to describe Buddhist monks. It stems from the stereotypical image of a bald monk riding a donkey while begging for alms.

BOWING AND CURTSYING: As is seen in other Asian cultures, standing bows are a traditional greeting and are also used when giving an apology. A deeper bow shows greater respect.

BUDDHISM: The central belief of Buddhism is that life is a cycle of suffering and rebirth, only to be escaped by reaching enlightenment (nirvana). Buddhists believe in karma, that a person's actions will influence their fortune in this life and future lives. The teachings of the Buddha are known as The Middle Way and emphasize a practice that is neither extreme asceticism nor extreme indulgence.

CALLIGRAPHY: Chinese calligraphy is a form of visual art and a central part of Chinese culture. It is considered one of the traditional "four arts" of gentlemen scholars, along with guqin, weiqi, and painting. Calligraphy by notable masters is highly sought-after by collectors.

CONCUBINES AND THE IMPERIAL HAREM: In ancient China, it was common practice for a wealthy man to possess women as concubines in addition to his wife. They were expected to live with him and bear him children. Generally speaking, a greater number of concubines correlated to higher social status, hence a wealthy merchant might have two or three concubines, while an emperor might have tens or even a hundred.

The imperial harem had its own ranking system. The exact details vary over the course of history, but can generally be divided into three overarching ranks: the empress, consorts, and concubines. The status of a prince or princess's mother is an important factor in their status in the imperial family, in addition to birth order and their own personal merits. Given the patrilineal rules of succession, the birth of a son can also elevate the mother's status, leading to fierce, oftentimes deadly, competition amongst ambitious members of the imperial harem.

CONFUCIANISM: Confucianism is a philosophy based on the teachings of Confucius. Its influence on all aspects of Chinese culture is incalculable. Confucius placed heavy importance on respect for one's elders and family, a concept broadly known as filial piety (孝). The family structure is used in other contexts to urge similar behaviors, such as respect of a student toward a teacher, or people of a country toward their ruler.

COUGHING OR SPITTING BLOOD: A way to show a character is ill, injured, or upset. Despite the very physical nature of the response, it does not necessarily mean that a character has been wounded; their body could simply be reacting to a very strong emotion.

CROWS: An inauspicious symbol in Chinese culture. A person "has the beak of a crow" if they are prone to saying inauspicious things.

CULTIVATION: A practice in Daoism-inspired Chinese myth through which humans can achieve immortality and non-human creatures can acquire higher forms, more humanoid forms, or both.

DHARMA NAME: A name given to new disciples of Buddhism during their initiation ritual.

DAOISM: Daoism is the philosophy of the dao (道 / "the way"). Following the dao involves coming into harmony with the natural order of the universe, which makes someone a "true human," safe from external harm and able to affect the world without intentional action. Cultivation is a concept based on Daoist beliefs.

DRAGONS: There are several kinds of dragons in Chinese mythology. Jiao (蛟) or jiaolong (蛟龙), "flood dragons," are hornless, aquatic dragons that can summon storms and floods. Zhenlong (真龙), "true dragons," also have water-related powers, but are capable of flying through the clouds. "True" dragons are a symbol of the divine and the emperor, hence the translation as "imperial dragons" in this story. According to myth, flood dragons can transform into true, or imperial, dragons by cultivating and passing heavenly tribulations.

ERA NAME: A designation for the years when a given emperor was on the throne (or some part of those years). This title is determined by the emperor when they ascend the throne, and can be used to refer to both the era and the emperor himself.

EYES: Descriptions like "phoenix eyes," "peach-blossom eyes," or "triangular eyes" refer to eye shape. Phoenix eyes have an upturned sweep at their far corners, while peach-blossom eyes have a rounded upper lid with gentle upward tilt at the outer corners and are often considered particularly alluring. Triangular eyes have eyelids which droop at the outer corner and are considered harsh and keen.

FACE: Mianzi (面子), generally translated as "face," is an important concept in Chinese society. It is a metaphor for a person's reputation and can be extended to further descriptive metaphors. For example, "having face" refers to having a good reputation, and "losing face" refers to having one's reputation hurt. Meanwhile, "giving face" means deferring to someone else to help improve their reputation, while "not wanting face" implies that a person is acting so poorly or shamelessly that they clearly don't care about their reputation at all. "Thin face" refers to someone easily embarrassed or prone to offense at perceived slights. Conversely, "thick face" refers to someone not easily embarrassed and immune to insults.

FIRESTARTER: An ancient "lighter" made of easily flammable material inside a bamboo tube. It can be ignited by shaking or blowing on it.

FOOT BINDING : A process used to create artificially small feet, which were seen as an attractive trait for women during certain periods of Chinese history. The process involved breaking and tightly binding the foot to mold its shape. The foot might also be bound with pieces of broken crockery in order to induce necrosis in the broken toes and cause them to fall off, leading to a smaller final result.

GODPARENTAGE RELATIONSHIPS: Similar to the idea of "sworn brothers," gan (干) relationships are nominal familial relationships entered into by non-blood-related parties for a variety of reasons.

In the setting of *Stars of Chaos*, the border towns have a tradition where a debt of gratitude that a person could not repay by other means would be recognized by either the recipient or their descendants naming their benefactor as their godparent. Entering this relationship means that the recipient (or their descendant) now acknowledges filial duties toward their new godparent, such as making sure they are taken care of in their old age.

INCENSE TIME: A common way to tell time in ancient China, referring to how long it takes for a single incense stick to burn. Standardized incense sticks were manufactured and calibrated for specific time measurements: a half hour, an hour, a day, etc. These were available to people of all social classes. "One incense time" is roughly thirty minutes.

IMPERIAL EXAMINATION SYSTEM: The official system of examinations in ancient China that qualified someone for official service. It was a supposedly meritocratic system that allowed students from all backgrounds to rise up in society, but the extent to which this was true varied across time.

JIANGHU: The jianghu (江湖 / "rivers and lakes") describes an underground society of martial artists, monks, rogues, artisans, and merchants who settle disputes between themselves per their own moral codes. For members of the jianghu, these moral codes supersede laws mandated by the government. Thus, the jianghu typically exists outside of or in opposition to mainstream society and its government, with its members customarily avoiding cooperation with government bureaucracy.

The jianghu is a staple of wuxia (武侠 / "martial heroes"), one of the oldest Chinese literary genres, which consists of tales of noble heroes fighting evil and injustice.

LOTUS FLOWER: This flower symbolizes purity of the heart and mind, as lotuses rise untainted from the muddy waters they grow in. It also signifies the holy seat of the Buddha. An extremely rare variety known as the bingdi lian (并蒂莲) or "twin lotus" is considered an auspicious sign and a symbol of marital harmony.

MANDARIN DUCKS: Famous for mating for life, mandarin ducks are a symbol of marital harmony, and are frequently featured in Chinese art.

MOURNING PERIOD: The death of a parent was a major event in historical Chinese culture. Children who survived them would be expected to observe a mourning period during which they wore only plain white clothes, stayed at home, and ceased to partake in entertainment and social events. The exact length of the mourning period varied, and there could be exceptions if, for example, the child had important duties they had to attend to.

SHA PO LANG: Sha Po Lang (杀破狼) is the name of a key star formation in Zi Wei Dou Shu (紫微斗数 / "purple star astrology"), a common system of astrology in Chinese culture. It refers to an element of a natal star chart in which the stars Qi Sha (七杀 / "seven killings"), Tan Lang (贪狼 / "greedy wolf"), and Po Jun (破军 / "vanquisher of armies") appear in four specific "palaces" of the sky.

Sha Po Lang in a natal horoscope foretells change and revolution, a turbulent fate. The fortunate among those with this in their star chart gain talent and fortune amidst chaos, while the less fortunate encounter disaster and destitution. Those with this formation in their natal horoscope will encounter great ups and downs, yet have the potential to make their name in dramatic fashion. Many great generals of ancient times were said to have been born under these stars.

THREE IMMORTAL SOULS AND SEVEN MORTAL FORMS: Hun (魂) and po (魄) are two types of souls in Chinese philosophy and religion. Hun are immortal souls which represent the spirit and intellect, and leave the body after death. Po are corporeal souls or mortal forms which remain with the body of the deceased. Different traditions claim there are different numbers of each, but three hun and seven po is common in Daoism.

TIGER TALLY: A token used as proof of imperial authorization to deploy and command troops. In *Stars of Chaos*, there are three Black Iron Tiger Tallies total, which can command the eight branches of the Great Liang military in times of emergency. They are held by Gu Yun, the imperial court, and the emperor, respectively.

TITLES OF NOBILITY: Titles of nobility are an important feature of the traditional social structure of Imperial China. While the conferral and organization of specific titles evolved over time, in *Stars of Chaos*, such titles can be either inherited or bestowed by the emperor.

In the world of *Stars of Chaos*, a notable feature of the ranking system with respect to the imperial princes is that monosyllabic titles are reserved for princes of the first rank while disyllabic titles designate princes of the second rank.

Princes of the second rank are also known as commandery princes, so named for the administrative divisions they head. The title of commandery prince is not solely reserved for members of the imperial family, but can also be given to meritorious officials and rulers of vassal states.

TRADITIONAL CHINESE MEDICINE: Traditional medical practices in China are commonly based around the idea that qi, or vital energy, circulates in the body through channels called meridians similarly to how blood flows through the circulatory system. Acupuncture points, or acupoints, are special nodes, most of which lie along the meridians. Stimulating them by massage, acupuncture, or other methods is believed to affect the flow of qi and can be used for healing.

Another central concept in traditional Chinese medicine is that disease arises from an imbalance of elements in the body caused by disharmony in internal functions or environmental factors. For example, an excess of internal heat can cause symptoms such as fever, thirst, insomnia, and redness of the face.

QI DEVIATION: A physiological and psychological disorder believed to result from improper spiritual or martial training. Symptoms of qi deviation in fiction include panic, paranoia, sensory hallucinations, and death. Common treatments for qi deviation in fiction include relaxation (voluntary or forced by an external party), massage, meditation, or qi transfer from another individual.

UNBOUND HAIR: Neatly bound hair was historically an important aspect of one's attire. Loose, unbound hair was seen as highly improper, and is used as synecdoche to describe someone who is disheveled in appearance.

WEIQI: Also known by its Japanese name, Go, weiqi is the oldest known board game in human history. The board consists of a nineteen-by-nineteen grid upon which opponents play unmarked black and white stones as game pieces to claim territory.

WILD GEESE: A classic motif in Chinese poetry, the wild goose, or yan (雁), has come to embody a host of different symbolic meanings. As a migratory bird, it can represent seasonal change as well as a loving message sent from afar. Famous for mating for life, a pair of geese can allude to marital bliss, while a lone goose can signify the loss of a loved one.

WUXING THEORY: Wuxing (五行 / "Five Phases") is a concept in Chinese philosophy used for describing interactions and relationships between phenomena. The expression 五行 (literally "five motions") originally refers to the movements of the planets Mars (火星 / "fire star"), Mercury (水星 / "water star"), Jupiter (木星 / "wood star"), Venus (金星 / "metal star"), and Saturn (土星 / "earth star"), which correspond to the phases of fire, water, wood, metal, and earth, respectively. In wuxing cosmology, people are categorized according to the five phases and relationships are described in cycles.

Xiangke (相克 / lit. "mutually overcoming") refers to a cycle in which one phase acts as a restricting (and oftentimes destructive) agent on the other. The phase interactions in the ke (克) cycle are: wood breaks through earth, earth dams up water, water douses fire, fire melts metal, and metal chops through wood. When applied to

408 ✦ STARS OF CHAOS

people, these interactions take the form of karmic consequences, which are oftentimes directed at the children and other family members of the original actor. An example of one such cycle might be: An emperor killed many people to expand the nation → the adverse effects of his great deeds are directed toward his children in the form of early death.

Chinese superstition also holds that, due to their phase categorization, certain people's fate can "suppress" (克) the fates of the people around them. For example, if someone is categorized as metal, they may suppress people who have been categorized as wood. Similarly, if someone's fate is determined to be more tenacious than others, they may bring harm to their familial relations. In the case of Gu Yun's unmarriageable status, people have observed the misfortune that befell his family and concluded that he inherited a similar fate. Thus, any woman who marries him will suffer misfortune as her fate is suppressed by his.

YIN AND YANG ENERGY: The concept of yin and yang in Chinese philosophy that describes the complementary interdependence of opposite or contrary forces. It can be applied to all forms of change and differences. Yang represents the sun, masculinity, and the living, while yin represents the shadows, femininity, and the dead, including spirits and ghosts. In fiction, imbalances between yin and yang energy can do serious harm to the body or act as the driving force for malevolent spirits seeking to replenish themselves of whichever they lack.

THE WORLD OF STARS OF CHAOS

COPPER SQUALL: A horn-shaped device made of copper that amplifies the voice of the speaker when spoken into.

GIANT KITE AND RED-HEADED KITE: A large, amphibious airship, the giant kite is powered by steam and equipped with thousands of wing-like structures called fire pinions, which burn violet gold.

A variation of the giant kite is the red-headed kite. Unlike the giant kite, the red-headed kite is a small pleasure vessel that does not see use in the military.

HEAVY ARMOR: A class of armor used in the military, heavy armor is powered by violet gold, allowing its wearers to traverse thousands of kilometers in seconds and lift objects weighing hundreds of kilograms. A single suit of heavy armor has the power to annihilate a thousand soldiers.

IRON CUFF: The part of light armor that encircles the wrist. Highly convenient, iron cuffs can be removed from full suits of armor and used on their own. A single iron cuff can conceal three or four silk darts.

LIGHT ARMOR: A class of armor used in the military, light armor is typically worn by the cavalry and can only support a small amount of propulsion. It relies primarily on man- and animal-power, and its primary advantages lie in how light and convenient it is.

LIGHT PELT: The lightest class of armor used in the military, the light pelt is specially designed for riding and weighs less than fifteen kilograms.

PARHELION BOW AND ARROW: A giant mechanical bow that runs on violet gold. When fully powered up, arrows released from such a bow can pierce through a city wall a dozen meters thick.

SILK DART: An extraordinarily thin knife that can be concealed in and fired from wrist cuffs.

VIOLET GOLD: A substance mined from beneath the earth which can be burned as fuel in high-quality mechanical devices. It is of such strategic importance that it is called the "lifeline" of Great Liang.

WINDSLASHER: A weapon used by the Black Iron Battalion. It looks like a staff when at rest, but spinning blades release from hidden incisions in one end when the weapon is spun.

WU'ERGU: A slow-acting poison of northern barbarian origin. It is purported to have the ability to transform someone into a great warrior, but those afflicted with wu'ergu are plagued with nightmares and eventually driven insane with bloodlust.